Nina wanted to believe him. Something rebellious inside her fought the caution her aunt had taught her, ignored the warning signs, and clamored to invite this dark-eyed man and his battered brother into her big empty house. Surely a man who worked on computers and troubled himself to take care of his young brother couldn't be dangerous. She wanted to say yes. Thirty years of experience told her she was insane if she did.

"Mr. Smith, I just don't think this is a wise idea," she answered slowly, avoiding looking at the way his muscles rippled when he stretched to reach the higher plants. Why couldn't the man wear decent shirts like anyone else instead of those formfitting T-shirts?

He set the empty watering can down on the worktable and crossed his arms over his chest.

He was staring at her with curiosity, but she wouldn't return his look.

"What is it you want most in life, Miss Toon?"

Also by Patricia Rice:

PAPER MOON
DENIM AND LACE
WAYWARD ANGEL

GARDEN OF DREAMS

Patricia Rice

FAWCETT GOLD MEDAL • NEW YORK

A Fawcett Gold Medal Book
Published by The Ballantine Publishing Group
 Published in the United States by The Ballantine Publishing Group, a division of Random House, Inc., New York, and simultaneously in Canada by Random House of Canada Limited, Toronto.

http://www.randomhouse.com

Library of Congress Catalog Card Number: 97-90652

ISBN 0-449-15062-3

Manufactured in the United States of America

First Edition: February 1998

10 9 8 7 6 5 4 3 2 1

To all the good friends I left behind in Western Kentucky:
You gave me the best years of my life.
Thank you, and God bless you all.

Author's Note

I have lived in the beautiful Western Kentucky area for twenty years, and I'm quite familiar with the Land Between the Lakes and its environs. For fictional purposes, however, I've invented a composite town I've called Madrid, Kentucky. It borrows bits and pieces of all my favorite places and rolls them into one. The characters come completely from my imagination, although I'd surely love to meet a Nina Toon who might donate acreage for a botanical garden!

ONE

"Three weeks. Unless we run into a major fault, we'll have the finished program in three weeks, Harry. If you and your friends would leave me alone, we might have it even faster."

JD jotted notes across his desk pad while staring at the jargon on the screen. The sleek modern curves of the desk with its assorted computer equipment and the staggering skyline outside the bank of windows behind him formed a cocoon of expensive technology that obliterated any signs of humanity from his surroundings.

Unfortunately, technology couldn't shield him from his uncle's Arkansas whine over the telephone. In the electronically controlled coolness that shut out the muggy pollution LA called air, JD made a quick slash beneath one of his notes, then scowled at something said on the line. "No, Harry. Absolutely not. I'm not allowing a single bleeping stranger on this floor until the program is packaged and out of here. *No*, Harry!"

As his uncle continued, he flung his marker across the desk and didn't notice as it bounced off a gleaming metal stress toy and skittered to the floor. He ran his hands through his tousled hair and swore violently as he glared out his office window at the crowded LA freeway below.

"To hell with family, Harry. They may be *your* family, but

they're not mine. Stall them, Harry. I don't want to hear another word about it." JD slammed the phone down and swore vividly and fluently for two minutes before grabbing the receiver and punching a button. A man couldn't trust anyone, not even himself sometimes. He'd learned that lesson long ago.

"Dillon," he growled into the receiver, "what the hell were you doing letting us sign a loan contract that allows a damned financial officer on the premises? Are you out of your mind? Read the blamed thing again. We've made every payment promptly. There's no reason for this." He listened for about thirty seconds, gnashing his teeth at his lawyer's weak excuses. He despised people who couldn't accept responsibility for their own mistakes.

"They're threatening to pull the loan if we don't bring him up here," JD interrupted. "This is a serious matter, Dillon. Have you ever seen Harry's damned friends? They all carry Magnums in their underwear and pigstickers in their socks."

JD suffered the lawyer's hemming and hawing just long enough to escalate his fury to murderous, bit his tongue before he could recklessly fire the company's only legal representative, and slammed the phone down. Impulsiveness did not become a CEO. Before he could punch another button, Jimmy MacTavish bobbed into the office.

"JD, I've gotta leave early today. Barbara wants me to attend some function or other, and I've gotta rent a monkey suit. Katy about has that ATM debit loop under control. We're still on schedule." He loosened his narrow knit tie as he entered.

If anything, Jimmy matched the public's image of the quintessential computer nerd. Tall and string-bean rangy, he wore wire glasses he'd taped together and forgotten to take in for repair. His hair straggled into his eyes more often than not, and his entire wardrobe consisted of white shirts, narrow ties, and interchangeable baggy suit pants without the matching jackets. Compared to JD's more compact, muscular build and his wardrobe of T-shirts, jeans, and cowboy boots, an observer couldn't be blamed for thinking Jimmy the CEO of Marshall Enterprises.

"We've got trouble, Jimmy. That loan contract Dillon let us sign allows a financial officer on the premises. Harry's friends are threatening to come in on us."

JD noticed Jimmy seemed more nervous about missing his date with Barbara than about Harry's threats. No one was afraid of Harry. Anybody in their right mind would be afraid of Jimmy's bloodsucking girlfriend. JD waited for the day Jimmy came in with two holes in his neck.

"What can bankers do? They'll look at some printouts, ask a few questions, pull a few invoices. You're getting paranoid, Marshall. No one knows what we're doing. No one cares. We're not exactly Microsoft."

Maybe he was paranoid. JD worked his shoulders beneath his T-shirt in hopes of releasing some of the tension. What he really needed was time in the gym so he could work off enough steam to keep him from killing somebody. If Harry walked in here right now, he thought he might throttle him. Since his uncle had called from his car phone, that possibility appeared imminent.

"Word is out, Jimmy, don't kid yourself," JD reminded his partner. "We went to half a dozen banks for that loan. We presented precise plans of what we would accomplish with the money. They know we're competing with the big boys on this one. That's why they turned us down. There's nothing to stop them from spreading the word. They may be laughing, but they'll be watching."

"If you're so worried about Harry's friends, why don't you go ahead with your plans and go public? We could make enough off a stock offering to cover the loan on the basis of the game software alone." Jimmy loosened his tie even more and began to pace nervously, occasionally throwing a glance at the escape hatch of the door.

"We haven't got time for that now. Besides, once we have

the banking program copyrighted, the stock will be worth fortunes. We'll need that money for operating expenses to get the program through production and sales. We discussed all this, Jimmy. We've got to find some way of stalling Harry."

"I still think you're nuts. If you can't trust your uncle, who can you trust? Listen, I've gotta go. Barbara's waiting downstairs. I'll see you later." He loped off, leaving the office door open behind him.

JD didn't envy Jimmy's henpecked state, but he still wished he had the freedom of running out like that. Once upon a time he'd amused himself and released a lot of angry tension by creating video computer games with ghouls crashing down hallways and space aliens zapping dinosaurs. Then he'd developed the biggest video game of them all, Monster House, and sales had slammed through the ceiling. He'd turned into a damned executive with a multimillion-dollar company to run, and his life hadn't been the same since.

Particularly not after he'd had the brilliant idea of applying that fascinating loop he'd created for Monster House to a program that would facilitate on-line computer banking. The principles were the same; he just used debits and credits instead of gorgons and three-headed dwarves. Once he'd realized that, there had been no going back. He'd sunk all his profits into research and development and hired the best staff available. Then a few months ago he'd discovered that the big software companies were closing in on him. With their huge facilities, they could develop the program fifty times faster once they discovered the key he already possessed. He'd gone out hat in hand, begging for money to speed up his own production.

Only Uncle Harry had come through. JD glared at his secretary as she walked in bearing the ubiquitous phone messages. She didn't flinch. Miss Hartwell had almost twice JD's years and a head full of gray hair as thick as his own black locks. Sometimes, he swore she used the same barber.

"You've had two calls from Mr. Dillon, another from the

stockbroker, one from a Mr. DiFrancesco who says your uncle Harry told you about him, and another from some youngster who wants to know if you came from Tempe, Arizona." Her usually clipped tones held a quizzical note when she mentioned the last.

Tempe, Arizona. That's all JD needed on a day like this, to be reminded of Tempe. He didn't come from anywhere, precisely. He'd lived in Germany, Italy, Alaska, and half the United States at one time or another. Tempe had been one of his father's last stops. JD had been sixteen at the time. He had no desire whatsoever to recall that disastrous period of his past.

"Tell them all I've gone to hell for a vacation and won't be back until I meet the devil. I've got work to do." Spinning in his chair, JD ignored the messages his secretary dropped on the desk and returned to his computer screen. He had no intention of ever creating a computer program that talked. He much preferred his silent companions to the ceaseless nattering of the people around him. He hadn't always been that way. These last years he had just gravitated in that direction. On the whole, the people in his life were a major disappointment. Computers, on the other hand, he understood completely, even when they broke down and went haywire on him.

"The guard downstairs said Mr. Marshall is on the way up. Shall I keep him out, too?" she asked without inflection.

Miss Hartwell had an admirable machinelike quality that JD appreciated. If he ordered Uncle Harry pushed down the stairs, she would do her best to oblige. Unfortunately, Miss Hartwell's skinny sixty-five-year-old frame was no match for Harry's 250 pounds.

JD stared longingly at the neat lines coming together on his screen. He thought he'd just found the right piece that would put this particular part of the puzzle together, and he longed to try it out. But he could see the time had come for donning his CEO hat and growling authoritatively. He didn't have to ask when life had become this complicated. He knew. It had happened just as soon as he'd allowed people in instead of machines.

Harry bustled in without waiting for anyone's permission. Miss Hartwell obediently bowed out, closing the door behind her. Harry didn't give her a glance.

"DiFrancesco's on his way over here, Johnny. You'll like the man. He's a good friend of Frank. Smart as a whip. He'll turn your finances around in no time, boy. Just look at what he's done for Frank. He's got one of the best casinos in Vegas, and he's opening a place in Tahoe. We'll all be millionaires by the twenty-first century."

Harry flung his bulk into the wide leather chair next to JD's desk. JD winced and absently contemplated the cost of new springs. He'd impulsively purchased the leather furniture last year upon the suggestion of a particularly willowy interior designer. The relationship hadn't worked out—no surprise—but he rather liked the furniture she'd chosen.

"That's just fine, Harry. As soon as we get this program packaged and out of here, your friends can help us with the stock offering. But we don't have any finances to manage right now." JD tried reason, but he knew from long experience with his few scattered relations that reasoning didn't play a large part in Marshall lives. Of course, he didn't exactly have the habit of looking before he leaped either, or he wouldn't be in this predicament today. "I want them out of here for just a while longer, Harry. This is important."

Harry wiped his sweaty brow with a handkerchief and distributed his bulk more comfortably between the wide arms of the chair. "We don't have a choice, Johnny. Either DiFrancesco comes in, or they'll pull the loan. I told you I didn't have that kind of money on my own. It's a package deal. Frank's real careful how he loans out his money. They're good guys, Johnny. Don't be such a bigot. Not every casino owner in Vegas is mob."

No, probably only half. Maybe one quarter, JD mused as he

played with his swordlike silver letter opener, another gift from a delusional female. Hell, all of Vegas could be Ivory pure except for one character, and Harry would latch onto that one impurity. Marshall luck ran that way.

"I haven't got the patience for this guy, Harry. I'm telling you that time is of the utmost importance right now. I've got to finish this program in the next six weeks or we're dead in the water. We'll be a quarter million in the hole and no chance of payback."

"No problem. I'll show him the ropes myself," Harry said cheerfully, reaching in his pocket for a mint. "I know everybody. We'll just ask for what we need and take care of ourselves. You won't hear a peep out of us, Johnny. We'll be good as gold."

Oh, God, save him from Harry's clichés, JD prayed fervently. He never expected any response to his prayers, so he felt free in wasting them as he liked. Harry had been more father to him than his own father had, but that didn't say a great deal. Harry meant well. He'd offered JD a home and a garage to work in when he'd first started out. And though he'd genially approved each new employee JD hired, helped locate new facilities when the company's sales took off, chewed gum and shot the bull with sales executives when JD didn't have time for them, Harry never really *did* anything. He didn't even have an official position with the company. His only ambition in life was to be friends with everybody.

JD couldn't formulate a response to Harry's naïveté before the intercom buzzed.

"A Mr. DiFrancesco to see you, Mr. Marshall. He's coming in. He's smoking." Miss Hartwell's voice dripped disapproval even through the wires of the intercom.

Harry squirmed a little nervously as JD glared at him. "He doesn't like people telling him what he can or can't do," he whispered as the door swung open.

JD didn't find that reassuring.

Shorter by some six inches than JD's modest five-eleven, DiFrancesco entered as if he imagined himself John Wayne in a pinstripe suit. JD detested him on sight, even if the cigarette hanging out of the corner of his mouth hadn't already pissed him off.

"This is a nonsmoking facility, Mr. DiFrancesco," JD said icily. "We have too many valuable properties on location that can be damaged by smoke."

The shorter man glanced around JD's spartan office. "Not that I can see." He took a chair without asking and dropped cigarette ash into his trouser cuff just like in an old forties movie on TV. JD wondered where he found his tailor. MGM?

"I've come to inspect your operation, Johnny. We're making certain we've invested our money wisely. We'll start with the R&D department you expanded." He glanced impatiently at his Rolex. "If you'll show me the way, Johnny, you can introduce me around before the staff goes home for the day."

JD felt his blood pressure escalate to terminal. No one but his uncle called him Johnny. Rudely, he stood up, using the full effect of his greater height over the seated man. He hadn't spent all his time in the marines playing with computer documents. He'd built up a certain amount of muscle he kept in shape with regular workouts. He hadn't done it for the purpose of intimidating people so much as for a release of energy and frustration after a day in the office, but if his size threatened this slimeball, he wouldn't apologize.

"I've told Harry I don't have time for this. If you'll make an appointment with my secretary, I'll be happy to talk another day." Without waiting for a reply, JD walked out, leaving his visitors staring after him. He thought he saw DiFrancesco's cigarette drop onto his expensive gabardine trousers. A pity it couldn't burn a hole in the devil's hide.

Slamming his office door after him, JD stopped at his secretary's desk. "I'm going home, Miss Hartwell, where I might possibly get some work done."

Miss Hartwell covered the phone receiver with her hand and whispered, "It's the boy from Tempe, again. What should I tell him?"

To get the hell out of Tempe was JD's advice, but no one had asked him. Grabbing the receiver, he said curtly, "Marshall here."

A quaky adolescent male voice asked, "Is this John David Marshall from Tempe, Arizona?"

"I haven't seen Tempe in sixteen years," he replied impatiently, wondering what kind of joke someone was perpetrating on him now. It wasn't as if his fame and fortune preceded him as it did Bill Gates.

Following a moment's hesitation, the voice cracked anxiously. "Then I'm your son."

TWO

“I know what you’re going through, Nina,” the man behind the desk said sympathetically, leaning forward to show his earnestness.

Nina contemplated saying, “No, you don’t,” but stopped herself. She’d just come from a confrontation where she’d insanely held a shotgun on the cell phone people, but a lifetime of caution came easier. That’s why she was here, doing things the proper way.

Matt Horne had a young politician’s blond good looks and polished smile. Nina figured he had the county attorney’s job locked up in the next election, and after that, the sky was the limit. In the meantime, he walked a careful line in the cases he took. She could see his agile mind weighing the pros and cons of this one.

“I’m doing this for Hattie,” Nina insisted. “I’ve put it off as long as I can, but the doctors say she’ll never get better. Her lucid moments are fewer and farther between. It’s not the money, Matt. You know that. Heaven only knows, there’s little enough of that. It’s the land. Hattie’s life was that land. I can’t let them steal it.”

“You can’t stand in the way of progress, Nina.” Matt steepled his fingers against his chest as he retreated into a leaning position against the back of his leather chair. "I think we can keep the incompetency hearing fairly quiet. People know how hard you've worked to help Hattie. They'll understand this is just a legal maneuver. But the cellular tower has to go in there, Nina. It's the only suitable hill in the whole county."

"They can put the blamed thing on top of the bridge, then," she said emphatically as she rose from the chair. "If you won't do this for me, Matt Horne, I'll take it to a lawyer in Paducah. There are plenty of people behind me on this one. I'll get a petition. And if I find you're working for those damned phone people, I'll tell the world how you're robbing a sick old lady."

Matt rose with her, holding out a steadying hand. "Now don't go off half-cocked, Nina. We go a long way back. I've never seen you like this. Hattie's illness has been too hard on you. You're stressed out. You should take a break, have a vacation, get away from all this for a while. I'll have the papers all ready when you return. It will be very simple, very quiet, just a legal transfer giving you power of attorney. You don't have to worry about a thing."

"I have to worry about a damned phone company coming in and tearing up Hattie's Hill while I'm gone. I'm not quite that much of a fool. You get those papers drawn up now, Matt. If you don't, I'm out of here."

Furious for the second time that day, Nina slammed from the inner office on the second floor of the one and only bank building in Madrid, Kentucky. *Take a vacation,* she fumed. *Stressed out.* Hell, yes, she was stressed. But she damned well wasn't a hysterical female who needed placating. If she had any money at all, she'd hire an attorney in Paducah and have him research ownership of that mobile phone company. She'd bet a week's wages Matt Horne was on their payroll.

Not stopping to gossip with Matt's secretary in the outer office, Nina stormed down the stairs, furious at herself for losing her temper, furious at Matt for treating her like a mindless infant.

He'd been one year behind her in school, for pity's sake. He knew damned well she was twice as smart as he was. She just didn't have the money for the fancy schooling Matt's family had provided for him.

Hitting the glaring sun outside, Nina stopped long enough to let her eyes adjust to the shimmering heat waves. Groceries, she reminded herself. Groaning that she still had to add shopping to a list of irksome chores, she headed across the street, promising herself a treat to make up for the day's frustrations.

"Just tell me if I can keep that refrigeration unit running another year, Nina, that's all I ask. I can pay the new registers off in a year if that unit doesn't kick out."

Holding her paper sack of groceries with the precious box of Breyers chocolate ice cream ticking inside like a time bomb, Nina gazed impatiently at the Piggly Wiggly owner. As with Matt, she and Howard had attended grade school together. Except for thinning hair, Howard hadn't changed one iota from the mama's boy who'd sucked his thumb then.

"Howard, I'm not a psychic. I haven't any idea if your refrigerator will give out this year or next. But if you don't start setting it at zero, your ice cream won't be worth diddly-squat. I'm tired of taking home cream soup."

"You told me when that other unit was about to crash," he reminded her. "But you didn't tell me until after I'd already signed a new contract for roof repair. I don't want to make that mistake again."

"Then you'd better start saving more money out of your profits for repairs to this ratty old building instead of spending it on new bass boats, Howard. That's what I tell my students. No one saves money against a rainy day anymore. It's spend, spend, spend. You'd do better to build a nest egg and pay cash." Knowing she sounded like a prosy, frustrated spinster, Nina shifted the heavy sack from one arm to the other. She hated it when she sounded like this, but people never *learned.*

Somebody had to teach them. "And I'll give you one more piece of advice. You won't increase profits for that nest egg unless you start stocking the kind of items tourists expect in a real grocery store. Why can't you try some of that fancy Häagen-Dazs ice cream, or some of those Oriental vegetables they have in the Kroger up in Paducah?"

"My customers won't pay a dollar and a half for ice cream bars, and can you imagine Ethel and Harriet buying Chinese walnuts or whatever? Don't be ridiculous, Nina."

"Chestnuts, Howard. They're water chestnuts. And they're good for you. The tourists would buy them."

"Well, the tourists are only here three months out of the year, and I have to make a profit for twelve. Don't tell me how to run my business and I won't tell you how to teach school."

Nina grinned and surrendered before that familiar attitude. "I know. You're running the place the way your daddy did, and what was good enough for him is good enough for you. If it ain't broke, don't fix it. Good luck with your refrigerator, Howard. But you'd better take a look at that meat grinder Sadie's using. It's grinding mighty peculiar."

She swung out into the parking lot, smiling at having thrown Howard into another dither. They'd grown up together in this town, known each other forever, and he still hadn't learned she knew how to push all his buttons. But then, his mama never had been real smart either.

She wouldn't let the level of intelligence—or lack thereof—in Madrid bother her today. She had half a gallon of ice cream in her sack to top off the double fudge brownies she'd just bought. After a day like today, she intended to reward herself with absolute decadence. If she had someone to share with, she would have added real whipped cream, but cream separated if it didn't get used up quickly. She couldn't eat an entire bowlful by herself.

She still hadn't quite got the hang of living alone. Aunt Hattie used to join her in these occasional bouts of indulgence.

They'd turn an old Andy Williams record up loud, sit on the front porch, put their feet up, and eat bowls of double fudge chocolate whipped cream surprises. This time of year, they'd cover it with strawberries. Then they'd laugh and make plans and just enjoy the sunshine.

Nina did that on her own now, pretending Hattie still sat beside her. She couldn't get over to Hopkinsville today to visit Hattie, so she would turn up Andy Williams and talk to herself about the plans for the new greenhouse. On Nina's teacher's salary, Hattie's dream of a botanical garden was progressing slower than a snail through sand, but Nina kept working at it. Even though Hattie didn't understand Nina's grand dreams these days, Nina still related her latest achievements when she visited.

Each summer she inched infinitesimally closer toward the basic assets needed for the garden. By building her own greenhouses she figured she could grow most of the more common plants needed in this area. So she worked hard, saved every penny, and dreamed.

Nina frowned as a rust-red pickup chugged into the BP filling station next door. Lowering her sack of groceries into her aging Toyota hatchback, she hollered at a teenager heading across the parking lot in the direction of the BP. "Billy, tell that driver he'd better have his engine looked at before he takes off."

The teenager waved his icy Pepsi can in greeting. "Sure thing, Miss Toon." Grinning, he glanced at the truck's out-of-state plates. "But he ain't gonna listen."

Nina shrugged. That wasn't her problem. In her experience, men seldom listened when a woman told them something they needed to know. Examining the idea further, she supposed they seldom listened, period. She knew perfectly well the stranger getting out of his pickup and filling up the tank would look at Billy as if he were some kind of backwoods con artist trying to rip him off for a valve job. She supposed she could go over there and inform him that Billy gained nothing by the warning, but that would lead to other explanations, and she didn't handle explanations well. People around here just accepted her warnings the way they accepted Miss Tansy's eccentric hats. Except for Howard, of course. He always wanted more.

As Nina cranked her engine, she glanced over at the small tableau at the filling station. Sure enough, Billy stood there earnestly talking to the stranger, while the stranger merely nodded with impatience. She didn't have her glasses on and couldn't see the man clearly, but judging by the long hair on the back of his neck and the athletic set of his shoulders beneath a tight black T-shirt, she'd say he wasn't a typical fishing enthusiast.

Swearing at herself for forgetting to put on the wretched new glasses again, she rummaged through her purse. The ice cream would melt if she didn't get it home soon. She found the blasted glasses, untangled the gold chain she'd hoped would keep her from losing them, and jerked them on.

The stranger entered the station to pay for the gas. Nina glanced at the huge motorcycle in the back of the pickup. Harley-Davidson, no doubt. The man looked like that kind. She bet he had a leather jacket slung over the truck seat.

As she pulled out of the lot, she caught a glimpse of a long-haired teenager in the passenger seat. Brothers, she figured. A man with black hair that thick and unmarred by gray couldn't be old enough to have a kid that age. Why would two motorcycle thugs come to this backwater fishing retreat?

It didn't matter. She had enough worries of her own without borrowing others.

At a signal from Ethel Arnett, Nina stopped her car in the middle of Main Street. "Main Street" was a euphemism for the two-lane county highway running through the town's center. The Piggly Wiggly and other businesses on either side of the highway had installed sidewalks for the convenience of their customers, but they may as well have left the dirt roads and boardwalks of a prior era. The inhabitants still treated the road as a horse trail.

"Hi, Ethel. How's the bake sale coming?"

The older woman leaned against Nina's car door and fanned herself. "We'll have a hundred cakes or more, I reckon," Ethel drawled. "We oughter raise more than last year. The committee thought flowers might look nice on the tables. Have you got anything we can use?"

Nina grinned. She'd known what Ethel wanted when she hailed her. The church ladies had more sense than to ask her to bake a cake. "The roses are gorgeous this year. Why don't you send Dottie out for what she needs? You know I can't arrange them like she does. I've got ice cream in the back. I'd better get going. See you later, Ethel."

The old pickup from the gas station gave a roar of disapproval and sped around her before she could shift into drive. Strangers in the area didn't take kindly to the local custom of stopping cars in the middle of the road so pedestrians and drivers could gossip.

Nina didn't waste much time worrying about what tourists thought. They came and went with the seasons. The rest of the town relied on them for a living, but she didn't. She thanked the good Lord and Aunt Hattie for that. By the time school started in the fall, Nina had usually mended her frayed patience by puttering in her greenhouses and was ready for the high-energy chaos of high school again. If she dealt with the summer tourists as others did, she'd not have any patience left to mend.

Instead of turning up the road to the interstate, the pickup ahead of her roared on toward corn and soybean fields. Nina shook her head in dismay as she carefully steered her aging Camry in the same direction. That pickup wouldn't make it the fifty miles to the next town. The driver would find himself stranded in a cow pasture. He could count himself lucky if he didn't get shot by some farmer defending his marijuana crop in the woods. That had happened once a few years back.

Well, he'd better hope the truck broke down before she turned off on Hattie's Lane. She wasn't about to let that half-gallon of Breyers chocolate melt in this heat going after him.

With thoughts of ice cream floating through her mind and heat mirages puddling the highway, Nina almost didn't see the van turning out of the gravel road ahead. She supposed some stupid tourist thought he'd find a shortcut to the lake that way, but she wouldn't recommend anything but a four-wheel drive down that road. He was lucky the van still had its bottom.

The van picked up speed and disappeared around the wooded curve ahead. She hated that curve. The kids liked to fly down the road doing ninety at night. They inevitably took the wrong lane while cutting the curve, and drivers coming from the opposite direction didn't know it until they came up on them. A carload of kids lost their lives just the previous year pulling that stunt in front of a semi.

She took the blind curve at a cautious pace, prepared to pull over if someone cut it too sharply coming the other way. Aunt Hattie had always said caution never hurt, and Hattie was seldom wrong.

Nina winced as she rounded the curve. The rusty pickup had stalled half off the road near the embankment ahead. The engine must have died before the driver could pull over. The boy stood in front of the cab, pushing it backward while the driver steered. She hoped they'd made it far enough down the road from the curve for the driver of the van to see them, because he was picking up speed rapidly.

Even as she thought that, Nina watched in horror as the van accelerated without veering into the left lane to avoid the stalled vehicle. Screaming, Nina slammed her own brakes as if she could halt the van that way. Fingers clenched around the wheel in helplessness, she watched the van slam into the pickup's engine compartment where it angled half on the road. She winced and shuddered at the resounding crash. The pickup spun off the road into the soybean field. The van never slowed down.

Sick to her stomach and trembling, Nina clutched her steering wheel and edged the Toyota off the side of the road. She couldn't see more than the pickup's spinning tires from here. The words "He didn't stop" formed a continuous refrain in her head as gravel crunched beneath her wheels. How could he not stop? Was the driver insane? What in hell could she do?

"Missouri. LAW 119," Nina muttered, halting the car near the spinning tires and disengaging the engine. "LAW 119." She'd heard repeating something helped to remember it. She would remember that license plate number. She would have that scoundrel by the neck. But she didn't have time to rummage for pencil and paper. She leapt from the car as soon as the engine stopped.

She heard the boy's shouts of fury and breathed a momentary sigh of relief. She'd had a horrible dread of finding both occupants lying dead and bloody between the soybean rows.

The road had been built high between the low-lying fields, to avoid the traditional spring flooding. She stood on the edge and looked down. Apparently having jumped free of the collision, the boy appeared unharmed. He'd climbed up on the driver's door where the truck lay turned on its side at the bottom of the embankment. Movie images of cars exploding upon impact unreeled in Nina's head as she ran through the gravel and slid down the hill in her cheap Keds. Aunt Hattie had never given her instructions for a situation like this.

The boy had opened the cab door by the time Nina reached them. She didn't see any imminent danger of flashing fire or smoke. The rear wheel still spun idly, and the gleaming chrome of the motorcycle now lay crumpled in the middle of soybeans. Heat waves rose off the black dirt. A cardinal chirped "pretty-pretty" somewhere in the trees behind them. She didn't smell gas.

"Is he all right?" she called up to the teenager leaning in the open doorway.

"He's out cold! We've got to get him out of here."

The kid sounded slightly hysterical. Nina couldn't blame him. "We shouldn't move him until we get the medics. We might make something worse." Even as she said it, she realized how long it would take for an ambulance to arrive. The town never had organized an ambulance service. Some of the volunteer firefighters had training, but most of them would be out in their fields right now. And she didn't know that she could trust them with a serious injury any more than she could trust herself.

"We've got to get him out!" The level of panic in the boy's voice rose considerably.

"All right. Get down from there." She was an adult. She could handle this situation. As a teacher, she had learned the trick of taking command. "You get out on the road and flag someone down." She glanced back at the road. They'd come almost ten miles from town already. This far from the interstate, traffic dwindled, and the road led nowhere in particular. He'd be lucky to spot a combine.

The boy jumped down. Face pale with fear, he turned to her with brief hope in his eyes, hope that died as he caught a good look at her. "You can't get him out," he announced bluntly. "I'll have to push the truck back up."

Since the truck had slid down the embankment on its side, the wheels rested on the hillside. Pushing the truck up would do nothing more than set it at a precarious angle that would only turn it over again. Nina thought it safest lying flat just where it was, but she didn't bother arguing with the terrified teenager. She already knew she didn't have the strength for lifting a truck. She needed three-inch heels to reach five-four and managed a hundred pounds only when soaking wet.

"Let me get a look at him. I've had some first-aid courses.

Can you drive?" she asked as she climbed up to where the boy had perched moments before.

"No. My ma wouldn't let me," he said with anger. "Now look. I could've taken your car and gotten help." His voice brightened. "How about a car phone?"

Like bloody hell would she give him the keys to her car. She'd thought he might take the motorcycle. She snorted at the notion of a car phone. If he only knew . . .

She glanced inside the truck and wished she hadn't. The stranger had apparently smacked the windshield when the van rammed him. He'd probably had his seat belt off so he could climb out. Blood crawled down a face too bronzed even for this southern climate. She winced at the bloody gash in his scalp. No wonder he was out cold. His doubled-up position against the far window didn't look too comfortable either. One boot-clad foot tangled with the gearshift at an awkward angle.

Clenching her teeth against the sight, Nina contemplated some way of prying him out of his unconscious sprawl. If they could lift the pickup high enough, they could possibly slide him out the passenger door. The alternative was hauling him up by the thick ebony hair of his head. She figured the battered brown Stetson on the floorboard belonged to him. Too bad he hadn't been wearing it. Then again, she'd never seen a motorcycle thug wearing a Stetson. Maybe it belonged to the boy.

The boy watched her anxiously, as if she held the answer to all his problems in her hands. Nina imagined that at any other time he had the tough fifteen-year-old swagger that matched his long hair and earring, but right now he barely looked twelve.

"You're right. If we could lift the truck just enough to open the door, we could slide him out. I'd better drive back to town and see if I can find someone to help us." She didn't like the idea. It meant a twenty-minute round-trip at best. She searched her brain for someone who might live closer, but she couldn't think of anyone who would be home at this time of day. Even the farmer who owned this field worked in the factory up at Calvert.

The kid looked dubious. "I can lift the truck, but how will you slide him out?"

Hell if she knew. Twisting a short lock of stick-straight white-blond hair, she stared out over the soybean field. The beans were barely peeking through the ground. All that wet weather earlier this spring, she supposed.

Wet weather. Canvas. "Stay right there," she ordered, as if the kid could go anywhere else. Sprinting up the hillside, she dashed back to the battered Camry. She'd protected the carpet in the trunk with canvas when she'd hauled plant trays in all that rain.

Seldom did she find occasion to appreciate her petite size, but she did now as she climbed down inside the cab with the canvas. The truck cab was smaller than a double bed. She felt extremely awkward sitting on the stranger's head while determining the extent of his injuries. The man beside her wasn't terrifically large, but the muscular shoulders she'd noticed earlier pretty well filled the doorway. He groaned as she tried stabilizing his neck.

Nina pulled her hand back from the heated warmth of him as if burned. The blood disguised his features, so she assumed her sudden breathlessness had to do with the heat. She couldn't tell from this angle, but she figured him for six feet of dead weight. As she worked around him, bile rose in her throat at the sticky sweet smell of blood. Damn good thing she'd never wanted to be a nurse.

By the time she had him situated, an RV and two pickups towing fishing boats had roared by on the road above. None of them stopped. Blasted tourists.

"Why didn't you flag them down?" Nina asked in irritation as she climbed out and watched another truck cruise by.

The kid shrugged and spit on his hands as he looked for just the right spot to heft the truck. "Dad wouldn't want strangers nosing around."

Dad? She'd like to know where the damned hell Dad was and if the asshole would want his son baking in an overturned pickup, but she didn't ask. She'd better quit swearing while she was at it. One of these days she'd let those words fly in a classroom and the parents of her students would take off her head.

"I'm a stranger," she replied, wishing she could growl.

"You're a woman."

Oh, good. Oh, really good. And she supposed that attitude came from the boot-wearing stud inside. If he hadn't already had his block nearly hacked off, she'd gladly take it off for him.

It was too hot and miserable to argue the point. Fine. She was a woman. Nina wiped her forehead with her arm, got beside the twerp, and with a shove to match his, dug in her heels and felt the cab lift all of three centimeters.

They inched around and shoved some more, gaining another inch or two. The man inside groaned more loudly than before.

"Use the door for a wedge," Nina gasped. "Get it open."

Still holding the truck cab with one hand, the boy eased the other down to the door handle. It opened a crack and dug into the dirt.

"He's going to be mad about those computers," the boy muttered as something inside slid around.

Nina figured the heat had affected her hearing. Motorcycle thugs didn't know the word *computer* as far as she knew. For that matter, ninety percent of Madrid thought computers a necessary evil designed by the outside world for the single purpose of making their lives crazy. She didn't respond but pushed from a different angle. The hot metal scorched her hands.

A furious curse roared out of the interior. Nina blinked, and the boy jumped. The cab slipped back to the ground again. This time a stream of curses sailed through the open window, each one more inventive than the one before.

"Jackie!" the voice roared. "Where the f—— are you?"

Now that was one particular word Nina never used, even in her own head. She didn't think anyone should fling it around a teenager. Swiping at the perspiration pouring down her face, she yelled at the truck roof, "Trying to get you out of there, you puling fool! Where do you think he is?"

The boy's eyes widened in surprise and admiration as if she'd invented a new curse word. Nina knew the reaction. That particular word never failed to send half her class to the dictionary. The other half threw it around for weeks, sometimes months after. She'd even had one valedictorian work it into his graduation speech. The power of words never ceased to amaze her.

The silence in the truck grew so long that Nina feared he'd passed out again. But then a blunt-fingered, sun-browned hand clamped over the edge of the driver's door at the top, and she heard another onslaught of swear words, only slightly less loud than the first outburst.

She glanced at the boy. "Maybe we'd better climb up there and see if we can help him out."

The boy nodded and scrambled back up the engine side of the pickup. Nina didn't see how both of them could fit up there, but she didn't see how a seriously injured man could pull himself out either. Cautiously, she judged the nearness of the truck bed to the door. Maybe if she lay flat against . . .

Another hand wrapped around the doorway edge. Before she could contemplate climbing up, a pair of powerful shoulders emerged, followed by muscular arms in a tight black T-shirt with the sleeves rolled up. She hadn't seen anyone roll up T-shirt sleeves since the last James Dean movie. She stared as muscles bulged with the strain, and then a narrow waist and a blue-jeaned rear end settled over the side.

He looked ready to tumble backward off the truck. Nina leapt on the pickup bed and crawled up beside him while the boy looked on helplessly from the engine end. For just a second, long-lashed brown eyes stared into hers. Wide and momentarily unguarded, his gaze reflected a pain that pierced her soul. Then, with blood still running down his face, the stranger closed his eyes wearily and murmured, "Send in the clowns," before slumping backward into her arms.

A fine way to greet a rescuing angel. Nina could tell right now she'd just rescued one of those smart-mouthed hillbillies who couldn't utter a gracious word. She just couldn't immediately think why a hillbilly would know the words to Stephen Sondheim's music. Send in the clowns, indeed.

"Jackie!" she screamed as he began to slide back down. But the boy had already jumped up beside her and grabbed the man's other arm.

Between Nina and Jackie, they laid him on the side of the truck. A combine stopped on the side of the road, and Nina whistled in relief as Gary Thomas slipped down the embankment toward them. She didn't think she had the strength left to drag a full-grown man up that hill. In fact, she figured she'd pass out from the heat and exertion in another thirty seconds.

The boy beside her stiffened nervously, but he simply didn't have a choice. They had to get his brother somewhere cool and safe, then have a doctor look at him.

Gary was a stocky farmer, father of two little girls in her Sunday school class. Nina nodded, gave him a hasty explanation, and let him take over. Gary seldom said much. At the moment she rather admired that particular trait.

"Get him in the back of my car," she ordered as they hauled the unconscious man up the hill. "I'll drive him over to the clinic."

"We've got to get the bike first!" the boy yelled as she opened the back door. "And the computers! Dad would kill me if they got stolen."

Dad again. Either this boy had a strange notion of what fathers thought important, or he had one mean bastard of an old man. Nina was inclined toward ignoring him, but Gary turned and answered reassuringly, "There's room in back. Go unload the computers. I'll take care of the bike later."

Obviously Jackie trusted strangers more than his old man did. After watching fearfully while they arranged his brother partially across the backseat and into the hatchback's trunk, he dashed down the hillside and began lugging boxes up the hill.

There for a while, Nina thought the kid contemplated putting a few of the boxes on top of his unconscious brother in his efforts to get them all in, but he finally stored the last one under his feet on the passenger side of the car. Then he looked anxiously at Gary. "You won't let anyone steal the bike?"

Gary wiped his sweating brow with his handkerchief and shook his head. "I'll haul it over to Miss Toon's while you're at the clinic. It'll be safe enough there." He glanced at Nina. "Should I call Bob to tow the truck out?"

Nina slammed her door and turned the key in the ignition. "Not yet. The sheriff may need a look at it. I'll call him when we get back. Thanks, Gary."

Checking the road before pulling out, Nina didn't notice the boy's silence until she had the car under way. Her heart thumped nervously at the look on his face when she finally turned in his direction. "What's wrong?"

"You can't call the sheriff," he said adamantly.

"That van ran you off the road. The driver has to be caught before he kills someone."

"We can't call the sheriff." He crossed his arms over his scrawny chest and glared out the windshield. "They'll put Dad in jail."

Behind them, the injured man groaned and began swearing again.

Remembering the ice cream, Nina sighed. This had certainly turned out to be one of those days.

THREE

JD clenched his eyes closed and groaned. Lord, he ached. He thought he'd given up drinking. He didn't have a masochistic bone in his body, and he had an aversion to pain. Drinking led to pain; ergo, he didn't drink. But he still ached.

His head felt muggy. He heard voices, but he didn't feel inclined to tune them in. If he didn't think too hard, maybe he could drift back to sleep again. He could count line numbers in the banking program. That usually worked, if he didn't get caught in a particularly sticky loop command. But he couldn't remember what line he was on.

The voices jogged other memories. He winced and tried forgetting, but the memory slashed a fresh gash across his brain, and the wound still bled. How could Uncle Harry do this to him? He still couldn't believe it. Maybe he didn't trust people much, but Uncle Harry? Harry had been closer than a father to him. There was something wrong with this picture, only he couldn't put his finger on it.

Finger. Fingers. On his forehead. Cool ones. Smooth and slender. JD instantly jerked back from whatever world he drifted in. The voice that spoke over his head had no resemblance whatsoever to Harry's.

"He's not feverish. The doctor said he'd come around soon. Go ahead and finish your hamburger. He'll be all right."

JD didn't think so. He thought he might die first. Imps of hell pounded sledgehammers in his brain, and now that he'd been dragged back to consciousness, he realized his foot throbbed and ached as if he'd pulled it off and stuck it back on wrong. He couldn't remember a time when he'd hurt worse. Maybe that time when the horse threw him . . . Or the day he slammed the bike into a tree. But that had been a long while ago. He was too old for those stunts now. Remembering the son he hadn't known he had, he groaned. Entirely too damned old.

The cool fingers slipped away, but he sensed their owner hesitating beside him. He didn't suppose he'd see the face of an angel if he opened his eyes. His luck didn't run that way. But a she-devil might be just up his alley.

Wincing against the pain of movement, JD squinted into the dim light of the room. The slender figure outlined against the glare through the window blinds reminded him of someone, or something, but he didn't strain his brain remembering.

"Awake?" she asked quietly, stepping farther away, almost out of his sight.

He tried nodding and realized the mistake at once. He closed his eyes again. "Jackie?"

"He's wolfing down a pound of hamburger right now. I'd say he's fine. Can I get you something to drink? The doctor said you shouldn't eat anything just yet."

He thought he heard a trace of amusement in a voice almost as slender as the figure he'd seen. Or could voices be slender? Thin? Tinkly? He concentrated on the words rather than the sound.

He definitely didn't want to eat anything. He didn't particularly want to sit up either, but his mouth felt like the inside of a toaster. "Beer?" he asked cautiously.

"Not likely. This is a dry county. How about Coke?"

He grimaced and regretted the effort. "Water."

JD had managed a semisitting position by the time Jackie bounded in with a tall glass of ice water. The mysterious voice had evidently closed the window blinds, and he could open his eyes a little better. He still couldn't focus on Jackie without narrowing them. "You all right?" he asked gruffly. He hadn't yet acclimated himself to this tall young man who claimed him as father. He'd certainly set a hell of an example so far. Lack of paternal behavior must be another of those genetic flaws he'd inherited.

"I'm fine," the boy acknowledged. "It's you they sent spinning off the road. The bike's dented, but the engine still starts. I don't know about the computers, though."

The computers. Oh, shit. JD sipped the water and nearly gagged. Tap water. Or worse. But he was too thirsty to argue. He drank some more and tried to orient himself. The truck had died on a road to nowhere. He'd shifted to neutral and had started climbing out to help Jackie push. He couldn't remember any more than that. He squinted back at the boy.

"What the devil happened?"

"Some clown pulled out and rammed right into us, sent the truck flying. I've been trying to persuade Miss Toon not to call the cops." He lowered his voice. "I used some of the cash in your wallet for the doctor and told them your name is John Smith. Was that okay?"

Oh, shit. Oh, double shit. JD gritted his teeth and leaned back against a surprisingly comfortable pillow. He wasn't in a bed. He'd gathered that much. His elbow poked against a couch back. A man could get used to a couch as soft as this one. Even his legs fit on it without coming off the other side. Which was a good thing, he decided, peering blearily at his feet. The damned arms of the couch must be a foot high. He blinked as he looked at his feet again. Instead of seeing the black square-toed boots he favored, he saw a bundle of white bandages. Oh, shit.

"What's wrong with my foot?"

"Cracked a bone when it hit the gearshift, apparently. Doctor said he couldn't do much for it but keep it wrapped so you couldn't bang it around more. You're supposed to stay off it, though."

Shit. Horse manure. Chicken droppings and cow flop. He couldn't think of a word bad enough. He sipped the nasty water again and wished for whiskey. Maybe he should take up drinking again. It couldn't make his life any worse than it had become this last month or so.

"Where are we?" JD calculated how much cash he'd brought with him. Would they trace credit card receipts? Bank card transactions? He couldn't imagine Uncle Harry or his cohorts being that smart, but he sure as hell didn't like taking chances when the odds were against him. And then he remembered Nancy and the police. Double damn hell.

"Just across the lakes. Miss Toon saw the accident and took you to the clinic. They don't have hospital beds or anything there, and I told them you didn't have insurance, so she brought us back here until you could wake up and decide what you want to do."

"Good thinking." He reassured the anxious boy while his brain whirled. Miss Toon must be the slender shadow he'd seen when he woke up. The image of spiky white-blond hair surrounding a petite face of sharp bones and huge green eyes came to him, but he couldn't place it. He and Miss Toon needed to talk. Calling the cops wasn't such a hot idea at all.

He could do surface charm well enough. It was relationships he bungled. He didn't want a relationship with Miss Toon. He just needed her temporary cooperation. Maybe charm would work. "Go get Miss Toon."

Jackie disappeared, and a moment later JD caught the fresh scent of some flowery fragrance. It made him aware of his own ripe aroma. Rubbing his eyes, he focused on the woman drifting on the edge of his vision. He wanted to yell at her to get over where he could see her, but in his experience women frequently didn't respond well to orders. They were a mysterious gender he'd avoided whenever possible. Obviously, if Jackie were any indication, he hadn't avoided them enough.

Although his head ached like hell, he tried reason and politeness. "Miss Toon?" His voice croaked, and he took another sip of water.

"I'm here, Mr. Smith. How does your head feel? You've got a rather nasty cut there."

Well, that explained something, anyway. Gingerly, JD explored the bandage taped across his forehead. "Jackie tells me we have you to thank for rescuing us. It's not every day someone goes out of their way for strangers. I appreciate it."

"You're quite welcome, but anyone would have done it. I couldn't leave you out in a bean field. Your brother tells me we can't reach your father. Is there anyone else I can notify? Someone must be getting worried by now."

"Brother?" JD squinted up at the silhouette hovering somewhere behind his left elbow. What in hell was she talking about? He wished he could get his head in focus. The doctor must have given him something for the pain. "We're traveling," he managed to get out. "There's no one expecting us. What time is it? Do we have time to find a motel?"

She drifted closer and took the glass he'd emptied. "It's almost nine, and you're in no condition for driving, even if the truck is, which I doubt. And the next motel with any chance of a vacancy this time of year is about fifty miles down the road. I told the sheriff I'd keep you here for the night. He said he'd talk to you in the morning."

"Crap!" He didn't realize he'd roared the word until Tinkerbell stepped backward, away from him. He considered apologizing, but "Damn it to hell" came out instead.

"My feelings exactly, Mr. Smith," she said dryly. "It's been one of those days. I'd offer you some ice cream, but it's melted all over the rug of my car. It blends well with the blood. But my aunt wouldn't like it if I offered any less than my full hospitality. May I fix you some soup, perhaps?"

He damned well didn't want soup. The ceiling fan whirling lazily over his head created something of a humid breeze, but it sure as hell didn't cool things off any. Hadn't they heard of air-conditioning out here? JD felt his shirt sticking to his back. That ice cream would have tasted good right about now. "I'll pay for your rug," he grunted. He had too many things to think of at once, and his head just wasn't up to it. "Just bring me some more water, please."

"How about iced tea? And perhaps some cheese and crackers? They're not too heavy. Maybe they'll stay down."

He hadn't had cheese and crackers in years, not unless it was goat cheese on fancy rye crackers of some sort at one of those parties Jimmy had insisted he attend. Somehow, JD knew Tinkerbell didn't mean goat cheese on rye. Soda crackers and Velveeta would suit him nicely right now. He nodded.

He kept his eyes closed and pretended the breeze from the fan was cool as she drifted away again. He didn't hear her coming or going, but he could catch her flowery scent as she passed. The kitchen must be nearby. He could hear her talking to Jackie. She talked with the kid much more easily than she did with him. Of course, Jackie probably didn't swear at her.

Jackie came back with the tray, and JD almost felt disappointment. He didn't waste time puzzling on that. He glanced at the boy's pale, wary face and decided he'd better sit up and pretend he wasn't dying. Learning the responsibilities of fatherhood at his age and in this condition seemed pretty ludicrous, especially after thirty-two years of doing what he damned well pleased.

Just throwing his foot over the edge of the couch warned he would die sooner than later if he tried that again. Gritting his teeth, JD propped the bandaged foot on a convenient coffee table and sat up against the back of the couch. It had a good high back, one a man could feel comfortable with. The seat sank down deep so he could sprawl, and he sighed with relief once his foot settled. He sipped the iced tea and decided Miss Toon was right. He definitely preferred this over water.

"What are we going to do about the sheriff?" the boy whispered.

"Why does she think you're my brother?" JD whispered back.

The kid shrugged. "Heck if I know. You don't look much like a father, I guess."

If his head didn't hurt so damned much, that thought might make him laugh. Ever since he'd discovered he had a fifteen-year-old son, he'd felt like Methuselah. "All right, we'll just let her think that. You're my brother, Jackie Smith. A hick sheriff doesn't need to know more."

Jackie nodded uncertainly. "I guess. She's kind of nice. She teaches at the high school here and knows all about Monster House."

And probably disapproved of the video game thoroughly, but JD didn't add that. "Well, we wouldn't want her mixed up in all this then. We'll talk to the sheriff in the morning and be on our way. She won't ever know."

The boy squirmed uncomfortably. "I don't know about that. The engine died before the truck got hit. The whole thing's in pretty bad shape now. And the doctor said you should stay off that foot. That's your gas-pedal foot. I don't see how we can go anywhere."

"What about the Harley?" JD demanded.

"What about the computers?" Jackie asked.

Stalemate. They couldn't haul computers on a Harley. He couldn't hold the blamed bike up with one foot either. Not for long, anyway. "All right. Send Miss Toon back in here. I'll see what we can do."

He was too tired to think. If it hadn't been for Uncle Harry and Nancy, he could just catch a ride to the nearest dealership and buy a new truck. But he couldn't let either of those two connivers know where he and Jackie were yet. Maybe this impulsive jaunt across middle America hadn't been such an intelligent idea, but it was all he'd thought of when the walls started crumbling around him. It was what he'd always done when things turned bad and he could trust only himself. In his eagerness to escape, he'd promised Jackie the ocean, but maybe the kid would settle for those lakes. Maybe.

The pixie drifted in again. Jackie had turned a light on, and this time JD could see trim, suntanned legs running up into hideous wide-legged denim shorts that carried up past her hips into a bib over her breasts. If she had breasts, that is. A man couldn't tell beneath all those denim pockets. Bib overalls, for crying out loud. He really had landed in the outback of nowhere.

But then JD's gaze reached her face, and he figured the blow to his head had smacked him into another dimension. Wide green eyes filled the area above sharp, high cheekbones. If it weren't for the pouty pink lips, he'd vote her as best model for one of those velvet paintings of wide-eyed waifs. Of course, those paintings didn't have spiky white-blond hair. Tinkerbell did. And she was a schoolteacher? They didn't make schoolteachers like that when he was kid, or he'd have gone to school a little more often.

"If you're tired, I thought Jackie might help you into Aunt Hattie's room. It's on this floor, so you won't have to climb stairs."

She spoke with such soft diffidence that he scarcely heard her. How could a schoolteacher keep a roomful of teenagers in order when she talked like that? JD ran his fingers through his hair and winced as they came in contact with his throbbing head. A bed sounded incredibly good right about now.

"I don't mean to impose," he answered stiffly. "I don't want to put your aunt out of her bed." Miss Toon might look like an alien, but he felt like one. He'd never lived in the country, never had an aunt of any sort, had never relied on the kindness of strangers. He'd been insane to cross the country in that old pickup, but he hadn't wanted Harry and Nancy tracing airplane tickets. Damn. He still couldn't believe Harry.

The pouty lips smiled shyly. "I don't think she'd mind. She's over in Hopkinsville."

JD didn't know where or what Hopkinsville was and didn't bother asking. "If you're sure she won't mind," he agreed wearily. He hadn't the strength left for arguing.

"I'm sure she won't," she answered with a hint of amusement. "Shall I call Jackie? I thought he might like a cot in the room with you, but I can make a place for him upstairs, if you'd prefer."

"I don't want to trouble you. You'd best leave him with me." Tilting his head, JD looked at her long and hard, drinking her in as if she were the tall, cool beer he needed. He couldn't fit all the pieces together. The hick clothes, the punk hair, the shy voice.

She retreated from him even as he stared. "It's no trouble at all. I've got plenty of room." She slipped away before he could say anything else.

As she left, JD contemplated with bemusement the new ache she'd aroused, the one forming a hard lump behind his zipper. He didn't think this was a particularly appropriate time to end his jinx with women. But his rebellious body had never had a lick of sense.

Great. Just great. He groaned, leaning his pounding head against the pillow as he considered his new predicament. He'd stolen his own program and computers, practically kidnapped a kid he didn't know to keep the kid's stepfather from killing him, and now his only means of transportation lay in a cornfield—while he sat here with a broken foot and a hard-on for a woman who looked like Tinkerbell.

Wasn't life just a bowl of cherries?

FOUR

"Miss Toon."

"Nina," she responded absently, beating the eggs.

"Nina Toon?"

She thought she heard laughter in her guest's tone and watched him warily. More stocky than tall, with narrow hips that emphasized his muscular shoulders, John Smith permeated her kitchen, making her pretty wicker stools seem small and unstable in comparison. She couldn't remember ever seeing a man in Hattie's kitchen. Maybe that's why he seemed to dominate the butcher-block counter. She glared at his smirk. Nina couldn't call her unexpected guest a handsome man by any standard she knew. Pierce Brosnan was her ideal. Or Sean Connery. Polished, sophisticated men with charm and wit and spectacular smiles. This man had broad cheekbones, a long jaw and powerful nose, a chin that stuck out entirely too far, and a smirk she'd like to wipe off his face. And he needed a haircut.

"That's right. Nina Toon. Do you have a problem with it?" she asked warily.

"Kind of like Looney Tunes? Cartoons? Ninatoons. It fits. Where'd you get a name like that?"

She suspected she should whop him upside the head with her frying pan, but she didn't have much experience with strange men, and she certainly had none at entertaining them as houseguests. "Most of the Toons around here live across the lakes," she replied stiffly. "They and a few other families formed a Catholic community back in the 1800s. We just kind of proliferated, I guess. I think it was my grandfather came over this way, but I've got about ten zillion relatives back at Fancy Farm. I go over to the picnic every once in a while."

"The picnic?"

Well, she knew he wasn't from around here. She poured the eggs in the pan. "The Fancy Farm picnic. It's the oldest picnic in the world. It's in the Guinness book. They've been holding a kind of homecoming picnic over there the first weekend of August since 1880. All the politicians come. It's kind of a kickoff for the fall political campaigns."

"All that hot August air and politicians, too. I imagine it's delightful. Is it time for me to pop the bread in the toaster yet?"

She knew he poked fun at her, but she couldn't think of any way of politely telling him where to jump off. If Jackie had made those snide remarks, she would have clipped his hair to the scalp. But John Smith wasn't a teenager. John Smith. He really did think she was a fool.

"By all means, Mr. Smith. Where did you leave Pocahontas?" Her eyes widened, and she bit her lip as that slipped out. She didn't know where it had come from or what perverse quirk of her tongue let it slip. She didn't dare turn around to see how he took it.

"Back in Arizona with her other Native American friends."

The toaster clicked as he pushed the bread down, and she dared a quick peek at him. He didn't seem put out by her sarcastic question. In fact, he was watching her with a Cheshire-cat grin on his face. Nina hurriedly returned to scrambling the eggs. "Pocahontas was an easterner, Mr. Smith. I'd think she would find herself a trifle out of place in Arizona."

"That's okay. I'm a trifle out of place here. What is this place called?"

"Kentucky," she answered dryly.

"I knew that, Miss Toon. My geography may be poor, but I can read a map. I just don't know where in Kentucky I got knocked off that map."

She reminded herself he was a guest and not one of her students. She really didn't need this complication in her life right now. "Madrid," she answered with a sigh.

"Muh-*drid*?" he repeated, pronouncing it like the city in Spain.

"*Mad*-rid," she corrected, accenting and flattening the first syllable. "Like the New Madrid fault. You know, where the huge earthquake fault is. It's just across the Mississippi from here. They keep telling us we're ripe for a big one any day."

"Oh, swell. I've come all the way across the country to go from one earthquake fault to another. With my luck, the big one will hit while I'm here. I don't suppose you see a big black cloud hanging over my head with lightning bolts shooting out of it, do you?"

She laughed. A large man with long hair sitting at her counter popping toast from her toaster was surreal enough for one morning. The thought of a black cloud floating around her kitchen with lightning bolts shooting out of it was just too close to how she felt right now. "Every cloud has a silver lining, Mr. Smith," she chirped.

She could feel his glare clear through her new cotton chemise dress. Ignoring him, she scooped the eggs into a blue willow bowl.

"JD," he answered, without any seeming relevance.

She turned and squinted at him. "JD?"

"John David. People call me JD."

She grinned. "As in, juvenile delinquent?"

"Juris doctorate," he threw back at her, carefully spreading a thick hunk of butter on the soft toast.

"James Dean." She took the rest of the toast slices and cut

thin slivers of butter to melt on them while he struggled with his hunk.

"James Dean was a stupid punk with no ambition. He liked making an ass out of himself. I do not and will never resemble James Dean." He took a hungry bite out of the toast.

"You look more like a victim of war this morning." She amazed herself. She talked with this stranger as if she'd known him all her life. Better. The boys she'd grown up with had been tongue-tied most of the time.

She'd grown up here on the farm with Great-aunt Hattie, a confirmed spinster, and she'd seldom had an opportunity for bantering with any man. The boys she'd gone to school with didn't count. She still thought of them as boys. She'd never had a man in the kitchen or any other room in the house, except when the preacher came calling, and he scarcely counted. She'd never related well to strange men. She'd hoped college would change that, but not many men attended teaching classes, and she'd commuted, so she hadn't had time for hanging around afterward in the pizza parlor or wherever men hung around. Anyway, according to her aunt, all men were predatory. And she distinctly felt like prey when this one looked at her the way he did now.

He didn't seem to notice her ignorance. Rather than get up and hobble around on his good foot, he continued sitting at the counter as he hollered "Jackie!" at the ceiling. The sound of the shower had stopped some minutes ago.

"I can keep his eggs warm. Teenagers like to make sure their faces haven't been rearranged overnight. I suppose I must have spent inordinate amounts of time in front of a mirror when I was that age, too."

"When was that, last year?" He sat back so she could ladle a generous helping of eggs on his plate.

He made her feel giddy. Nina wanted to laugh like a teenager. Instead, she placed Jackie's eggs in the warming oven and scraped out the pan. "Not unless I was a child prodigy, which I assure you, I was not."

"I was, but no one knew it." He gestured at the stool beside him. "Sit down and eat before your breakfast gets cold."

"I'm not much of a breakfast eater." She remained standing by the sink as she sipped her tea. Looking for a different direction for her thoughts than the man filling her kitchen, she glanced out the window. The roses needed watering before it got any hotter. This early heat wave would shatter the blooms before the bake sale Saturday.

The buzz of the hair dryer filled the awkward silence. Then the doorbell rang, and the hair dryer shut off. Jackie must be listening from upstairs.

Jackie had said they would put his dad in jail if she called the sheriff. She wondered where their father was and how this man felt about that. Nina watched her guest at the counter, but he had casually returned to eating his eggs and sipping his coffee, as if the ringing bell had no significance for him. Maybe he wanted their father put in jail. She couldn't quite understand cause and effect here, but she'd had to call the sheriff. If she hadn't, Gary would have. Or Bob, when he towed the truck out.

Without a word, she swept past Mr. JD Smith into the front room. At this hour, it could only be Sheriff Hoyt.

He stood on the front porch, hat in hand, revealing his crew cut. She'd known Hoyt forever. He'd been a short, fat little boy in grade school, but he'd begun growing in junior high. He'd started working out in the gym after he made the football team. Now his shoulders stretched considerably broader than his stomach, but she still saw him as that boy who couldn't bend over to tie his own shoes. She gestured for him to come in. His size didn't make her feel uncomfortably aware of his physical presence as the man's in the kitchen did.

"We're having breakfast in the kitchen, Hoyt. Come on back."

As he followed her into Aunt Hattie's spacious kitchen, Nina contemplated the overabundance of males cluttering her hitherto all-feminine domain. The stranger gave the sheriff a short nod. Hoyt took the mug she handed him but didn't add cream or sugar. Neither spoke. She'd seen two male dogs size each other up in much the same way. She wondered when they would begin circling and growling.

"Sheriff Hoyt Stone, JD Smith. Have a seat, Hoyt. I don't like people towering over me."

Hoyt gave her a vaguely surprised look, as very well he might. She'd just said more to him than she'd probably ever said in her life. She hadn't thought she got chatty when she was nervous, but there was a first time for everything. Or maybe having the stranger behind her gave her an assurance she hadn't possessed before. Foolish thought.

"We ran a check on that license plate you gave us, Nina," Hoyt said as he took a stool on the other side of the counter. "It was stolen a few days ago."

"That's why the van didn't stop then," she said with satisfaction, glad to have the mystery explained. "It must have been stolen, too."

"License plate?" JD raised his rugged eyebrows. "You got the license plate?"

She shrugged diffidently. "It was either that or chase after the van like on TV. I didn't think the Toyota would catch up though. Four cylinders have definite drawbacks."

Her stomach did belly flops at the slow grin forming on JD's chiseled lips. Nina gazed in astonishment at the warm look of approval in his dark eyes. She couldn't remember any man, anywhere, anytime, looking at her like that. She had an instant understanding of all the love stories she'd ever read. A look like that could lay a woman flat and roll right over her. She tore her gaze away and dutifully returned it to Hoyt.

"Chasing after the van would have been dangerous, Nina," the sheriff said with disapproval before turning back to JD.

"Mr. Smith, I'll need a look at your driver's license for the report."

JD shrugged and reached for the coffeepot Nina had left on the counter. "My wallet wasn't in my pocket when I went to bed last night. It must have fallen out in the truck. Has anyone towed it in yet?"

Nina opened her mouth to protest that Jackie had the wallet when he paid the clinic last night, but for some reason, she closed it again. Maybe she was protecting Jackie.

"Bob was out there working on it this morning. I'll have him look for your billfold." Hoyt gave JD a suspicious look. "We ran a make on your tags, too. They're registered to a James Robert MacTavish in California."

JD shrugged again. "He loaned me the truck to transport the Harley. I hope you haven't called him yet. I've got to figure out some polite way of telling him I've wrecked his baby. He was in the process of completely restoring it."

"I'll need to call and confirm the story. I've been waiting for a decent hour out there."

JD glanced at his watch. Only then did Nina notice it looked like real gold with an exorbitantly expensive number of fancy dials. She couldn't put the fancy watch together with the T-shirt and the battered pickup. Maybe he'd stolen it.

"He'll be up in another hour. Just make sure you tell him JD says he'll pay for the repairs. How good is the town mechanic? MacTavish will want all original parts and no jury-rigging."

Hoyt took another sip of his coffee and stood up. "Bob's good. I'll tell him what you said." He put his hat back on and turned to Nina. "Thanks for the coffee, Nina. See you at the bake sale?"

"You'll see my flowers, Hoyt, but I doubt you'll see me. There's a lawn and garden show over in Hopkinsville I plan on attending when I visit Hattie."

Hoyt looked as if he wanted to say something, but Nina headed toward the front door without giving him a chance. She thought her teeth might start chattering at any moment. She didn't know if she imagined the tension in the kitchen, or if it was all on her part. She had the strangest feeling that Hoyt had asked all the wrong questions and that JD had led him down a garden path. What in the devil was she doing letting a man she knew nothing about stay in her house? She had to get him out of here right away before he turned out to be a serial killer. She couldn't imagine what had come over her. She'd never done such a reckless thing in her life. It must be the boy. She was used to looking after teenagers.

After letting Hoyt out, she marched straight back to the kitchen with every intention of telling Mr. JD Smith he'd have to leave. Only, when she got there, she found him sitting on a stool at her kitchen sink, filling the basin with sudsy water to wash her dishes. Jackie came in behind her, and instead of saying all the things she should say, Nina found herself retrieving the warming dish and preparing more toast.

"If you've got a phone book and could tell me what to look under, I think I'd better call that Bob and talk to him." JD turned around on his stool as Nina poured a glass of milk and set it in front of Jackie.

"You're not supposed to walk on that foot," she reminded him. "If you're going to hobble all over the house, you should use one of Aunt Hattie's canes." She couldn't believe she'd said that. Had her brains flown out the window the moment this dark-eyed stranger entered her house? He wasn't even good-looking, her mental guardian screamed. But he was very much male, her libido replied. Nina could almost hear it talking. JD's muscular physique made her feel feminine and petite instead of like an unappealing shrimp. She noticed his bulging biceps and his flat stomach, for pity's sake. She really should have her head examined, except it wasn't her head that was in trouble. She was almost thirty years old, and for the first time in her life she had the hots for a man. At least, she thought that was what the kids called it.

Without another word, she went in search of one of Hattie's walking sticks. She usually kept them in the umbrella stand near the front door. By the time she returned, she knew the brothers had discussed her and reached some decision. Nina didn't like the way they looked at her at all.

JD took the stick and hefted it in his hand. Admiring the hand-carved cedar with the fire-breathing horse on top, he smoothed the polished wood. "This is a fine piece. Someone has a lot of talent."

"A lot of people have talent. Not many people appreciate it," she answered absently. She'd seen sticks like that most of her life. They were pretty, but seldom useful. That was half the problem with handicrafts. They made lovely ornaments with no particular purpose. Of course, she pretty much had the same problem with her garden.

"Creativity is a lost art. The business world demands logic, not creativity. Without government funding of the arts, society will lose all beauty and originality, and stifle in its own lack of imagination," JD said as he took the stick and wandered down the hall to the front room and the telephone.

Nina stared after him as if he'd mentioned he'd met Shakespeare. He'd just nailed the crime of the twentieth century and wandered off as if it were common knowledge. She couldn't think of one single person in the entire town who could have phrased the problem so neatly. And he threw it out like discarded paper.

Shaking her head, she caught a glimpse of Jackie watching her. She hastily turned her attention back to him. "Can I fix you anything else?" she asked politely. He'd devoured the eggs and toast as if starved, but she'd seen him put away four hamburgers with all the trimmings last night. Teenage boys had hollow legs.

"May I fix myself some more toast?" he asked politely. "That jam's awful good."

"Freezer jam. I made it from last year's strawberries. Help

yourself." She set another loaf of bread on the counter and let him fix his own.

"My d— JD's pretty smart, isn't he? My mom says he's too smart for his own good, whatever that means."

Nina had a strong feeling she knew exactly what that meant, but she couldn't describe it in words. She still had difficulty grasping the concept of intelligence as acquainted with a man his age wearing T-shirts and driving beat-up pickups with Harley-Davidsons in the back. She'd about decided the computers must be stolen.

She picked up her garden gloves from the table on the enclosed porch. "I'm going out to water the plants. Just holler if you need anything." She hadn't had to tell anyone where she was going for the last year or more. She couldn't quite decide if she liked the feeling it gave her now. Perhaps she had been a little bit lonely since Hattie left.

JD found her some time later as she stared up at the river birch Hattie had planted at the corner of the house.. He limped on one foot and the walking stick, but he did it with a grace she could never have managed. Athletic, she added to the tags she'd applied to him.

"I'm losing this blasted tree," she muttered—mostly to herself—as he came up beside her. "How do other people keep them alive?"

He looked up at the still green leaves and back at her with a quizzical expression. "How do you know you're losing it? It looks fine to me."

She shrugged and pulled off a single yellowing leaf from a bottom branch. "I can just tell. If you'd listened to Billy's warning yesterday, you wouldn't have stalled out when you did. You should listen when people talk."

"MacTavish just overhauled that engine. It shouldn't have gone out," he protested, limping after her as she headed for the greenhouse.

"You'd better sit yourself down somewhere, Mr. Smith,

before you hurt something." Nina considered asking him when he would leave, but she didn't have the gumption. She'd never had enough gumption. She'd apparently used up all her reserves yesterday. She really should get busy on the phone-company problem, though. Would Matt do the job, or should she start looking for someone else? Remembering she'd also started him on Hattie's incompetency hearing shut down any further thought in that direction.

"I need to talk with you. If you'd sit still a minute, I could sit, too." JD hobbled into the greenhouse after her, then stopped and gazed around.

Nina ignored him. In here, she knew who she was, what she was doing, where she planned to go. The plants welcomed her. If she talked to them, they didn't talk back, except to wave an occasional frond or sprout another blossom. Plants had their own lives, their own whims, but they didn't bite the hand that fed them. She liked the sense of appreciation she felt in here. She certainly didn't get it from teaching.

She checked her begonia cuttings for moisture, then watered her granddaddy fern. She'd practically supplied the entire county with ferns from this old fellow.

"I thought Jackie said you were a teacher. Are you a florist, too?" He still stood at the entrance of the greenhouse, gazing at the jungle she'd created.

"Plants are just a hobby. I barely cover my costs by selling a few cuttings here and there. I raise a few poinsettias and Easter lilies for the church, a few begonias and petunias and things for the Piggly Wiggly to set out in the spring. The rest is for my own benefit. What did you want to talk about, Mr. Smith?"

"Why are we back to this Mr. Smith business? What happened to JD?" He hobbled down an aisle for a better look at an orchid climbing up a support post toward the roof. She'd covered the post in bark and moss so the plant had something to grasp.

"I thought I'd wait to see that driver's license before

committing to any name," Nina answered idly, putting the watering can down and checking the geranium seedlings to see if she should separate them yet.

He remained silent for a moment longer. "Jackie could have been a little more imaginative in his choice of names, I suppose," he admitted reluctantly.

Nina shot him a suspicious look. He'd smoothed the long tangle of his black hair off his forehead, revealing the stark white swath of bandage against bronzed skin. Gary had brought up their duffel bags with the motorcycle, and she noticed her guest had apparently dug out a brown leather vest to cover a clean T-shirt. But the attempts at civilization only emphasized her guest's features. He definitely had Native American blood. She should have seen it earlier and not made that joke about Pocahontas.

"When did Bob say your truck would be fixed?"

"Will you believe me if I tell you I'm protecting you by not using my real name?" He ignored her question about the truck.

Nina ran her fingers through her cropped hair and glared at him. "Look, mister. I've done everything any decent law-abiding citizen can do. You, on the other hand, have done nothing but lie. You'll excuse me if I ask what I can do to help you leave."

He took another look at the orchid, then gazed around the lush greenhouse before turning back to her. "If I offer you a thousand a month in rent, will you let us stay?"

FIVE

Miss Nina Toon looked as if he'd dropped a ton of bricks on her. Maybe he had. JD didn't know the rent in an area like this, but he assumed it in no way equaled the extortionate sums commanded in Los Angeles. He'd impulsively thrown out the first number coming to mind that might have some impact on her finances. He could remember living on a marine sergeant's salary. A thousand extra a month would have opened whole new horizons. A teacher would fit in a similar category.

As much as the greenhouse fascinated him, JD couldn't take his eyes off the petite statue frozen in the aisle ahead of him. She wasn't wearing those atrocious bib shorts today. She'd apparently dressed for guests by donning some breezy, flowery long dress that she wore over a tight ribbed shirt. He personally thought the combination awful, but he admitted to some prejudice against long skirts over those lovely legs. If she had breasts, the dress's loose bodice disguised the fact. He rather thought if she had anything to show, she would. Women usually knew their most attractive assets. So he could assume she hid what she didn't have. Lust-crazed idiot that he was, that didn't keep him from wanting to see more.

Since she didn't answer him immediately, JD tried explaining in a manner that might reassure her doubts. "Look, I just talked to the mechanic. It will be weeks before he can put the truck together. I promised Jackie we'd have a little fun together this summer. A friend of mine offered the loan of his summer house on Myrtle Beach. I figured I could work on my programming while Jackie made some new friends, and we would have plenty of time to get out and enjoy ourselves." He strangled his walking stick in helplessness. "Now we're stranded here in the middle of nowhere. I've already checked, and it's too late to reserve any of the cabins or rooms at the state parks. Everything is booked for the summer all over. If we could just have a place to stay, I figure I could make the best of it, take him swimming, waterskiing, whatever. He's got a learner's permit. I don't know what the state law is around here, but I thought I could take him out on the Harley. I just need time to get this job done, then the truck should be back together and we can head out for the beach again."

She still seemed slightly dazed, but she picked up her watering can again and began working on another overgrown green monstrosity. JD had never seen so many plants in one place, and he lived in California, for pete's sake. He had the feeling if he took a machete through here, he might uncover a Mayan ruin or two.

"I don't even know you," she finally murmured, reaching for a fern hanging over her head. "You could be a serial killer for all I know. Maybe if you'd let Hoyt check you out, if you'd given your real name . . ." She hesitated, making even that possibility seem remote.

JD knotted his fist around the walking stick. The more she resisted, the more he intended to push. His first decision might have been reckless, but the more he thought about it, the more he realized it was the right one. It answered a dozen problems without his even contemplating the slender woman tempting his vision right now. Add her to the mix, and he settled in concrete. He had every intention of staying here. He hadn't gotten where he was today by quitting.

"Look, if I tell you the truth and you see how innocent it is, would you give me a chance?"

For someone of her pale coloring, she certainly had noticeable lashes. Long and cinnamon-colored, they flapped closed now, creating soft brown arcs across her cheeks, as if she squeezed her eyes shut in hopes he would disappear. When she opened them again, JD moved a little closer. He didn't know why he did that. He had rotten luck with women—probably his own fault, he admitted honestly. But he'd never learned to curb his impulses.

Nina backed away slightly, as if shy of his proximity. He took the watering can from her hand and easily watered the plant she strained to reach.

She clasped her hands in front of her as she watched him. "I can't believe a thing you say," she reminded him.

"You can check with Jackie. He'll tell you exactly what I'll tell you now."

He still saw suspicion in her eyes, but she didn't instantly tell him to go to hell. Like she ought to. Even he admitted that.

"Jackie's mother married a man who beats her. Jackie's tried stopping the guy several times and got smashed against the wall for his efforts. Now his stepfather has taken to carrying a gun, and Jackie is terrified of him. It isn't a healthy situation. With school out for the summer, it could quickly become explosive. Jackie tracked me down and called me and asked if he could live with me. I didn't even know about the kid, but I couldn't leave him there."

The effort of this explanation exhausted him; JD leaned against one of the tables. He wasn't used to explaining himself, and the half truths made everything more difficult. He still shuddered at the situation he'd found in Tempe. He might never forgive himself for not knowing about Jackie. And his anger at himself had led to still another reckless decision. He should never have run off with Jackie without telling Nancy.

"I went down and tried persuading Jackie's mother to come

with us, but she refused," he said carefully. "She, Nancy, thinks the creep will come around now that he's working a steady job. She agreed that the situation would be healthier if Jackie isn't around so much. But she didn't agree to let me take him across the country. She doesn't know where he is right now, and she's probably called the police on us. I don't want him back in the situation he just left, but if the police find me, that's what will happen. Do you understand?"

She held her arms crossed in front of her as if to ward off a blow. "I understand that you're running from something, most likely the law, and you've got an innocent child mixed up in it. Your intentions may be perfectly honorable, but you can't leave the boy's mother scared to death. That's a criminal act in itself."

His little spiel could have raised a dozen questions, but she zeroed in on the gist of it, undistracted by all the other clouds he'd thrown in her way. Damn, but she was good. JD picked up the watering can again. "You've got a laser for a brain, you know that, don't you?"

"I work with kids. It's my job. You learn to see through the dust they kick up. Are you going to call Jackie's mother?"

Tenacious, too. Uncomfortable, JD twisted his shoulders inside the tight shirt. The humidity in here made him itch. Or maybe her razor-sharp gaze had cut invisible gashes in his hide. He didn't want to call Nancy. He couldn't trust her any more than he did Harry and his cohorts. He didn't like taking chances on anyone but himself. But Nina was right. Nancy had enough problems without worrying about Jackie, too.

"I can't call her. She could have the call traced. But I'll get word to her. Will that suffice?"

"What can you possibly tell her that will make her feel easy again?" she asked, watching him with those wide cat eyes.

"I'll tell her we're at the beach and having a great time. I'll give her my friend's number in case she wants to reach us. She thinks I'm an irresponsible idiot, so she'll buy that."

"What about your friend? Won't Jackie's mother send the police to question him? I would."

"It won't do any good. He'll just tell her that I'm sending messages through the computer. By the time the police figure out how to trace a computer message, if they even bother, I'll be back home."

Nina wanted to believe him. Something rebellious inside her fought the caution her aunt had taught her, ignored the warning signs, and clamored to invite this dark-eyed man and his battered brother into her big empty house. Surely a man who worked on computers and troubled himself to take care of his young brother couldn't be dangerous. She wanted to say yes. Thirty years of experience told her she was insane if she did.

"Mr. Smith, I just don't think this is a wise idea," she answered slowly, avoiding looking at the way his muscles rippled when he stretched to reach the higher plants. Why couldn't the man wear decent shirts like anyone else instead of those form-fitting T-shirts?

He set the empty watering can down on the worktable and crossed his arms over his chest. His biceps bulged even more than Hoyt's. Nina had the strange notion that all her hormones had shot straight to her brain. They'd never done that once in her entire lifetime. Maybe she was one of those insane women who fell for criminal types.

He was staring at her with curiosity, but she wouldn't return his look. She began filling a seed starter.

"What is it you want most in life, Miss Toon?"

Startled by the question, Nina jerked her head around. Big mistake. Dark eyes had turned serious, and his mouth had pulled into a straight line that almost made him . . . intriguing. Not handsome. Just intriguing. She shrugged. "I've never given it much thought. I have a house and all the land I could want. I have dozens of children every winter that I can get rid of in the summer, an ideal situation if I ever heard one. I've never felt the need for a man in my life. I can't think of anything else that I could want."

She felt his glare cut into her back as she returned to her work.

"No dreams at all? Anyone of intelligence has dreams. You don't strike me as particularly stupid. There must be something, even if it's just a glassed-in porch or a new red sports car."

He was trying to bribe her! That thought jolted her out of her near complacency. Only a criminal would throw around those kind of dreams. Nina dropped her spading shovel and faced him squarely. "I have dreams, all right, mister. I have big dreams. I don't squander wishes on tawdry red cars or pretty windows. If I'm going to wish and dream, I'll do it right. What I want is an entire botanical garden. I want those acres out there turned into a wonderland of plants and trees. I'd show the world the true beauty of this area, draw tourists in year-round so the town doesn't starve every winter. I want fern forests and Japanese pagodas, lily ponds and English mazes. There's swampland down the back near the lake that I could turn into an environmental learning center and habitat for wildlife. I could spend a lifetime creating a living monument to my aunt. Now how's that for dreams, Mr. Smith?"

His startled expression slowly turned to a genuine smile as she spoke. His whole face lit up when he smiled. Crinkles formed in the corners of his eyes, and a dimple actually formed on one side of his mouth. That dimple caused chaos inside her, and Nina gave up spinning dreams to clutch the table behind her with both hands.

"I like the way you think, Nina Toon. I like it real well. Nothing in this world would ever get accomplished unless someone, somewhere, had the dream first. All right. I'll help you on the road to your dream. I don't know much about botanical gardens. You'll gave to sit down and make plans of what needs doing first. You'll need cost estimates. I can't finance the whole thing. No one could. But I can find investors, government grants, whatever. If you've got the land, half the problem is already solved."

She couldn't believe he'd said that. She couldn't believe she was hearing it. The sudden bright red balloon of hope nearly blinded her. A white knight galloping to rescue her from phone companies, crooked lawyers, inertia, and poverty sprang up wildly in her imagination.

Nina stared at JD in incredulity until it finally sank in that she was talking to the world's best con man. She'd heard all about the fast-talking salesmen who talked lonely old ladies into parting with their life savings. They drove through here with regularity. She'd just never encountered one before. She felt a certain amount of admiration for the way he carried off the act. He came in here wearing little more than jeans and underwear, with next to no money, no credit cards, no insurance, in a battered pickup truck, and he had the incredible gall to claim he'd help her build a multimillion-dollar botanical center. She'd always liked the movie *The Music Man*. Come to think of it, except for the deep tan and straight hair, JD Smith held a certain resemblance to Robert Preston.

She grinned at the thought. "You should sell used cars," she informed him with amusement. "I haven't heard a line that big since I bought the Toyota. I want the thousand dollars rent up front, Mr. Smith. And I want reassurance that the boy's mother knows he's all right. I want her address, too, in case the cops pick you up and the boy gets left stranded. I don't want him handed to Social Services if I can prevent it."

He looked startled and suddenly wary. She couldn't blame him. She knew she looked like a pushover. She had this dumb-blonde face, and her lack of stature compounded the childlike impression. She supposed if she wore three-inch heels and grew her hair out and wore it in a bun she might eventually garner some respect, but she had this dread of turning into her aunt. So she let people think what they would. They found out they were wrong sooner or later.

She couldn't really fear him when he stood there, balancing himself on her worktable with his one good foot, a huge white bandage covering the gash on his forehead. He looked like a war veteran. What could he possibly do to her except lie? She doubted if he could top the lies her students came up with when they missed class or didn't do their homework. Kids were smooth, but she could see through them. Just as she'd seen through this one.

"I'll give you the address and phone number if you promise not to use them except in an emergency," he said cautiously.

Nina nodded agreement. "I'd suggest you get a lawyer if you want custody of the boy, but that's your business and none of mine."

For a moment, she thought she almost saw a glimmer of respect behind his eyes, but then he picked up his spiel again, and she nodded impatiently, waiting for him to go away so she could work.

"I'll get you the rent today. I'll see how damaged the computers are first. Once I get this program under control, I can begin on your idea for the garden, so start putting your facts together. You'll need aerial photographs and copies of your deeds, I suspect. I can arrange for that as soon as I get a computer up and running. Be detailed and don't overlook anything. If you're not a landscape professional, you should start considering who else you want on the project. I'd suggest drawing on local people as much as possible, maybe professors from the regional university."

Perhaps her tapping toe gave him some indication that she wasn't listening. JD stopped and gave her a quizzical look; then a dangerous light gleamed in his eye. Nina wasn't prepared for his impulsive movement toward her. She definitely wasn't prepared for the strong hands suddenly clasping her waist. Before she could even consider screaming, he kissed her cheek.

"Thank you, you're a lifesaver," he murmured.

"Nina!" Dottie's shrill voice carried faintly through the thick air. "Nina, I saw your car. Are you in the greenhouse, dear?"

Dazed, amazed, Nina pushed away from his embrace and stared at the terrifying whirlwind who had just swept into her life. She backed away carefully, as if he might reach out and sweep her away again. She knew she should say something. She knew she should stop this right now.

Instead, she took to her heels and ran out of the greenhouse as if the hounds of hell chased after her.

JD followed her progress with equal amazement. He knew he didn't understand women, but more often than not, they ran after him like lemmings to water. He'd never had one actually run from him. Then again, he'd never had a pixie turn him into a toad before, and that was precisely what he felt like now as he hobbled after her. One big ugly toad. One big ugly *horny* toad.

SIX

"My, my, you look flushed, dear." Dottie clasped and unclasped her flower basket handle. She wore a loose flowered cotton dress over her slightly humped and thickened figure. A sound pair of SAS brogans completed her gardening ensemble. "It's much too warm for working in that greenhouse." Her eyes widened as she peered over Nina's shoulder.

Nina didn't turn around to see what prompted her curiosity. Catching Dottie firmly by the elbow, she steered her toward the rose beds. "The heat is opening the blooms too quickly. I'll get you a bucket of water. You'll need to immerse the roses as soon as you pick them. I've got some gorgeous Oriental lilies that might fill out the bouquets, and we can snip some of those feathery ferns you like. If you see anything else that will work, just holler. You know Aunt Hattie likes sharing her garden."

Dottie kept glancing over her shoulder. "Dear . . . ," she said nervously, "there's a man back there. I think he's coming this way."

Drat the man. She'd thought she'd made it perfectly clear that she didn't want his company. How in the name of heaven could she face him in front of Dottie? The dear old lady would have talk all over the town, not from anything she knew but just from her dreamy speculations. And Nina really didn't think she could face him without turning red under any conditions.

Weren't computer people supposed to be antisocial nerds or something? The computer part must be one more lie, Nina decided as JD propped a hand on her shoulder. She didn't believe for a moment he needed the support for his lame foot. She wanted to glare at him, but she still couldn't look at him. She wished him away, but the silence was growing a little thin as Dottie stared at JD and he waited expectantly for introductions. If he dared to try selling Dottie a new roof or something, she'd throw him in jail herself.

"Dottie, this is John David Smith, the man whose truck got knocked off the road yesterday. JD, Dottie Henson, from our church. She makes the most delightful bouquets."

"Pleased to meet you, ma'am." Clenching the walking stick in one hand, he took Dottie's with the other. The old lady's eyes lit as if she'd just walked into a ballroom.

"My, oh, my, it's a pleasure to meet you, Mr. Smith. Will you be staying in Madrid long? We'd love having you at church Sunday."

Nina felt a certain satisfaction in the way JD began a hasty back step. Men of his ilk and churches did not go hand in hand.

"Miss Toon has graciously agreed to let my brother and me rent some rooms until our truck is fixed. We'll see what our plans are by Sunday."

Dottie's eyes grew even wider as JD made his farewells and limped up the walk to the house. When he was safely inside, she turned expectantly to Nina. "My, he's a handsome rogue, isn't he? Are you sure you know what you're doing, dear?"

Remembering that kiss, Nina didn't think she had any idea at all what she was doing. But she fully intended to correct that situation shortly. She might be backward around men. She might not speak her mind as often as she should. But that didn't mean she didn't have a mind at all. JD Whatever-his-name-was would get a piece of it as soon as she summoned the courage.

* * *

Jackie had sprawled across the spacious couch and turned on the TV by the time JD returned to the house. He looked up as JD walked in.

"There's no cable. She doesn't have any video games. What am I going to do all day around here?"

"Make your bed. Wash your dishes. Offer to mow the lawn or whatever manly task needs doing. Once I see what condition the computers are in, I'll take you down to the lake, and we'll see what's happening there. Get off your butt and do something useful in the meantime."

"You sound just like Mom," Jackie grumbled as he flicked off the TV. "Do this, do that," he mimicked. "This is supposed to be a vacation. I shouldn't have to do anything."

"Five-year-olds don't do anything. No one said you get a free ride for life." JD circled the front room, checking for electric sockets. He found a tangle of extension cords plugged into an ancient ungrounded socket behind the couch. Swearing at the fire hazard, he located an even older single-socket outlet behind the TV. Wondering if he could trade his rent payment in exchange for updating the wiring, he limped toward the room he'd slept in last night.

At one time the wide room with big front windows had probably served as a dining room, but illness must have made it difficult for the absent Aunt Hattie to get up and down the stairs. Apparently her illness had required electrical appliances of some sort. He found new outlets along one wall that might support at least one of the systems.

"Whatcha gonna do if they're broke?" Jackie inquired, following him rather than going about his chores.

"Turn the air blue," JD answered idly, looking around for surfaces he could rearrange to sit the hardware on.

Jackie grimaced. "Do you think she's got a lawn tractor for the lawn? I could do that."

A lawn tractor, the adult equivalent of a child's toy. JD didn't think his landlady would much appreciate a kid playing with it if she had one, but the kid should do something useful, and the boy could learn. This father business was a definite strain on the mental muscles, but he couldn't think of any way of denying him. JD wished he'd had a good example to follow, but all he could muster was a stern look. "Go make your bed and wash your dishes first. Then ask Miss Toon if she wants her lawn mowed."

Gloomily, he figured he should feel guilty at letting Nina decide what to do with the kid, but she apparently didn't have the same problem as he did in dealing with teenagers. As Jackie wandered off, JD began arranging the furniture to suit himself.

By the time Nina returned, he had his main hard drive up and running. He'd rerouted the on-line charges and modem to his own private telephone number since he couldn't find any local network access, and he didn't want the calls traced. Then he'd e-mailed Jimmy to call Nancy. Jimmy could trace the call if he wanted, but JD didn't have a problem with that. He and Jimmy had built the business together. They had an equal interest in protecting the banking program. He could trust Jimmy that much. His partner could play computer-ignorant marketing director for all it was worth should anyone question him.

Satisfied that he'd done all he could in that quarter, JD concentrated on the best way to make the money transfer from his bank account without anyone tracing it. If he could set up a local bank account . . .

His skin prickled. A breath of fresh air mixed with the fragrance of roses permeated the room. He never noticed such things. His secretary frequently walked through his office, rearranged his desk, and filed correspondence without once disturbing his train of thought.

Frowning, he concentrated on the monitor, but even though he'd focused his thoughts two thousand miles away, JD knew the exact moment the pixie alighted. He felt her furious vibrations before he even lifted his head.

"My services are not included in the rent," she informed him in ominous tones.

Maybe if he didn't look up, he wouldn't have to acknowledge that curious statement. Perhaps he could pretend he was lost in thought. JD rested his chin on his hand and stared at the computer screen, but he had the overwhelming notion she would take his head off in about two seconds. Reluctantly, he glanced in her direction.

"Jackie and I can fix our own meals," he answered politely, still slightly bewildered about what answer she expected. "We can make our own beds and clean up after ourselves, if that's what you mean. I'm certain you have enough to do without keeping up with us."

Nina stared at her uninvited houseguest in confusion. The motorcycle lord of earlier had donned a pair of horn-rimmed glasses that made him look like an absentminded professor. He'd even covered the T-shirt with a blue denim shirt, apparently for easier access to the assortment of pens and pencils he kept in the shirt pockets. The bottom of one pocket had already absorbed ink stains of black and green. The disheveled lock of hair once again fell over his bandage. He looked far different from the smooth-talking con man who'd appeared back in the greenhouse. Did this man have an evil twin brother or just two personalities? Or had her imagination just gotten the better of her again?

It had taken Nina this long to gather the courage to come in here and make that statement about her services. She'd practiced for a good five minutes. She thought she'd made herself perfectly clear without using any embarrassing phrases. Now he looked at her as if she'd lost her mind and talked about cooking and cleaning. She didn't give a good flying damn about cooking and cleaning.

"Fine," she stormed, incoherently as usual. "You do that.

You can take care of *all* your own personal services. Just leave me out of it. Are we completely clear on that?"

He stared at her as if she'd just thrown a temper tantrum for no particularly good reason. Could he have forgotten that kiss in the greenhouse already? Her cheeks flamed at the thought. She'd not thought of anything else this last hour. It would be just like a man to think nothing of something that had practically set her on fire. Preferring not to remind him, she stalked out, leaving him thinking what he would. Living with a man would be pure hell, she could tell already. But she damned well needed that rent money so she could fight the phone company.

Fascinated, JD watched the pixie flap her irate wings and flee; then reluctantly he turned back to his computer screen and stared at it without comprehension. Personal services? Is that what she called a little kiss? Other women would have been charmed. This one called it "personal services"? He grunted and returned to his work. He'd never understand women if he lived for a thousand years.

Leaning on his walking stick, JD counted out hundred-dollar bills on the counter in front of the teller. He'd left Jackie outside with the Harley. "It looks like I'll be around for a while, so I thought I'd better start an account," he told the teller as he filled out the deposit slip using his new name. Any sensible bank officer would see through his statement quickly enough, but he counted on the stack of bills cutting through the questions. Thank heavens Jackie had found his wallet. JD had known when they'd left that they would travel on cash, and he'd brought plenty.

His assumption proved correct. The clerk nodded eagerly. "Sure thing, Mr. Smith. We can give you some counter checks today. Your new ones will arrive in the mail within a week."

"You're set up for electronic deposits, aren't you?"

The clerk looked a little bewildered but, after consulting with the head teller, returned with the answer JD wanted. "Yes, sir. We don't have much call for it hereabouts, but we can handle that."

He hadn't fallen entirely through the rabbit hole then, JD thought in relief. He'd experienced enough culture shock these last two days without discovering a bank that didn't handle electronic transactions. Being rescued by a combine and waking up in a hundred-year-old farmhouse with two electric plugs per room had already severely shaken his concept of middle America.

As JD took the new checks from the teller, he glanced up to see a familiar face. He hadn't been precisely conscious when they'd hauled him out of the bean field, but he didn't know too many people around here. He expected this must be the Mr. Thomas his son had told him about.

JD approached the farmer and held out his hand. "I want to thank you, Mr. Thomas. If you hadn't come along when you did, I'd have been in a heap of trouble."

The shorter man shrugged diffidently as he shook JD's hand. "No problem."

JD could deal with men if he must. Growing up without a mother, living on military bases the better part of his life, he'd learned about nontalkers like Thomas. He could communicate better with men who said nothing than with women who never stopped talking. He pounded the other man on the back. "I owe you one."

"Sorry about your truck. Is Bob fixin' it?"

"It's going to take some time. Miss Toon is renting us some rooms until it's done. Thought we'd take in a little fishing while we're here. Know any good fishing holes?"

They wandered out of the bank discussing the best fishing spots for this time of year. Thomas greeted Jackie, admired the Harley, commiserated with them over the damaged chrome, and, after inviting them to church on Sunday, ambled off to the farm store.

"Church?" Jackie asked with distaste. "We don't have to go

to church, do we? Mom made me go a couple of times, and it's *boring*."

JD had never had a mom to make him go. He remembered attending Bible school one summer when he'd grabbed the opportunity to escape a sweltering slum for air-conditioned church rooms. He hadn't been impressed with the ambience, but he'd stayed cool for a week.

He swatted Jackie on the side of the head. "We're in the Bible Belt now, son. We'll see what's expected of us. Can you imagine what your mom would say if the police told her they'd traced us to a church out here?"

Jackie grinned and didn't argue more. Looking at the boy, JD tried finding a piece of himself in that mop of long hair, the long nose and sulky mouth, but he couldn't. He could barely remember Nancy, but he supposed the kid resembled her. Still, he couldn't help feeling some kind of pride that the kid claimed him for his father. He'd been all of sixteen when he and Nancy had run away from their respective homes to start what they thought would be a new and better life. Hell, they'd made a new life, apparently, but not the kind they'd had in mind. He hadn't even thought Nancy might be pregnant when her old man had dragged her home. He'd just felt relief that he didn't have to figure out how to put food for two on the table any longer. He'd hit the road the next day and never looked back.

He'd been an immature jerk. Back then, taking precautions hadn't occurred to him. He'd teach Jackie better. Lord, the kid was almost as old as he was when he'd fathered him. JD would damn well make certain the boy knew how to take care of himself and any partner he picked up. There was no point in passing on the Marshall legacy of incompetence with women.

As he and Jackie rode the Harley toward the lakes, the sheriff stepped out of the Piggly Wiggly and flagged them down. JD had the sudden sense of falling into some old Western movie where the town sheriff knew everything and everybody. He rolled the bike to a halt and winced as he forgot his sore foot and set it down as a brake.

The sheriff looked properly sympathetic. "Sorry about that. Shouldn't you be resting that foot?"

Now that the man wasn't looking all dopey-eyed at Nina, JD could tolerate him. And Jackie should learn respect for the law. He couldn't believe he was thinking like that. Age certainly had a way of catching up with a man. He was actually being polite to a hick sheriff so his son would learn respect. Once upon a time JD would have just given the man the finger and ridden off in a cloud of dust.

"Promised the kid I'd take him fishing. The accident kind of wrecked our vacation plans, so I'm looking for some way of making it up to him."

"This is a great place for a vacation," the sheriff informed him proudly. "It's a shame it's not hunting season. I could take him down some trails and show him some deer. If you want to rent a boat, there's a marina just off on the right as you reach the lake. They'll take good care of you."

"I'm obliged to you." JD nodded, hoping he'd picked up the local lingo. "Gary Thomas just told us where to find the best fishing holes. Reckon we'll take some fish back for Miss Toon this evening."

That clouded the man's expression quick enough. Sheriff Hoyt definitely had intentions in that area, JD decided.

"Bob said he didn't find your billfold in the truck anywhere. Have you found it yet? I've still got to fill out that report."

Double damn shit. Here he was driving the Harley through town without a license as far as this backwoods sheriff knew. He should know better than to expect the law to be on his side. Grinding his teeth, JD summoned a polite reply. "Damn, I'm sorry, Sheriff. I'm so used to having the thing in my pocket, I'd forgotten it went missing." It didn't take much of an act to look crestfallen. "What do you reckon I should do? I hate burdening Miss Toon with driving us around until I get a new one. I'm not even sure I can replace it since I'm not at home. It's kind of like being in a foreign country and losing a passport. Where's the nearest embassy?"

That almost brought a grin to the sheriff's face. "Well, if you carried your birth certificate around with you, you could go over to the courthouse and take the driver's test and get a Kentucky license. Just give me your social security number, and I'll use that on the report. Try staying away from any more stolen vans while you're around here, and I'll pretend I don't know you haven't got a license on you."

JD gave him a number with a wrong digit that would throw off any search the sheriff might make. Anyone could mess up a number. Hoyt would never know if it was his own fault or JD's. He'd done the same at the bank. If they stayed only a few weeks, it wouldn't hurt. It would just slow down anyone tracing him.

"I'd offer to take you out for a beer, Sheriff, but Miss Toon tells me I can't do that around here, so I guess we'll just bring you a mess of fish when we get some. Appreciate your understanding."

"Bring the boy over to church on Sunday so he'll meet a few of the other kids. You might find this is a good place to live." Tipping his hat, Hoyt sauntered back in the direction of his car.

Behind him, Jackie gave a whistle of relief. "Wow, you played that one close. He can't find Mom that way, can he?"

"Quit worrying about your mom. She'll be okay now that she knows you're safe. We're here to have a good time, remember?"

The boy accepted that, but then again Jackie didn't know about Harry. As he gunned the bike down the road, JD tried not to let that minor matter get to him.

Jimmy's return e-mail had said that Harry and his "partners" had gone looking for him.

SEVEN

Maybe he should have tried harder to get rid of DiFrancesco. Maybe he should have found somewhere safer for Jackie. Hell, maybe he should just have his head examined. What had ever given him the idea that he could become a corporate businessman? His credentials leaned more toward backwoods mechanic.

With Jackie chattering excitedly beside him about the fish they'd caught, the ones now simmering in the frying pan, JD wondered if his life would have been better if he'd stayed married to Nancy, found a mechanic's job, and settled somewhere. Jackie's life might have been better for it, anyway. Guilt churned his guts every time he looked at the boy, even more than his fury at Harry and his cohorts. He could choke on guilt. Fury merely gave him a path of action.

"Hey, Dad! Look at the eyeballs! They're rolling around—"

JD made a hushing motion as he pointed toward the front room. He didn't need their pixie landlady recognizing his relationship to Jackie. He'd told her about Nancy, but he preferred erring on the side of caution otherwise. As the Smith brothers, they weren't so easily identified if someone came through town looking for them.

Jackie popped a hand over his mouth and nodded. Lord, it

hurt just looking at the boy. He was so eager to please, but a wariness lingered behind his eyes at all times. JD knew that feeling of waiting for the next blow to fall. He wished he could reassure Jackie that he would protect him from any future blows, but he couldn't. The predicament they were in now gave sure evidence of that.

Well, he might be totally incompetent at relationship building, but he had a few other talents he could rely on. With a smirk, he winked at Jackie, and still carrying the greasy spatula, JD wandered toward the front room.

"Miss Toon? Would you care to join us? We're about to partake of the biggest, fattest catfish these lakes have ever given up. There's plenty enough for you."

The house had only the one ancient TV. His addlepated landlady sat cross-legged in front of it, watching the evening news with a pencil between her teeth as she worked her way through several gardening catalogs, apparently comparing prices. No wonder she was addlepated. He'd have blown a gasket by now concentrating on both activities at once.

She waved her fingers, indicating she'd heard him, popped the pencil from between her teeth to mark notes on a legal pad beside her, then finally replied, "That's okay. You two enjoy yourselves. I'll catch something later."

"Catch something? As in flies? Like a spider? If you go down to the lake right now, all you'll catch is mosquitoes. Come on. It won't take ten minutes to eat. I still owe you for saving my life, remember?"

She gave a mighty sigh and shoved her fingers through her hair, making it stand on end more than before. Finally, she sent him a look over her shoulder. "Okay, you'll know my guilty secret. I *hate* fish. I particularly hate *catfish*. They're full of nasty little bones that aren't worth the trouble to pull out. I'll just have some cheese and crackers later."

JD leaned against the door frame and admired the delicate tilt of her narrow chin. For some insane reason, he felt the same protective instincts for this little bit of fluff and bone that he felt for his son in the other room. She didn't seem capable of looking after herself. She lived in this huge gloomy house all alone, drove a rickety car that shouldn't be trusted ten feet from safety, and she'd developed some decided peculiarities that would worsen with age unless someone pulled her out of the empty shell she'd buried herself in. He had the urge to tug her into his arms and teach her what she was missing. Stupid inclination given his own paranoid tendencies.

"Then come and eat your cheese and crackers with us. Tell us about the local flora and fauna. Or better yet, tell us how we can get out of church on Sunday. So far, you're the only person who hasn't invited us."

Nina threw another look at the TV where the local newscaster expounded upon the latest protest over the TVA's mishandling of the lake properties. With a shrug, she switched it off. She didn't know what made people think large corporations would do anything else but mishandle property when the bottom line was all that mattered to them. They hadn't learned yet how to put beauty, nature, or the environment on a financial statement. Climbing to her feet, she followed JD into the kitchen.

She despised eating alone, and besides Jackie had been awfully proud of his fish. She should congratulate him on his catch at least.

He grinned at her as she entered, and she saw a flash of family resemblance between the brothers. They both had that wicked grin that could turn a woman's heart upside down. Returning the smile, she accepted the chair JD pulled out for her.

"If you're going to catch this many fish, you'll have to start a fish market," she teased Jackie as JD opened the refrigerator, apparently in search of her cheese. She tried ignoring the male in blue jeans rummaging through her refrigerator. He'd taken off his denim shirt in deference to the heat in the kitchen and was back to a T-shirt again. She turned and concentrated on Jackie.

"Could I make money at it?" he asked seriously.

She should have known better. She didn't know if the enormous check JD had presented her earlier was any good. She was afraid to find out. If their clothes were any evidence, they didn't look as if they had enough to live on. Of course the boy's thoughts would turn to money. Maybe she shouldn't try cashing the check.

"Well, you'd have some pretty stiff competition," she pointed out. "Everyone out here fishes."

He shrugged without looking too deflated. "Then I'll find something else. I want to own my own business like Dad."

A guilty look darted over his face as JD dropped the cheese and crackers on the table. Nina pretended she didn't notice. She wouldn't delve into family history. She suspected the two must share the same father but different mothers. She found it surprising that Jackie would admire a man who beat him, but children always adored their parents, right or wrong. Or had JD said it was Jackie's stepfather? It wasn't any of her concern.

"Owning your own business is pretty risky," she said as JD took his seat. "Most small businesses go under in the first few years. You'd better make sure you get a good sound education in business management, then learn your trade really well from an expert before venturing out on your own."

JD raised a quizzical eyebrow as he passed the bowl of cole slaw. "Shall I guess what subject you teach?"

She grinned at his satirical tone. "Economics, accounting, and math at the high school, bookkeeping and typing at the vo-tech school in the evening. I've also subbed in biology when desperation calls, which it frequently does. I keep telling them my minor is in botany and they should change it to a botany course if they're going to keep putting me in there."

Nina didn't know if she liked the look of amazement she saw in JD's eyes. Did he think her a total idiot? Of course he did, after that performance this morning. Coloring, she returned her attention to her food.

"I suppose I shouldn't ask, but with that kind of background, why didn't you get another degree and teach at the college?"

"Stupid question," she replied more curtly than she'd intended. "The nearest college is on the other side of the lakes. I made that drive for five years through ice and rain and fog. There's no way I'll drive it for the rest of my life."

"You could move to the other side of the lakes," he pointed out reasonably.

"Aunt Hattie lived here." She didn't embellish the topic. Aunt Hattie had raised her since she was a lonely child of nine. Her great-aunt had taken on a responsibility that had belonged to Nina's irresponsible parents. Without Hattie, she might never have had a home at all. And Hattie had started losing her mental faculties shortly after Nina finished her master's degree.

"She doesn't live here anymore," he prodded. "Have you ever lived anywhere else?"

"No. This is my home, and I'm quite happy with it. I wasn't cut out for an ivory-tower environment."

JD's eyes narrowed shrewdly. "You're afraid of the unknown. You're staying where it's safe."

"What in hell difference does it make to you?" She bit her lip, and her eyes widened as she realized she'd sworn in front of Jackie. Glaring crossly at JD, she turned her attention back to the teenager who had instantly retreated within himself as soon as she'd raised her voice. "How does your fish taste, Jackie? My first fish tasted like heaven. I never thought I'd eaten anything so good."

He regarded her warily and poked at the remains. "All right, I guess. How come you don't eat fish now?"

Nina wrinkled her nose. "A steady diet of fish when I was growing up, I guess. Sometimes, too much of a good thing ruins it."

He regarded her solemnly, absorbing that piece of information without comment. It suddenly struck Nina that behind that long hair and earring was a mind of significant intelligence . . . like his brother's. That knowledge made her stir uncomfortably. She'd easily dismissed the boys she'd grown up with by allowing them to acknowledge her intellectual superiority. Teenage boys disliked girls who earned straight As and made them look stupid. Instead of acting dumb for their benefit, she'd kept them at a distance by garnering every academic honor available. She had the distinct feeling that she couldn't get away with that kind of arrogance with her new boarders.

That night, Nina returned to her childhood bedroom and lay sleepless, staring at the ceiling. Come daylight, she would see the crack that she had decided as a child resembled a stairway to heaven. She had lain awake nights wondering if her parents had climbed that stairway and looked down on her from above, watching out for her in death as they hadn't in life.

She didn't grapple with that image these days. She couldn't precisely remember when she'd figured out that her so-called parents hadn't actually died. They'd just left. She remembered struggling with their desertion as a child, wondering if it was something she had done, wondering if they might have stayed if she'd been a better student, if she hadn't outgrown her clothes so fast, if she'd been prettier. She'd never voiced her doubts aloud. She'd simply tried to be as good as any angel so Aunt Hattie wouldn't abandon her, too.

Somewhere along the line, she'd grown tired of explaining where her parents had gone, and she'd started telling people they were dead. People accepted that easily enough. She'd tried creating fiery spectacular deaths for them one year, but Hattie had put an end to those tales. After that, she'd just allowed the images to die a natural death, and she'd quit expecting cards at Christmas or surprises on her birthday. Like crabgrass, hope dug in and sprouted for many years, but she'd finally succeeded in smothering it.

She hadn't given her parents any thought these last few years. She didn't know why they came to mind now. At some point she'd heard Hattie tell someone they'd married too young. Knowing people as she did, Nina imagined her father had left first, her stepfather actually. Her mother didn't know who her real father was, Hattie had said.

Nina had vague memories of screaming arguments in the little house at the far end of Hattie's farm where they'd lived at the time. Her stepfather had come home drunk once and broken a window when he discovered her mother had locked him out. He'd disappeared from her life some time after that.

Her mother had left her with Hattie not much later. There'd been talk of returning to school, finding a job, and she'd even come home once or twice that first year. But obviously Nina hadn't been important enough to remember after a while. She imagined her mother's car driving off the huge bridge over the lake, disappearing forever, and no one ever knowing what became of her. That made it easier to accept and explain the desertion.

Nina didn't like the pitying looks some of the older townspeople gave her, so she continued the charade of saying her mother was dead. No one could prove otherwise. She didn't need anyone now, anyway.

But lying here on this empty bed, Nina felt the loneliness building inside of her. Hattie had helped fill it for a long while, though even she couldn't fill it entirely. She'd given Nina a home, taught her how to behave, but her great-aunt hadn't known how to play with a child or give her the unstinting love of a parent. She'd just been another student for Hattie to teach.

Nina had the desperate feeling she would turn out just like Hattie if she didn't make some major changes in her life, but she didn't know where to begin. She'd lived in Madrid all her life. The prospect of taking off and finding a job and a home in another city after all these years terrified her. Besides, she had the farm and her dream of a botanical garden. What would she have elsewhere?

Listening to the television playing softly in the room below, hearing JD or Jackie turning on the water in the kitchen, Nina wondered if she couldn't stay and still make changes. Maybe all she needed was people in her life. Maybe she should take Hoyt up on the offer of a ride in his new boat. Or she could go fishing with Howard. Maybe something would come of it. Maybe she'd been too stuck-up to see what was right in front of her face.

She might as well go to the bars in Paducah and pick up strangers for all the good that would do, she decided. She would most likely shove Howard in the water if he quoted his mama one more time, and she'd surely fall asleep listening to Hoyt recount his football days.

She tried concentrating on the chirping of crickets in the bushes below, but even insects didn't cooperate at this time of night.

With a sigh, Nina threw back the stifling sheet and fell asleep listening to the clickety-clack of JD's keyboard in the room below.

EIGHT

Not since her teenage years of primping and preening had Nina regretted the farmhouse's limited amenities. She regretted it now as she entered the upper story's one bathroom to find alien male shaving razors and accoutrements cluttering the counter. The small bathroom they'd added downstairs when Hattie became ill had little space and no mirror. Perhaps they should have been a little more generous in their expenditures, but they hadn't seen the point at the time. Even Hattie hadn't considered turning the place into a boardinghouse. Cooking and house cleaning had never been high-priority items with either of them, and that kind of work came hand in hand with boardinghouses.

As did this sudden lack of privacy. Nina felt a moment's guilt as she locked the bathroom door so she might shower in peace. She disliked inconveniencing guests, but it wasn't as if she'd invited them, she reminded herself. They would just have to adapt. As she would.

After years of scattering her underthings where she pleased, dropping towels until she got back to them, leisurely soaking for as long as she liked, it seemed odd to consider someone else. Hattie's bad hip had bound her to the downstairs these last years, so the upstairs had become Nina's private den. Now she had two strange men trampling through her domain. She didn't like it, but for a thousand a month, she'd live with it. She'd take JD's check to the bank this morning.

The sound of Jackie's boom box filtered through the wall from his room down the hall. For a thousand a month, she couldn't ask the two of them to share a room. JD had holed up downstairs last night and hadn't come out since. She was grateful they didn't need entertaining. She wanted to visit Hattie and attend the garden show this afternoon.

Nina heard the phone ring as she stepped out of the shower. Dripping wet, her hair sticking out in unruly spikes, she could only shrug and towel herself off. Whoever it was could call back. Even when living alone she had little inclination for streaking naked through the house to answer a phone. She didn't receive calls requiring that kind of response. Answering machines and cordless phones were for people with fast-lane lives, not her.

She was in the process of blow-drying her hair when the knock rapped at the door.

"Nina? The landscape designer from the university just called. He said he could come out this afternoon if that's all right with you. What do you want me to tell him?"

She almost dropped the dryer at the sound of a male voice not two feet from where she stood, stark naked. She collected herself enough to turn off the dryer. She didn't know how to respond. Inexplicably shy, she considered pretending she had evaporated. He had to know she was naked.

Lord! She was turning into Aunt Hattie.

Nina swallowed to ease her suddenly dry throat. "Designer? What designer?"

The voice on the other side sounded impatient. "From the university. The one you said was so good. I left a message on his voice mail, and I just talked to him. He seems interested."

"Albert Herrington? You have Albert Herrington on the

phone?" Dazed, Nina glanced around, grabbed a robe from the back of the door, and hastily pulled it on.

She practically dashed into JD's arms as she threw open the door. He caught her, gave her brief robe an upraised eyebrow, then released her before she froze up completely.

Ignoring the tempest of sensations his touch engendered, Nina ran for the phone in her room. The attention of Albert Herrington drove even JD's proximity out of her mind.

"Mr. Herrington? I'm delighted you called." Holding a hand on her chest to keep her pounding heart from leaping out, Nina listened to the faint British accent of the voice on the phone.

Not until she had breathlessly agreed to forgo the trip to Hopkinsville so she might show him around Hattie's acres did she realize JD had propped himself in her bedroom doorway. She glared at him as she hung up the phone.

"Has no one told you eavesdropping isn't polite?"

His gaze drifted to the place where her short robe met her bare thigh. "Since I initiated the call, I think I'm entitled to hear the result, but eavesdropping isn't what's on my mind right now." A slow, heart-stoppingly sexy smile curved his lips as his sleepy gaze swept downward. "Where did you get that silk robe, and how can I persuade you to wear one all the time?"

Nina slammed the door in his face.

Did the man have no decency? She couldn't imagine another man she knew making such a blatantly sexual comment. Of course, she couldn't imagine another man she knew standing there in the first place.

Sighing, she fished in her closet for something suitable to impress Mr. Herrington. She couldn't pay the man. She hoped JD had made that clear. She didn't have the funds for buying plants or paving walks or doing any of the things he would suggest. The more she thought about it, the more questions she had.

Grabbing a summer print Sunday dress from the closet, she

slipped it on and went in search of JD. What on earth had he told the man to get him out here this quickly?

She found him nibbling crackers as he searched the refrigerator. "He's coming out this afternoon," she announced, pulling the pitcher of iced tea from beneath his nose. "Did you tell him I have no money?"

"That's not precisely what I told him, no." He produced a jar of jam and opened a cabinet. "I told him a large corporation is interested in sponsoring the garden, that it would be good publicity and could lead to major referrals."

"In other words, you lied," she said flatly, setting a glass of tea in front of him before sipping her own.

"I did no such thing. Once we get this thing off the ground, we should have several corporations involved. This is the way big business operates. If everyone sat around waiting for the money to appear, nothing would ever get done. It's just a matter of timing." He matter-of-factly chewed his sandwich and glanced at his watch. "What time is he coming? Jackie met some kids at the cove, and I promised to drive him down there. I could use a few winks of sleep before your friend shows up."

Nina opened her mouth, but too many scathing words crowded her tongue, and she couldn't decide which to let fly first. She shook her head in disbelief. "There's a path to the cove from here. Jackie can walk it easily. I'll show him."

Why had she done that? Why had she let him get away with those whopping big untruths? When would she ever learn?

He nodded gratefully. "Wake me up before Al gets here. I'd like to hear what he says." He wandered off, half-eaten sandwich in one hand, tea in the other.

Nina wondered if he always ate like that and, if so, why he hadn't died of rickets.

As she led Jackie across the back field to the cove path, Nina tried prying out a little more about her lying bum of a boarder. She knew better than to write any checks against the rent money JD had paid her until she was certain his check cleared, but if she threw her boarders out for dire lack of morals, she would have to give the money back. She still wavered on the borderline of that one. She could put up with a lot for a thousand dollars. With a thousand dollars she could hire someone besides Matt for battling the phone company.

"Do you and JD go fishing a lot when you're home?" she asked casually, knowing better than to ask a teenager a direct question.

Jackie cast her an anxious look and swiped a thick lock of hair from his forehead. "No place to fish," he answered reluctantly.

"I hadn't thought of that. I'm just used to having water handy. Then you're from out west?"

He nodded, clearly hesitant about saying too much. That made Nina even more nervous, but she persevered. "The school here doesn't have too many computers, and I've not learned a lot about them. I bet with a brother like JD, you've learned a lot. Are you going into his business when you get out of school?"

The boy brightened. "I think it would be great working in a place where everybody sits around playing Monster House. I've got some good ideas for new games. Gnomes and trolls are old. They need cyberpunks and narcheads. Cool dudes could be the good guys, and then we could have a whole slew of metro-fuzz who could go either way."

He suddenly shut up and slanted Nina a shrewd look. "JD says ideas can get stolen and I'd better hang on to mine until I'm old enough to write programs."

Well, apparently the man did work in the world of computers in some form or manner. She still suspected him more apt to be the thief of ideas or purveyor of stolen hardware than someone capable of persuading large corporations into donating untold sums to lost causes. But judging by Jackie's statement just now and JD's wariness about giving his name or location to anyone, he definitely wasn't the trusting sort. Did that make *him* untrustworthy?

Nina halted at the top of the well-worn path to the cove. She liked Jackie. He acted tough, but he was a good kid. Her hand itched to brush that messy hair out of his face, but she knew better. "I don't think too many people could take your ideas and convert them into anything constructive. If you can write computer programs, you'll have it made."

Jackie gave her a quick, shy smile. "JD said he'd teach me. Thanks for showing me the path. See you later."

He hurried off to make certain she wouldn't embarrass him by showing up in front of his new friends. Nina chuckled and shook her head. Some things never changed.

So JD told him he'd teach him how to write programs. She had a rough time imagining a man with muscles like JD's as a computer whiz. She knew that the construction of computer programs required intense concentration, complete focus, and immense amounts of patience. JD might manipulate a keyboard, but she simply couldn't see her motorcycle-riding guest in the role of programmer. She could, however, see him as a man who could talk young boys into believing anything.

She hurried back to straighten up the greenhouse and a few of the garden beds before Mr. Herrington arrived. She didn't have much, but she could make what she had as presentable as possible. She was particularly proud of the way the pale pink shrub roses cascaded over the rock wall to mix with the pots of salmon geraniums in the driveway below. The combination had been accidental but quite effective. By next year the creeping sweet William would fill in the bare spaces around the roses and throw more color over the dreary wall. She wished she could have taken landscaping in college, but there had been no point. She could never have found a job in Madrid as a botanist or landscape designer, and she could never leave Aunt Hattie to work elsewhere.

Once convinced she'd neatened the outside as much as possible, Nina washed her hands and retreated to her desk to organize a file of the plans she'd made so far. She didn't have aerial photographs as JD suggested, but she had a surveyor's drawing of the land and a number of photographs to indicate the possibilities. She'd even taken some pictures last winter showing how a wildlife exhibit would work during the off-season.

By the time an old Jeep pulled up the drive, Nina's teeth chattered with nervousness. She was about to make a total fool of herself trying to convince this important man that a botanical garden would succeed in this outpost of nowhere.

She cast a panicky glance at the closed door of the front bedroom. Maybe she should wake JD. Obviously, he could fast-talk anyone into anything.

But she couldn't rely on him. She would manage on her own. In another month or less, JD would be gone. She would do this on her own, as she had always done. She had just never imagined everything happening so fast. Most likely nothing would come of it. Life usually went that way.

Straightening her shoulders and clamping down on her jittery stomach, Nina walked out on the front porch to greet her guest.

Albert Herrington wasn't exactly what she expected. For one thing, he was too young. She had expected an older man, a venerable professor with wrinkles of wisdom around his eyes. Or at least a respectable middle-aged balding Englishman. The lanky, sun-blond man loping across her lawn couldn't be much older than she.

"Miss Toon?" He held out his hand before he even reached the porch. "So happy to meet you. Where is Mr. Smythe? Am I too early?"

Smythe? The lying, conniving . . . Nina smiled brittlely. "Mr. Smith operates on his own time. Pleased to meet you, Mr. Herrington." She took his hand without shattering into little pieces. Oddly enough, her disappointment in the man's looks made it easier to relax with him. How could one be nervous around an overgrown puppy?

"It's quite an exciting idea he has for this area. You're to be commended for your willingness to donate so much land, Miss Toon. A botanical garden showcasing the wonders of Western Kentucky's wilderness areas, brilliant idea. I do hope Mr. Smythe appreciates the immensity of the project."

Translation: the enormous funding required, Nina thought wryly as she stepped down from the porch. She smiled politely and indicated the walkway to the side of the house and garden. "I'm sure he does. I see it as a community effort, Mr. Herrington. It will have a major effect on surrounding areas, so we must involve everyone in the lakes area to obtain the kind of support a project like this requires."

He beamed at her. "Quite so, Miss Toon. I understand and empathize with your sentiments. It wouldn't do to alienate the locals, would it?" He glanced back toward the road. "Shouldn't we wait for Mr. Smythe?"

"We might wait the entire day. Let me show you the way the land lies. If Mr. Smith comes, he'll find us easily enough." With any luck, Mr. Smith would sleep until midnight.

Sometimes, she had no luck at all. Just as Nina thought they'd neatly made their escape onto the wooded portion of the path, JD sauntered out the back door and raised a hand, flagging them down. To Nina's surprise, he'd actually donned a blue chambray shirt and almost-respectable khaki trousers. He'd also slicked his hair back and removed his rakish bandage, and he wore his horn-rimmed glasses. He looked more English than the Englishman, except for the bronzed coloring. Even the walking stick enhanced the image.

Nina fought back a scowl as she introduced the two men. The friendly puppy waxed enthusiastic while JD shoved a hand in his pocket and grunted unobligingly. So much for the fast-talker. She could kick him. What was the matter with the man? Didn't he understand how important this was for her?

Nina led the way, pointing out the high points of the land, the views of the lake, the slope begging for terracing, the woodland descending into wetlands and back to meadow. To her, the possibilities loomed as wide as the horizon, and she wanted Albert Herrington to see it. To her approval, he bubbled over with more ideas than she'd dared develop in years. JD remained noncommittal.

"The wetlands are unique in an inland area like this," Albert proclaimed as they strolled toward the house. They'd reached a first-name basis by this time, no thanks to JD's taciturnity. "The water fowl alone will draw tourists in the spring and fall. Your idea for wildlife feeding stations in the winter is commendable, but I'll have to do some consulting on the matter. Gardens and wildlife are not always compatible, and this place may be a trifle hazardous to reach when the weather turns."

"Not if the state four-lanes the main road as they've proposed," JD interrupted unexpectedly. "I calculate we can build an entrance not two miles from the highway. Heavy snow might cause a problem, but I understand that's unusual here. The whole point of this venture is to provide year-round income for the area."

Nina raised her eyebrows in surprise at how quickly he had grasped not only her intent, but the hazards of carrying it out. She refrained from expressing her surprise as Albert quickly agreed with JD's assessment.

"It will be a pleasure working with a man of your vision, JD." Albert stopped at the drive to shake JD's hand. "And you, Nina." He almost bowed over her hand before smiling at her from his lofty height. "I shall be delighted to work with as lovely a lady as yourself anytime. You are not at all as I envisioned. Perhaps we could have lunch together after I've made a few preliminary sketches?"

JD continued scowling, and Nina threw him a nervous glance. No mention of money had passed anyone's lips. She couldn't afford even preliminary sketches. Uneasily, she replied, "You do realize the funding isn't under way yet? This will have to be a long-term project."

"Of course, Nina," Albert responded cheerfully. "JD's company can only lay the foundation. The rest will come with time and effort. I'm honored you chose me to help with the foundation."

After several more optimistic remarks on the subject, Albert departed, leaving Nina standing uncomfortably close to her guest. She had no idea how she'd come to be there. She stepped away, creating the barrier of distance between them.

"What on earth did you tell that poor man?" she demanded. "JD's company?" she mocked. "Do you have any idea how much sketches on a project this size could cost?"

He glared down at her. "I thought he'd be a paunchy old man, one of those English gardener types with funny-looking hats and leather patches on their jackets."

Nina stared up at him. "Are you out of your mind? What do his looks have to do with anything?"

"Never mind." JD shoved his hands in his pockets and stared over the wooded hillside in the direction of the lake, retreating into some interior world of his own. "We discussed the sketches. My contacts can afford it. The next step is finding more financial support. I've got to get back to work."

He wandered back toward the house, leaving Nina staring after him. Why in the name of all that was holy did she see loneliness behind those dark, opaque eyes of his? A man like JD Smith didn't have time for loneliness.

And how could she come to such a conclusion when she didn't even know what kind of man JD Smith actually was?

NINE

JD returned to the house and maturely refrained from slamming the door of his room as he headed back to his computer.

He'd thought the foppish voice on the other end of the telephone line belonged to an old man, a bumbling professorial type. He'd meant to delight his hostess with his offering and keep her happy puttering in the garden while he finished this dratted program. He hadn't meant to provide her with a classic movie star from a Brit cinema, one who would gush all over her and make her eyes light with anticipation.

He should have known better. The Marshall luck with women wouldn't succumb just because he'd stepped out of the fast lane into this pastoral setting. Idiot idea thinking a pixie shepherdess might have more discerning tastes or understanding attitudes than California blondes or European sophisticates or any of the other assorted females he'd encountered over the years. He wouldn't even get into the ones his father and grandfather and uncles had won and lost.

Wincing as he brushed at his hair and hit the wound on his head, JD returned to his senses. He was behaving like a jackass. He could develop a whole new Monster House around his behavior today. He barely *knew* Nina, and he wanted to throw a protective shield around her and keep her to himself. Damned

Marshall hormones anyway. Didn't he have enough trouble without his caveman instincts kicking in now?

He needed to keep his nose to the computer, where it was safe. His foot would certainly appreciate it if nothing else. Propping the throbbing appendage on an open dresser drawer, JD returned to the tedious task of adding the final touches on the banking program. The explosion of creativity that had started this project had dwindled to monotonous fine-tuning. Someone else could do it, but he didn't want the entire program in anyone's hands but his own. He might be handicapped when it came to figuring out women, but he understood the greedy part of human nature only too well. After all, he'd applied his knowledge rather successfully on his schoolteacher landlady by handing her that thousand dollars.

A persistent knock intruded on his thought processes just as JD finally succeeded in immersing himself completely in his computer machinations. He frowned and hoped it would go away as he typed in the final set of instructions for one loop of the program. The knocking stopped, then returned more insistently, followed by a feminine call of his name. JD sighed and stared blankly at the screen. Just the sound of her voice decimated his concentration.

"What?" he demanded irritably, scraping the chair back and swinging his foot down. To his surprise, the room was almost dark. He switched on a lamp and tried to rise, but his leg had fallen asleep. Groaning silently, he massaged the pins and needles as Nina's voice carried through the door.

"Did you tell Jackie when to come home? It's getting dark, and I'm not certain how safe it is out on the lake on a Saturday night."

Jackie. Oh, shit. Rubbing his bleary eyes, JD staggered to his feet and swung the door open.

Nina stood there in a rumpled pair of camping shorts and a loose T-shirt smeared with dirt. Obviously she'd had a productive afternoon. The worry in those fine green eyes held his attention more than his fascination with the size of the breasts behind her loose shirt.

"I didn't give him a time. I just figured he'd show up when he got hungry." The angry flash of her eyes warned he made a lousy excuse for a father—or brother, as she thought him.

"You'd better drive down to the cove and see if you can find him. I'll take a lantern down the path just in case he got lost. A lot of beer drinking goes on at that dock. I wouldn't want him falling in with the wrong crowd."

She turned around and marched away, leaving JD feeling like a fool. Of course there was beer drinking at the dock, especially on a Saturday night, even in a dry county. He knew that. Why hadn't he considered it before he let Jackie go?

Because he didn't know a damn thing about being a father. He certainly had no example to follow. His father would have been one of the good old boys down at the dock tanked with beer. At fifteen, JD could have stayed out drinking until dawn if he'd wanted. No one would have known the difference. Or cared.

That didn't mean he should raise Jackie that way. If nothing else, JD knew how it felt knowing no one cared enough to ask where he'd been or tell him when to get home. He didn't want Jackie growing up feeling as if he could go to hell and back with no one watching.

He grabbed his motorcycle keys and limped for the door. When he saw Nina reappear with a lantern, he took it from her and set it aside. "It'll be dark soon. I don't want you out there looking for the brat. Stay here and I'll call you if I have trouble finding him."

She picked up the lantern again and headed for the door. "Don't be ridiculous. I've lived here all my life and nothing's ever happened to me. I'll just go down the back way and make certain he hasn't lost the path. It's scarcely a bear-infested habitat. The worst I might encounter is an amorous skunk."

He grinned at that, imagining the stern schoolteacher glare

the skunk would encounter. But he knew the other kind of skunks lurking in the night. He reached for the lantern again. "If you want to be useful, call for a pizza delivery. I'm starving. I'll pay."

She let him set the lantern aside without argument. That made him immediately suspicious. He might not know a great deal about women, but he didn't think this one was so easily dissuaded. He glared down at her deceptively innocent eyes. "I'll find him, all right?"

She shrugged. "You're the boss. I'll go call Mama Rosa's."

JD didn't like the way she said that, but he didn't have the inclination to stand there and argue. Without another word, he slammed out of the house, failing the manly in-charge image he wanted to convey when he limped and nearly fell down the damned stairs.

Nina watched him go with a smile of delight tugging at her lips. Whatever else JD Smith might or might not be, he was a concerned brother with a feudal attitude toward women. She rather liked his foolish attempt to protect her from the shadows of night.

She placed the call to Rosa and told her she would collect the pizza later. Delivery service had not yet reached Madrid.

Then she lit her lantern and went in search of Jackie.

She found him at the same time JD did. JD had the advantage of faster transportation and the directions of the unruly crowd congregating in the cove. She had the advantage of the shortcut. The thick saplings along the shoreline concealed any noises from the dock below, but the sound of violent gagging behind the sassafras shrubs on the wooded path led them both to their quarry.

"Dammit, you stupid young pup!" JD bellowed helplessly as Jackie bent over with another round of gagging. "I gave you credit for a little more sense than this!" The smell of beer permeated the air. Even the thick pine needles underfoot couldn't erase the taint.

"Yelling won't make it better," Nina commented dryly, closing the lantern shutter so it didn't reveal the boy's embarrassment too thoroughly. "I don't think he'll be joining us for pizza tonight. Jackie, if I leave the lantern, can you find your way back up the path?"

The boy shot her a pitiful look, but when she offered no sympathy, he nodded and wiped his mouth with the back of his hand. He took the handkerchief JD shoved at him but didn't look in JD's direction.

"If Jackie's taking the lantern, I'll accept your offer of a ride, Mr. Smith," she said, interrupting JD's useless growls. "We can stop at Rosa's and pick up the pizza on the way."

"I want to throttle the brat first." He continued glaring at the boy.

"I'm certain you can think of something much more constructive to do with him in the morning. Go on home, Jackie. I won't let him throttle you until daylight, at least."

Still holding the handkerchief to his mouth, Jackie nodded, picked up the lantern, and hurried back toward the house. His slender form quickly disappeared into the forest of saplings.

"What do we do now?" JD muttered.

"We wait and make certain he doesn't double back to avoid facing you. Does he do this often?" she asked with curiosity as even the sound of the boy's feet in the dry leaves died out.

"How in hell do I know?" he asked with equal parts frustration and irritation, running his hands through his hair. "His mother didn't mention it."

Nina found his concern touching, but she didn't understand why he made such a big deal of it. Most brothers would have thought it funny. "Then we'll assume it's just a matter of peer pressure for now. Let's go see who's down at the cove." She turned and marched toward the lake. As a high school teacher, she knew every teenager in the district. One of the advantages of small-town living was that she also knew all their friends and family. No one could get away with anything for very long around here.

The older men had congregated out on the houseboats at the end of the dock. The kids had a campfire just around the bend, out of sight of the adults. The boats might contain summer tourists, but the campfire belonged to the locals. Although JD caught her hand and tried to tug her back, Nina shook him off.

Ethel's seventeen-year-old nephew looked up at her guiltily. One by one the other young louts turned and caught sight of her. Several looked longingly at the shadowed shrubbery as if they wished they could disappear, but when the others didn't flee in the face of her wrath, they reluctantly held their places.

"Hey, Miss Toon," Ethel's nephew called nervously, glancing at JD behind her.

"You will stand and make appropriate introductions to Mr. Smith, Jackie's brother," she demanded curtly. "That is, if you're still capable of standing."

The boy looked rebellious, but the challenge to his manhood couldn't be ignored. He staggered only slightly as he stood up. "We ain't doin' nothin' wrong, Miss Toon," he sputtered belligerently after grumbling out a few names in introduction.

"You're underage and drinking. I know Sheriff Hoyt ignores it as long as you behave, but if I complain, he'll have to act. Tommy," she spoke sharply to a boy hastily shoving something under a deflated rubber raft, "hand that over. The lot of you have had enough for the evening."

"I ain't got nothin', Miss Toon." The culprit held up his empty hands in innocence.

JD stepped over the campfire, picked up the raft, and uncovered the hoard of beer cans. Without a word, he lifted the heavy bucket of ice and beer and strode toward the lake with it.

"Hey, mister! You can't do that! That's stealing." A couple of the older boys leapt to menacing positions, but JD continued on his course, unfazed. Cries of protest erupted all around as he waded out in the water and dropped the bucket into the lake. No one, however, made any move to stop him.

Perhaps they thought to rescue the cans later. If so, they were doomed to disappointment. JD walked back across the sand. "Aluminum pollutes," he said pleasantly. "You'll have to go in and empty those cans into the water so you can toss the empties back to me for recycling."

"Yeah, and who's gonna make us?" one of the larger boys demanded.

As JD reached for the ruffian's collar, Nina intruded calmly. "Sheriff Hoyt, your father, Mr. Clancy"—the football coach—"and Tammy, if I tell her what you were doing tonight. She works with Students Against Drunk Driving, I'm sure you realize."

The mention of the girlfriend was the deciding factor. Sheepishly at first, then making a game of it, they dived in after the beer, emptying it into the water and onto themselves and each other until a healthy stack of cans built on the beach.

JD didn't once crack a smile, but Nina had the distinct impression he fought back a bad case of chuckles. He confirmed her opinion after they gathered the cans and proceeded toward the road. His laughter came softly, mingling with the rattle of empty cans in the garbage sack.

"Defeated by a girl's name! Men don't stand a chance, do they?"

"Not as long as all they require is animal trainers." She could expound a long treatise on the subject, learned at the knees of her aunt, but she refrained. She hadn't listened blindly. Her own observations had led her to conclude some boys were capable of growing into intelligent men instead of bigger animals. Some, but not all. She wasn't sure into which category JD fell.

He didn't have the leisure for a reply. Sheriff Hoyt sauntered toward them, eyeing the rattling sack skeptically. "Partying, Nina?"

"Just doing your job for you, Hoyt," she answered sweetly. "Unless you want to arrest half the football team, you'd best not go any farther."

He frowned, glanced over their shoulders, and gave JD's cheerful grin a disgruntled look. "They're good kids, just sowing a few wild oats."

"Fermented barley, looks like to me," JD said as the sheriff took the sack. "If I find out where they got this stuff, you'll be minus one bootlegger in these parts. Maybe you should spread the word."

JD issued the threat in such a pleasant tone that Nina wasn't certain if she'd interpreted it correctly.

Hoyt obviously didn't have any problem digesting it though. He scowled. "I'll do my job. You keep your nose out of it."

"Someone, somewhere, hasn't done their job or the kids wouldn't have this stuff. I don't much care if adults drink themselves under the table, even in a dry county, but there's no excuse for selling to kids. I'm offering my help, if you want it."

Hoyt backed down a hair. "I'll get the word out, but I reckon it's one of the older boys buying it at a package dealer over in McCracken County. There's too many ways these kids can get it."

"Well, I don't know what you'll do with that lot back there, but I mean to make it a good deal less appealing to a certain fifteen-year-old of my acquaintance." With a nod to the sheriff, JD limped across the parking lot, dragging Nina after him.

"What will you do with him?" Nina asked as they reached the Harley. She gave the bike a look of misgiving. She'd never been on a motorcycle. She had no clue how to get on.

"Hell if I know," JD admitted, swinging his leg over the seat. "Hop on and tell me where to find the pizza place. I think better on a full stomach."

"Hop on, he says," Nina muttered, glaring at JD's broad shoulders and the narrow seat. He held the bike handles. How would she stay on?

He glanced over his shoulder as she hesitated. "Scared?" he taunted.

"Ignorant." She looked at the seat skeptically. "Maybe I should walk."

His reckless grin convinced her walking was the best alternative. "Throw your leg over the seat, Miss Toon, and wrap your arms around my waist. You won't go up in flames, I promise."

Nina seriously considered kicking a wheel to see if she could turn him over on his smug expression, but she decided that would be childishly unbecoming to a woman her age. Motorcycles had never fascinated her, but she could deal with one in the same way she dealt with horses—carefully.

JD had promised she wouldn't go up in flames, but feeling the heat of him through his shirt nearly burned Nina's fingers, and the play of his muscles beneath her hands as the Harley roared to life sent her thoughts straight to hell. She had never in her entire life, *never,* been aware of a man's physical presence like this. Her aunt had warned her about the dangers of teenage petting, and Nina had always managed a sufficiently frosty distance to keep the boys wary of coming too close, even as she grew older. She'd never particularly regretted it. The boys she'd grown up with held no enticement for her. But JD was definitely not one of the boys she'd grown up with.

Nina tried just crunching his shirt between her fingers, but JD turned the bike into a curve and she grabbed his waist rather than fall off. She pretended that clinging to a man's trouser band had no significance for her, but she suspected JD knew better. He struck her as a man of some experience.

After picking up the pizza, Nina found the problem multiplied. She had to wrap one arm entirely around him and lean against his back so she could hold the pizza in her other arm. Nina had the vicious urge to bite JD's shoulder blade when he chuckled at her awkwardness.

"I never thought I'd resent a box of pizza," he murmured as Nina adjusted her position to keep the box between them.

"Next time, I walk back with Jackie," she muttered in reply.

The motorcycle's roar drowned their words away after that. Nina tried not to think about the man's hard body vibrating against hers, or the smell of hot pizza in the warm summer air rushing around her, or the stars twinkling above the dark shapes of the trees as they flew down the road. She'd always lived cautiously, never stepping far from the beaten path of her existence. She had never considered the word *sensual* in terms of her life, but she thought she experienced it now. All her senses had the blood thrumming hotly through her veins, and deep down inside her, she knew JD was responsible for this awakening.

Nina almost felt disappointment when JD shut off the throttle and she realized they'd reached the house. She climbed off awkwardly, holding the pizza box and avoiding JD as much as humanly possible.

Returning his attention to a more important concern, JD glanced up at the darkened windows. "Think he's there?"

"Hiding in his room, most likely. It's such an awkward age. They think they're too old for coddling, but they miss it. Try to remember how you felt at that age when you talk to him," Nina replied, thankful for this return to sanity.

She couldn't interpret the grimace JD made in the porch light as they climbed the steps. Perhaps his foot pained him. He didn't carry the walking stick. Nina wondered—not for the first time—how there'd come to be such a disparity in the ages of the brothers, or why their father hadn't stepped in if his son had been abused by another man. The various complications of divorces amazed her. She had never thanked Hattie enough for stepping in when her mother and stepfather had gone their erratic ways.

The muffled sound of rock music drifted down from the

upper story, and they breathed mutual sighs of relief. Jackie had returned safely.

"May I eat first?" JD asked dryly as Nina hesitated at the bottom of the stairs.

"You're asking me?" she asked incredulously. "He's your brother."

"Yeah, but you have a better handle on kids than I do. I don't have much experience."

Nina halted and actually looked at the man beside her. She saw his physical strength, his beguiling features, and the worry in the depths of his dark eyes. He wasn't angry at the boy. He was genuinely concerned about doing the right thing. She found that oddly reassuring. He'd intimidated her with his size and his motorbike and his self-assurance, but he had his vulnerabilities, too. She would try to remember that.

Bravely, she touched his arm and nodded toward the kitchen. "There's no textbook answer that I know. Each one is an individual. You have to know how they respond, how they feel, what makes them tick. I really don't think there's a psychiatrist in the world who can make those calls better than a concerned parent. Let's eat first."

JD seemed unusually subdued as they consumed the pizza and a liter of Coke. His anxiety didn't affect his appetite, Nina noted wryly. The man could eat his weight in a single meal and not notice the difference. He could eat. He just didn't talk much. She began to think she'd just imagined the sexual innuendos of earlier.

"Kids learn best by doing," JD finally said. "He's learned drinking large quantities of beer makes him sick."

He was already looking for an out. Nina smiled at his logic. Maybe he didn't know much about the boy, but he didn't want to hurt him. "He hasn't learned to stand up against peer pressure," she pointed out reasonably.

JD glared at the last piece of pizza. "I was afraid you'd say that. What kid can stand up to peer pressure? Especially when he's the new kid on the block and has to prove himself?"

Nina wondered if he spoke from experience. She'd never felt that particular pressure, but she'd never been placed in a strange situation. She knew her peers well enough not to be influenced by them.

"A child who is sure of himself can fight peer pressure best," she answered thoughtfully. "I don't know how you go about providing that kind of self-esteem. I had stability on my side."

JD gave her a skeptical look. "You never felt inclined to make out with the captain of the football team so you'd be popular?"

"Hoyt was captain of the football team," she pointed out with a smile. "What do you think?"

He gave a rueful grin. "How about captain of the debating team?"

"No such critter. Familiarity breeds contempt, I fear."

"Hmm, there is that. If Jackie really knew those kids, he wouldn't be so interested in imitating them. What do those bums usually do with their summers?"

"Work at the Dairy Queen, or their fathers' farms, whatever. What did you have in mind?"

He grabbed the last slice of pizza and chewed a bite thoroughly before replying. "Your landscape friend said the scrub plants in the woods need clearing out to turn it into some kind of woodland garden, didn't he?"

Nina regarded him warily. "There are acres of junk trees out there. I'm inclined to think a bulldozer faster. And without a design, we don't know which acres need clearing."

JD shrugged. "They'll all need clearing some way or another. Let's say five strong guys at minimum wage, working whatever hours they want. Maybe a hundred hours a week at most between them?"

Nina's eyes widened. "I can do the math. That's over five hundred dollars a week plus taxes. There's no way."

"A bulldozer would be cheaper," he agreed, "but it'll keep Jackie and friends occupied usefully for a few hours a day, let them learn a little about hard work. And Jackie is smart enough to learn what jerks they are after a week or so."

"Five hundred a week? That's an expensive lesson. Even if you sell your watch and the Harley, it will cost more than we have." She didn't know where the "we" came from. It would cost more than she had, certainly. But the idea was his.

"The corporation can fund basic land preparations as well as design, I figure. I'll have an attorney file nonprofit papers for the foundation. You can talk to him about the specifics, purpose, goals, and so on. It's mostly gobbledygook. You can do it."

A nonprofit corporation. She still struggled with the concept of a landscape designer, and he had moved on to land clearing and corporations. Things were going way too fast here.

"Corporations need officers and directors and things, don't they?" she whispered.

JD shrugged and moved his chair back. "Round up a few of your friends, the minister, the principal, whatever. Now that I think of it, you'd probably best get a local lawyer, one who knows Kentucky laws. Put him on the board in exchange for his services. It's no big deal."

No big deal. He'd just sketched an outline for her future and told her it was no big deal.

Maybe not to him, but she had to live here the rest of her life. What happened when JD Smith walked out, leaving her holding an empty bag and a worthless corporation?

TEN

"So you see the predicament I'm in, Aunt Hattie. He's talking big, stirring up interest, but what happens when the money never comes through? No one will ever believe me. The garden idea will die deader than a doornail, and no one will listen if I ever raise it again. They'll laugh in my face and slam their doors." Sitting on the bed, twisting her hands in her lap, Nina poured out her story as if her aunt were actually listening. "Should I throw him out, shut him up, call the professor and tell him to forget everything? But how can I do that? He's already paid his rent, and you know we need the money."

The frail woman at the window picked at the blanket over her legs and muttered, "She's coming back. She's a good girl. She'll come back soon."

Nina sighed. The nursing attendant said Hattie had occasional bouts of sanity when she complained about her room and the food and wanted to know why Nina didn't take her home. She just wished Hattie would have those bouts when she was around. She desperately needed some advice right now.

No, she didn't. Not really. She knew what Aunt Hattie would say. She'd say taking the thousand dollars was short-term thinking, and she needed to plan for the long term. She'd scold her for risking everything on a stranger, particularly a strange man. She just needed Hattie's presence to remind her of all the lessons on caution she'd been taught.

Giving Hattie a hug and a kiss on her papery thin cheek, Nina straightened her covers. "She'll be back, Hattie," she said reassuringly. "I'll bring her with me."

A tear trickled down Nina's cheek as Hattie gave a firm nod of approval, just as in the old days. But the Hattie of old wasn't behind those vacant eyes now. This Hattie didn't even know when Nina left the room.

Eyes blurred with tears as she drove away from the nursing home, Nina fought the urge to pull over and collapse in an old-fashioned bout of weeping. She was almost thirty years old, for pity's sake. She could make decisions for herself. She'd made the decision to put Hattie in the nursing home. It was the hardest one she'd ever had to make, and she hoped she didn't have to make another like it in this lifetime. In comparison, the incompetency hearing scarcely rated.

She just felt so damned *alone* making these decisions by herself, without anyone's advice. Her damned mother could have at least left her a brother or sister to help. Nina had talked to the preacher, but the man had just nodded his head and agreed with everything she said, no matter which argument she used, for or against. Hattie's wandering off to the lake in the middle of the night had pretty well confirmed the final decision. Nina couldn't watch her every minute, and she couldn't afford around-the-clock private nursing.

That didn't make her any less heartsick. Her strong, independent aunt had lived and breathed for the land. Cooping her up in that cubbyhole in a nursing home would kill her. Hattie had deteriorated rapidly in this past year, and Nina blamed herself.

She wouldn't think about it. What's done is done, Hattie had always said. She'd decided on the nursing home for very good reasons, and those reasons hadn't changed simply because turmoil in the form of JD Smith had entered her life. She was a big girl now. She would make her own decisions.

Nina's choices didn't come any easier when she entered the house to the tantalizing aroma of cooking spaghetti sauce and the sight of Jackie sprawled across the living room rug, attacking a computer. He'd apparently unplugged the TV and had his brother's laptop hooked in its place. For some reason, the sight of the boy and the scent of a meal cooking drained whatever fight she had left in her.

"Is that spaghetti I smell?" Nina asked as she crossed the room in the direction of the kitchen. Underneath the smell of sauce came the distinct odor of something burning on the electric range.

"Yeah, I'm supposed to stir it every fifteen minutes," Jackie yelled back, still pounding away with the joysticks. He gave a yip of triumph as he apparently hit whatever target the computer game had thrown him.

Looking at the sauce bubbling and spurting in small volcanic eruptions, throwing molten lava down the side of the pot and across the stove, Nina estimated the sauce hadn't been stirred since the game started. Grinning, she pulled out a wooden spoon, stirred the sauce, and turned the range down, then tasted the pot contents. Not bad. She should get some fresh lettuce from the garden and fix a salad.

Not knowing what to make of a man who could cook real spaghetti sauce, Nina wandered back to the front room. She noticed JD's door was closed and could hear the frantic clicking of his keyboard over the noise of Jackie's game.

"Monster House?" she asked, sitting on the couch and watching the game flicker over the computer screen.

"Nah. This is a new one that's not out yet. Da—" He hesitated. "JD said as long as I'm grounded, I might as well do something useful and test it for him. It's really cool. Wanta play?"

She knew next to nothing about computers. She'd played

with a few at school just to see what they were all about but couldn't find any particularly good use for them in her life. She didn't need them for her classes, thank goodness, since the school scarcely had enough to go around. But as much as she hated the technology cluttering up the landscape, she couldn't contain her intellectual curiosity. Dropping down to the floor beside Jackie, she let him show her how to play the game.

His stomach rumbling in anticipation of the meal ahead, JD emerged a few hours later to find Jackie and their landlady totally enraptured by a computer treasure hunt. Leaving them engrossed in the game, he wandered back to the kitchen. From the stains he'd noticed on Jackie's shirt and the dirty plate in the sink, JD assumed Jackie had eaten. From the pot of cold, gluey pasta in the sink, he assumed Nina hadn't.

Cursing the lack of a food disposal, not to mention the absence of a dishwasher, he scraped the mess into the garbage and put on another pot of water to boil. Food obviously wasn't the way to his landlady's heart, or her bed. Remembering her slender arms wrapped around him, her slight weight pressed into his back, he'd stayed awake half the night planning ways to seduce her. Maybe he should invent a romantic computer game.

James MacTavish sat in his swivel office chair with the smoggy skyline of Los Angeles behind him, contemplating the depths to which a Monday morning could sink. He'd thought last week bad enough when it started out with JD wrecking his lovingly restored Chevy pickup and DiFrancesco turning the R&D department upside down before he'd taken off in pursuit of JD. Now he sat here with Harry's paranoid telephone messages about stolen plans, a letter demanding repayment of the loan to DiFrancesco's company, and a message from JD saying the software program had hit a snag. And across from him sat a beautiful, tearful woman demanding he find her son or she would call the police.

Jimmy briefly contemplated a quick trip to Hawaii until JD got his ass back here. Then he contemplated the streaks of tears down a soft, creamy cheek, blue eyes glittering with as yet unshed moisture, and his guts twisted into a knot. He'd finally figured out this was the mother of JD's son, the son his partner had known nothing about until a few weeks ago. JD sure had damned good taste in women, even if he never kept them around long. This one had endless tanned legs, golden curls clinging to a slender neck, and ruby lips that trembled when she spoke. She also had a purple bruise beneath her right eye.

"I've left my husband, Mr. MacTavish. JD was right. I should have left him when he started smacking Jackie around. But I couldn't bear to admit another failure. I don't like being a quitter. I wanted to make it work. But I refuse to be a victim. I want my son back, Mr. MacTavish. I should never have let JD take him away. I must have been out of my mind to agree to it. I've been out of my mind for some time now, it seems, but I've come to my senses. Where has that irresponsible idiot taken my son?"

Jimmy could tell her. He'd received the police report on the wrecked truck. But Harry's paranoid messages had made him slightly paranoid, also. What if this woman was just a front for DiFrancesco's organization? JD had sworn him to secrecy. Something had happened to send his partner careening off into Nowheresville like that. He and JD went back a long way, and Jimmy loyally supported JD's decisions, even if he didn't understand them. Without JD, this company wouldn't exist, he wouldn't have the hefty paycheck he took home every two weeks, or that lovely bonus at the end of each year that had bought him a house in Beverly Hills, a series of red Corvettes, and the attentions of a female like Barbara.

But this woman in front of him had a right to her son. She'd raised the boy for fifteen years. JD couldn't just walk off with him like that. Loyal as he might be to JD, Jimmy could admit his friend and partner had an impulsive streak a mile wide. And that reckless behavior was hurting this pretty lady rather badly.

"I'm sorry, Mrs. Walker. JD sends me messages on the computer, but there's no way of identifying where they're coming from. He said he was heading to Myrtle Beach, but he hasn't arrived yet. I've left word for him to call when he does. He said the boy's with him and doing fine. He wanted me to pass that on to you so you wouldn't worry. Could it hurt for them to take a small vacation and get to know each other?"

"For all I know, that damned JD Marshall is teaching him devil worship and using Jackie as a front for a car-theft ring. I wouldn't put anything past that man. I want my son, and I want him now. I didn't mind him bringing Jackie here for a weekend or so, but I never agreed to their taking off across the country where I couldn't find them. I'm calling the police, Mr. MacTavish. I'm sorry. I thought you might help me—"

The intercom buzzed. With an apologetic glance to Nancy Walker, Jimmy grabbed the receiver as if it were a lifeline. Swiveling his chair so he looked out the window and away from the weeping woman, he whispered harshly, "What is it?"

"Harry Marshall is on the other line. He sounds rather odd, almost hysterical, and he insisted I interrupt whatever you were doing. He says it's a matter of life and death."

Jimmy knew JD's terrifying automaton of a secretary too well. If she interrupted him, it could only be a matter of utmost importance. He wasn't sure he could handle another disaster just yet. With a mutter of agreement, he had her make the connection.

"Jimmy?" The voice coming over the line sounded weak and terrified. "Jimmy, you've got to find JD. They've got the program. They're out here looking for JD, and they're not happy, Jimmy. They may come after you next. Find him—" The rapidly rising hysterical note in his voice cut off when the line went dead.

Jimmy stared at the plastic receiver until it started beeping at him. Pulse pounding a little more erratically than earlier, he slowly lowered the phone. He wasn't a fast thinker like JD. He wasn't an impulsive man by nature. JD had the ideas. Jimmy carried out the meticulous details. But something told him he'd better think fast and make his own decisions right now.

"Do you have a car, Mrs. Walker?" he inquired carefully as he faced the weeping woman once again. Mentally, he wrote off Barbara without a single regret.

JD's ex-wife looked up at him, startled, but she nodded.

"It wouldn't happen to be a Chevy, would it?" he asked hopefully.

When she nodded again, he made a brave grimace. "How would you like to tour the USA in your Chevrolet?"

"Damn! Damn, damn, and double damn!" JD flung the hematite paperweight against the wall and sent his desk chair flying. The blue rock he'd found at the lake had fascinated him, but it shattered now from the force of the blow. The old wooden chair he'd used in front of the computer held up a little better, merely toppling over with a heavy thud. He noticed neither.

He couldn't believe he'd run into a snag he couldn't solve at this late date. He had the world by the ear with this program. A secured loop from consumer to business to bank and back again via the Internet had been impossible until now. He'd be richer than Gates if he completed this. He'd have the business world groveling at his feet. He had to finish this program. But he couldn't get around the snag.

Swearing, pacing back and forth, JD finally stalked out of the room he'd closeted himself in since last evening. To his surprise, sunrise crept across the floorboards through the wide mullioned windows in the front room. Nina never closed the blinds. The morning sun shone across old-fashioned braided rugs and that monster couch with all the pillows he could learn to appreciate, should he ever have enough time to lie on it again.

Suddenly tired, he rubbed his eyes and staggered down the hall toward the kitchen. Maybe coffee would refresh his brain. He was so damned *close*. He could taste success. He just needed to unravel that one lousy knot.

A sun-drenched vision in white poured water into the coffee-maker as he entered the kitchen. He blinked, and the ironic lift of a cinnamon-colored eyebrow at his appearance warned he had not encountered an angel. Feeling suddenly gritty in wrinkled jeans and torn shirt, JD ran his hand through his hair, realized it probably already stood on end, and grimaced.

"Good morning to you, too," she muttered, reaching for the refrigerator door. "If this is the way you always wake up, I'll set the timer next time so you can have the coffee *before* I get up."

He didn't see the need for explanations. The T-shirt advertising the one hundredth Fancy Farm picnic hung almost to her knees, but his weary brain fell into its usual rut, wondering just what lay beneath the folds of cotton. His physical awareness of his petite landlady had become a constant in his life since his arrival. He thought he discerned more of her breasts than hitherto revealed, but he wouldn't let himself fall into that trap. Grumbling about taking a shower, he stumbled back down the hall, wishing he were in his antiseptic modern home where spike-haired fairies didn't materialize at dawn.

JD returned to the kitchen, his hair freshly washed, his clothes once again in some respectable order, to find the kitchen empty except for the fresh pot of coffee. Frustrated that he'd cleaned up for nothing, he poured a big mug of coffee and wandered outside. Somehow, he knew the sprite had disappeared into the morning dew. He had the unreasonable belief that he deserved her company after going to the trouble of showering and changing clothes.

He found her frowning up at the supposedly dying birch tree while she ran water from a hose at its base.

"Isn't it a little early in the morning for playing nursemaid to a tree?" he grumbled. He hadn't meant to grumble. He wanted to woo the damned woman, not snap at her. But he couldn't get around the problem worrying at the back of his mind, and lack of sleep made him grouchy.

"Aunt Hattie planted this tree for my twenty-first birthday. Do you suppose it knows I've put her in a nursing home or that I'm declaring her incompetent? Maybe it's dying in protest."

JD squinted at her through the bright glare of the morning sun. The heavy heat of the day hadn't arrived yet, and it felt almost pleasant out here. But he thought Miss Nina Toon might be a twig short of a full tree at the moment. "That's the craziest thing I've ever heard," he muttered in reply. Then what she said finally sank in. The famous Aunt Hattie had been shuffled off to a nursing home, and this sprite meant to have her declared incompetent. Shaking his head to clear the cobwebs, he studied her more carefully.

"Alzheimer's?" he guessed.

She shrugged. "Senile dementia, whatever you want to call it. She's closing in on ninety. She has a right to check out of the real world, I suppose. I had just hoped to take care of her the way she took care of me."

JD sipped his coffee and contemplated the brilliant dawn and the mockingbird singing its foolish head off in the holly tree. Anything was better than looking at this diminutive female and feeling her pain. He didn't need any more people messing with his mind. But though she spoke in quiet, reasonable tones, her anguish penetrated his defenses. He didn't want it to. It was no business of his. But she radiated painful vibrations.

How was it that he could feel this woman's pain when he never noticed any other's? He had been known to work through an earthquake while people ran screaming from the building around him. Hell, his alcoholic old man had taught him all about ignoring pain, including his own. So why the devil was this sprite pounding open sores he hadn't known existed?

He didn't like feeling pain, hers or his. Maybe staying here hadn't been such a hot idea at all. He had Harry and his goons after him, and a program he desperately needed to complete. He didn't need this weird attraction to a woman who approached life with such fatalistic caution. Trees died. People got old. Life went on. Why worry?

For some reason, his usual careless attitude didn't work this time. Watching his landlady gnaw her bottom lip and frown, JD had the ridiculous urge to console her. He didn't have much experience at it, but the compulsion to reassure her was overwhelming.

"From what you've said," he ventured tentatively, "you *are* taking care of her. That tree is your Aunt Hattie. This house, this land, everything around it. They're all your aunt. You're doing what she wanted you to do."

She gave him a brief, unhappy look then nodded thoughtfully. "Maybe. I can live with that, I suppose. I just hate going into court and declaring her incapable of taking care of herself or her property. But it's the only way I can keep it."

Relieved that he'd not made a total ass of himself, JD sought an easy reply. "You'd lose it otherwise?" He told himself it was just an idle question, something to keep the conversation rolling while he rested his brain and drank his coffee. He didn't really care about the answer. Once he solved his little snag, he'd be on the road back to California. None of this had anything to do with him. He had his own problems, much bigger problems than this midwest farmer's daughter or whatever.

He snorted. Sure, and who was he fooling? That's why he'd dived headfirst into her idea for a botanical garden—because he was bored and needed a hobby. First thing he'd do when he returned to California would be to hire a shrink.

"The cell phone company wants a tower on Hattie's Hill. They're threatening to have the land condemned if I don't give them right-of-way. I can't fight them unless I have power of attorney."

Hattie's Hill. What in hell was Hattie's Hill? And that's when it came to him. He wasn't a lawyer. He only knew the bare bones of law as it affected him. But phone companies and powers of attorney struck a chord that resonated through his brain, and all the little pieces of one of his problems began snapping into place.

"Don't worry," JD informed her carelessly, his mind already back at the computer. "If you don't have power of attorney, you can't sign their damned right-of-way either."

With that, he strode off, leaving her staring blankly after him.

ELEVEN

"Yeah, JD's not bad," Jackie replied noncommittally to an earlier question as he swung his weed hook through the vines and brambles beneath an old pin oak. "He's only grounded me for the week. This work stuff stinks, but there's not much better to do."

His companion in travail stopped and wiped the sweat from his brow with a filthy rag, then rested on his long-handled shears. "Why doesn't Miss Toon just hire a bulldozer? That's what my dad would do."

Secretly relieved that the other guy had quit first, Jackie stopped working and took a deep drink of his bottled water. He glanced around at the small dent they'd cut in the thick undergrowth and gave a mental groan. "I don't know. She's pretty weird."

"Yeah. I remember last year she ran out of the classroom and yelled at the guys topping the trees in the school yard. Told them they were murdering the trees. She threw a fit when they wouldn't stop, and she got the principal. My dad said she told him that even if they didn't stop murdering the trees, the bucket truck was about to break down and the guy could get stranded up there."

Jackie grinned. "Yeah, she's got a thing about trees, for certain. What happened?"

His companion shoved the rag in his pocket and reached for the water. "The bucket broke down, and it took the volunteer firemen an hour to get the guy out. And the trees they topped died the next year. My dad says she's a witch."

"My dad would say she put sugar in the gas tank." Jackie promptly shut his mouth, remembering he shouldn't talk about JD that way. Reluctantly, he swung the weed hook at the next stand of brambles. He had mixed feelings about JD. The man had abandoned him and his mother and left them living on the limited generosity of his grandfather. It looked like a man ought to know when he had a kid. But he was angrier at his mother for not telling JD in the first place, so they could have been living in luxury all these years. The angers kind of balanced out. He just knew JD had rescued him from the rotten old man his mother had finally married. That didn't square things exactly, but it helped.

Of course, now JD thought he should act like a father, yelling at him to pick up his room and eat his meals and help out around the house, grounding him for drinking a little beer. But it wasn't any worse than what his mother had him do. His mom would have killed him for the beer thing. And living out here was pretty cool with the lake and all. He just wished Miss Toon would get air-conditioning. He was about to croak from the heat.

"Sugar in the tank. Yeah, I hadn't thought about that. Miss Toon is weird enough to do something like that," Laddie agreed. "What's she gonna do with all these old trees when we get the junk cleared out?"

"Make a garden. She wants a tourist attraction like they've got down in Florida. JD said he'd take me to Disney World if we had time, but with the truck broke, I guess it ain't gonna happen."

"She's gonna make a Disney World here?"

Jackie gave his friend a look of disgust. Brains weren't the biggest part of Laddie's character, he was discovering. "She's gonna make a garden, like Cypress Gardens, I guess. A place where all the rich people go and ooh and aah over the flowers. I heard her talking to JD. They think it will draw enough people that the town will need hotels and McDonald's and things like that. Miss Toon gets all excited when she talks about it."

"McDonald's! Cool. This place ain't got anywhere to go. Wait till my dad hears that. Maybe he'll let me work there so I can buy my own truck."

Vaguely uneasy that he might have said too much, Jackie swung his hook a little harder. It didn't matter what Miss Toon did about the garden or McDonald's or anything else. He and JD would be out of here before anything interesting happened.

Not certain how he felt about that, he gave the sapling in front of him a particularly vicious cut.

Nina was cleaning the spaghetti sauce off the burner when Jackie slumped in, clothes drenched and forehead dripping, stinking to high heaven of sweat and cut grass. She raised an eyebrow in his direction. "Did you jump in the lake, clothes on?"

"Nah. We shoulda." He reached in the refrigerator and helped himself to a can of root beer. "Can me and Laddie get paid so we can go into town and have a pizza?"

"I don't think JD plans on cutting payroll checks until Friday. That's how business works. You've got to hold out until payday. Is Laddie still outside? You both need to write down your hours so he'll know how much to pay you."

"He's out sticking his head under the hose."

Nina watched Jackie gulp the foamy soft drink, and her own stomach heaved in protest at the thought of the gas intake. Grimacing, she reached in the freezer and pulled out a couple of Eskimo Pies. "Why don't you take these down to the lake and cool off? Mama Rosa's isn't open until four, anyway."

Looking surprised, the boy accepted the ice cream. "Mom doesn't let me eat dessert until I've had lunch."

"So, you're on vacation. You're probably too hot to eat right now anyway. Cool off, then come back up here for hot dogs later. You'll be more ready to eat then."

Brightening, Jackie swiped his face with the kitchen towel and loped out the back door holding his prize. She could hear him yelling at Laddie from here. It didn't take much to please teenage boys sometimes. Food and something to do worked wonders.

The hair on the back of Nina's neck prickled, and she realized JD had entered the room behind her. She supposed he wouldn't approve of her sending his brother out with just ice cream for lunch, but she didn't care. The kids had worked hard all morning. They deserved a treat. She swung around and waited for his comments. After the strange ones he'd made this morning, she wasn't certain what to expect.

"Do you ever cook real food?" he asked mildly, opening the refrigerator door and examining the contents.

He was barefoot and sleep-tousled. She'd decided he must have stayed up all night working and had taken a nap after he'd disappeared back into his room this morning. Jackie had probably wakened him with his door slamming. She tried not to look too closely at the way JD's jeans slid down his hips as he bent over and rummaged through the refrigerator. She was grateful he actually wore a shirt, although she'd already noted he hadn't fastened it all the way up in front. She'd never realized just how attractive a man's hairy chest could be.

Feeling the odd sensation in the pit of her stomach again, she returned to cleaning. "I've not starved yet," she answered his question. "I find eating as boring as combing my hair. I only do it because I have to."

She heard the refrigerator door close, then felt strong masculine fingers running through her choppy hair. The intimate touch shot right through her nervous system, and Nina swung around, wielding the bottle of cleanser like a sword.

JD dropped his hand easily and set a jar of peanut butter on the counter. "If you eat as infrequently as you comb your hair, it's a wonder you don't starve. Are there any good restaurants in this town?"

"Carla's, if you want country-fried. That's about it." Still feeling his hand stroking her hair, Nina returned to polishing the stove, although she'd already eradicated all traces of spaghetti sauce.

"Country-fried," he groaned, rummaging for the bread. "It's a wonder everyone out here doesn't drop dead by the age of forty. Let's go to the grocery and see if we can't find something edible there. I'll buy. I didn't mean for you to feed us."

Thinking of Howard's Piggly Wiggly and the dearth of anything this man would consider edible, Nina grinned. "By all means, let's complete your education. Shall I draw up a grocery list?"

He gave her a suspicious look as he slathered the peanut butter on the bread. "What makes me think this will not be a pleasant experience?"

"Just call it a learning experience. Give me a minute to wash up. I'll be right with you."

JD watched her go with a hunger that had nothing to do with the peanut butter in his hand. She practically bounced when she walked. Her hips swung like a young girl's. That loose cotton dress swished around her knees and clung softly in all the right places. He suddenly realized tight tops and short cutoffs weren't half as feminine and enticing as that breezy halter dress. He didn't care what size her breasts were anymore. He just wanted that bundle of energy wrapped in his arms and her spacey attention focused on him.

Sighing with defeat, he finished his sandwich and drifted back to his room to put himself together before facing the Piggly Wiggly expedition. He couldn't believe anyone would call a store by that ridiculous name. He wondered what marketing genius thought grocery stores should be named after children's storybook characters. Maybe he should call his new software program Higgledy-Piggledy. It opened up whole new horizons of kindergarten tots lining up to play with automated tellers.

Still grouching, he brushed his hair and checked his e-mail. Still no reply from Jimmy. That wasn't like him. He was usually on any problem JD sent him like a duck to water. He considered calling the office. Could Uncle Harry and his cohorts actually summon the means of tracing a phone call?

Deciding he couldn't put Nina and Jackie at risk just so he could find out, JD typed out another urgent message and sent it while he waited. Jimmy might have a fresh approach to the program snag. With that solved, they could get the program canned and processed while JD manipulated legal strings to keep it out of DiFrancesco's hands. He wondered what kind of lawyers this town possessed. He sure as hell wasn't calling Dillon on this one. Visions of gutting Marshall Enterprises, declaring it the corporate equivalent of incompetent, and leaving the shell in his enemy's hands danced in JD's brain. Aunt Hattie would never know what a good turn she'd served him.

Nina appeared wearing a floppy-brimmed sun hat and carrying a rope tote bag like the ones JD had seen women use in Europe. With the long flowing flower-printed dress, she looked as if she'd stepped out of some television special on English gardening.

"Is the Piggly Wiggly a formal affair?" he inquired in amusement. "Shall I wear a tie?"

She gave him an exasperated look that made her cheeks rounder and her mouth pucker into a perfect shape for kissing. "Do you even own a tie?" She swept down the hall and out the door without waiting for a reply.

JD trailed after her, admiring the slender posterior view she afforded him. If he couldn't solve the snag, he might as well let his brain sleep while his libido took over. Hell, maybe what he really needed was a gym for working out his frustrations. Or a good roll in the hay.

Hobbling less now, he accepted the passenger seat she left him in the rolling wreck she called a car. There was something to be said for the planned obsolescence of American cars. At least their engines fell apart before they looked like traveling junkyards, unlike this Japanese-made one.

"I keep thinking I'll get a new paint job for this thing," Nina said as if she'd heard his thoughts. Turning the ignition, she continued, "The vo-tech classes paint cars for just the cost of materials. But I haven't figured out how to get back and forth to work while they're working on it. They tend to be rather slow."

"Maybe you should just retire it. You'll be putting your feet through the floorboard and pedaling it before long."

She gave him a look of irritation. "Do you have any idea how much a new car *costs*? And what I might afford couldn't be anywhere as well made as this one. These rubber bumpers have saved me a fortune in repair bills."

JD grinned and refrained from commenting on people who drove bumper cars. His Uncle Harry had sold him out to the banking equivalent of the Mafia. His partner had fallen off the face of the earth. The program he'd worked on for the last three years of his life had run aground. He had a broken foot, no vehicle, and a son he'd never known existed. And he was sitting here grinning like a fool in a bumper car beside a spike-haired wood sprite. Obviously, his brain had checked out entirely.

When she pulled off the main road he knew as the one toward town, JD gave her an inquiring look.

Again, she read his mind easily. "I'm stopping at Tom's place for fresh produce. Howard always trucks his in from Georgia, and it's never as good as homegrown." She maneuvered the car down a dirt drive. "It's too early for my tomatoes, but Tom has a greenhouse and gets a head start. I've got leaf lettuce, but Tom usually has spinach. And his wife is experimenting with mushrooms. It never occurs to Howard to stock mushrooms."

Not having the slightest idea who the hell Tom and Howard were, JD nodded agreeably, then grimaced as the car hit a pothole. "I thought you didn't cook. Why bother with fresh vegetables if you don't cook?"

"Who cooks them? I just throw them in a bowl and make a salad. Of course, when the corn comes in, I'll cook *that*. Fresh sweet corn is worth a few minutes of boiling water."

JD tried to remember the last time he'd had fresh sweet corn and couldn't. It if didn't come in frozen packages or served by a waiter at a restaurant, he generally didn't eat it. He might know how to use a kitchen, but he seldom had time, and California restaurants weren't much inclined toward serving corn on the cob, not the kind of restaurants he frequented these days, anyway. Maybe backwoods life had a few advantages.

After a convoluted discussion with Tom's wife involving tomato varieties and the uses of mushrooms, Nina finally filled her rope bag and returned to the car. JD had listened idly while munching a tomato in its raw, freshly picked state. Aside from wishing for some salt, he had spent most of the time admiring the way his landlady's fair cheeks pinkened with sun and exertion. The reason for the hat had become readily apparent.

"You should wear sunscreen," he admonished as he lifted his foot into the car and tried wiggling his toes. He didn't have any problem letting the lady drive, particularly in a heap like this one.

"I was only out a few minutes. Besides, I forget. Sunscreen is for the beach."

As they jolted from the dirt drive to the paved road, JD caught a glimpse of shining silver through the undergrowth, and he strained to catch a better view of the vehicle. "Who's the local driving a Mercedes? Now that's the kind of car to have. One-eighty on the autobahn, you could cover a lot of miles in that."

Nina glanced in her rearview mirror with a frown. "No one around here drives a Mercedes. The nearest dealer is probably two hundred miles away, even if anybody could afford one, which they can't. Even Dr. Rogers takes half his work on credit and can't afford better than a used Cadillac. Cadillacs are the only fancy cars we can get serviced around here."

JD turned around and watched the silver vehicle drop farther behind them. "Well, then, you have some wealthy tourists. That particular make could set you back a hundred grand, new." He knew. He'd considered one for himself, but he didn't tell Nina that. He somehow felt vaguely awkward flaunting that much ridiculously disposable income in front of a schoolteacher driving a fourteen-year-old used car.

Nina laughed. "The tourists we get drive pickup trucks and campers. Can you imagine a Mercedes owner camping out? This isn't exactly resort country."

"They must have tired of the interstate then and taken a more scenic route." JD repositioned himself so he could continue admiring flushed cheeks and bow lips. Contemplating kissing them kept him fully occupied.

"Then they're lost," Nina concluded. "This road goes nowhere, unless they turn on the state road at the junction."

JD felt a vague uneasiness at this knowledge, but he wouldn't let it intrude on his pleasant contemplation. Sometimes, diverting his mind from a problem made it easier for a solution to show itself.

They bumped back on the state road and turned toward town. Nina checked the mirror again and verified the Mercedes still followed. "That should provide some entertainment when we reach town. Reckon Howard could go out and lie across the road to make the guy stop and spend some of his money?"

"Not knowing Howard, I couldn't venture to say, but you

could always have Sheriff Hoyt flag him down if it's entertainment you want."

Nina grinned. "Got your hackles up, did he? Hoyt's like that. I think they teach it to them at sheriff's school or something."

Not caring for a discussion of Nina's homegrown suitor, JD let the topic lapse. They arrived in the tiny town of Madrid not long after. This time, it was broad daylight and he wasn't in a hurry, so he got a good look at it. One strong wind could wipe the crumbling old brick storefronts away. A tiny voice in the back of his head said it would be no major loss.

At least the Piggly Wiggly owner kept his windows clean, JD observed as he hobbled from the car. He could remember places as a kid that had a season's worth of flyspecks and dead insects on the panes. In that light, the town of Madrid reflected creditably. No junk cars—if he didn't count Nina's—littered the yards. Neat flower boxes lined many of the storefronts. And there were trees everywhere, even in the middle of parking lots. Countrified, perhaps, but pretty, he decided.

Nina interrupted his reverie by sidling up to him and touching his arm as they entered the store. "Don't look now, but the Mercedes stopped in front of the pharmacy. They must be asking for directions."

"Then the damned fools must not have a map. There's a road sign right in front of them." Not having any sympathy for idiots, wealthy or not, JD wandered toward the produce section. Nina was right. The tomatoes in here were a pitiful sight. And the strawberries had seen better days.

"Maybe we could take him home with us," Nina said cheerfully, picking through the baking potatoes. "Just tell the driver to follow us and we'll get him out of here. Then we show them Hattie's Hill and explain what a wonderful garden it would make, and he could throw a hundred grand away on something useful."

"Not damn likely. He'd probably sue for mental anguish or

something. You're better off leaving those types out of it. Where are the Chinese vegetables? I can make stir-fry."

Nina grinned even more brightly. "Howard thinks Chinese vegetables grow in China. They don't come from Georgia, anyway. Here he comes now. Ask him for the water chestnuts."

A pudgy, slightly balding man bumbled toward them, his tie loosened at the neck and the top button of his white shirt open. "Nina, I heard you've got a millionaire planning some kind of resort out your way! What in the world is that boy talking about?" He gave JD a suspicious but not unfriendly look.

"If you're looking for millionaires, go check out the Mercedes down at Ed's. I don't know any. What boy are you talking about?" Nina tied up the bag of potatoes and pushed the basket down the aisle, forcing Howard to bumble after them. JD grinned at the scene. He liked the way she put men in their places without even trying.

"Ethel's nephew. He just came up from the marina, said he'd been talking to Laddie Hancock." Howard sent JD a sudden look of recognition. "You must be that guy renting Nina's place." He stuck his hand out. "Howard Hughes, no relation."

"JD Smith." He shook the man's hand and watched hope and a twinge of greed leap to Howard's eyes. He waited for Nina to take over the conversation. No way would he admit to being the "millionaire." With mischief in mind, he asked, "Have you got water chestnuts?"

Beside him, Nina giggled as Howard's eagerness melted into chagrin. JD understood the need to get his jollies where he could, and watching the man wiggle like a worm on a hook did provide some amusement.

"No, sir, no water chestnuts at the moment. The shipment is late. I'm calling the transport company shortly." Desperately, Howard turned back to Nina. "Well, what is the boy talking about? Where there's smoke, there's fire. Something must be going on."

"Nothing more than usual, Howard. You know Hattie

always wanted a garden out there. I'm just looking into it, is all. How's the meat grinder?"

JD blinked at this abrupt change of subject. He'd thought Nina would be bubbling over with news of the garden. Her taciturnity puzzled him, but he didn't live here. He'd leave the nuances of local gossip to her.

"It broke down, just like you said. I've got a new one coming in tomorrow. Now if you would just tell me about those refrigeration units . . ."

Nina pushed the basket impatiently down the aisle. "I don't know anything about refrigeration units, Howard. Just use your own good sense. I'm in kind of a hurry here. Does the broken grinder mean I can't get fresh hamburger?"

JD gave up on this impossible conversation. Wandering off, he looked for his favorite cereal and settled for corn flakes. The ice cream was soft, and he didn't recognize any of the brand names, but he made sure he picked up chocolate. He owed Nina that. Prowling up and down the aisles, he understood Nina's remark about this being an experience. Accustomed to every brand on the market, salad and deli bars, gourmet aisles, and bakeries in the grocery stores in LA, he plunged back into the world of his youth here. The place didn't stock two brands when one brand would do. Generic goods and the local distributor's product seemed the only choices. And obviously Mueslix and water chestnuts hadn't reached this part of the country yet. He thought the PX in Germany stocked more than this place.

But he had an armful when he caught up with Nina at the checkout counter. Managing the cane and the groceries hampered him, his foot ached like hell, but he wasn't completely helpless yet. He still knew his way around grocery stores.

The clerk at the checkout counter was busily interrogating Nina about the proposed "resort." JD could sense Nina's temper rising simply from the compressed line of her lips. He didn't understand why she kept her idea a secret, but he preferred her in a good humor, not a cantankerous one. Hastily pulling out his wallet, he counted bills on the counter.

"I thought you couldn't find your wallet," she hissed as she pushed the basketload of sacks out to the car.

So much for keeping her happy. JD took her keys and opened the hatchback. "I explained that. I'm not harming anyone. Why didn't you tell those people about the garden?" he countered.

"And have them all getting their hopes up only to fall flat on their faces when nothing comes of it? I'd be a pariah. No, thank you."

The day had definitely taken a nasty turn. JD shut the trunk and, now that he had possession of the keys, headed for the driver's side of the car. "Is that a slam to my abilities or your own?" he asked angrily as he slid into the seat.

To Nina's credit, she didn't argue with him over driving privileges. She just slammed the door on her side so hard he thought the car would tumble off its frame. "It's happening already!" she declared furiously as he started the engine. "The rumors are already starting, and we haven't put plans to paper. There's not one penny of money or anything more constructive done than chopping a few weeds. I've seen it too often, and I'll not be a party to it. I don't know what you're here for, JD Whoever-you-are, but I'll not let my friends and neighbors down like that."

He didn't have the foggiest notion what she was talking about, but he quit concentrating on her tirade as soon as he pulled the Camry away from the curb. The Mercedes sitting at the pharmacy had just started its engine, also, and he didn't think taking it home with them was such a hot idea.

TWELVE

"This isn't the way home," Nina reminded JD patiently as he roared the Camry out of town as if it were his motorcycle. Or roared as much as four cylinders could, she amended.

The man in the small space beside her confused her too often. He looked like he belonged on a motorcycle, wheeling from one beer joint and pool hall to another. But as far as her limited knowledge could determine, he did seem to know his way around computers—to the extent that he carried them with him on vacation. He had manipulated a busy landscape architect into drawing up plans without producing a penny of money, and he spoke intelligently of the creative arts. The man cooked stir-fry, for heaven's sake! Maybe he came from outer space.

Maybe he was taking her back there with him. Watching his direction with alarm, Nina intruded on JD's obviously black humor. "We've got ice cream in the back, remember! We'll not get it home before it melts if you keep going this way. The air conditioner in this car isn't that great."

His square jaw hardened as he glanced in the rearview mirror. "I noticed. Where does this road go?"

"If you stay on it, you'll end up crossing the lake," Nina informed him, not in the least assured by this seemingly rational reply. "Unless you've taken a notion to go hiking or swimming, there's nothing over there but wilderness."

"Not a half-bad idea, but under the circumstances, probably not the best one. What about boat rentals?"

Thoroughly puzzled now, Nina glanced over her shoulder to see what he was watching in the mirror. Far in the distance, she could see the sun glint off shiny metal. The Mercedes? "Boat rentals?" she inquired absently. "What about them?"

"Can we rent boats across the lake?" he asked impatiently.

"No, it's all TVA-owned right now. No commercial enterprises, at least, until they can figure some way out of their promises. You can put your boat in the water over there, but you can't rent one."

JD jerked the steering wheel hard and swept around one of the road's more treacherous curves without slowing. Nina thanked the reliable Camry's road-hugging qualities and wished she could afford a new one. JD's next question shattered that little daydream.

"How do we get to the nearest marina then? Besides the one back in town."

"You've lost your mind, haven't you? You've taken me grocery shopping like any normal human being, then as soon as you get your hands on my car keys, you turn into a raving lunatic."

He gave her a frustrated glance that should have curled her toenails. She really didn't want to see this man angry. He hadn't shaved this morning; his beard-stubbled face and long hair gave him the look of one of those unforgivably menacing men women loved watching at the movies, men any sane woman would avoid in real life. She hated those movies.

"The Mercedes is following us," he replied curtly. "I really don't think you want to take them home with us. Where can we rent a boat?"

She still didn't see the connection, but she didn't want her neck wrung either. She nodded at an upcoming intersection.

"Turn left up there. That road takes you down the commercial side of the lake. There's a resort with boat rentals a few miles down the road. Why don't we want a Mercedes following us?"

He ignored the question and made a hard left. Accelerating, he drove over a hill at a rate that left Nina's heart in her throat and her head on the ceiling. She checked behind them. She could no longer see the intersection. Maybe they'd lost the Mercedes and JD would calm down. She didn't have much experience dealing with paranoia.

"I thought you said this place doesn't have resorts?"

He sounded almost normal again, and Nina regarded him cautiously. "If you're thinking in terms of luxury hotels, forget it. Boat rentals, miniature golf, maybe a pool and restaurant, and some campgrounds. That's luxury around here."

The land here was too flat, the road too winding and tree-lined for a good view of the road behind them. Not until the Mercedes topped the small rise did she know if it still followed. From JD's grunt of disgust, she gathered he saw it, too. Now he was making her nervous.

"Maybe the owner of the Mercedes just wants a scenic view of the lake," she said uneasily, watching for the road signs to the marina. She knew they were there, but she never had occasion to rent boats. This was unfamiliar turf.

"Then he'll get one," JD responded without humor. "At least he's not running us off the road this time. Doesn't want to damage his pretty fenders, I imagine."

Really alarmed now, Nina tried to read his expression. His mouth was set in a grim line that didn't bode well for someone. "What do you mean, 'this time'?"

"I recall what happened with the van. It was kind of hazy there for a while, but I remember it now. That clown deliberately smashed into the truck. He could have killed Jackie. There wasn't any oncoming traffic at the time, was there?"

"He was speeding," she protested. "He was probably drunk

and misjudged the distance. Why would anyone deliberately run into you?"

"That's what I want to know." Seeing the directional road sign without Nina's help, JD jerked the wheels in a hard right down the narrow lane toward the marina.

"There's a word for people like you," Nina complained as he kept the Toyota at an unconscionable speed. "Nobody out here knows you. Even if that van driver decided you'd make good roadkill, that doesn't mean he knows who you are. Who are you hiding from anyway, the Mafia?"

"Something like that." With practiced skill, JD steered the Camry into the parking lot, slammed into a space, turned off the engine, and hopped out. "Hurry up. With luck, they won't know how to drive a boat."

"And you do?" Nina asked sarcastically. "What about the groceries?"

He gave her a look of irritation, opened the hatchback, and picked up a sack. "This is gonna look like one hell of a picnic lunch."

He hadn't answered her question about driving a boat. Nina briefly considered asking for her keys back, but JD's long legs had already carried him halfway across the parking lot.

Grabbing the other sack of groceries, Nina raced after him. Before she followed him into the rental cabin, she glanced over her shoulder. The Mercedes was nowhere in sight. Maybe JD had turned before the driver of the other car saw them.

JD was laughing and acting perfectly normal when she entered the cabin. The man behind the rental counter gave her a swift look and grinned. She didn't want to know what they'd been saying about her, so she wandered on through to the boat dock. To hell with men, anyway. Who needed them?

JD sauntered out a little while later, swinging her tote bag and the keys in one hand, carrying the paper sack already dripping ice cream in the other. Well, she should lose a few pounds anyway. She didn't need the damned ice cream.

She dropped her sack of groceries behind the seat of the boat JD climbed into. She'd lived on the lakes all her life, but she could count on the fingers of one hand the number of times she'd been out in a boat. She gave the low seats a wary glance and tried to figure out how she could gracefully descend into the rocking, bouncing, narrow little front seat without making an idiot of herself.

Looking up from the boat equivalent of a dashboard, JD shot her a glance, noticed her hesitation, and stood up, offering his hand. "Come on. It won't get away from you."

"I don't understand any of this," she warned as she reluctantly took his hand and climbed down. The toughness of JD's hand and the strength with which he practically hauled her into the boat reassured Nina somewhat. She wasn't much used to having men around, certainly not strong ones. She bet he could dig out her overgrown daylilies in a third of the time it would take her.

As she settled in the seat, he turned his attention back to the boat. She didn't like the way he studied the lake as he threw off the rope tying them to the deck. "Do you know how to drive this thing?" she asked warily.

"It's a machine. I'll figure it out."

Before Nina could make a hasty exit at these unpromising words, JD had the engine roaring. As he pulled away from shore, Nina caught the side of the boat with one hand, her hat with the other, and closed her eyes against the wind smacking her face.

Assured they wouldn't instantly sink or smash into any of the other boats bobbing in the marina, she peeked out from beneath one eyelid. They'd already hit open water. The sun glancing off the rippling waves nearly blinded her.

"I think you owe me a good explanation," she demanded through clenched teeth, reaching for the sunglasses in her purse.

"Haven't you ever been out in a boat before?"

JD looked as if he were having the time of his life. The wind blew his thick dark hair straight back, and his teeth gleamed white against his tanned skin as he accelerated and the boat responded. He gave her a laughing glance when she didn't immediately answer.

"Aunt Hattie was sixty years old when I was born," Nina replied, irked. "Do you think we went for regular Sunday boat outings?"

That slapped the grin off his face. Slowing down, he steered past the buoys and headed north. "You've lived with your aunt all your life? What about your parents?"

"Great-aunt. She let my mother live in a house she owned farther down the road. Hattie had retired from teaching by then, and she used to baby-sit me." Nina didn't know why she was telling him this. She had ten thousand questions of her own. But it helped to talk about the familiar while her teeth chattered and she watched the water widen all around her. Still holding her hat on, she glanced back at the marina parking lot, but she wasn't wearing her glasses, as usual. She couldn't see if the Mercedes had arrived.

"Your parents could have taken you out on the weekends," he pressed on.

"My mother and stepfather went their separate ways when I was nine. Hattie filled the gap. If anyone took me out before then, I don't remember. Why are we running from a Mercedes?" There, she finally got it out—again. Maybe she would push him overboard if he didn't answer this time.

He hesitated, obviously choosing between two equally explosive subjects. He finally offered the reply she sought. "I'm trying to avoid some rather unsavory characters. It would be just like them to show up in a Mercedes. I don't want them knowing where you live, if they're who I think they are."

"So we're going home in a boat and leaving my car at the marina?" Nina asked incredulously.

"Looks that way. Do you think I could persuade Sheriff

Hoyt to go back and pick it up?" He flashed her the crooked white grin that turned her insides into flapjacks.

"I think you're crazy. I don't have a landing dock. I want my car in the driveway where it belongs. You can't keep a rental boat out forever. The Mercedes probably went right on. And why are these unsavory characters after you? Does this have something to do with Jackie's mother?"

Ignoring all the more pertinent demands, he zeroed in on the last one. "Nothing to do with Jackie. I've got something the bad guys want. I didn't think they'd follow me all the way out here, though. I can't figure out how they found me in the first place. I didn't even tell Uncle Harry."

Nina stared at him, not at all certain how to take this answer. She didn't watch television often because there were far too many unbelievable melodramas cluttering the airwaves on the few channels she picked up. In any given month, how many car chases could really happen? How many spies almost got caught? How many insane people stalked perfectly innocent bystanders? It was all fictional nonsense. But he seemed quite serious. She didn't believe him.

"I assume that means you didn't expect your creditors to go to such lengths to get back whatever it is you bought from them?" she asked tentatively. She understood bad debt and repossession. The furniture company had taken back practically everything her mother owned.

He didn't even bother glaring at her. He seemed to be watching the shore. Nina didn't know what Hattie's property looked like from this angle. How would he know where to stop?

"They might think of themselves as creditors," JD admitted, still concentrating on their direction, "but I've made every payment on time. I can pay them the balance of the loan as soon as I get this program canned and on the market. It's not the money they want. It's the program."

When had she tripped into the rabbit hole and met the Mad

Hatter? Nina wished she had a spoon so she could get some of the ice cream before it turned into soup. A sugar high might help about now. Of course in this heat, she might be able to drink the ice cream without need of a spoon. Holding her hat, she watched the shoreline for landmarks. "Why do they want the program?" she asked in exasperation, playing along with the game.

"I can only guess. Aside from the fact that it will earn them a hefty bundle if marketed correctly, I suspect they have some means of using it for money-laundering. If they put their experts on it, a loop could be added that might make their bank accounts undetectable. I can't imagine they're that smart, but someone must be. They'll have a damned difficult time marketing the program as theirs. I'll sue their pants off."

The intensity of his reply indicated he really believed it. Nina still thought him a paranoid delusional. But she saw the Madrid marina ahead and breathed a sigh of relief. "We could just stop there and walk up to the house," she pointed out.

"You want to carry dripping ice cream half a mile?" JD slowed even more, scanning the shore. "Besides, I don't want anyone knowing where we take the boat. If we're lucky, the jerks in the Mercedes will think we're on a little outing and will wait in the parking lot for our return. If we're not lucky, they're somewhere behind us waiting for us to dock. They can spot us at the marina too easily. That place only has fishing boats. If I can find a cove and cover up the boat, they'll spend the rest of the day looking."

"I quit reading Nancy Drew when I was nine," Nina informed him coldly. "You can't hide a blamed boat."

Seeing something ahead, JD grinned. "Watch me. I was tops in my camouflage class."

With that scarcely reassuring news, he steered the boat directly toward the cypress-tree-littered shore.

Nina wondered if now was the time to remind him that this

lake was created by damming a river and backing water up over acres of farmland. The original trees still lay directly below the water's surface.

THIRTEEN

JD grimaced as he heard an underwater branch scrape the bottom. He'd known the danger of these shallow waters. Losing the boat didn't much concern him, although he suspected the sprite beside him would have a fit if she knew that. Hell, she'd croak if they lost the damned groceries. Her priorities just didn't match his. Give him expediency over caution any day.

Easing the boat over the snag, he breathed a sigh of relief as it pulled free without ripping out the hull. He hadn't really wanted to hear Nina's cries of horror if he wrecked the thing. He steered toward the stand of cypress trees. The old beaver dam ahead would provide the cover he needed.

Easing into the narrow channel, JD cast a quick glance over the water. Because it was a weekday, the number of boats visible was minimal. He didn't see any suspicious craft slowing down or coming within easy range. He despised this cloak-and-dagger stuff in real life. On computers, he could make it amusing. He didn't find this even vaguely funny. Especially since now Nina and Jackie were in danger.

JD roped the boat to a dead cypress stump, knotted it securely, then glanced at the swampy water between the boat and the bank. "How's your water moccasin population?"

"Small," Nina replied with what he took as a resigned sigh. "I can wade to shore. I just don't like any of this."

"I've got news for you," JD replied as he climbed into the murky water, "neither do I. Give me the groceries. I'll set them on the bank first." He found some solid ground on which to deposit the paper sacks, then waded back to lift Nina out of the rocking boat. She weighed scarcely nothing, and despite her vehement protests, JD simply carried her to shore.

"I'm perfectly capable of walking," she said indignantly as he deposited her beside the sacks.

JD managed a halfhearted grin. "Yeah, but let me get what jollies I can here. I'll cover up the boat. You go on and see what the boy is up to."

"Up to his ears in hot dogs, probably. I showed him how to boil them on the stove. Can't I help you cover the boat?"

"Not unless you're carrying a hatchet in that purse. Go on, I'll be right with you." JD watched as she reluctantly filled her arms with sacks and trudged up the slight embankment toward the house. She'd felt awful damned good in his arms. He'd even kind of liked her protests that she could do it herself. He didn't know too many women willing to soak their shoes and themselves in this scummy water. Independence and spunk. He'd look for that when he got back to California.

If he got back to California. It was beginning to look as if someone wanted him dead, and DiFrancesco was the first villain who came to mind. Using his pocketknife to saw off some small cypress branches, JD considered the possibilities. The R&D department had led DiFrancesco by the nose for a week before the financier had realized what they were up to. They'd had him playing the latest Monster House version, working his way through the reading program they'd developed for the Literacy Foundation, and reading through long scripts of the new game he'd created. DiFrancesco had understood little to none of it, so JD had thought himself safe at the time.

Then he'd heard Harry explain that the banking program

was top secret and nobody could see it. That had set the jerk off, all right. Cursing his uncle's stupidity, if that was what it had been, JD lashed the branches to the boat and inspected the impromptu camouflage job. Harry never knew when to keep his mouth shut. He shouldn't really blame Harry. He just wanted to be friendly to his friends. Some friends.

Grunting approval of the temporary concealment, JD slogged through the water toward the bank. DiFrancesco had insisted on seeing the banking program immediately. JD had refused. The building had been broken into that night. Fortunately, the thief wasn't aware of the new technology guarding the lab. *Unfortunately,* the thief had escaped before the police arrived. In any event, he hadn't come near the information he was after, as far as JD could tell.

He'd backed everything up the next day, removed all the disks from the lab, cleared out the hard drives, and taken off before Harry's "friends" could make another attempt. He had to trust that none of his staff had taken anything home with them. Security was supposed to check, but he knew well enough the holes security overlooked. JD rather suspected DiFrancesco and his cohorts had broken into the homes of everyone on the staff by now, including his own. He could guarantee no one had the latest revision, because he'd just created that himself on the way out here. But DiFrancesco didn't know that. The question was: What exactly *did* the bastard know?

It didn't make sense. If the rat had a working version, he might want the creator dead so JD couldn't make claims against him when he sold it as his own. But no working version existed. Everyone knew that, except maybe Harry.

As JD carried the last sack of groceries up to the house, the answer finally dawned on him. DiFrancesco had contacts with JD's competitors.

Damn! How stupid could he be? He'd thought only Uncle Harry naive enough to deal with warped characters like that.

Instead, he'd been the one who was naive. The Mafia had nothing on huge industries with their greedy fingers in every pie. Industrial espionage was big business, particularly in his high-tech world.

DiFrancesco must have found enough information to send the other developer into ecstasies thinking they had enough for a working program. That's when they'd tried to bump JD off, although how in hell they'd found him, he couldn't say. Unless Jimmy had told them. Or someone had followed him.

But by now they'd discovered they still didn't have a working program, and they probably weren't any closer to solving the snag that finalized the software either. So they were tagging him, waiting for the final answers.

Maybe he was paranoid. Nina had certainly looked at him as if he were insane. Maybe this business was making him crazy. He had imagined DiFrancesco and the Mercedes. He had imagined the whole damned thing. Nobody wanted him, nobody cared. The van had just shoved him off the road because he was there. It happened all the time.

JD had just convinced himself of that by the time he reached the house. The kitchen smelled of overcooked hot dogs and root beer. Nina was just putting up the mop, probably after cleaning chocolate ice cream drips. He wondered if she'd tried to save it. Smiling at the thought, JD glanced at Jackie and the ketchup-laden paper plate in front of him.

"Hey, Dad, I heard you've got a boat! Can I go for a ride?"

Deadly silence descended like a pall over the previous cheer. Jackie gulped and turned a sheepish gaze back to his plate. Removing a box of cereal from the grocery sack, JD gave Nina a quick glance. He had to give the woman credit. She never missed a beat. But she didn't say a word.

"I'll take you out for a ride some other time. Isn't there something else you can do right now?"

Realizing escape was his best bet, Jackie leapt up. "Laddie's camping out at his cousin's tonight. Can I go?"

"There are sleeping bags and equipment in the front hall closet," Nina informed him, not once looking at either of them. "I don't know what condition they're in."

"Gee, thanks, Miss Toon." Giving her his best manners and charm, Jackie sped out of the room.

JD wished he could go with him.

The silence thickened. He didn't owe her any explanations. Obviously, she had come to the same conclusion. She offered no questions. Instead, she chopped viciously at a green onion as if she'd make juice out of it.

JD grabbed one of the tomatoes they'd just bought and hacked at it equally viciously. Ignoring the juice spurting across the table, he talked to the back of her head. "I told you, we're keeping a low profile."

"Right." The knife sliced sharply into the cucumber she picked up next, and JD winced at the graphic image.

"You're the one who assumed we were brothers," he reminded her. "I never said a word."

"You certainly didn't." Chop, another chunk rolled off the cucumber.

JD plowed his hand through his hair. He didn't have to deal with this. He could just remove himself to the other room and let her steam. With any other woman, he probably would have. He just couldn't find it in himself to treat Nina like that. He didn't bother examining the notion. He wasn't much on introspection.

"Okay, so I lied by omission. I just did what seemed safest at the time. I didn't want Jackie involved in any of this, or you. If the sheriff had an APB out for a man and his son, I figured this would slow him down. And I suppose I was kind of flattered. I've been feeling ten thousand years old since I found out about him."

That brought her around. Her big green eyes widened into circles. So much for showing his sensitive side. She looked as if she didn't believe one word he said.

"Since you found out about him? You mean, you didn't know you had a son?"

Oh, hell, he was in for it now. Grabbing a bunch of spinach leaves, JD ripped them in half. He'd never realized how much stress cooking could release. He viciously ripped a few more leaves before replying. "She never told me. I was sixteen, and she was fifteen. When her old man got the marriage annulled, I joined the marines and left town. I didn't even think about the consequences. I probably sent her a few lovesick letters at the time, but she never replied. That's the last I heard of her until a couple of weeks ago."

"My God." Blinking, she opened the refrigerator and produced boiled eggs and a packet of shredded cheese. By the time she finished, this would be one whopper of a salad, JD decided, thinking of anything but the conversation.

She remained silent as she chopped up the egg and added the cheese to the growing bowl of ingredients. Finally, she gave him a swift glance over her shoulder. He should have been concentrating on the greens, but he was aware of every nuance of her presence. He didn't want her angry with him, or disgusted, or even pitying him. He wanted their relationship clear-cut and aboveboard. He was renting a room from her. He didn't want to be thrown out on his ass. He'd like to have her in his bed, but he didn't need her respect or approval for that. He just wanted those shapely legs wrapped around him. That was it. No more. Or so he told himself.

"How did you find out about him?" she finally asked.

JD shrugged. "He found me. When that bastard Nancy married started beating up on him, Jackie didn't just get mad. He went searching for me. He's not dumb."

"I didn't think he was. I'm not so certain about his father." With that scathing remark, she opened the refrigerator again.

"What did you want me to do?" JD exclaimed. "I found out I had a kid I knew nothing about. I've got a madman trying to steal my business out from under me. And I was supposed to sit there and let the hound dogs rip me apart while leaving Jackie for his old man to beat into a pulp?" He couldn't believe he was demanding she understand his actions. Why should he care if she understood? Damn, but the heat in this place was rotting his brain. "Why don't you have a damned ceiling fan in here?" he asked in disgust.

"We tried, but it kept shorting the fuse. So we put it in the living room. What kind of dressing do you want?"

"Like I have a choice," he answered grumpily. "You have low-fat ranch and an ancient Thousand Island. I'll mix some vinegar and oil."

"You should have bought more at the store if you wanted something else." She withdrew the ranch dressing and reached for the salad bowls.

They were bickering like a married couple. Damn. JD closed his eyes and shook his head, listening for the sound of Jackie in the other room. He'd been rummaging in the closet earlier. He was on the phone now. He had to get Jackie out of here before he returned the boat to the marina.

"Laddie's father will pick him up," Nina said, as if reading his mind. "The boys camp out down there all the time. I haven't figured out the fun of fighting off mosquitoes and burning marshmallows, but it keeps them occupied. There's not much to do in Madrid otherwise."

"It's a good place to bring up a kid," JD grudgingly admitted. "Back home, they all think it's a parent's duty to keep them entertained. Thanks for suggesting the camping. I wanted him out of here before I moved the boat."

Jackie burst back into the kitchen. "Did you get any cookies? We need grub."

"Cookies aren't grub," Nina reminded him patiently. "Take some apples and that jar of peanut butter along with the cookies. At least you'll get some nutrition."

Jackie made a face but did as told. JD admired the no-nonsense way she ordered the boy around. If he'd said that,

Jackie would have griped and complained, then grabbed the cookies and left.

They sat down with their cold meal and didn't discuss anything of relevance again until they heard the truck pull up, and Jackie yelled his farewell from the front room. An uneasy silence descended as the door slammed behind him.

"I'll take a look at your wiring when I get a chance." JD finally broke the quiet. "You could probably burn the place down with some of these sockets in here." He picked at one of the cucumbers in his salad. He had some sympathy for the vegetable. Women were damned hard on a man.

"That's what the electrician said when he installed the wiring in Hattie's room. But he wanted the earth and two moons to redo it, so I figured he was just out to earn a buck." She scooted her lettuce around in the bowl and avoided looking at him.

"I suspect you'd blow the place up if you installed air-conditioning. You'll have to do something to this old place one of these days. Houses don't hold together all by themselves. What did you decide to do about the incompetency hearing?"

"I'm going ahead with it. I can't even borrow money against the equity in the house until I have some legal authority over the place. So I guess that means I'll have to hire someone to fight the phone company before they condemn the land. I imagine that's what they intend to do anyway. I think my lawyer told them Hattie was in a nursing home and wouldn't protest."

She looked so dispirited sitting there, JD wanted to reach out and hug her. He definitely didn't need that kind of complication right now, though. He had enough problems of his own.

"Let me check my resources for an attack lawyer. He'll clean the phone company's clock fast enough. You might want to junk the local guy, too, if you think he's working against you."

She jabbed a slice of tomato. "I went to school with him. He's running for county attorney next election. I have to live with these people. I'll give him the incompetency case, but I'd appreciate the name of a fancy lawyer if you can drum one up. I don't think Matt would want the hot potato of the phone company even if he's not in cahoots with them." Finally, she looked up from her salad bowl and met his gaze. "How much danger are we talking about from your unfriendly Mercedes people?"

"I don't know for certain it's them," he warned her. "I could just be paranoid." He read the blink of agreement in her eyes and the slight relaxation of tension in her shoulders. So, she'd come to the same conclusion. "But I've got a lot of evidence that says otherwise. I'll check my mail again. I haven't heard from my partner and I'm worried. If they've gotten to him, I may have to leave. My main problem is leaving you or Jackie unprotected if they do know I'm here, and I can't keep moving on, setting up in new towns all across the country until I get this puzzle solved. I don't suppose you have any relatives you could visit for a few weeks?"

"Doesn't matter," she said. "I've got too much to do around here to leave now."

JD slumped back in the kitchen chair and examined the pale face of his hostess in the sunlight from the big kitchen windows. She was made so delicately, a man couldn't be blamed for thinking her weak. But though carved in petite dimensions, her features were strong. Her chin might be narrow, but she had it thrust out now, as if daring him to turn her out of her own home. The spiky hair added its own kinky strength to the image. He really liked what he saw, liked it too much if he admitted the truth. Unsettled, he crossed his arms.

"I've pretty much concluded that they've run into the same snag as I have. Until someone solves the problem, the program is essentially useless. In that case, they need me alive to see if I can fix it. I think they're keeping an eye on me right now. The danger will come when they think I've got the program ready for market. What do you think? Are you ready to play the game with me?"

"I don't want Jackie going back to an abusive father," she warned.

JD understood. She didn't care what happened to him, but she would watch out for the boy. He could accept that. He could take care of himself. Nodding, he took his bowl to the garbage can and scraped it out. "I'll try taking the boat back to the marina and picking up your car later. If the Mercedes is still there, I may have to make other arrangements. But I suspect they've given up for the day. They're not particularly patient people. They're looking for easy alternatives right now. In the meantime, I'll see if my partner has left any messages."

He put the bowl in the sink and left her sitting there with the sunlight playing through her nimbus of silvery hair. She didn't look very happy with his solution. He wasn't particularly thrilled himself. Something inside him just wouldn't pick up and run this time.

A few minutes later when he discovered Jimmy's e-mail box was too full to accept more messages, JD thought about reconsidering the notion.

FOURTEEN

Nina listened to JD's frantic pounding on his keyboard. He hadn't even bothered closing his door. When she went out to pick up the mail, she'd seen him hunched over the computer, notes scattered on the floor all around him, a pen crunched between his teeth as he scowled at the monitor. She suspected he hadn't moved an inch for hours.

His thick hair had grown long enough to pull into a small ponytail in back, and he'd apparently grabbed a rubber band and jerked it away from his face. It made him look more like a motorcycle thug than ever. To her utter dismay, she liked it that way.

Not wishing to contemplate the knot of tension or whatever it was she felt when around JD, Nina retreated to the garden. It hadn't rained in days. Everything needed watering.

Once upon a time she could have lost herself contemplating rows of corn in the vegetable garden, new climbing roses for the fence, a trellis for the walkway. Her mind would focus on which plants were thriving, which seemed to be failing, and she would wonder what foul insect had skeletonized her geraniums. Today, she scarcely saw where the water fell.

The incident with the Mercedes had puzzled more than terrified her. JD's behavior, on the other hand, churned her stomach. Either he was insane, or someone was really after him. Neither alternative appealed to her.

She'd known kids in school who lied about everything. They just made up stories as they went along, making their lives more exciting, more interesting than anyone's around them. It got them the attention they didn't receive at home. Surely a grown man wouldn't do the same. But she could think of one or two women around town who were prone to exaggeration. Maybe a man would think it made him more attractive.

But the Mercedes had been there. It had followed them. She found it hard to believe anyone driving a Mercedes would have any interest in a motorcycle bum or a battered Toyota. The possibility that everything JD had said was true did not make her any happier. How much damage could one computer programmer do to another? Surely they weren't violent.

The van "accident" implied otherwise.

Gritting her teeth and glaring at an innocent lily, Nina set the whole idea aside. JD "Smith" rented her front room and played with computers. That's all she needed to know.

At dusk, he sauntered down from the back porch, tucking in his T-shirt as he glanced around, looking for her. Nina contemplated remaining hidden behind the fence, but she supposed she should see if he needed anything. Southern hospitality demanded an awful lot of a person.

She liked the way his bronzed face lit up from inside when he smiled. She liked it when he smiled at her approach. She liked it altogether too well. She couldn't manage a scowl in return, but she kept her voice neutral. "Did you need anything?"

His smile became a crooked grin, but he didn't tease her for a change. "I'm taking the boat back. You'll need your car. We can't leave it parked at the marina. Is there a barn or something on the property where we can at least keep it hidden?"

She definitely didn't like these games. She pointed at the next stand of trees. "There's an old equipment shed over there.

The roof is falling in, and half the slats are gone from the side. I won't be responsible if it falls on your head. But it's deep. No one could see the car in there."

He followed the direction of her finger. "That'll do for now. I don't know if they have any way of breaking into court computers and obtaining your address from license plate records, but I'd rather not take chances."

"Even if they got my name, it's a rural route address on the records. I've never persuaded the clerk to correct it to the new post office numbers. The only way they can find me from a rural route address is by asking at the post office. I'll go in and talk to Joe Bob tomorrow, tell him not to give out my directions to strangers. Beyond that, I can't promise. Everyone knows where I live."

And they would all think someone driving a Mercedes was the financier behind the garden plan that didn't exist. Nina could kick whoever had started that rumor. She didn't think JD had strayed anywhere outside the farm without her. Jackie must have said something. How could she tell a whole darned town not to talk to strangers?

JD obviously didn't like the idea that everyone knew where she lived. He frowned, but there wasn't anything the mighty JD Smith could do about it. Shrugging, he said, "There's only so much we can do. I've hidden the program, so even if they break in, they won't find it. Will you be all right until I get back?"

Stupid question. As if she hadn't lived here alone this past year. Nina nodded and watched him walk off with the easy stride he managed even with a cane. The rough field and broken ground through the trees didn't slow him, despite the limp. He took it all with a muscular gait that had him disappearing into the woods within seconds.

The air seemed suddenly still. Not even the mockingbird sang its silly song. Nina listened for a bobwhite or a catbird, a car engine, anything. The heavy humidity weighed on her skin like a soggy blanket as she watched the place where JD had disappeared. She should get back to work. She had plenty to do. But she stood there until she heard him start the boat engine, then waited a while longer until the sound grew fainter and she could hear it no longer.

She finished watering the garden, but her heart wasn't in it. She'd fought this depression when Hattie had gone to the nursing home and she'd rattled around the empty house alone. She should be over it by now. Hattie was safe and comfortable where she was. If she'd stayed here, she could have wandered into the lake and drowned. Sometimes, Nina wondered if her aunt wouldn't have preferred that, but she simply couldn't bring herself to allow it. At least this way, Hattie had her lucid moments. It wasn't as if she were gone entirely.

The mosquitoes got too thick to endure. Nina gave up and returned to the house. The old rooms were ominously silent without Jackie's boom box or the click of JD's computer keyboard. She should be used to silence. Even when Hattie lived here, it had been quiet in the last few years. Her aunt had been too ill to make much noise. The rush of water as Nina turned on the faucet couldn't fill the vacuum.

She fixed herself a sandwich and turned on the TV news. She could get the local channel without cable. She supposed she should ask about cable sometime, but she'd never particularly missed it. The garden and lesson plans usually occupied the majority of her evenings, and she didn't want more wires littering the countryside.

She got out her notes on the landscaping project and studied them. She'd scarcely begun listing the possibilities. The costs escalated with each new idea. She didn't know why she was wasting her time, but it gave her something to do. It wasn't as if the plans would be totally wasted. Someday, she would find the funds for Hattie's garden. Maybe she would win a lottery.

* * *

JD saw the gray flicker of the television through the front window as he strolled up the walk. It was past midnight, and it had just occurred to him that he hadn't asked his absentminded landlady for a key. He hadn't needed one until now.

Nina didn't look up as he entered. Deeply engrossed, she sat cross-legged on the floor in front of the TV, scribbling like a crazy woman across the notebook in her lap while sorting through the pages of notes and drawings scattered on the rug around her.

She'd waited up for him. JD knew it instantly. He supposed he could call it arrogance, but he knew her habits. She was waiting for him to come home safely. No one had ever waited up for him before. No one. He didn't know if he liked the idea or not. It was kind of like the air he sucked in between his two bottom teeth when the dentist gave them a good cleaning. It took some getting used to.

"Can I fix you some warm milk or anything?" JD asked awkwardly, not knowing how else to intrude upon her reverie.

She glanced up in wide-eyed surprise, and he fell once again for those elfin features. He remembered them now, staring down at him from the pickup, all puckered with concern. He'd made some stupid remark about clowns because he hadn't believed what he was seeing. He still didn't. But he knew better than to offer facetiousness now.

"Warm milk sounds appalling," she replied without inflection, leaning over to turn off the TV. She didn't own a remote either. JD suspected the ancient TV could receive twelve channels at most. How could anyone live in such a technological backwater?

"I thought that's what people recommended when someone couldn't sleep. Are those notes on the garden?" He nodded at the papers in her hand.

She started gathering the pages and snapping them into a three-ring binder, the kind he used to carry in high school. "I want to be prepared when the professor calls back. Did you get the car?"

She didn't ask where he'd been all these hours. She probably wouldn't have liked it if she knew, which was probably why she didn't ask. Miss Nina Toon had a very perceptive head on her shoulders. "It's in the shed. I didn't see any sign of the Mercedes. Maybe it was all a fantasy. I'll hit the sack now and get off to an early start in the morning. The sooner I get that program running, the sooner I can get out of here. That's probably best for everyone."

She nodded slowly, not taking her gaze from him. The look made him itchy, but she didn't say any of the things she was obviously thinking. "Did you get any supper?"

"I stopped and had a bite. I can take care of myself." Damn, now he sounded surly. If he could just get his hands around her for a few minutes, pull her into his arms for a little while, kiss her until both their heads spun, maybe he would lighten up. But he didn't see any chance of that happening before the world ended. He didn't want to be accused of buying her "services" again.

"All right. Good night then. I'm just picking up here before I turn in."

Realizing he'd been right, that she'd waited up for him, JD felt a moment's smug satisfaction. So, she wasn't entirely invulnerable. A person had to care just a little if they worried, didn't they?

Not wanting to carry that thought too far, JD strolled off to his room, whistling.

"I heard about that botanical garden your fancy boarder is helping you plan." Matt Horne bounced the eraser end of his pencil against his shiny desk. "Do you think that's a good idea before you get this cellular phone business settled?"

Nina skimmed her fountain pen across the bottom of the pages he'd given her to sign. She wouldn't take her anger out on Matt. He wasn't worth the effort. Capping the pen, she straightened and faced him coolly. "There is no garden, my boarder has nothing to do with anything, and none of it is any of your business. You should know by now how rumors grow. The kids just got to making something out of nothing. Wishful thinking, I guess. How soon will this go to court?"

"The docket's pretty full. It might be next session," he admitted with a small shrug.

Her temper soared. Lately, she'd lost it entirely too often. So far, she hadn't vented it on anyone but the imbeciles from the phone company, but if she'd had her shotgun here right now, she might rethink that position. "If you can't get it in any sooner than that," she replied bitingly, "I'll go over to Hopkinsville and find an attorney and file it in that district. Don't play politics with me, Matt Horne. I don't care what the damned phone company is paying you. File that paper now or I'm taking my business elsewhere. And it won't just be the incompetency hearing when I do."

His baby-blue eyes widened innocently. "Are you threatening me with something, Nina? You know I've always handled your aunt's affairs. Do you have a problem with the way I've carried them out?"

"Not until now. It shouldn't take two seconds for the judge to sign that sheet of paper. Are you going to get it on the docket or not?" Heaven help her, she sounded like JD. No wonder Matt looked at her as if she were losing her mind.

"I'll see what I can do, Nina. I didn't think you were in any hurry. Hattie's been in the home for a year now."

"I foolishly hoped she would improve, but now I know better. There's no sense hoping anymore, and the place needs repairs. I can't do it until I have her power of attorney. I need it this summer, not after school starts."

He stood, patted her hand soothingly, and murmured reassuring sympathies as he walked her out of the office. Nina wanted to throw a bucket of manure in his face. Did he really think her a flighty old spinster with no brains in her head? She hoped JD had the name of a good attorney by the time she got home. Gad, but she hated politicians.

The next stop on her list was the post office. Nina almost turned around and walked out with Joe Bob's greeting. "Heard you're building a theme park out at your place, Nina!"

She supposed, if it had been any other person but herself, she would have felt the same excitement and curiosity about the rumors. She just couldn't find the patience for them right now. Too many bombshells were exploding around her head, and it wasn't even the Fourth of July yet.

"No theme park, no garden, no nothing but a couple of kids with overexcited imaginations. Hattie wanted a botanical garden to draw tourists, but there's no money for it yet. I'll be sure and let everyone know if I win the lottery, however." She handed him a manila envelope containing her home-study test answers. "If any strangers ask for directions to my place, I'd appreciate it if you'd not give them any. I've had some persistent telephone salesmen after me, and I'm afraid they'll show up out here one of these days."

"Sure, Nina. I usually don't give out that information unless I know there's an honest reason. A woman living alone needs protection. You ought to get yourself a big dog."

Nina grinned in spite of herself. "I've got one. His name is Smith."

Job Bob looked a little startled, but since she'd left money for her postage on the counter and walked away, he couldn't comment.

Humming to herself, she delivered a vase of roses to one of Hattie's old friends, sat and chatted awhile, then moved on to the pharmacy to pick up a few items she hadn't the nerve to purchase with JD hanging around. As she stepped from the frigid air-conditioning of the poorly lighted pharmacy into the glaring heat of the noonday sun, she stopped and let her eyes adjust.

The sun's glare reflected off the sidewalk, shimmering the air with heat waves. Nina took a deep breath and nearly choked on the stench of hot asphalt. Country in the summer, she mused wryly, turning toward the Toyota.

The figure hovering under the bank awning nearly stopped her in her tracks.

It couldn't be. The heat was playing tricks with her mind. The loose flowered dress and white straw hat belonged in another era. She had spent too long in front of the television last night. She hadn't had enough sleep.

Imagination was a terrible thing. Her mother couldn't have returned from the dead to haunt her. She'd been gone twenty years. As far as Nina was concerned, she could stay gone another two hundred. She wouldn't recognize her mother if she saw her in any case.

Jerking her gaze back to the Toyota, Nina hurriedly opened the door and climbed in. A nice cold shower would straighten her head out quickly enough. She would never watch any more old TV movies, she vowed. Never again.

Turning the key in the ignition, she pulled away without looking back.

She turned down the highway toward Hattie's Lane and looked in the rearview mirror.

The Mercedes followed behind her.

FIFTEEN

"Oh, shit. Oh, double shit." Nina hit the accelerator and continued on the highway toward the interstate instead of taking the turnoff toward Hattie's Lane. She couldn't believe she was doing this. She should stop the car right here and wait for the Mercedes to slow down, then get out and demand to know what he thought he was doing.

But caution wouldn't allow it. She could only handle so much rebellion in a morning. If she had any more shocks to her system, she might go into overload and explode, but right now, caution prevailed.

She didn't watch enough TV to know how one went about shaking a tail, as she thought they called it in detective stories. Quaint term. Four cylinders certainly couldn't outrun eight. She'd just have to count on her knowledge of the territory and hope his lack thereof would be his downfall. Whoever that "he" might be.

She was quite certain it was a man, even though the other car stayed well behind her. The windows were too heavily tinted to see inside, but the shadow she'd seen through the windshield definitely looked masculine. Maybe she should just pull up to Sheriff Hoyt's and ask him to take a look.

And have him think she definitely had gone around the

bend? No sirree, Bob. She wasn't dealing with any more men who thought she'd dried out and gone to seed. Not on your life.

With a tiny feeling of glee, Nina hit the interstate. She couldn't roar into the traffic and blend in with the crowd, not in this car. For one thing, it didn't roar anywhere. It just kind of trundled into the biggest gap she could find. The Mercedes almost caught up while she looked for an opening. And for another thing, a brown hatchback Toyota with rusted fenders didn't blend anywhere. Toyota hadn't made hatchbacks in ten years or more. She probably had the last one on the road. For a brief moment, she wished she had one of those anonymous white Tauruses or something. Just for a moment. Then she remembered her plan, and she smiled again.

She didn't need to rent boats to shake a tail. She still had all her wits, despite any apparitions she thought she'd seen. Maybe the stress of admitting Hattie no longer could handle her affairs had ticked something off in her brain, bringing back images of her mother. Hell, maybe she was losing it. Senility was probably inherited. It didn't matter. She knew precisely what she was doing now.

Nina checked the rearview mirror. The Mercedes was just far enough behind her to be barely visible. Smiling at the exit sign ahead, Nina hit the accelerator, swerved down the ramp, and immediately turned into the truck stop on the right. Sandwiching the Camry between two semis, she watched as the Mercedes glided down the ramp, hesitated, and turned right, the driver apparently figuring he could see her if he traveled down the road a little farther.

As soon as he disappeared into the dip down the road, Nina hit the gas, pulled out of the truck stop, and took the entrance ramp toward home. Let the damned man find her now. She hoped he enjoyed the scenic view of the gravel pits.

The triumph carried her as far as Hattie's Lane. By the time Nina turned up the gravel road, the elation had faded considerably. She didn't like the idea of someone following her all over the countryside. She didn't like the notion that she could lose her head so far as to imagine her mother had mysteriously appeared on the sidewalks of Madrid. She hadn't even seen her mother in twenty years, for pity's sake. She wouldn't know her from Adam. And she certainly wouldn't look as slim and beautiful as her pictures from twenty years ago, even if she were alive, which she probably wasn't.

If Nina wanted irrationality, she could imagine she had a sister and God had sent her in answer to her plea for help on the decision of Aunt Hattie. Now that was at least somewhat rational. For all she knew, she could have half a dozen sisters and brothers. Wouldn't that be a circus and a half? She didn't even want to think about it. JD Smith and his son were more trouble than she could handle right now.

She would take a nice cold shower and not leave the house for the rest of the summer. Except to visit Hattie. Maybe the Mercedes driver would like visiting Hattie. She could invite him in, and they could share lukewarm coffee and listen to her aunt talk about people neither of them knew.

Not even bothering to park the car in the damned shed, Nina pulled it up beside the house, slammed the door, and stalked in through the kitchen. She'd led a sedate life, a boring one if anyone wanted to know, and she liked it that way. She didn't like surprises. She didn't like her routine disturbed. And her routine was definitely disturbed these days.

And the minute she saw JD standing at the kitchen sink, she knew she lied. She couldn't think of anything more disturbing than having a tall, long-haired stranger standing at her kitchen sink, regarding her with quizzical dark eyes as if he had every right to know all her secrets. She liked the disturbance all too well. Something hot flooded through Nina's veins when he looked at her. He didn't just look through her, discarding her as a dried-up old teacher. He looked *at* her, sizing up her mood, giving her one of those admiring glances that curled her toes, watching her patiently while she flung her purse on the counter and kicked off her shoes. She really, *really* liked knowing he wanted to hear anything she had to say. At the same time, she could almost feel the heat of his look as it traveled up her legs. Damn, but that was unsettling.

"What do you want?" she asked with irritation, refusing to let him know how he disturbed her. Then he really would think he could take advantage of a horny old maid.

"Your mother called," he said casually, sipping from the glass of water in his hand.

Just that small announcement knocked her into an out-of-control tailspin.

Panic exploded, panic and nausea. It was one thing *seeing* ghosts—*hearing* from them blew out her already frayed wiring. Motorcycle bums who made her heart race, fancy cars, cloak-and-dagger intrigue, Aunt Hattie and the phone company, all combined to short-circuit what remained of her nervous system. She simply couldn't deal with one more thing.

Certain she would crash and burn, tears stinging her eyes, hands shaking, Nina aimed blindly for the door.

"I don't have a mother!" she yelled, stalking out of the kitchen before she collapsed in front of him.

"Well, pardon me then," JD shouted back. "I thought all women *liked* talking to their mothers!"

Showed what a fat lot he knew about women. Running up the stairs, Nina escaped into her room, slamming the door so hard the hinges rattled.

The slamming door shook the whole house. JD stared over his head, amazed that the ceiling didn't fall in. From the cracks in it, he was surprised the house remained intact at all.

What in hell had he said? Was he supposed to ignore the ringing phone? He didn't get angry easily, but his blood heated now. He hadn't done anything to deserve that reception. Except admire her legs a little too obviously. Maybe that was what had set her off. She had damned fine legs. Most women would want legs like that appreciated. But not the irritating Miss Nina Toon. Oh, no, she was too far above that kind of thing. JD wondered if she'd ever lowered herself to sleep in the same bed with a man. Heaven forbid.

He slammed his glass down on the counter, fully intending to return to his computer. Machines appreciated him, even if women didn't. He didn't know why he'd thought he might develop some kind of tenuous relationship with this eccentric female. He would never understand women. Hell, he didn't understand men half the time. His Uncle Harry made a big "for instance." He'd stick with something logical, like computers.

But despite all his best intentions, JD followed his feet up the stairs. Maybe he didn't know a lot about women, but he knew enough about this one to realize she didn't explode that readily. If she'd wanted to explode, she would have done it yesterday when he'd driven her halfway to forever and scared the daylights out of her. Something had gone wrong. Nina had a tendency to wander in an absentminded daze that gave one cause to wonder about her sanity, but her look when she came in hadn't been absentminded. Dazed, maybe, but not the gentle kind of daze he'd come to know. Something definitely had happened out there. The thought of the Mercedes spurred him on.

If that sucker had returned and tried to harm her, he'd find the bastard and personally strangle him with his bare hands. People didn't mess with what was his. *And Nina was his.*

Now that was definitely irrational. Slamming his fist against the closed bedroom door, JD ignored the mutterings of his logical mind, focusing on the fury of his illogical one.

At Nina's weepy "Go away," he tried the knob. As he'd suspected, the effort of locating the key for the old-fashioned lock had eluded her. The door swung open.

A pillow hit him square in the face. JD batted it aside and towered over the prostrate form on the bed. "What happened out there?" he demanded.

Or maybe he yelled. She reached for another pillow quickly enough. Damned good thing it was a pillow or he'd be in a great deal of pain right now, he thought as she swung it smack against his crotch. She certainly knew the proper target.

Jerking the pillow from Nina's hands, JD flung it to the floor, then removed himself from the field of battle by taking an upholstered armchair against the wall. With interest, he gazed around her bedroom, anything to keep from looking at the slight feminine form huddled around a pile of pillows. He had entirely too much interest in the juxtaposition of his hostess and a bed.

He didn't know much about antiques, but he figured the room was full of them. They looked a thousand years old and brooded over the high-ceilinged space like dark giants frozen in time. The headboard of the bed alone rose at least eight feet and sprawled unrelentingly across half the wall, looking more like an out-of-place sleigh than any bed he'd ever seen. An old-fashioned armoire filled most of another wall. If it hadn't been for the corner windows, the room would resemble a black hole. He couldn't imagine a child growing up in here. He couldn't imagine the sprite who loved flowers surviving in this oppressive darkness. His gaze slid to Nina.

She'd turned her back on him as if he weren't there. Her silence didn't fool him, however. His insides clenched at the sight of her slender shoulders shaking with the force of her quiet sobs. He'd generally found it easiest to walk out on weeping women. That's what he should do. For some damned reason, he just couldn't bring himself to leave this one. The room reeked of her misery.

"What happened, Nina?" he asked firmly. Maybe if he handled her as he did Jackie, he could get some answers.

"Go away," she sobbed into her pillow. "Get out!"

JD's temper rose again. It didn't make sense, but nothing he felt around this capricious female made sense. "Not until you tell me what's wrong!" he shouted back.

"Nothing's wrong! Everything's wrong. Just go away. I'm tired."

"Did that lawyer give you a hard time?" he asked suspiciously. He could straighten out lawyers well enough.

"Matt Horne thinks I'm an addlepated female. But I'm not. So get out of here." She didn't turn around, but she sat up with her back turned toward him, clutching a pillow to her middle as if to keep from throwing it. "I'm perfectly fine. Women are entitled to bouts of PMS," she informed him haughtily, her tone defying him to back out on that one.

JD didn't buy it. "Bullshit. If you are, so am I. Once a month I lose my cool and blow up. I'm about to do that right now. What in hell did that lawyer say?"

"Matt Horne is a jerk. He didn't say anything. He has nothing to do with anything. Go ahead and blow up; just don't do it in here. Go shoot a computer or something."

He should. He really should. He had no business in here. He had no idea how he'd got here or why. But looking at the slim line of her back on that god-awful bed had him bleeding in places he didn't know he could bleed. She wore another of those dainty slip kind of dresses that hung all over her, with a tight ribbed shirt underneath. He couldn't figure out if she looked like some avant-garde form of his grandmother or a twelve-year-old. In either case, it made him one sick pervert because he couldn't tear his gaze away.

"If that wasn't your mother on the phone, then who was it?" Deciding on another tack, JD waited impatiently for some sign that he'd broken through her barriers.

"A ghost. How in hell do I know? Maybe your imaginary villains have found imaginary playmates. I don't have a mother."

"Right. Your aunt found you under a cabbage leaf. A veritable gardening genius. Have you had this miracle written up in *Scientific American* yet?"

She twisted quickly, flinging the pillow hard and accurately, slamming him in the face again. JD flung it to the floor. Had she been anyone else, he'd have lifted her off that bed and either pounded her against the wall or against himself. The latter seemed more likely, so he stayed where he was.

"My mother died in a fiery car crash off the lake bridge," she said angrily. "Want to know all the gory details?"

JD contemplated that bit of information with interest. If her mother really was dead, then the phone call had been from a ghost. He couldn't imagine anyone stupid enough to pretend they were her mother if the woman had died so spectacularly. Everyone in half the state would know about it.

"That was quite a feat of engineering," he replied laconically after thinking about it. "Did she smash the car through the concrete or fit it between the girders? And was the lake on fire at the time? I didn't think there was enough oil in there to produce quite that effect."

"Get out!" she screamed. "Just get out, will you?"

"What do I tell the ghost when she calls back?" He shouldn't egg her on like that. He had seen the tears streaking her cheeks when she'd thrown the pillow at him. She was in pain, and he didn't know how to handle it. He despised feeling helpless.

"Tell her I don't live here anymore. Tell her I died and went to hell. Tell her anything. What in hell does it matter? She's dead anyway."

"How dead is she?" JD asked with interest, finding this conversation so perverse he could almost get into it.

"Over twenty years' worth of dead. I haven't seen her since Christmas, 1977. Not a birthday card, not a call since then. Maybe she slit her wrists and Hattie didn't tell me about it. She's gone. It's just some jokester having a little fun."

Twenty years. That would have made her about nine years old as far as he could determine. He'd lost his mother about then, too, but she was definitely dead. He'd found her out cold on the bedroom floor. Drugs and alcohol, the doctor had said. Fatal combination. JD would never forget the blank, wide-eyed expression on her frozen face when he'd come home from school that day. It made him want to vomit even now.

"My mother killed herself when I was ten," he mentioned conversationally. "Be glad yours had the decency to just disappear."

She stared at him in horror, and JD remembered why he hadn't offered that particular tidbit to a female before. Revealing any kind of vulnerability invested them with a power he didn't like. He liked being invincible. But she didn't seem to take it as an admission deserving pity. Maybe he'd said it because he thought she could relate a little bit.

"How?" she demanded. "Did you find her?"

"Drugs and alcohol, and yes, I did. So don't give me any more of your sorry little tales about being abandoned. I can top anything you can tell. At least you had a family to take you in."

"And you didn't?"

She looked at him in disbelief, more interested in his disclosure than her own. Well, to hell with that little turnaround. This was her day for disclosure, not his. "That's not the topic under discussion. You had Aunt Hattie. What about your father?"

She shrugged, crossing her legs beneath her as she faced him. At least she wasn't crying anymore. JD gave silent thanks for that.

"I don't know who he is."

JD squinted at her suspiciously. "Is this another of those fiery-car-crash tales?"

She shook her head, and the spiky tendrils of ash-blond hair danced. "No. Not unless Hattie made it up. She said my mother didn't know who my father was. My mother married some guy who left us when I was eight. Hattie said they were both too young when they married. Stupid excuse if you ask me."

"It happens. I only have to look at Jackie to know how. Didn't you ever fool around when you were a kid?"

She looked properly appalled. "With that kind of example to

follow? Are you kidding? I'm not that dumb. I followed my aunt's example and got a college education instead."

Wow, that opened a whole new can of worms. JD wouldn't touch it with a ten-foot pole. "How come it was your aunt who took you in and not your grandmother or somebody?" That seemed a neutral path to take.

Nina rubbed the back of her hand across her face, scrubbing away the tear tracks. "Family history. My grandfather died in World War II, so my grandmother moved back here when my mother was little. This was my great-grandfather's house, so my grandmother shared it with her sister, my aunt Hattie. But they got along like cats and dogs. Hattie taught school, and my grandmother thought she should farm. My grandmother was a housewife, cleaning and cooking and all that, but when Hattie refused to farm the acres, my grandmother decided to do it herself. She turned the tractor over on herself on that hill out there." She nodded toward the window overlooking the fields.

JD shook his head in disbelief. "Are there no men in this picture at all?"

Nina gave a weak smile. "Just enough to father women. This was my grandmother's room. Jackie's sleeping in my mother's. I don't know much about my great-grandparents, except they had two daughters and raised them here. What about you?"

JD didn't want to get into all that right now. It made a piss-poor story anyway. He shrugged. "Family of men. My father raised me. When he died, Uncle Harry stepped in. Now there's Jackie. Don't think any of us have learned from our experiences. Now will you tell me what happened in town today?"

She grimaced. "I saw my mother, and the damned Mercedes followed me." Her voice wavered, and she hurriedly scooted to the edge of the bed and stood up.

JD jumped up at the same time. She seemed so small and frail, he feared she would crumble into pieces right before his eyes. He couldn't bear seeing her cry again. He couldn't deal with tears. And he couldn't distinguish between his terror of her tears and the terror of her announcement about the Mercedes.

So he did the only thing that came naturally to him. He caught her before she could escape, pulled her into his arms, and kissed her.

SIXTEEN

Lord God in heaven above, JD blasphemed silently as Nina sank into him as naturally as a hot breeze on a summer day. He wrapped his arms hard around her and pulled her up against him so he could delve deeper into her kiss. She weighed no more than that ephemeral breeze. He feared she would disappear just as easily. He knew better than to catch the wind.

He tasted the salt of her tears on her lips, but that didn't stop him. Her lips parted so willingly beneath his that he couldn't have stopped now even had he wanted. And he most certainly didn't want any such insane thing. He wanted inside her. He wanted to climb in and crawl around and make her so entirely his that she would never escape again. Not considering where that thought led, JD taunted her tongue with his and nearly groaned as the blood surged in his groin at Nina's tentative response.

Her slender arms slipped around his back, and he exploded at the stroke of her soft palms through the T-shirt. Yanking her from her feet, he demanded more of her mouth, ravishing it as thoroughly as he needed to take the rest of her. She moaned against his lips, quivering slightly but moving against him in all the right places. Her hands clung now instead of stroking, and he could feel the heated desperation of her kiss.

Satisfied that the lust wasn't all on his part, JD allowed himself the pleasure of sliding his hand beneath the loose bodice of her dress, caressing the pert breasts she hid there. She wasn't so small as he had imagined. She filled his palm like a plump California peach, a peach that wouldn't bruise when he squeezed it. The moan she emitted at this caress heated his blood beyond boiling. Touching wasn't enough. He needed more. He needed so much more it scared the hell out of him.

"Nina," he growled against her mouth, instinct demanding that he ravish her now while the time was ripe, conscience nagging that she wasn't the kind of woman who would treat this lightly. JD cupped her breast through the tight ribbed shirt and stroked the pointed nipple. Her arousal heightened his. "Nina, I want you now. Tell me yes."

She moaned helplessly in reply, arching her breast into his hand and letting him fill her mouth with his tongue again. He couldn't hold out much longer. With other women, he could pet and tease half the night away if they wanted. Not with this one. He needed her now, sprawled across the bed and wrapped around him, raising herself wantonly to his plunge. He couldn't remember ever being aroused to the point of savagery. He didn't know what it was about this woman that turned his guts inside out, and he wasn't about to contemplate it now.

When she made no protest, JD cupped her buttocks and carried her to the high bed, settling her on the edge while he tormented her more with his tongue. Her legs parted instinctively, allowing him closer. Giving up any claim to conscience, he leaned over her, pushing her down into the soft mattress, propping his hands on either side of her head. The elation of conquering his prey spiraled through him as she not only accepted this position, but wrapped her hands in his hair.

He ignored the clamor of the downstairs door knocker. Whoever it was could come back later. He didn't give a damn about Nina's tears or her aunt Hattie or her missing mother. Desire alone drove him. He wanted all this flowery cotton out of the way so he could sink his fingers into naked flesh. He could almost feel the satiny softness now. She wore no restricting undergarments beneath her flimsy bodice. JD caught her long skirt in his fist and yanked it upward.

The knocker gave a more imperative pounding. Cursing mentally, JD slid his hand along a silken thigh and was rewarded with the urgent cry of "JD!" as Nina pulled her mouth from his and brushed her hips upward. He was almost there. The heat of her skin burned his hand. Just a few minutes more. His fingers slipped beneath the elastic of her panties.

"JD! No, stop! No!"

Those weren't the words he wanted to hear. All thought processes blurred with the pounding need of hormones; JD didn't heed the warning but dipped his fingers into the moist heat of her. Nina arched against him with a cry, but her fingers dug into his arms as she uttered another feeble protest.

The knocker continued pounding.

And then the back door slammed, and Jackie's voice carried up the stairwell. "Someone's at the front door! Anyone home? Miss Toon, you there? Want me to answer it?"

Nina jerked upright and out of JD's grasp.

"Shit. Damn." Insides roiling, JD pulled back. The pain of unquenched desire shot through him, and he closed his eyes against the temptation of the sexily rumpled wood sprite on the bed. He couldn't look at those wounded green eyes as she scrambled away from him. Damn Jackie. Damn this town full of Andy Griffith look-alikes. Damn the whole rest of the world. Why couldn't he enjoy just this one simple pleasure before the whole universe toppled down on him?

He collapsed against the bed as Nina brushed past him. Even with his eyes closed, he could see her nervously pressing at her dress, rumpling her hair even more as she attempted to right the damage he'd done to her composure. It couldn't be done. She couldn't wish away her kiss-swollen lips or the dazed glaze of her eyes. That knowledge offered JD some satisfaction as he opened his eyes and admired the splendid sight of the intrepid Miss Toon mussed from his lovemaking.

"We could lock the door," he suggested, knowing full well her response to that yet wanting to see the sudden flush of her cheeks at the idea. Idly, he wondered if she understood just how close he'd come to losing it completely. She didn't seem particularly triumphant at her conquest. Mostly, she looked very flustered.

"I'll answer the door," she said nervously, still pawing at her hair as she opened the bedroom door.

Since he could hear Jackie talking to the visitor, JD thought that a flimsy excuse for leaving, but he understood her need for escape. He was pretty rattled himself. He wasn't precisely certain what had happened here. He just knew he wasn't ready for it to end. His whole body ached when she slipped away. His head pounded once she was out of reach and his mind functioned again. She'd said the Mercedes had followed her. JD shut his eyes and groaned.

Utterly terrified by what she had almost done, Nina slowly walked down the dark hallway, readjusting to the real world of gloomy shadows. For a few moments, the world had shone with light and glory and an all-encompassing happiness that still left traces in her soul. She hadn't thought anyone could make her feel like that. She'd never felt like that in her life. She could still taste JD's lips against her own, and his hand had seared a permanent brand against body parts that embarrassed her just thinking about. For a few minutes, joy had ruptured the husk of her narrow life.

But then, she'd once believed in Santa Claus, too.

Realizing Jackie stood in the doorway, keeping the visitor on the front porch, Nina hurried to correct that inhospitable situation. The interruption might have irritated her, but she supposed it had been timely. The thought of how far she might have gone if the real world hadn't intruded . . . Her visitor deserved some measure of appreciation in return.

Not until Jackie stepped aside and she had a full view of the person standing on the porch did Nina remember why she had tried so desperately to drown in JD's kisses—her mother.

The woman glanced up as Nina faltered on the last few steps. The gauzy broad-brimmed hat sheltered her face in shadows, but Nina could see her own eyes in this woman's, see the narrow bones of her face, the delicate turn of her jaw. Aunt Hattie had often remarked on her resemblance, and there were all the old pictures in the photo album. Even twenty years couldn't erase the likeness. It would have been simpler if she'd gained fifty pounds and waddled like a duck, but she looked the same, only a little older, with a little more flesh sagging about her chin and harsher lines around her eyes.

"Nina," the woman said as she approached, her inflection revealing none of her thoughts. "Am I intruding?"

Nina flushed, certain that everything she had done these last few minutes was spelled out across her face. Even Jackie gave her a quizzical look. Unnerved, she couldn't find a suitable response. Curtly, she said the first thing that came to mind. "What are you doing here?"

The woman looked slightly taken aback. Nina couldn't think of her as "mother." Aunt Hattie had been the only mother she knew. The arrangement hadn't always been satisfactory. Hattie had often been annoyed by a young child's energetic rambunctiousness. Nina had wished for a younger woman to understand her teenage angst. But they'd worked around the bumps. They loved each other, each in her own way. This woman had no such claim.

"I'm sorry. I . . ." The woman twisted the handle of her purse, gazing from Jackie back to Nina. She needed only short white gloves to complete the picture of fifties matron. She had so obviously dressed for the occasion that Nina almost felt sorry for her. And then the woman glanced over Nina's shoulder at the stairs behind her, and Nina's heart instantly hardened.

She turned and watched the man striding down the stairway,

only a slight catch to his walk betraying his injured foot. JD had tucked his shirt back in his pants and brushed his hair out of his eyes, but nothing could disguise the blatantly masculine and proprietary way he looked at her. Though the heat of his gaze blazed up and down her spine, she was almost grateful for his chauvinistic presence at the moment. She didn't want to handle this situation on her own. When her insides lurched at the pressure of his hand on her shoulder, Nina hastily rethought that assessment.

"Unless she's selling cosmetics, perhaps you should invite your visitor in?" he suggested gently, steering Nina away from the doorway where she had supplanted Jackie in blocking the entrance.

The boy watched with curiosity, his gaze darting back and forth between them. Nina would have liked it if the earth had just opened up and swallowed her whole, but without such a miracle, she had no other choice. Not even summoning a smile of welcome, she nodded toward the living room. "Come in, please. Would you like some iced tea?"

Without waiting for a reply, Nina hurried down the hall toward the kitchen, leaving JD to see her guest seated. He didn't remain there long. Apparently leaving Jackie to entertain the visitor, he appeared in the kitchen just as Nina reached in the freezer for ice.

"I'll get that. You'd better go in there and see what she wants. In my experience, people don't return from your past without a reason."

That utterly sensible, immensely pragmatic statement instantly purged all Nina's nervousness. Glancing up at JD's rock-solid form and impassive expression, she nodded agreement with some amount of wonder. He had taken an emotionally devastating situation and turned it into a practical problem akin to mathematics. She would be eternally grateful for his logically grounded mind.

"You're right. I'm sorry. I'm being overly dramatic. I'll see what she wants."

Nina started to leave the kitchen, but JD stopped her by brushing her cheek gently. The affection of the gesture astounded her, making her go soft and warm inside. She met his eyes with a dazed wonder.

"You're so beautiful, she must seriously regret leaving you behind. Feel sorry for her for missing all those years she could have enjoyed with someone as special as you."

The smooth-tongued con man spoke again, but Nina needed to hear those words, to feel them deep down inside her. She had little or no confidence on her own. JD gave her what she needed. She didn't know that she should feel grateful that a con artist like him wanted her or thought her special, but she would take what little reassurance she could get. With a small smile of thanks, she escaped his hold and went to meet the mother she had never known.

"Yeah, I really like computers. My mom won't let me have a modem, but JD promised to let me surf the Internet when we get home. He says there's no net access here and we can't run up Miss Toon's phone bills right now."

Jackie's voice carried down the hall, and Nina smiled at his enthusiasm. She hoped JD and the boy's mother worked out their differences somehow so Jackie could have the father he so obviously needed. Whatever JD might be, he would make a good father. She didn't know how she knew that. Motorcycle bums and con artists weren't her idea of good fathers. She just knew it somehow.

Her mother's gaze instantly traveled to Nina as she entered the room. Nina gave Jackie's long hair a quick brush and smiled at the boy's flush. "JD's bringing out the tea. Why don't you go see if there's anything to eat? You must be starved after camping out all night."

Jackie popped out of the chair with alacrity. "I'm about to die. Laddie ate all the peanut butter."

Nina felt a tug of dismay at the affection she felt for the boy as he disappeared from the room. She should have children of her own by now. She'd always wanted children. She'd just never wanted them enough to marry. She turned her attention back to the woman sitting on the upholstered armchair.

"You could have written," she said as she lowered herself into Hattie's rocker. She needed the reassurance of that rocker right now.

The woman looked uncomfortable. "What would have been the point? I had no intention of coming back here, ever. And the situation I was in, I couldn't take you with me. It just seemed better that way."

"So what brings you back here now?" Nina asked conversationally as JD appeared carrying the glasses of tea. She noticed he didn't bring one for himself. She supposed he had the right to stay out of a family argument. He wasn't family, after all.

Her mother glanced nervously at JD as she accepted the tea. "Shouldn't you introduce us, dear?"

"JD Smith, my mother. I don't know what her name is these days." That was a low blow, and Nina saw her mother flinch. It didn't give her much satisfaction.

"Helen McIntyre, Mr. Smith. How do you do?"

The easy charm and the gracious smile made Nina's hands twitch. Her mother knew how to woo men, seduce them with her femininity, even with the difference in their ages. JD looked completely taken in by the act. It would have been nice if she'd had a mother to teach her those things instead of Hattie, who hated men and wouldn't dream of seducing them. But Nina refused to lose the battle on the grounds of ignorance. She rocked the chair until it squeaked and JD turned in her direction.

"Thank you for the tea. We won't keep you from your work," Nina said pleasantly as he handed her the icy glass.

JD shot her a look she couldn't interpret. She thought she discerned a predatory gleam in his eyes behind that hawklike nose, but she wouldn't acknowledge it. She'd lost her head briefly, but that didn't mean he owned her. He was just a paying guest. She wanted him out of here. Now.

"Invite your mother to dinner. I make a mean taco." He leaned over and kissed her cheek as if he had every right to the gesture.

Nina almost kicked him, but JD beat a strategic retreat. He had no right behaving that way, but her mother didn't know that. She rather liked the sense of power she felt as the woman across the room regarded her with curiosity and a certain amount of jealousy. She felt a little less incompetent, as if she could attract a man like JD without any of her mother's artifices. It almost made her feel wanted.

"Your Mr. Smith is a handsome man," her mother acknowledged, sipping her tea. "I thought I understood from gossip in town that he was just a boarder."

"I assume the gossip in town didn't bring you here." Nina dismissed the subject. She might not have her mother's Southern charm, but she had a head on her shoulders. She could turn a conversation around.

Helen nervously slid her fingers up and down the perspiring glass. "I almost didn't come. I probably shouldn't have. I just didn't know what else to do. This was my home once. It's the only home I know. I heard Hattie's still alive."

Ten years ago, Nina might have fallen for those short, breathless sentences, the sense of desperation attached to them. Perhaps she was still a trifle naive. She didn't go out into the world much. The people of Madrid in general treated each other with honesty. Nina didn't associate much with the kind of people who used others and threw them away, but she knew about them. She had firsthand experience with them. One sat across from her now.

"Hattie's almost ninety and senile. She was ill for years before she went into the nursing home. I cared for her myself. I visit her every week. I don't think she misses you." Even as she said it, Nina realized she lied. The mysterious "she" that Hattie mumbled about could only be Helen, the niece she had adored to the extent of providing her a house and home, then taking in her daughter when that hadn't been enough.

"I'm sorry again. I should have realized. Hattie was always the strong one. I just never thought anything could happen to her. She was good to me when no one else was."

Nina waited impatiently for the "but" that would fall at the end of one of these sentences. She found it difficult believing that her mother had returned after twenty years to tell her she loved her and had made a huge mistake leaving her behind. If this were a TV movie, Nina might believe her mother had returned with a millionaire husband prepared to right all wrongs. But real life didn't work that way.

"Well, I'm taking care of her now, so you don't have to worry," Nina finally replied in hopes of dragging out the real motive for her mother's return.

Helen lifted her chin and removed her hat. A flash of defiance crossed her features. "I'll do it now. After all, I'm Hattie's heir. I should be the one looking after her and seeing to her property. Is my old room still vacant?"

Numbly, Nina wondered where she'd put the shotgun.

SEVENTEEN

Leaving the heavy traffic of the interstate behind, the Geo flew past the golden rubble of wheat fields and dusty fence rows of blooming honeysuckle and wild roses. Nancy Walker glanced uncertainly at the gangly man in patched eyeglasses beside her. He had been a true gentleman from the moment they'd thrown their hastily packed travel bags into the trunk and left LA. But after two days of almost nonstop travel, she had begun to wonder about his obsessiveness. Perhaps it took a man with this kind of driving obsession to accomplish the goals James MacTavish had conquered. She didn't know too much about men like that. JD was the only other one she'd known, and he'd only been sixteen at the time, scarcely a comparison for this man in his thirties.

"I thought you didn't know where to find them?" she inquired cautiously. They'd scarcely left the interstate in the past two days. The fact that they now traveled country roads made her suspicious. This definitely wasn't Myrtle Beach.

"I don't. I just know where to start. I wish I'd brought the adapter for that lousy laptop. JD might have e-mailed me by now. Keep an eye out for computer stores. Maybe I can find a battery out here."

Nancy glanced at the emerald bean fields whipping past the

car window and grinned to herself. "You had a better chance in Vegas, unless rabbits have taken to using laptops."

"I didn't know the battery was dead in Vegas. I can't believe there's so much empty countryside out here. Doesn't anyone build cities anymore?" Hitting a straight stretch of two-lane, he accelerated to a dangerous speed.

"The interstates were designed to bypass cities," she replied pragmatically. "You have to get off them to find stores."

"Whose stupid idea was that, anyway?" Crossly, he slowed down as a farm truck loaded with round bales of hay pulled into the lane in front of him. "Damn idiot is asking to get run over," he muttered.

"Not by this little bitty car." Amused despite herself, Nancy turned off the static of the country music station and turned on the tape player. In the past two days, she had learned Jimmy MacTavish had a decidedly warped vision of the world. She suspected he had spent his entire life in LA, and the rest of the country was a foreign planet to him. His observations on the changing countryside around them had tickled her thoroughly, distracting her somewhat from her concern about Jackie. At least she didn't have to worry about her husband coming after her. He'd never find her out here, and the divorce lawyers could handle everything just as well without her. For the first time in her life, she felt free as a bird. She rather liked the feeling.

"What are we going to do when we find Jackie? I don't think he'll fit in the backseat," she asked idly, just to keep the conversation going.

"JD can buy you both plane tickets anywhere you want to go. And if you're smart, you won't argue with him. He's a rich man. You could do worse."

"I have done worse," she answered wryly. "But I couldn't live with a man like JD. I want someone who knows I exist."

The man beside her broke his desperate stare at the road

ahead and shot her a startled look. "How could any man in his right mind not know you exist?"

She thought he almost blushed before he returned to watching the road. Realizing that was a compliment, Nancy felt an odd warmth inside. She hadn't heard a man's compliments in a long time. "Some men think of me as more or less an appliance, like their televisions or toasters. People don't generally notice appliances until they need to use them."

Jimmy made a rude noise and leaned over the steering wheel in a vain attempt to see around the farm truck. "People notice appliances that rattle and clank constantly. I figured that was why most women talk so much."

"Are you saying I talk too much?" she asked, surprised. He hadn't said anything vaguely personal in two solid days. Now he'd made two entirely different observations.

"Not you." Satisfied he could see far enough ahead, he hit the accelerator and practically pumped the four-cylinder engine around the truck, barely avoiding collision with an RV traveling in the other direction. "Any other woman would have whined and complained and worried the whole way out here. You've been a good sport. I can't believe JD let you go."

"You know the wrong kind of women." Releasing her breath and her grip on the door handle, Nancy turned to observe her companion a little better. He wasn't a bad-looking man once she mentally removed those impossible wire-rimmed glasses. He had a kind face. She needed a kind face right about now. "And I let JD go, not the other way around. I let my father annul our marriage, and I never answered his letters or phone calls. I was much too young, and he was much too old."

Jimmy frowned slightly. "I thought the two of you were almost the same age."

Nancy shrugged. "In terms of years, maybe, not in any other way. JD was born old. Any other kid in his situation would have turned into a hoodlum. JD joined the marines. He could have released all his anger by shooting people. JD built computer programs that shoot people. We were together less than a week, and he had found two jobs and an apartment without cockroaches that we could afford on his pay. This is not normal teenage behavior."

Jimmy looked as if he were trying to digest this information. "And what did you do?"

"I stayed in the apartment and cried and polished my fingernails. Like I said, I was too young. I don't know what he saw in me."

The look he gave her was definitely complimentary. Nancy felt a slight thrill when it focused on her legs. She knew she had nice legs. That's why she wore shorts now.

"I can guess," was all he said before diverting his attention back to the road.

Just that dry statement sent a shiver of excitement down her spine. It had been a long time since any man had made her feel sexy. She trod dangerous waters here. Pulling back slightly, she directed the conversation to safer ground. "Where are we going?"

"Madrid, Kentucky. That's where JD wrecked my truck."

Nina sat on top of Hattie's Hill, gazing over the view the slight rise afforded. She had spent her entire life on this farm. She had built her dreams and her future around this land. Her friends were here. Her job was here. She didn't know anything beyond those waving fields of soybeans. Oh, she'd visited the city a time or two, gone to Opryland with the class on trips, poked around Paducah, and once, even traveled as far as St. Louis. She'd never had any inclination to live in those places. She liked it here, with familiar surroundings, where she felt safe.

And now the woman making herself comfortable back at the farmhouse, the same one who had torn her life in two at the tender age of nine, threatened to rip it in two a second time. If Helen McIntyre was Hattie's heir, she could let the cell phone company install whatever it liked. She could sell the land and the house. She could leave Nina homeless; all the work and toil she'd put into this place over the years would become nothing. Nina simply couldn't believe life could be so cruel.

She didn't cry. She was still in too much shock to cry. Had that damn Matt Horne known this all along? He must have. He was Hattie's attorney. No wonder he was so confident about the phone company. Maybe he'd even written Helen and told her what was happening. She couldn't believe that lousy turd of an attorney would have known where her mother was all this time and never once mentioned it to her. It didn't make sense. Everyone thought her mother dead. Why should Matt Horne know differently?

Because Hattie would have told him. That betrayal hurt more than any other. Hattie had known where to find her mother. Hattie had known she was alive. And Hattie had never said a word. It couldn't have hurt worse had her aunt stuck a knife in her gullet and twisted it.

Tears formed at that knowledge. Shattered into little splinters by the betrayal of those she thought closest to her, Nina couldn't pull together the strength to fight. She felt more battered than if they had taken a bat and broken all her bones. She didn't know if she could ever get up again.

Within sight and smell of the joyous abandon of her rose garden, Nina's dreams gradually crumbled into dust. Letting her gaze drift over the greenhouses, the vegetable and herb garden, the saplings she had nurtured through winter frosts and summer droughts, she sobbed brokenly. She couldn't believe she'd lost it all in one fell swoop. It didn't seem real right now. Those trees and bushes and flowers were her children, her life, her future. How could anyone rob her of them with just a few words? Murder her life before her eyes?

She couldn't let them. She wouldn't. Gradually, that knowledge sank in. She would fight.

Sobbing with righteous anger, Nina straightened her spine

and rubbed furiously at her tears. She'd worked and slaved here for twenty years. She'd paid the taxes with her meager teacher's salary. She'd installed the new wiring when Hattie got sick. She'd built the greenhouses with her own money. They were hers, and she wouldn't let anyone take them away.

She still had JD's thousand dollars in the bank. The check hadn't bounced. She would get the name of that fancy lawyer he'd talked about. She'd hire some city lawyer to come in here and walk all over Matt Horne and Helen McIntyre. She wouldn't be a victim this time. Damn them all to hell, she would fight tooth and nail for what was hers, and not with the rusty shotgun she'd taken to the cell phone people.

Leaping up and heading back down the hill, Nina supposed on the face of it, it would look bad fighting her own mother over land that had belonged to her mother's mother. It would look nasty in the newspaper. But she didn't care. Helen McIntyre had abrogated her responsibilities a long time ago. She should be made to pay for her carelessness now.

Only, it was Nina's own carelessness that had caused this. She'd known the taxes had come in Hattie's and her grandmother's name. Her grandmother hadn't left a will that she knew of. No one had ever questioned the legality of Hattie's running the farm. As long as the taxes were paid, no one cared. But now Nina was paying for that negligence.

She couldn't let Matt know what she was doing by asking for copies of wills and deeds. Someone from out of town would have to research them for her. There had to be some legal angle she could play. If they wanted to strip her of everything that mattered, she should be compensated for her expenses in some manner. She could play dirty, too. Hell, if nothing else, her mother owed Hattie for her support over all those childhood years. The debts outstanding mounted faster than she could think of them. Only the beneficiary remained in question.

Nina fought the sense of betrayal sneaking up on her. Maybe

Hattie had believed Helen would return one day, but Nina was absolutely positive her aunt never meant to surrender their dreams of the garden. Maybe Hattie thought Helen wanted the same things they did. It no longer mattered. This was a fight for survival, and she would win.

Nina supposed that sounded cold and calculating, but she hadn't chosen the circumstances. They had been thrust on her by Hattie's illness, by the cell phone people, by Helen's declaration of ownership. She simply couldn't leave her life and the land in the hands of the kind of woman who would abandon her own child. She cared too much to give up Hattie's dream.

Nina saw JD leaning against the pin oak, watching her storm down the hill and across the field. Fine. She'd pick his brain first. She didn't have time to worry about kisses that reduced her to pulsating jelly. She needed his brains and his knowledge, nothing more.

Not acknowledging the look in his eyes as she approached, Nina waited until she was close enough not to have to yell. "Have you got the name of that fancy lawyer yet?"

He calmly raised those devilish eyebrows. "Jimmy isn't answering his e-mail. I'm looking for another source. Your professor friend called. He wants to meet with us over dinner and show us his plans."

"To hell with his plans. I need a lawyer first. I'll call the bar association." Planning on stalking straight past him, Nina nearly stumbled as JD stepped in her way. She glared up at him and tried skirting around him again.

JD caught her arms and held her still. "I don't know what happened between you and your mother, but we're meeting with the professor. I don't start something and then quit."

Eyes widening at all the implications of that statement, Nina let his words chase through her. She thought she liked him better when he was wearing those horn-rimmed glasses and the loose work shirt. This JD with the unwavering dark eyes and tight T-shirt scared her a little. She couldn't break his grip if she tried. She didn't like him telling her what to do. She didn't like his moving into her life and stirring things around. She liked it even less when he was right.

"I might not have control over the land," she threw at him in self-defense.

He didn't flinch or back down in the least. "We'll worry about that when the time comes. Go get cleaned up and ready to go out. We're meeting him over at Grand Rivers. And splash your face with cold water before you let your mother see you. Always present a confident appearance in front of your adversaries."

She wavered a little. She hated it when he was right. At the same time, she felt the overwhelming desire to fling herself into his arms and weep uncontrollably against his broad chest. She wanted to dump the whole gigantic problem in his competent hands and let him deal with it. Which was an absurd notion from beginning to end.

Stiffening, she gave a curt nod. "Patti's?" she inquired, naming the best restaurant in Grand Rivers, and the entire region for that matter.

"That's what he recommended." Releasing her arms, JD asked, "Do I need a tie?"

That put her back on firmer footing. She should insist on both jacket and tie. She'd like to see him dressed up and uncomfortable for a change. But it wasn't JD's fault that her entire world had just turned over. She managed a weak grin and shook her head. "Just not a T-shirt, please."

He eyed her long skirt and loose bodice skeptically. "I don't suppose I could persuade you to wear a T-shirt instead of one of those things, could I? Now that I know what you're hiding under there, I'd like to see a little more of it."

Nina felt her cheeks flush crimson. She wanted to smack his face as hard as she could, but surprisingly, the temper wasn't there. Instead, an unexpected heat swept through her, and she squirmed slightly at the knowledge that she had given him every right to talk that way.

"Forget it," she said curtly. "That won't happen again. I've more important things on my mind."

She stalked off, leaving JD with an ache in his crotch and his gaze fastened on the tempting sway of her hips as she paraded back to the house. More important things on her mind, had she? Well, hell, so did he. That had never stopped him from seeking a physical release from his frustrations before. He thought the uptight little teacher might benefit from that same release. All he had to do was make her realize it.

Why not move the moon and the stars while he was at it?

Jackie watched as they came down the stairway. He didn't know how he felt about the way his father was looking at Miss Toon. He'd just found JD. He wasn't ready to share him. And yet, at the same time, he had this niggling understanding that came from thinking of JD more as a brother than a father. Man to man, he could see what JD was seeing.

He watched as the silky soft stuff of Miss Toon's skirt swayed and clung in all the right places. The dress was old-fashioned as far as Jackie was concerned, worse than anything his mother would have worn. It had a full skirt that stopped just short of her knees, a big wide belt, and huge, prissy lapels. But the whole thing was some kind of optical illusion, he decided, because he could practically see the curves of Miss Toon's breasts beneath the V of that neckline, and her legs looked shapely and tanned in those high-heeled sandals. No wonder JD looked like some slavering beast hanging over her shoulder.

He'd kinda hoped JD and his mom would get together again, but his mom never looked like Miss Toon. His mom looked like a mom, but Miss Toon looked like some funky movie star. She wasn't really pretty, but she was cool in a way he couldn't define. He liked her a lot, and so did JD from the looks of it. Jackie felt kind of crawly under his skin just feeling the electricity between them when JD took her arm and Miss Toon jerked it away. He didn't know what they were fighting about, but he didn't think it was the kind of fighting his mom and stepfather had done. They weren't angry and throwing things. They were bouncing off each other like pinballs, but each time they bounced a little less. He figured sooner or later they'd end up snuggled together at the bottom when the game ended.

Feeling pretty cocky with that observation, Jackie gave a wolf whistle that made his father scowl and Miss Toon smile. She tousled his hair, which Jackie hated but kind of liked, too. She smelled good, and he could see she actually wore lipstick for a change. That made him wonder if she really was holding JD off or just leading him on. Women, he thought with disgust. He'd never bother with the lot of them.

"Hold down the fort, tiger, and I'll bring you back one of those huge slices of meringue pie Patti's is known for."

"You could take me with you," Jackie pointed out. "It's just a business thing, isn't it? Not like a date or anything."

JD affectionately clipped him upside the head. "Don't give the lady ideas, son. We've got a moonlight drive across the lake ahead of us. I left the makings for tacos in the refrigerator. You won't starve before we get back."

"I don't have to eat with *her*, do I?" Jackie asked anxiously, rolling his eyes toward the ceiling. The woman who'd appropriated the empty corner bedroom upstairs reminded him of pictures of a barracuda he'd seen on the Discovery channel.

"I doubt she'll want to share your taco. Just be polite is all I ask." JD caught Miss Toon's arm and steered her toward the door. Jackie noted with interest that this time she didn't pull away.

"Yeah, right," he replied, suddenly eager to see them gone. They made him itchy and anxious at the same time. To hell with them. He could find better things to do than sit here all evening eating tacos and waiting for spider woman to come downstairs and gobble him up.

He ignored all his other rioting emotions as he watched them pull away in Miss Toon's battered Toyota. He wouldn't think about them. They'd left him free for the evening, and he would take full advantage of that freedom. They'd never come right out and said he couldn't go anywhere.

Raiding the refrigerator and putting together a cold taco, Jackie hurried out the kitchen door before spider woman could come downstairs. It wasn't dusk yet. He could see the path toward the cove well enough. Maybe he'd run into some of the other guys down there.

He liked it out here in the woods. Maybe if they stayed, JD would get him a rifle and teach him how to shoot. Jackie didn't think he particularly wanted to shoot deer, but he could aim at bottles and tin cans. He kind of liked walking down this path as the sun set, watching the rabbits dart out in front of him. He'd seen a raccoon washing a fish in the lake once. And he'd seen deer running across that big field Miss Toon called Hattie's Hill. This was a thousand times better than watching the guys at home beat up the video machines at the game room, especially since he had his own private computer for playing those same games without someone shoving him around.

All in all, he wasn't doing too badly out here. Let JD boff Miss Toon if he liked. Maybe they would stay longer if he liked her enough. Jackie wished his mom could be here, too, but he hadn't been gone long enough to miss her too much. She smothered him. A guy needed his freedom. He wasn't a baby anymore.

Taking a shortcut through the trees to the lake instead of the cove, Jackie slid down the embankment, keeping himself upright by grabbing saplings and branches as he passed. Maybe the fish were biting. JD had shown him how to make a pole out of a willow branch and some string. He'd left that last pole down here. The guys probably wouldn't be at the cove until twilight anyhow. He could kill some time fishing.

Reaching the tangled debris of dead leaves, plastic milk bottles, and old logs at the lake's edge, Jackie halted quietly and checked the water for air bubbles as JD had taught him. The sun was setting on the far side of the lake, so the shadows of the trees hadn't reached the water here yet. Light sparkled off the ripples, dancing over a fish leaping upward farther out, catching on some shiny metal near the shore.

Intrigued by that last glint, Jackie worked his way through the underbrush in the direction of the dark shape bobbing beneath the twigs and leaves JD had said made up an old beaver dam. Sunlight sparkled on the metal again, but this time, Jackie caught his breath. Excitement rippled through his veins. That looked like a silver belt buckle, the kind the country music singers wore on TV.

Not until he realized the belt buckle was attached to the bloated shape of a body did Jackie begin to yell, and he didn't stop yelling until he dashed into the safety of the marina.

EIGHTEEN

Restlessly, Nina tugged the brushed silk of her dress through her fingers. Refusing to look in JD's direction as he steered the car up the lane toward the house, she tried staring out the window and sorting her thoughts instead. They wouldn't sort. They bounced from one subject to another and always ended back at the man beside her.

Despite Albert Herrington's presence—or maybe because of it—JD had asserted a proprietary attitude toward her all evening. He'd caught her elbow going into the restaurant, teased her hand beneath the table, given her those damned intimate smiles over the menu until she thought she'd have to walk away or melt into butter. The butter part won out all the way.

The truth was, she'd never, but *never*, had a man look at her like that before. Back in school, she'd had boys tease her by pulling her hair. They'd occasionally carried her books or tried to cop a feel after a school dance. She'd had boys in college offer to take her out for coffee after class. But they'd all been boys. And she'd been busy with studies, with the garden, with Hattie, with so many adult things that their childish attempts had never stirred much more than a condescending smile on her part. She'd always been too damned adult for the males around her. And now that they were men, she still thought of them as boys. But not JD. Not by any shot.

JD made her feel all the dangerous things Aunt Hattie had warned her about. Nina knew better than to fall for meaningful looks and warm touches. She knew better than to believe the heat of his kiss. But somewhere along the way, her mind had parted company with the rest of her. Some part of her craved the touching, the smiles, the intimate looks, the feeling that they shared something special together. Now she really knew what it was to lose her mind. She'd totally misplaced it and couldn't find it anywhere.

She tried concentrating on the problem of her mother and hiring an attorney. JD had already disappointed her by not coming up with the name of a good lawyer as he'd promised. She knew in her mind that all men were a disappointment. If she kept a running list of disappointments, she might convince herself that JD was like all other men.

Of course, the problem with that was that he'd turned up Albert Herrington and fueled his enthusiasm for a plan that had no money and no backing and no future. On the basis of a few promises, she had a landscape designer and an entire pad full of sketches. The meeting tonight had been stimulating and exciting, and blissful rose gardens floated in her head. JD made her believe it could happen.

And now she faced the crash back to reality. As they pulled up the long graveled drive, Nina closed her eyes against the impossibility of it all. JD's curses and the sudden gunning of the accelerator jerked them open again.

"The sheriff 's car!" she exclaimed as he swung the Toyota in behind her mother's aging Cadillac. All the lights in the house were blazing, and Nina had her door open before JD turned off the ignition. "Something's happened to Jackie!"

Nina flew up the walk and into the house before JD could catch up with her. Feeling a boulder caught in his throat, he followed her with a more measured tread. He was never in a hurry for bad news, and in his life, law enforcement officials always meant bad news.

He wiped the perspiration from his forehead and felt an enormous burden lift from his shoulders when he saw Nina hugging his embarrassed son. The boy looked all in one piece. If this piercing pain in his middle at the sight of a sheriff's car was what fatherhood was about, JD didn't want any part of it. He gave the boy's pale face and haunted eyes a quick look, then swung toward the sheriff, prepared to defend his son for all he was worth.

"What's this about?" His angry, defensive tone reminded JD of his own father, and he bit his tongue before he made it worse by saying more. From the corner of his eye he noticed Nina's mother sitting calmly on the couch, flipping magazine pages. If she had anything to do with this . . .

"The boy found a body down in the lake. I've been sitting with him until you got home. We'll need you and Nina to see if you can identify the deceased, since he was found on this property."

Nina gasped. JD didn't know how he felt about it himself. He'd seen bodies before, some still pouring their life's blood into the street. He hadn't lived in the best neighborhoods growing up. He didn't want Nina experiencing it. It revolted him knowing Jackie had.

Ignoring the sheriff, JD turned and placed his arm around Jackie's shoulders. "You all right, kid?"

Jackie nodded and pulled away, taking a chair to avoid any more embarrassing displays of affection. "It was pretty horrible. He was all bloated up and everything. I thought it was a beached whale."

JD saw Nina's wry grimace at the description and knew he couldn't put her through that. Dropping his arm around her shoulders, JD met the sheriff's gaze again.

"I'll go with you if you insist. I don't think Nina should. I can't imagine either of us will know the man. I don't know anyone out here, and Nina knows the same people you know."

Hoyt shrugged uncomfortably inside his uniform shirt. JD guessed he didn't like the way Nina stayed where she was, not objecting to his arm around her shoulders. Her acceptance surprised him a little, too, but she felt right there. He traced his fingers up and down her arm a little as he waited for the sheriff's reply.

"You and Nina would know if any strangers came out here. He didn't look dressed for boating or fishing. I've got people working on that end, but we usually know about any boating accidents within minutes. There haven't been any reported. If he slipped and fell in the water, he must have been on this property when he went in. One of you might have seen him."

Nina spoke before JD could reply. "There haven't been any strangers out here, Hoyt, except the cell phone people. They wear those uniforms with their names on them so people won't shoot them when they show up and start wandering around. And like he said, everyone's a stranger to JD. If anything, Jackie would know more about anyone wandering around the lake. He's up and down that path and in those woods all the time. If he didn't recognize the man, then none of us will."

"He says he's never seen the body before. Of course, it's been in the water a few days. That distorts things somewhat." Hoyt looked hesitant, as if unwilling to force the issue.

"I'm the only stranger around here these days," the woman on the couch announced. She had found an emery board and was shaping her nails while following the scene before her as if it were a television program. "Shall I go down and see if I can identify the body? Maybe it's someone from my past returned to haunt me."

She made it sound as if it were a joke, but a cloud of suspicion instantly rose in the room. A body appearing on the same day as Helen McIntyre returned from the dead seemed an odd coincidence.

"If you'd all come down in the morning, I'd appreciate it," Hoyt finally said, twisting his hat in his hands. "We have to send him in for an autopsy, so you'd better come early. I'm sorry for the inconvenience, but I've got to cover all bases."

"No, I don't think so, Sheriff." JD removed his arm from Nina's shoulders and started toward the door. "I've seen dead bodies before, and I'll not put these women through that unnecessarily. There's been no one on the property since I've been here. If the man is from around here, someone else can identify him. If he's not, then we can't identify him either. I appreciate your looking after Jackie, but the nightmare ends there."

Over the years, JD had learned to speak with authority. He'd commanded troops of marines and corps of employees. One country sheriff wouldn't tell him what to do. And if the body had some relation to DiFrancesco and his gang, he didn't want to know about it.

Hoyt moved awkwardly toward the door. "It might not be a matter of choice. When the results come back, we might have to subpoena everyone. Maybe it won't come to that. Maybe someone will file a missing-person report before long."

"That's most likely." JD nodded his agreement, strove for a pleasant countenance, and firmly closed the door once the sheriff stepped outside.

He turned and found all eyes on him. He sought Nina's first, wanting reassurance that he'd done the right thing. When she nodded with gratitude, he looked at his son. Jackie was still pale, but he no longer looked frightened. JD thought this might be part of being a father, also, protecting his offspring from the world's unpleasantness until he was ready to deal with it. He gave the boy an awkward pat on the shoulder.

"Go on up to bed. I think you've had enough excitement for the night."

"It was gruesome," Jackie agreed obliquely. "Do you think he fell out of a boat?"

"I don't think about it at all. You shouldn't either. That's the sheriff's job. You just get a good night's sleep. You need to get back at that clearing project early, before it gets too hot."

JD prayed that was enough to distract him. He didn't know how else to keep the boy from having nightmares. He knew how he'd keep Nina from having them, but he didn't think she was quite ready for his methods yet.

"Well, now that the excitement's over, I think I'll retire, also," Helen said brightly from the couch. "Had I known what fascinating lives you led out here, I might have returned sooner. Good night, Nina. And you, too, Mr. Smith. You look as if you've had some experience handling cops."

JD ignored the dig as the woman headed for the stairs. He'd met plenty of poisonous females in his time. He was immune to their venom. What he wasn't immune to was the innocence of someone like Nina. She looked at him with those wide eyes so open and defenseless that all his walls crumbled and fell. Locked and rusted gates creaked open, letting her in where no other had gone before.

He watched her now, seeing the green of her eyes haze and cloud over as she stared up at him. He stroked her cheek gently, wishing the day could have ended better. Nothing in his life had ever been easy. Why should it start now?

"Maybe we should go in the morning," she whispered uneasily. "It doesn't seem right, that poor man. . . ."

JD placed a finger over her lips. "That's your overdeveloped sense of duty talking. Believe me, you don't want to see what a drowned corpse looks like. It might be difficult to identify even if you did know him."

"Do you think my mother? . . . I mean, it is odd that she arrived and . . ."

JD shook his head. "That's her problem, and the sheriff's. You have nothing to do with it. Concentrate on your own problems. I'll get the name of that attorney in the morning, one way or another."

She nodded, grateful again. He didn't want her grateful. He wanted her all hot and bothered as she had been this afternoon. He had absolutely no experience at seducing women who didn't want to be seduced. He'd always let the women make the first move rather than bother himself with what they wanted and didn't want. This woman wasn't like that. He knew she'd never make a move on her own. It was up to him, and JD felt totally inadequate for the task.

"Stay with me tonight," he whispered, stroking her cheek, not daring more for fear of producing that wounded look he'd seen once too often in her eyes.

She just looked at him, not answering, as if she didn't know what he was talking about. A man would think she'd never heard of sex before. Vaguely remembering an earlier remark she'd made about men and the lack thereof in her life, JD discarded the thought. It made him edgy as hell. Instead of trying fancy words of persuasion, JD lowered his head and did what he'd wanted to do in the first place. He kissed her.

She was so damned soft and giving. She curled up against him like a purring kitten whose contentment rested on his stroking and fondling. He didn't want contentment right now. He wanted fiery swords and slain dragons. His arousal pressed against the confinement of his trousers, demanding the thrust and parry of conquest. And she purred and licked at his lips as if he were no more than another pussycat.

Baffled by his raging lust and a surge of protectiveness, JD cuddled Nina close and thrust his tongue between her teeth at the same time. She responded willingly to both, but not with the heated hunger he needed right now. He wanted to rip that sexy dress off her back and take her on the floor. But Nina trustingly wrapped her arms around his neck and brushed against him with such eager naïveté that JD couldn't imagine doing anything so crude.

He stroked the side of her breast through the heavy silk, cursing at the wired undergarment he felt when he wanted something much softer. "Let's go somewhere we can close the door," he murmured against her ear, steering her toward the hall and the bedroom across it.

She stopped and froze at once, pulling her arms away so fast that JD reacted as if doused by an icy splash of lake water. The cloudy haze of her eyes flashed with the cold glitter of emeralds.

"My mother and your son are upstairs, and you want us to make out like a couple of teenagers behind closed doors? What kind of example is that setting?"

Make out? He wanted a hell of a lot more than making out. With no idea of the source of her anger, JD stumbled about in bewilderment. "You'd rather do it out here, where they can see us?" He didn't like the angry edge of his voice, but he wasn't precisely in control of himself at the moment. "It's not as if we have anything to hide. We're two consenting, unattached adults. This is the nineties, for pity's sake. There's no shame in it. We can be circumspect. We don't have to flaunt it, if that's what you want."

Nina stared at him with mixed terror and horror. She was terrified at herself, at her response to this man she scarcely knew. And she was horrified at the suggestion she thought he was making. She shouldn't be, she knew. She might not watch TV much or go to the movies often, but she knew men and women indulged in casual sex. But she didn't. And no one had offered her the opportunity before. Those things just weren't done around here, were they?

Stupid. Of course they were. That's how her mother had ended up in trouble, and that had been thirty years ago. Of course JD thought she would want the same thing he wanted. Hadn't she just practically offered herself? Hattie would be horrified. She horrified herself. She couldn't believe a little gratitude and consolation could flame out of control so quickly. She'd just wanted someone holding her for a little while. It felt good having strong arms around her. She'd not had much of that in her life. She liked it altogether too well. Truth was, she wanted more of it. But not on his terms.

Nina's shattered thoughts grasped words she'd used before, words she'd entrusted to memory, words that erupted spontaneously. "I don't believe in sex without commitment," she announced firmly, as if that ended the subject.

It didn't. JD's eyes narrowed, and his fingers strayed daringly close to her nipples, to the point that Nina shivered in anticipation. She couldn't pull away. She simply stood there, waiting for him to understand.

"You want this as much as I do," he accused—rightly. "I don't know what they teach in this backwater town, but sex is something perfectly natural, just a release of tension and hormones. We'd quit sniping at each other so much if we could work out some of this chemistry sizzling between us. This isn't the nineteenth century. I can protect you, if that's your concern."

He spoke in perfectly, wonderfully logical tones while his hand played havoc with her senses. Nina could read the earnestness in JD's eyes, the passion in his expression as he tormented her with his touch. In another minute, he would find the hidden button behind her lapels, and her gown would fall open beneath his exploring fingers. She thought he might really believe what he was saying. She should feel sorry for a man who believed that there was nothing else in this world but the mindlessness of animal sex. Instead, he was rapidly persuading her to his way of thinking. It would be so easy to throw it all away, all her beliefs, a lifetime of teaching and learning, just for the pleasure of his lovemaking, to know for once in her life, someone wanted her. She desperately needed to be wanted, particularly with the return of the woman who had thrown her away. If she could believe someone cared, someone saw her and wanted her just as she was . . .

But JD Smith or whatever his name was didn't care, or he'd never ask this of her in such cold, logical terms. JD simply wanted a female body in his bed. He didn't care who she was or what she was or what she wanted. She mentally shook herself and stepped away from his encroaching fingers.

"Chemistry and hormones are not enough. I see that every day in my high school classes. I'm not a teenager. I'm a woman with needs and desires beyond what you're offering. I'll thank you to keep your hands to yourself from now on. Find someone else to release your damned tensions."

Teeth chattering from the strength of her anger and her tears, Nina stormed from the room, leaving JD to figure things out all by himself.

She was probably the only twenty-nine-year-old virgin in the world. And the hell of it was, she didn't *want* to be. She'd just reached a point where she was too terrified to be anything else.

Just the image of JD Smith leaning over her, naked, would keep her awake the rest of the night.

NINETEEN

"Helen! Look at you. I knew you'd come home."

Wrinkled and so shrunken that she looked as if she'd wasted away, leaving only her skin behind, Hattie sat alertly in her wheelchair, observing the two visitors entering her small room. Intelligence gleamed behind pale eyes as they focused first on Helen, then on the younger woman behind her. "It's about time you got here, young lady. I'm ready to go home now."

Nina's heart sank to her stomach. Of all the days for Hattie to be coherent, she had to make it the day Helen visited. For months now, she'd prayed for a day when she could talk with her great-aunt, get her advice, her assurance that she did the right thing. Her opportunity had finally arrived, and she had to share it with this stranger who claimed to be her mother.

"Hattie! How wonderful to see you again." Helen hugged the old woman. The cloud of her perfume wafted through the tiny room, and Hattie immediately waved the scent away as her niece stepped back, smiling.

"See you still haven't learned subtlety, girl," Hattie grumbled. "You smell like a bitch in heat. Open the window, will you?"

Nina smothered a laugh, kissed Hattie's cheek, and bounced down on the bed beside her. "Oh, Aunt Hattie, it's so good seeing you well again. I've got so many things I want to tell you. I've found someone who's making landscape designs for the garden for free. They're the most marvelous things you'll ever see!"

"With what you're paying to keep me in here, we could be planting the gardens," Hattie grumbled. "My hip's all better. I can go home now."

"Of course you can, Hattie." Apparently deciding the hermetically sealed window wouldn't open, Helen returned and took the small chair stuffed in the corner. "I'll talk to your doctor today. Now that I'm back, I can look after you."

Hattie gave her an approving look. "I always knew you were a good girl. That husband of yours wasn't ever any good. You married too young. But I taught Nina better. You're just like your grandmama, but Nina takes after me," she said proudly, patting Nina's hand. "She's too smart to let any man talk her into throwing her life away."

Nina sighed. This wasn't the direction she wanted the conversation to take. If she had only a few minutes of coherency to update Hattie on current events, she didn't want her wandering down dead-end byways. "The cell phone people want right-of-way to your hill, Aunt Hattie," Nina said quickly, before Helen could find some suitably sugary reply. "They want to put a tower right where your rose garden is. I've told them they can't have it, but they're talking about having the land condemned. Do you mind if I hire a lawyer to keep them out?"

Hattie didn't even look in her direction. Nodding sagely, she stayed with the one path her mind could find. "We all must come home someday. You'll be glad I held on to that farm for you, Marietta. We can raise Helen the way we were raised. These modern ways lead to the devil."

Helen bit her lip and threw Nina an uncertain look. Nina shrugged and surrendered. "You've done the best job any woman could, Aunt Hattie," Nina answered warmly. "If I ever have children, I'll raise them just the way you taught me."

"She's right, Hattie. You've done a wonderful job with Nina. I can't tell you how much I thank you. But I'll make it up to you now. I'll take you home, where you belong." Helen reached over and held Hattie's spotted hand.

"The roses are so pretty this time of year," Hattie said dreamily. "I want my granddaughter to have them. Hank would have loved her. I'll have that tea now, Marietta. Fetch it for me, will you?"

Nina handed her a glass of ice water from the pitcher by the table, but Hattie didn't see it. Her mind's eye had slipped beyond the landscape outside the window.

"Hattie, I'll go talk to the doctor now," Helen said nervously, standing and inching toward the door.

Hattie didn't notice her departure.

A single tear streaking down her cheek, Nina held her aunt's hand and patted it. "Who's Hank, Hattie? Does he love roses?" She didn't expect an answer. Figments of Hattie's past flitted in and out of her conversation frequently these days. The reference to a granddaughter was something new, but she supposed Hattie might think of her as the granddaughter she never had. It didn't seem significant.

"Hank loved roses. He had one painted on his airplane, he said. He promised me a rose garden." Hattie lifted her clouded eyes. "Helen had too much of Hank in her, but you're my spitting image. Take care of her for me."

Nina's heart caught in her throat at this sentiment. She wanted to protest Hattie's orders but wasn't certain how far her aunt's mind had wandered. She just clung to the affection Hattie had never expressed before.

"Men can't be trusted, child. Don't ever give your heart to a man."

Nina sighed. She had heard that countless times before. Like the phrase she repeated by rote to JD last night about commitment, her aunt apparently repeated memorized phrases now. Sometimes, it made Nina wonder about her own mind. "I know, Hattie. Only trust the land. I'm doing that. I'm looking out for it for you. You'll love the new garden."

Hattie nodded. "Just don't let any man poke you and you'll do fine."

A moment later, her chin fell against her chest, and she slept. Contemplating her great-aunt's frail form, Nina pondered the strange pathways of the mind. Stroking her aunt's thin hair, she didn't immediately set out to find her mother. Hattie was the only mother she really knew.

Helen returned without a doctor or nurse in tow. Nina had known she wouldn't find anyone. The doctors never made themselves available during visiting hours, and the nurses had their hands full. Without bothering to listen to anything Helen might say, Nina rose from the bed. "Are you ready to leave now?" she inquired politely.

"Of course not. I've got to get Hattie out of here. I thought you said she wasn't in her right mind. There's not anything wrong with her."

Nina thought she heard a hint of uncertainty behind the belligerent words, but she didn't have the patience for ferreting out her mother's innermost secrets. The woman in the room with her now exuded all the female self-confidence Nina had never possessed. Let her handle the situation. "Fine. If you want to sleep in the room with her so she won't wander down to the lake in the middle of the night, I'll leave word at the desk to have an ambulance transfer her back home. She has spells when she won't get out of bed, so you'll have to change the bed linen and persuade her to use the bedpan. And she's as likely to throw her food as to eat it. But I'll help where I can."

Nina disliked the bitterness she heard in her own voice as she hurried down the antiseptic corridor of the nursing home. She hated this place. She hated the soft squish of the nurses' thick-soled shoes, the smell of disinfectant, the querulous tones and harsh cries from all the closed doors around her. She knew

Hattie would hate it, too, if she knew where she was. Sometimes, Nina took comfort in knowing Hattie lived in a world inside her head now.

"I suppose I should talk to the doctor first. What's his name? Can I call him from here?"

"His name's Karpatik. He's in the Hopkinsville phone book. He won't get back to you until this evening. I've tried a dozen times before. Do you want to wait here until then?" Impatiently, Nina kept hurrying toward the door. She couldn't get out of here soon enough.

Helen hurried right alongside her. "Then I'll call when we get home. We can't leave her in here. Hattie hates it."

"I know. But there isn't a damned thing I can do about it." Nina slammed open the glass front doors and stalked out to the parking lot. They'd arrived in her Toyota because her mother had claimed her Cadillac had a brake lining that needed work. From the looks of the ancient vehicle, Nina suspected a great deal more than the brakes needed work.

"You've turned into a heartless monster," Helen accused as she bent her willowy height into the small front seat of the Toyota.

Nina's fingers clenched the steering wheel as she set the car in motion. "I'm a heartless monster?" she asked in incredulity. "You desert me for twenty years, and *I'm* the heartless monster? Do you have any idea, any idea at all what my life is like? Where were you when Hattie fell and broke her hip and couldn't walk for six months? Where were you the night she nearly drowned in the lake? Where were you when I had to call the ambulance and have her placed in that horrible home because I couldn't keep working to pay the debts and maintain the house and watch Hattie at the same time?" Nina fought the tears blurring her eyes. She didn't even ask about all those years when she'd needed a mother to explain the facts of life, to sew her Halloween costume, to attend her first band concert. Those years were long gone. She needed support *now*, and instead, she got this mealymouthed tirade on the way things should be done.

"Well, I'm here now," Helen answered huffily, crossing her arms over her ample chest. "You can go play footsie with that criminal of yours. I'll take care of things from now on."

"Do me a favor and don't bother," Nina said wearily. "Just go back wherever you came from and leave me alone. I don't need the hassle."

"You can't throw me out. I checked with a lawyer. Even if my mother didn't have a will, by law, her share goes to her children. Half that house is mine. And Hattie always said it would all be mine someday. So if you don't want the hassle, go live with your lover elsewhere. I don't need you any more than you need me."

"He's not my lover, he's my boarder. And I've poured most of my salary into that place for these last ten years, so don't go telling me who it belongs to. If it weren't for me, the taxes wouldn't have been paid, and you wouldn't have any land at all. I don't know how the hell you think you'll pay for taxes and maintenance if I move out, unless you've stashed away a small fortune these last few years. About the only job available around here is waiting on tables, and I can tell you right now, that won't pay the electric bill."

"There's over a hundred acres out there," Helen said stiffly. "It should bring a pretty good price."

Oh, Lord in heaven above, forgive her please, but she would have to throttle her mother. Gritting her teeth and glaring at the ribbon of two-lane highway in front of her, Nina said nothing until the thick cloud of her temper cleared sufficiently to speak without shouting. "Eight hundred an acre is the going price for undeveloped land. Good luck. You'll need it when I sue for every penny I put in it."

Neither of them spoke for the rest of the hour-long drive home.

* * *

As the clock in the church tower chimed nine, Jimmy MacTavish steered the cherry red Geo into a parking space in front of the cubicle labeled "Sheriff's Office." Beside him, Nancy Walker nervously fiddled with her hair. They'd taken rooms at a hotel near the interstate last night after they'd arrived too late to find anyone in the sheriff's office. Nancy had insisted they drive up and down the streets of Madrid looking for Jackie until it grew dark. Jimmy had thought it a waste of time, but he had nothing better to do. This town didn't have a computer store that he could find either, but he rather admired the tree-lined residential streets, the huge green lawns, and the neat beds of colorful flowers everywhere. Accustomed to the car-clogged highways and modernistic architecture of LA, he'd enjoyed the trip back in time presented by the towering Victorian mansions behind the town's business district. It looked like a good place for raising kids.

Nancy was out of the car before he could open the door for her. Her high heels clicked firmly on the pavement, and he breathed a silent sigh of appreciation at the long legs they accented. She'd taken care with her appearance this morning. Until now, she'd worn shorts and pulled her hair back in a knot. Today, she looked as if she'd just stepped off a movie screen.

The only person in the office was a bespectacled, overweight woman of indeterminable age. She looked up at them with curiosity, obviously more than eager to abandon her project on the ancient electric typewriter.

"I'm looking for Sheriff Stone. Is he in?" Jimmy felt foolish asking since the only other desk in the place was empty, but he saw no other means of getting to the point. He'd never had an aptitude for communication.

"He's over at the morgue with the state police. They found a body in the lake last night, and they're sending it in for autopsy. Could you state your business, please?"

Nancy took over before Jimmy could formulate a reply. "I'm looking for my son, Jackie Marshall. He was in a car accident here with his father a few weeks ago. Do you know anything about it?"

Jimmy gave an inward groan and almost covered his face with his hand before he thought better of it. JD would kill him. He would slice him into little pieces and feed him to the fish in the damned lake. Putting his hand to better use, he caught Nancy's arm and pulled her gently behind him. Smiling just a little nervously, he adjusted his glasses, remembered the broken nosepiece, and pushed at it gingerly. "Ummm, I think Mrs. Walker is a little confused. A friend of mine, JD Smith, had a little problem with my truck out here a few weeks back. He was giving Jackie a lift to his father's place when someone ran them off the road. We were wondering if you know where they went from here."

The woman behind the desk beamed with enlightenment. "Mr. Smith! Of course. He's the man staying out at Nina's place. I heard all about the garden he's planning out there. It's the most exciting thing that's ever hit this town, let me tell you. My sister is already thinking of opening a flower shop where visitors can buy baskets and pretty pots and things. We're waiting to see if Nina means to sell her flowers out of the greenhouse as part of the garden, or if we should do it. Our daddy owns a real nice lot out on the highway that should make the perfect location to catch the tourists when they come in."

Jimmy frowned, took off his glasses and polished them, and sought desperately for some response. Garden? Had the world gone berserk and he hadn't noticed? JD knew diddly about gardens. He didn't know a houseplant from an azalea. And he'd damned well better be working on the program loop or the business would crash down on their heads any day now. Maybe it wasn't JD out there. Maybe somebody had stolen the truck and crashed it. He didn't like the idea of mentioning that possibility to the anxious woman at his side.

"Does Mr. Smith have a young boy with him? Is Jackie living with this Nina?" Nancy asked before Jimmy could find his words again. At least this time she used her head and followed his lead. Calling JD by his real name could cause real havoc.

"Well, yes, I believe there's a boy out there with him, but I thought he was Mr. Smith's brother. I didn't know his name was Marshall." The clerk gave them a look of suspicion. "You say you're his mother?"

Nancy reddened, and relieved to come to the rescue, Jimmy jumped in. "Jackie's mother. Different fathers. Jackie's name is Marshall. Could you tell us where this Nina lives?"

"Who's asking?" a deep male voice rumbled behind him.

Jimmy spun around to discover a stocky, muscular man wearing a badge and a khaki uniform glaring at them from beneath a scowl that would suit a good John Wayne movie. Dealing with the law was up JD's alley, not Jimmy's. He'd never had much contact with the police except what he read in the newspapers or saw on television. Neither source reassured him much as he confronted the sheriff's unpleasant expression.

"I'm James MacTavish, sir." He almost stuttered as he had back in school, but he managed to remember he was one of the chief officers of Marshall Enterprises and an important person in his own right. "You filed a report on my truck," he said, straightening his shoulders. "We spoke on the phone some weeks ago. I came for my truck, but I understand JD and the boy are still in the area, and we'd like to see them. Your clerk tells us they're with"—he hesitated—"a Miss Nina? We were just asking for directions."

Nancy clung to his arm as the sheriff glowered at them some more. Jimmy wanted to reassure her, but he was feeling a mite edgy himself. What in hell had JD gotten himself into this time?

"I was just heading out that way. You can follow, if you like." Turning on his booted heel, the sheriff stalked out of the office.

Jimmy bit off the curse word he'd like to utter. Something was very, very wrong. Maybe he'd been just a little bit hasty in bringing Jackie's mother into whatever preposterous scheme JD had concocted this time.

TWENTY

Keys clacking beneath his fingers, JD gave a diabolical grin as the "execute" file fell into place. Anyone opening this cartridge would get the latest, greatest version of his newest Monster House game. Let Harry's thieves find the banking program now.

Finally, something was going right. Car accidents, dead bodies, mothers returned from the dead, and sons appearing from nowhere aside, he finally had one piece of his life in order. The banking loop worked. Champagne, caviar, and a monthlong celebration were called for. He'd settle for a night in his landlady's bed.

Whistling merrily, he plotted his way to that goal as his fingers added the finishing touches to the program's disguise. Now, he only had to get the cartridge to Jimmy. He kept a backup of his own, and a spare he would send to a post office box. Basic. For challenge, his mind worked over the problem of seducing one commitment-minded lady.

JD wasn't averse to commitments. He'd married Nancy, after all. He just knew from experience that his luck with women batted somewhere in the zero range. Sooner or later, Nina Toon would discover all the flaws in his character and speed into someone else's arms. But he damned well couldn't give up women just because his luck was bad.

He supposed, if he had any brains at all where females were concerned, he'd steer clear of women like Nina, women who expected commitment in return for emotional and/or sexual involvement. But he wasn't much on planning ahead in these matters. He hadn't wanted a woman like this in longer than he could remember, and he wasn't given to forethought when he wanted something. The challenge of cracking open the emotional fortress behind Nina's fey facade excited him more than the idea for a new program. That kind of excitement didn't come around often at his age. With Nina, anticipation sizzled through his veins again. He didn't analyze why.

Now that he'd finished the program, he could turn his mind to the things that would pave his way into Nina's heart. He had already sent out a query about lawyers in the vicinity. He expected a reply shortly. He'd get the nonprofit corporation formed at the same time as the lawyer investigated the legal entanglement involved in Nina's land. Or her mother's land. JD heartily suspected the old girl could be bought off for a nominal sum. Money wouldn't matter. In a few weeks, he could be one of the richest men in the country. He chuckled as he imagined Nina buying into that fantasy. She definitely had no trust in his financial capabilities.

Turning off the computer, JD contemplated his next move. The wiring. Nina would definitely appreciate his accomplishing something concrete and visible, like good electrical wiring. Or he thought she would. Sometimes, she didn't seem aware they lived in the twentieth century. He would drag her kicking and screaming into the technology age if he must. Images of installing a Jacuzzi on that wide back porch danced in his head.

He peered out the lace-curtained window at the sound of tires screeching to a halt in the gravel drive. Cursing at the sight of the sheriff's car, JD blinked in puzzlement at the tiny Geo chugging up the road behind it. He couldn't remember Nina having any friends with Geos, but it certainly fit local habits more than a Mercedes. Thank heavens Nina and her mother were still in Hopkinsville. He could straighten out Sheriff Hoyt Stone and his bullying tactics once and for all.

Jackie and friends were still carving order out of wilderness. JD didn't have to act the part of upstanding citizen for the kid's sake this time. Tucking in his T-shirt, he threw open the front door before the sheriff could knock. The sight of Nancy climbing out of the Geo blew away every angry word JD had reserved for the interfering sheriff.

Hell and damnation. How had the woman found him all the way out here? Images of Nina and Nancy trading information on him like baseball cards blew every gasket left in his mind. They'd fry him alive. Damn, but he'd known things were working too smoothly.

"Friends here to see you," the sheriff said dryly when JD said nothing.

"So I see." Jerking himself back from his first gut panic, JD settled his gaze on Nina's would-be suitor. "Nina probably has some iced tea made. She's in Hopkinsville right now with her aunt, but you're welcome to come in and cool off."

"Just might take you up on that." The sheriff waited patiently for JD to move from the doorway, but JD waited for Nancy to join them first. His lips tightened as he watched Jimmy unfold himself from the tiny car. He should have known. Jimmy was a sucker for any woman who batted her eyelashes.

Growling something irascible, JD stood back and let the trio troop in. "Jackie's out working in the woods," he replied in answer to Nancy's darting gaze. "They'll be in shortly looking for something to drink. You might as well make yourself comfortable while you wait."

"Couldn't I go out and look for him?" Nancy didn't take the seat offered but stood in the hall, glancing anxiously toward the kitchen, then up the stairs, as if expecting a wild horde of motorcycle thugs to descend on them.

Conscious of the rubber band in his hair and the ragged hole in his jeans, JD shrugged. She had every right to think of him as that mixed-up kid she'd married sixteen years ago. He hadn't precisely behaved any differently by dragging Jackie into this mess. "He won't appreciate it," he said in response to her question. "He's with his friends, trying to act as if he's grown-up. You have to let up on him, Nancy. He's fifteen, going on a hundred."

Biting her bottom lip, she nodded uncertainly. JD couldn't help but contrast her uptight, hovering anxiety with Nina's relaxed ease with the boy. Of course, Nina wasn't Jackie's mother. Maybe that made the difference.

"We've gotta talk, JD," Jimmy said from behind Nancy.

"Sometime after I punch your lights out, MacTavish. Go get a chair with the sheriff while I bring in the tea." JD jerked his head toward the living room.

"Tea?"

JD heard the question behind the question and grinned. "It's a dry county, and our hostess doesn't believe in stocking beer or alcohol. Tea, milk, or various ghastly carbonated beverages are available. I don't recommend the water."

By the time JD returned to the living room with a pitcher and glasses, his three unwanted guests had struck up a somewhat stilted conversation that seemed to center around the plans for Nina's garden. Pleased that they'd found the one thing he preferred talking about, JD plunked the tray down on the coffee table and left them to help themselves.

True Southern gentleman that he was, Sheriff Hoyt poured a glass for Nancy first, then poured his own. Before he took a drink, he pinned JD with his glare. "The state police came in this morning. The corpse didn't drown."

Holding the glass of iced tea against his sweltering forehead rather than sipping from it, JD glared back. "And?"

"He was shot in the back."

Nancy's shocked gasp created just the reaction the sheriff expected, but JD didn't fall for it. He shrugged. "I have no notion what firearms are kept on the place, but if you suspect any of us, I guess you'll need a search warrant. I'm not familiar with the area, but I imagine if you've got bootleggers in these parts, you've got other criminal types, too. People don't change much wherever you live."

"Nina threatened the cell phone guys with a shotgun a while back. You don't happen to know where that is, do you?" The sheriff sipped complacently at his drink.

"Nope. And knowing Nina, she probably doesn't either. But I'll have a lawyer after the phone company shortly, so she doesn't need a gun anymore. I'm sure she'll tell you you're welcome to it when it shows up."

The sheriff's expression indicated JD had hit the mark of Nina's behavior pretty accurately, and Hoyt didn't like it a bit. Score one, round one, JD thought smugly.

The conversation lapsed uneasily. "The lady back in town told us about the garden, JD," Nancy offered hesitantly. "What kind of garden is she talking about?"

Smiling, JD sipped his drink. Nancy had grown into a lovely, polite woman. Boring as hell, maybe, but polite. "A botanical garden. Nina thinks she can turn these acres into a tourist attraction that will draw people year-round. We're in the process of drawing up a nonprofit corporation to handle it. That's what Jackie's doing now, clearing some of the woods that the landscape man wants to make into a woodland garden."

Jimmy contributed little to the conversation, inhaling his tea and tapping his toe while glancing around at his surroundings. JD imagined him mentally tallying the cost of the ancient sagging sofa, the wooden rocker, the television that would fit in a museum exhibit, and coming up with lots of zeroes. JD knew

Jimmy made no judgment on these factors. He just calculated costs out of habit.

When the conversation did nothing more than sputter and start in his presence, Hoyt finished his tea and stood up. "Thanks for the hospitality. Tell Nina I said hello and ask her about that shotgun. If we don't identify the body, we may have to subpoena her to have a look. If he was shot, it was almost certainly on her land."

"Water doesn't move in these parts?" JD asked, following the sheriff to the door.

"Not much along the bank. There's too much timber in the shallows, and the main current is out beyond the buoys. Nina owns most of that land up toward the dock. I suppose he could have been shot out there, but seems like someone would have heard it that close to civilization."

"Seems like." JD could be agreeable if the sheriff would get his rear moving. He needed to talk to Jimmy, and his patience had worn thin.

The sheriff tipped his hat and swaggered back to his car. JD closed the front door just as the back door flew open. Wondering if his timing was good or bad, he waited for Jackie and friends to storm through the house, adolescent feet clattering like a herd of elephants across the uncarpeted floor.

"Saw the sheriff's car! Have they found who done it?"

"No, he was directing your mother out here. She's in the living room. Give her a hug, then go get your friends something to drink. And for pity's sake, wash your faces off. You look like savages." Stank like them, too, but JD didn't remind them of that. Short of lending them all his personal deodorant or hosing them down, he couldn't think of an immediate solution to that problem.

"Mom?" With both dismay and surprise, Jackie turned and met his mother as she rushed to hug him.

Wishing he had a beer instead of the tea, JD watched as Nancy sensibly stopped short of hugging her malodorous son, tousling his hair instead and kissing his cheek. He supposed she would take the boy back now. JD didn't know how he felt about that. He'd scarcely gotten to know Jackie. Hell, he'd scarcely had a chance to realize the boy was his. For fifteen years, he'd had a kid and never known about it. If he thought about it, he'd resent the hell out of missing all those little things like first words and baby steps and baseball games. But then, he'd have to remember what he'd been doing during those years and realize he'd have missed them anyway.

"I've got to get the guys something to drink. Miss Toon keeps Popsicles and things in the freezer for us. We'll be back after we clean up." Jackie tugged away from his mother's affectionate gestures and herded his wide-eyed friends back down the hall, not giving JD a look either. JD figured Jackie was probably pretty confused by all this, too. Food and drink always eased confusion.

"Who precisely is this Miss Toon?" Nancy asked acerbically when JD returned to his chair.

"Teacher. Her aunt owns the place, but she's in a nursing home. Nina's visiting her right now. She'll be sorry she missed you," JD added quickly, showing his obvious hope for an early departure.

To his surprise, Nancy suddenly looked uncertain. She threw another anxious look in the direction Jackie had taken, then settled back in her chair. "He looks happy." She didn't sound thrilled by the news.

"He's a good kid. You raised him right. We've got him and the others working off some of their energy, and paying them just enough for pizza and movies to keep them out of trouble. He's learning to fish, and now that I've got a little spare time, I'll take him out on the lake so he can learn boating." JD didn't think about what he said until he'd said it. If Nancy took the boy back, he wouldn't be teaching him anything. He may have already blown his opportunity to know the boy better. He'd worked right through it. Damn, but he made a lousy father.

Jimmy's head bobbed up at the mention of his having spare time, but JD couldn't say anything in front of Nancy.

"I left Bob," she said, apropos of nothing. She wrung her hands a little, staring down at them instead of at the men around her. "I've gone back to my daddy's place. I have a job with an insurance company making pretty good money. We'll be able to get our own place shortly. I want to take Jackie back with me."

JD definitely wanted something stronger than iced tea. Setting his glass down, he ran his hand down the back of his neck, striving desperately for the words that needed saying. To his relief, Jimmy wandered out of the room, leaving them alone.

"I owe you support for all those years," he said awkwardly. "You should have told me about the boy."

Nancy shrugged. "Daddy didn't want you coming back and claiming him. We didn't starve."

"I could have given him a lot of little extras, even when I was in the marines. I didn't make much, but I could have listed him for insurance and such. I owe you for those years, Nancy. And I can provide a lot more for him now. There's college ahead. Cars. Computers. I can help."

She looked mildly alarmed. "I want Jackie, not your money, JD. I won't let you have him."

Furious, but with no outlet for the fury, JD stalked to the big window overlooking the front lawn. "I can't take him away from you. Boys need their mothers as well as fathers. But he does need a father, Nancy. Don't fool yourself. Give me a chance."

"How?" she asked mournfully. "We live in different worlds. I can't trust you to bring him home when you're supposed to. I haven't even known where he was these past weeks. I've worried myself sick. I can't go through that again, JD. I need him with me."

Fighting back an anguish he didn't know he could feel, JD swung around. "Look, it's been crazy these last few weeks, all right? I didn't mean for any of this to happen. But it's over now. I've got the job done, and Jimmy can take it back with him. I promised Jackie a real vacation. He's happy here. Nina looks after him. She's the one who made me call Jimmy and assure you everything was all right. She won't let me do anything I shouldn't. I'll admit, I don't know beans about kids, but she'll keep me straight. You've had him all these years. Give me a chance with him. I won't take him away from you. I just want him for the summer. You've got a new job. You don't need to be worrying where he is all summer while you're working."

She hesitated for the longest time. JD wished he'd learned to be a persuasive talker. Until he'd spoken the words, he hadn't realized how much he'd relied on Nina's help with Jackie these last weeks. Maybe he shouldn't have mentioned it. For his own sake, he wished he hadn't thought of it. Nina was taking on a greater aspect than just an object of lust. He didn't need that complication right now. Maybe he was the one who should get out of here.

"I think I'd like to meet this Miss Toon," Nancy finally replied.

Ah, hell. Running his hand over his hair, JD nodded reluctantly. "You'll like her. Why don't you go out and check on the kids while I talk with Jimmy?"

He took a deep gulp of air when she nodded and wandered out. Maybe he could deal with women when they were reasonable. Maybe his luck was changing. Maybe a carnival could fit on a spoon, too.

JD found Jimmy at his computer, naturally. "You haven't answered your e-mail." He flung himself on the bed while Jimmy punched in his password to do just that.

"I've been on the run," Jimmy replied absently, running through the list of senders for any important messages.

JD waited. "From what?" he growled when Jimmy didn't explain.

"Damned if I know. Harry called, said something about someone having the program and they're out to get you and they might come after me next. Hell of a thing to hear, let me tell you."

JD sat upright. "Where's Harry now?"

Jimmy swung around in his chair, finally facing JD. "That's what I'm here to tell you. I think he's in trouble."

TWENTY-ONE

Nina pulled up behind a red car she didn't recognize, watched Jackie tackle one of his friends in the front yard, and climbed out to find a strange woman sitting on the front porch rocker, following her progress with interest. Maybe God was showing her what life would be like once she turned the farm into a tourist circus.

Resolutely, she carried her sack from the mall up the stairs, ignoring Helen trailing behind her. For some idiot reason, Nina had actually agreed when her mother asked to stop and pick up a few things before visiting Hattie. She didn't go to Hopkinsville often, and the stores there offered a wide assortment of merchandise she couldn't buy in Madrid. She'd actually come away with a new dress she'd bought on sale and thought JD would like. Stupid. Why should she care if JD liked it? And then she'd gone and bought one of those ribbon things for her hair. He'd know she was trying to impress him if she wore it. She didn't want him thinking any such thing.

Her disgust with herself still didn't distract her from the attractive woman rising from the porch rocker. The woman was taller than Nina by a head. She had lovely long hair that brushed her shoulders in a neat pageboy. She wore lipstick and smiled with teeth resembling a TV commercial for toothpaste. Nina hated her on sight.

"Miss Toon?" the stranger inquired, throwing a glance over Nina's shoulder to Helen, then back again.

"Nina." Not offering her hand, she stood there, waiting impatiently. It was well past noon, and she was starved, irritated, hot, and ready to kill anyone who looked at her crooked.

"Nina." The woman nodded politely. "I'm Nancy Walker, Jackie's mother."

That did it. That really blew it. Jackie's mother, of course. JD's wife, ex-wife, whatever. She should have known the woman would be a fashion model. "Fine, how are you?" Nina muttered and pushed past to enter the house. Maybe she could fry JD. She sure couldn't take her temper out on an innocent bystander.

She didn't care whether the Walker woman or her mother followed or not. The air outside had reached a hundred in the shade, with humidity to match. And the Toyota's air-conditioning had given out. She needed ice, and lots of it. She might start by putting it under her collar.

Nina screeched to a halt as she entered the kitchen and discovered JD standing on her kitchen table, tinkering with a shiny new ceiling fan, while a strange man handed him tools and looked worried. He had a right to look worried. Dropping her sack on the floor, Nina proceeded toward the freezer. "I hope you removed the fuses before you started that project," she threw over her shoulder as she passed.

"Why? I pulled the main one. That's all it should take," JD called down from his position near the ceiling.

Luckily for him, he'd removed the screwdriver from the socket before answering. Electric sparks arced between the loose wires, startling JD into jumping backward, off the table and onto the floor.

Holding a frozen Popsicle still in its wrapper to her forehead, Nina leaned against the refrigerator. "Because the box is sixty years old and doesn't work right, that's why," she answered calmly.

JD leaned his elbows against the countertop and shook his head in amazement. Nina tried to fasten her attention on the gangly man with the broken glasses, but she had difficulty pulling her gaze away from the tight shirt pulling across JD's shoulders and chest. Maybe she should run the Popsicle down her front.

"How do you keep from frying yourself every time you plug something in?" JD asked with curiosity.

Nina shrugged. "I know when things aren't working. Like the toaster. It's about to go. I don't plug things in where it feels dangerous." She shouldn't have said that, but she had a need to set him back a step or two. It felt too damned intimate standing here in her kitchen, exchanging mutually admiring glances in front of strangers. The man with the glasses would think the wrong things about their relationship, and that notion really heated the air.

Instead of regarding her weird statement with wariness, as he should, JD grinned. "How do you know the toaster is about to go?"

She jerked the wrapper off the Popsicle. "It hums, all right? Toasters shouldn't hum."

She could see him holding back his laughter. "Off-key or on? Does it hum a particular tune? Prefer rock to country?"

She flung an apple from the basket at him. JD caught it easily and munched a hole in it—while keeping his warm gaze firmly focused on her. She could almost read his mind, envision where his thoughts had strayed, and the part of her anatomy his teeth might nibble. She thought she might scream in frustration.

At the sight of juice trickling temptingly down his chin, she hastily turned her gaze to the stranger. "Since Mr. Ape there won't make the introductions, I'm Nina Toon. You really don't have to electrocute yourself for my sake."

The tall stranger almost blushed, then pushed his glasses back up his nose. "That's okay. I'm just here to clean up the mess after JD fixes things. That's my job. I'm Jimmy MacTavish, JD's partner."

Nina watched the grin disappear from JD's face as they shook hands, but he offered no objection to the introduction. She wondered why JD was playing with her wiring while his drop-dead gorgeous ex-wife idled on the front porch, but she didn't have the nerve to ask. She wasn't much at complicated personal relationships.

"Glad to meet you, Mr. MacTavish. I don't envy you your job. Does he fix things often?"

Jimmy coughed and sent JD's implacable expression a nervous look. "He fixed the toaster. It doesn't hum anymore."

"Does it still work?" she asked dryly, but she knew it would. Somehow, she knew JD could fix almost anything he set his mind to. The self-satisfied air of confidence around him confirmed it.

"Seems to." Jimmy cleared his throat again, then glanced from JD to Nina. "I'll go down and remove the rest of the fuses."

JD waited until he was gone before speaking. "I suppose you met Nancy coming in?"

Something around Nina's heart pinched, but she nodded. "She seems nice enough. Is she taking Jackie back?"

"Unless I can persuade her to leave the boy with me for the rest of the summer. She wanted to meet you first. She doesn't trust me."

The heat in the kitchen was stifling. Nina licked the Popsicle, telling herself she was just overheated, that there was nothing in JD's gaze to make her think he needed her help. A strong, confident man like JD didn't need anyone. He certainly didn't need a backwoods spinster like her.

He didn't move a muscle, didn't touch her in any way. He just leaned against the counter, arms crossed over his chest, giving out vibrations stronger than any damned toaster. Nina had the same feeling with him now as she did with a dangerous plug. If she ignored the warning, he wouldn't just break, he'd explode.

He desperately wanted Jackie, and he needed her help to keep him.

Nodding acquiescence to the inevitable, Nina caved. "I like having Jackie around. This house gets lonely. But I thought you were taking him to the coast?"

Relief rose off JD in almost visible waves as he straightened and dug his hand through his hair. "He's happy here. Nancy would feel better if she knew exactly where he was, and with whom. I never meant to impose on you for so long. If it will inconvenience you in any way . . ."

The thought of having JD with her all summer made Nina dizzy, but whether with excitement or nervousness, she couldn't tell. She felt no small amount of relief in knowing she wouldn't have to deal with her mother alone. The idea of two men occupying the space that had held only Aunt Hattie all these years didn't terrify her quite as much as it had at first. If she froze up now, allowed fear to rule her decision, she might be giving up far more than the rent JD would pay her. She was almost thirty years old. Somehow, she must overcome her fears and explore some small part of the world beyond Hattie's door. If that world contained men like JD, she must learn about them.

Resolutely, keeping things light so he wouldn't read her the wrong way, Nina glanced at the wires hanging from the ceiling. "I don't think it will be an inconvenience, just an experience."

He chuckled, and before Nina knew he'd moved from the counter, JD gripped her elbows. His strength should alarm her, but somehow, it reassured instead. The kiss he pressed against her cheek sent shock waves through her system. The one he pressed against her mouth when she moved the Popsicle nearly melted her bones.

He licked her lips and tasted her tongue before he pulled away, his dark eyes sparkling with laughter. "Um, yum, grape."

She should swat him for his presumption, but she still trembled too much to make such an assertive move. The hollowness opening inside her as she looked up at him didn't help her case any. She read things in his eyes that shouldn't be there. She hadn't given him any right to look at her like that. He assumed too much.

"I'll behave," he promised, reading her expression all too well. "I'll be an angel of discretion. Just don't wave too many of your boyfriends in front of me, or I'm likely to take them apart. I didn't have any siblings, and I never learned to share."

Nina did swat him then, but JD dodged and left the room, still chuckling. She never knew how to take his teasing. Nobody had ever teased her before.

Apparently her mother and Nancy had entertained one another on the porch until JD broke up the little gab fest. They came back chattering about hairdressers, depressing Nina even more. She hated hairdressers. She'd rather chop her own hair until it reached a stage beyond control than go to a salon. But Helen and Nancy were the kind of women who'd grown up having their hair done every week. Her inadequacies were piling up woefully.

Nina tried entering the conversation while they discussed dinner, but when they began exchanging recipes, she gave up. She didn't have recipes. She just threw things in a pot and cooked. She felt like a stranger in her own kitchen as her mother and JD's ex-wife rummaged through the refrigerator and pantry, exploring possibilities, ignoring Nina's timid suggestions. Obviously intent on impressing the men, they debated a meal that would take an afternoon to cook. Nina had better things to do than play one-upmanship with professionals.

Jackie found her some time later in the greenhouse. The slowly rotating fans created a small breeze, driving out some of the humidity, but perspiration still poured down Nina's forehead as she fed fertilizer to the newly transplanted geraniums. She smiled at Jackie, feeling comfortable for the first time that day.

"You look wiped, kid. Sit in front of the fan and cool off."

Jackie did as told, inching his skinny jean-clad bottom over a rough table to sit directly in front of one of the huge fans. "Is my Mom gonna let me stay?" he asked without preamble.

"I'm betting she'll do almost anything you ask." Nina smiled and handed Jackie a watering can. "While you're up there, water that fern, will you? Do you want to stay?"

He clambered onto the table without complaint, reaching to water the granddaddy fern. "It's a lot more fun here than back at my grandfather's. He never wants to do anything, and there's no place fun to go."

"That's because you've seen it all before and this is different. You'll get bored here after a while, too. But JD will think of things you can do, I imagine."

Jackie nodded eagerly. "He's cool, isn't he? I mean, for a dad and all. None of my friends have dads who ride motorcycles or play computer games."

"Yeah, well, I imagine your friends' dads have other advantages," Nina replied dryly. "That's enough water. When it starts dripping out the bottom, it's wet clear through."

Jackie jumped down again. "Who do you think that man was I found in the lake?"

The abrupt change of subject didn't startle her. Teenage minds worked like the videos they watched on MTV, hopping around like Mexican jumping beans. She shrugged in answer. "Maybe some tourist fishing alone whose boat sank. Maybe a worker from one of the barges. It could be anyone."

Jackie settled in front of the fan again. "Nah. He wore one of those long-sleeved white business shirts like my granddad wears to work. Tourists and bargemen don't dress like that."

No, she couldn't say that they did. The news made her uneasy, but Nina didn't pursue it. She had enough on her mind without worrying about the sheriff's problems. "Well, we'll let Sheriff Hoyt take care of it. What are your father and Mr. MacTavish doing now?"

"They've got all the fuses pulled, and the stove and refrigerator and all the lights are out. My mom and your mom went into Hopkinsville to get some KFC."

Nina giggled at that. So much for superwomen. Maybe, just once in a while, life smiled on her.

Long after Nancy and Jimmy had driven off in the little red Geo, JD found Nina sitting in the darkness of the porch swing, idly pushing herself back and forth. Nancy's decision to leave Jackie with him had unnerved and delighted JD at the same time. People usually didn't express that kind of confidence in him. He thought a lot of Nancy's confidence had to do with Nina. And maybe, a little to do with Jimmy. He had been in a hurry to get back to the better-known environs of LA and the production of the program. Neither of them would rest comfortably until the copyright had been filed. Harry could come out of hiding then, and all would be right with the world once more.

Riding the comfortable cloud of his successes, JD took the place beside Nina without asking, propping his arm along the seat back behind her. When she didn't object, he took over pushing duty.

"Your mother and Jackie are inside playing checkers," he said without prompting, reassuring her that they wouldn't immediately be disturbed. Sometimes, she appeared to be a sprite on the brink of vanishing at the sound of human voices. At least he'd finally reached a stage where she didn't jump and run when he appeared.

"She must have run out of boyfriends to entertain," Nina replied without inflection. "Or maybe she's just decided she prefers them young."

"That's a nasty crack. You have no idea how she's lived

these last years." JD didn't know why he defended the woman. It certainly had nothing to do with his upbringing. His father had taught him how to steal and lie, not how to behave like a gentleman. But he had nothing in particular against women, and his strength had always made defending the weak easy.

Beside him, Nina practically bristled with little porcupine quills. He had some inkling of the source of her frustration and anger, but there was nothing either of them could do about it. Her mother had as much right to live here as either of them. Probably more. He didn't know why he was getting involved. Maybe now that the program was done, he just needed new challenges.

He should take up the one Jimmy had presented him concerning his uncle Harry, but he had a nasty feeling he'd be in way over his head. He couldn't trade protecting Nina and his son for chasing Harry across the country. Chances were, Harry had gone to ground just as he had. He'd sent out some inquiries to Harry's usual bolt-holes. He'd wait and see what came of them first. This wouldn't be the first time Harry got in over his head—it was a Marshall family curse.

"My mother wants to sell the farm," Nina stated baldly. "She's here to get as much money out of the place as she can. If she had a truck, she'd probably start carting furniture off to sell to the antique stores."

JD thought that a mighty practical idea, but he'd never learned attachment to material things. Except maybe that picture book his mother had given him a few eons ago. If Nina felt the same way about her ratty old furniture as he did about the picture book, then he could understand some of her anger.

"How did the visit with your aunt go?"

Nina stiffened even more, if that was possible. "Hattie was alert when we arrived. Helen wanted to take her home right then. I talked her out of it, but she insisted on talking to Hattie's doctor when we got back here. I notice she never made the phone call."

"It's been a little hectic. Maybe she decided you knew best."

Nina gave an unpleasant snort but didn't reply.

JD pushed the swing and wished he could find a topic that would soften her just a little. He wanted to kiss her, but he figured with Nina in this mood, he would be lucky if she didn't take his head off. How did other men do it? How did they woo women who didn't want to be wooed? Or did everyone take the easy way out and let the women do the chasing these days? It sure was a lot healthier on a man's ego. JD had an aversion to rejection. He'd suffered enough of it in his life. He didn't need it from some slip of a woman who shouldn't mean anything to him.

That was the whole problem in a nutshell. For some reason beyond his comprehension, this woman *did* mean something to him. He'd always avoided sticking his neck out so some woman could chop it off, but with Nina, he was willing to take his chances.

If he had any brains at all, he'd walk away now, leave Nina alone, and spend his time with Jackie. But if he kept sitting here, empathizing with the anger boiling inside her, aching to hold her and fix her problems, he would have to make a move of some sort or he'd explode. He couldn't simply sit here and pretend they were no more than friends, that the chemistry between them wasn't so potent that it practically crackled like her bad wiring.

"I found a lawyer." His voice sounded sepulchral in the thick gloom among the squawks of the katydids and the croaks of the frogs down by the water. It was almost as if he could feel himself casting fate to the winds.

She jerked slightly, then looked at him. JD could see little of her expression in the darkness, so he doubted if she could see his either. That was a relief. He thought terror might be the predominant emotion at the moment.

"Have you called him?" she asked quietly.

"I have an appointment for tomorrow. Are you ready?"

She sighed and leaned her head against his shoulder. "I'll never be ready. Some things I just have to do."

JD gathered her against him as the implications of her statement shivered through him. He suspected he was one of those things she would just have to do. If she thought about it, she would run screaming in the opposite direction.

TWENTY-TWO

Wearing a hat against the baking heat of the morning sun, Nina spritzed the roses on Hattie's Hill with fungicide. The heat boiling her blood, however, had little to do with the sun and more to do with the woman behind her.

"I've asked Matt Horne to file a petition giving me Hattie's power of attorney," Helen continued her earlier conversation.

"Have you now? And did Matt mention that I've already filed the same?" Nina wished she could at least like this woman who'd given birth to her, but Helen had done everything possible to rub her the wrong way ever since she'd arrived last week. Nina suspected Helen wanted to make it impossible for her to stay in the same house, figuring possession was nine-tenths of the law. She certainly didn't know her daughter very well, if that was the case. Nina could outlast a revolution, if necessary.

"Well, then I guess the court will decide. I'm sorry if I've interrupted all your plans, Nina, but the fact remains that the land comes to me. I'm sure we can work out some arrangement."

"I doubt it seriously." Nina straightened and scanned the acres rolling all the way to the horizon. Tom had brought over his bulldozer and speeded up the clearing of the worst part of the undergrowth down by the creek. She could see Albert Herrington out there now, making more notes and testing the soil. As far as she knew, the nonprofit corporation papers hadn't been filed yet, and they had no money to pay the man, but he was here every day now. He apparently had a light summer class schedule.

Laddie Hancock's father had taken an interest one day when he'd been out with the boys, and he was over on the other side of the farm, chainsawing dead trees into firewood. Howard from the Piggly Wiggly had offered some maple saplings to line the front drive. Nina suspected his mother had made him do it, but she appreciated the offer just the same. The brilliant red and yellow of the maples would be a sight to see when they were grown. Albert had said they needed plantings for every season, and the maples worked nicely for autumn.

If Helen had her way, all these people were working for nothing, merely improving the land to bring Helen a higher price. Nina wondered if she should tell everyone that, but the project had taken off like wildfire, just as she'd feared. Everywhere she turned, people told her their excited plans for the influx of tourists the garden would surely bring. Everyone wanted to help. It had brought the town together in ways that no one had experienced before. If she disappointed them now, they might never work together the same way again. Maybe she could find another project they could work on before this one fell through.

Nina would rather believe JD's fancy lawyer could haul her mother across the coals. He hadn't made any promises. Like all lawyers, he spoke with caution, promising to research the issue, but Nina didn't hold out much hope. Considering the tax bill, the land must still be in Hattie's and Marietta's names. Since Helen was Marietta's only living child, it seemed logical that at least half the land belonged to Helen, as she'd said. Nina didn't like believing Hattie had left the other half to Helen, too, but she supposed there was logic in that also.

Sighing, she watched Ethel drag her bulky figure up the hill in her direction. Ethel's flowered cotton dress blew around her thick legs, making the climb even more difficult. Taking pity on the elderly woman, Nina started down the hill, leaving Helen to follow or not, as she would.

"Nina! I just had to tell you." Ethel stopped and caught her breath, holding her hand to her ample bosom as if she could press the air into her lungs. Flushed with the heat, she didn't belong out here, but Nina was in no position to tell her so. She merely led the way down the hill, toward the house and cooler air.

"My son said he can get a wholesale discount over in Tennessee on some of the plants you need. He'll truck them back himself if you and Mr. Herrington put together a plant list. He says it's mostly shrubs and trees, not flowers, but you'll need those, too, won't you?" Ethel asked eagerly.

They needed everything, including God's will and Lady Luck, but Nina didn't mention that. "That's marvelous, Ethel," she said as she led them into the relative coolness of the kitchen. JD's fan whirred efficiently overhead, drawing the heat up and out. She must admit the addition accomplished wonders.

As she poured the ubiquitous iced tea, she watched her mother settle into one of the kitchen chairs beside Ethel. Not once had Helen mentioned her plans to any of the townspeople. She merely gossiped cheerfully and led them down the yellow brick road. Nina thought it ironic that she had suspected JD of doing the same, but it was JD who was working the hardest to see her goals accomplished, while her mother undermined their every achievement like a gopher in a tulip bed.

As if Nina's thoughts had conjured him from thin air, JD appeared in the kitchen doorway. He still spent hours in front of the computer, but now he came out with his hands full of printouts with multiple sources of plants, price lists, and offers of help and encouragement from other botanical gardens across the country. The power of his computer amazed her, but she didn't tell him that. She spent a lot of time not telling a lot of people a lot of things, Nina mused idly as she poured another glass of tea.

JD triumphantly waved a stack of papers as he entered and brushed a mischievous kiss across Nina's cheek. He did it to annoy her, she knew. Every person in here probably thought they were sleeping together. But she disliked scenes, and his proprietary show of affection thumbed his nose at her mother, so she didn't object aloud. Besides, it kind of made her feel warm inside, as if he really thought of her with affection. Except for Hattie's occasional gruff words, Nina had never known that kind of casual approval. She definitely liked it a little too much.

She knew JD's *Music Man* behavior built a fantasy world she had no right to believe. She told herself she needed the crutch of his support temporarily, while she recovered from the blow of her mother's arrival and Hattie's betrayal.

But the fantasy seemed terribly real with the reassuring weight of JD's arm around her shoulders and the warmth of his gaze resting approvingly on her. She wanted the room to clear of all but the two of them so she could explore his kisses a little further. Aside from his proprietary behavior, he had treated her with complete circumspection this past week, just as he'd promised. Frustration had become as much a part of her life as breathing.

She didn't know what she would do without him. He kept the wheels of the garden operation rolling. Without JD, she'd still be sputtering instead of starting. She'd never known anyone with such enthusiasm and drive. She should be afraid of throwing away all Hattie's carefully taught lessons on caution. Instead, the joy and hope he fed her erased the bleakness and opened her eyes to a wide world she longed for yet feared entering.

She was definitely better off not examining how JD made her feel.

"A fax of the nonprofit papers," JD announced proudly, flinging the printouts onto the table. "The lawyer is mailing the originals, but he wants us to start rounding up a board of directors. Any suggestions, ladies?"

Ethel burbled her admiration as if she'd never known anyone who could start a corporation. Maybe she hadn't. Smiling at JD's uneasy sidestepping of the older woman's enthusiastic pats on his arm, Nina picked up a few pages and scanned them. She noticed her mother didn't jump right in and offer her help. Helen merely rummaged through the refrigerator and ignored them entirely.

Nina looked up and caught JD's gaze. He seemed as eager for her approval as any kid in her class. Odd, that she would think such a thing about a man who obviously thought he could accomplish anything he put his mind to. But he'd actually followed through on most of his promises so far. She couldn't withhold her gratitude forever.

"This is scary, JD," she whispered, so only he could hear. "It's getting a little too real." Dreams didn't come true. It wasn't possible, especially since she might not have the land or a house or the right to do anything, thanks to her so-called mother. But she couldn't rain on his parade, not when he'd worked so hard to give her what she wanted.

JD massaged her shoulder and threw the papers back to the table. "You know the old saying about being careful what you wish for, you just might get it. It's coming around, Nina. Are you ready?"

Yes. No. She didn't know. Her natural caution feared this whirlwind of activity but her desire for it was so strong that she couldn't combat her elation, and she grinned. "Are you jockeying for a board position?"

"I'm jockeying for a position, but the board has nothing to do with it," he murmured insinuatingly into her ear.

"Now, now, children. We have business to conduct here. I think we should ask Mr. Herrington and Mr. Hancock to be on the board. They've offered so much help, it seems fitting." Ethel chose that moment to turn on her church-lady officialdom and bring the meeting back to order.

Something in the combination of JD's encouraging words and Ethel's practicality gave Nina the courage to fling caution to the winds. She needed the garden plans to erase the bleakness and keep her going forward. If she didn't occupy her mind with the business of the garden, she'd spend her days worrying over Hattie and her mother and things over which she had no control. With luck, maybe things would go so far even her mother couldn't stop them. She needed to believe that somehow, despite all obstacles, the garden of her dreams would come true.

Besides, JD's warm words and looks were wearing her down. She knew he did it on purpose. She knew he would return to California one of these days and she'd never see him again. But she'd about reached the point where she purely didn't care. If she had only one opportunity for the kind of fling other women engaged in with some regularity, why shouldn't she grab it?

She knew why, of course, but she found it harder and harder to remember when JD stood close. Nina no longer saw him as the long-haired motorcycle thug or the glasses-wearing computer nerd, or any of the stereotypes she'd painted him with. She saw him as a man who wanted his son to know him, a man who carried out his promises, a man who had an oddly old-fashioned protective manner toward women. Or toward her, at least. That notion made her uneasy and excited at the same time. Once she disposed of caution, she had no anchor at all.

"I think you're right, Ethel. Maybe we should bring them in and have our first directors meeting now. And how about you, Ethel? You're good at organizing." Shaking off her personal problems, Nina dived into the more important ones. "How many directors do we need, JD?"

"The lawyer recommended at least six. People with an

interest in the outcome are a good idea." JD set down his tea and cast a questioning look at Nina. "Want me to go get them?"

Terrified, knowing every one of her plans could fall through if the land wasn't hers, Nina froze with uncertainty. "It's too soon," she finally responded. "We should wait and see. . . ."

JD caught her chin and forced her to look up at him. "Nothing ventured, nothing gained, remember. We're not doing anything irrevocable yet. We're just getting organized. We're showing our intent, Nina. Remember what the lawyer said?"

She damned well couldn't remember anything when he touched her like that. The warning thunk of a Coke bottle against the kitchen table brought her back swiftly enough. Jerking from JD's hold, Nina caught the wary expression on her mother's face and, with sudden resolve, nodded her agreement. "If you'll get Mr. Hancock, I'll get Albert. Maybe they can suggest others who might join us."

As she walked through the sweltering sunshine in the direction of the woods where she'd last seen the landscape designer, Nina knew she had never done anything so irresponsible in her entire life. She was committing an earnest, eager group of people to a project that had no funding and possibly no assets. And she was doing it to spite her mother. She must be insane. Could senility strike at the age of thirty?

Maybe it could. It didn't matter. Throwing out a lifetime of caution, Nina grabbed the opportunity JD offered.

She had a board of directors to organize.

Nina breathed a sigh of relief as the last of the newly formed board of directors of the Western Kentucky Botanical Garden Association drove down the driveway. Ethel meant well, but Nina hadn't been able to focus on paperwork once Helen had disappeared into the front room with the telephone. She couldn't trust her mother out of her sight for two minutes.

She wished JD had hung around, but he'd refused the honor

of joining the board. A tiny cynic in the back of her mind warned he'd refused the offer because he didn't want to sign his real name on any legal papers. But her weak side, the one obviously influenced by her frustrated libido, said he just wanted to take his son out fishing, as he'd promised. And of course, since one of these days he'd return to California, he didn't really belong on the board anyway.

Nina glanced up at the threatening sky. JD and Jackie had been gone for hours now. She had no idea if they were fishing close by or had rented a boat. She wished they would get home before the storm broke though.

A brisk wind blew through the treetops, and she cast another anxious glance at the clouds, watching for the greenish hue that often signaled hail or worse. She had insurance on the greenhouses, but the deductible was outrageous. She couldn't pay it if the storm destroyed the expensive glass panels. She should have used plastic. Stupid idea thinking the glass would be more attractive to tourists.

The wind whipped at her long skirt as she dashed around the house to fold up the patio chairs and haul them into the cellar stairwell. Surely JD had seen the storm coming and had made for shore by now. Even JD wouldn't risk Jackie's well-being by attempting to outrace a storm.

She couldn't very well go down to the dock to see for herself. That wouldn't bring them in any faster. Grateful she didn't have any animals to worry about, she tied down what she could, put away what she could carry, and ran inside just before the first fat drops of rain splatted against the rooftop.

Hauling the porch rocker into the front hall, Nina unplugged the television, and hesitated at the door of JD's room. The sharp crack of thunder overhead provided the impetus she needed. Breaking the barrier of his privacy, she flung open the door and hastily disconnected the computer equipment from its various outlets. Lightning had blown up Aunt Hattie's radio and fried her heating pad the last time she'd neglected this room. She didn't think computer equipment would fare any better.

She tried ignoring the rumpled state of JD's bedding and the assorted articles of clothing scattered about the room, but he'd made the room so definitely his own that it almost took her breath away. The quilted comforter that usually adorned the end of the bed now padded the kitchen chair JD had appropriated. His desk was actually the old-fashioned vanity Aunt Hattie had once covered with antique colored-glass perfume bottles. She didn't know where he'd moved the bottles, but a computer and printer now covered almost every inch of space. A denim shirt hung where Hattie's robe used to be, and a large pair of man's shoes occupied the place beneath the bed where fluffy slippers once resided.

Nina waited for a wave of anger or sorrow or some emotion to roll over her at the changes, but to her surprise, her spirits lifted at the sight. The hollow emptiness Hattie left behind had depressed her. JD had returned the room to vibrant life. That wasn't all JD had changed around here, but she wouldn't think about that either.

Carefully closing the door behind her, Nina hurried down the hall to the kitchen. She didn't have many electrical appliances, but she would unplug the toaster at least. The stove and refrigerator she couldn't move, but they'd always survived previous strikes, for whatever mysterious reason.

She hadn't seen her mother since the Western Kentucky Botanical Garden Association's first directors meeting. The official name gave her a kind of thrill, as if a name could make a dream become real. She shoved the excitement back into its box as soon as she walked into the dimly lit kitchen and saw her mother at the counter mixing a drink that included the contents of a whiskey bottle.

The sordidness of the scene repulsed her. Perhaps she had seen one too many movies about alcoholics and the evils of drink. Perhaps her Puritan upbringing had narrowed her mind.

The sight of a whiskey bottle where one had never sat before struck Nina even more forcefully than JD's masculine presence that first morning. The sight of her sophisticated mother lifting the alcohol-polluted glass to her lips shocked her worse.

Acknowledging Nina's frozen expression with a salute of the glass, Helen threw back a healthy swallow before returning the glass to the counter.

Hating her own rigidity, Nina forced herself to enter the room and unplug the toaster. The quart bottle of gleaming brown liquid glittered mockingly in the soft light from the stove hood. She had always preferred the shadowy light to the glare of the overhead lamp, but the shadows only made the scene more sinister.

"Aunt Hattie never allowed alcohol in the house." Nina tried not to sound disapproving, but the comment sounded just like her aunt. Disgusted with herself, she opened the refrigerator and grabbed a peach. She couldn't remember if she'd eaten supper. Probably not.

"Well, Hattie isn't here and I am, so get used to it." Carrying the bottle and the glass to the table, Helen sat down, crossed her stocking-clad legs, and pulled a cigarette from the case already lying there.

She was doing it on purpose, Nina told herself as she bit into the peach rather than say the first thing that came to mind. She had the urge to cram her mother's cigarette into the drink and heave them both into the storm, along with the woman who held them, but she hadn't the strength, physically or emotionally. She'd never truly known bitterness, but it roiled inside her now. The best thing she could do for both of them was go upstairs and get out of sight, but her newly formed rebellious streak kept her planted where she was. People had walked all over her once too often.

"Cigarettes are a fire hazard. The house isn't fully insured, and I can't afford higher premiums. As long as I'm paying the bills around here, I think I have a right to make the rules. Drink yourself into a stupor if you like, but put the cigarette out. I take my health and safety seriously, even if you never have."

Helen blew a smoke cloud and considered it briefly before stamping out the cigarette against the polished oak of the table. "That's the problem here, isn't it?" she said thoughtfully, not bothering to look at Nina as she spoke. "I never looked after you, so I have no business walking in on you now. It doesn't work that way, dear daughter."

"That is not the problem here, and you know it. It's not even the tip of the iceberg. We can let the lawyers solve the worst of it, but in the meantime, we need a few rules. No smoking is one of them." The declaration shocked Nina. She didn't know where it came from, but she didn't know herself very well anymore. She'd never laid down rules for JD, except for that one embarrassing scene the first day. JD had uncomplainingly adjusted to her habits as if he'd lived here all his life. She'd taken it for granted until now. She really should show her appreciation sometime.

"Rules won't make the real problem go away. You despise me, and you'll never give me a chance. You're just like my mother. The irony hasn't escaped me." Helen sipped more reasonably at her drink, finally turning her gaze in Nina's direction.

"It's a little difficult despising someone I don't know," Nina replied carefully, wiping the peach juice from her mouth with a paper napkin and heaving the remains in the trash. "In general, I don't like alcohol or drunks or adults who expose impressionable children to them. And while smokers can kill themselves all they like, I don't want the house burned down around my head or stunk up with secondhand smoke. And as long as we're being blunt, I have a fairly low opinion of parents who abandon their children. I realize there are occasionally circumstances beyond anyone's control, but I find it difficult believing that applies in your case."

Nina moved away from the refrigerator door and decided to get out of there before she lost all sense of propriety, but a sudden flash of light and crack of thunder directly overhead blew out the lights.

"Oh, shit," she heard Helen mutter. In silent agreement, Nina felt her way along the counter to the back door.

Although it was early evening, the storm had blotted out all remains of the setting sun. The security light had gone out with everything else, and only the lightning illuminated the swaying trees and pouring sheets of rain. Nina prayed Jackie and JD had found shelter. This was no weather for being near water.

Her mother echoed her thoughts. "Do you think your boyfriend and the kid had sense enough to get in?"

"He's not my boyfriend, and unless something happened, he has more than enough brains to come in out of the rain." Nina didn't like thinking about that "something." Evil villains in Mercedes took on a certain reality on a night like this.

"You damned well need a boyfriend," the woman behind her muttered. Nina could smell the scent of a match as she lit another cigarette. "You'll turn into a frustrated old woman like Hattie."

"Hattie's enjoyed a healthy, respectable life," Nina protested wearily. She'd had this argument with herself enough times lately to repeat it by rote. "She didn't need a man to make her whole."

Helen snorted. "Fat lot you know. My mother was the tight-laced one, not Hattie. My mother would have thrown me out in horror when I came up pregnant with you and had no husband to show for it. Had she been alive, she would have scratched my name out of the family Bible when I divorced Richard. But Hattie always understood. She might have despised men, but she knew all about them."

That didn't sound like a promising road to follow. Since the lights hadn't immediately come back on, Nina figured a wire must be down. She reached in the cabinet and brought out the oil lamp and matches.

"Aunt Hattie raised me to respect myself," Nina replied

without inflection. She really didn't want to start an argument over so foolish a subject. "She didn't despise men. She just didn't need them. She had everything she needed here. So do I."

Helen laughed harshly. "She must have decided she was such a failure at raising me, she'd better follow my mother's example. Hattie didn't need men because she had me, then you, to raise. And a classroom of kids every year, of course. Hattie liked raising things—dogs, cows, roses, trees, kids, anything. She liked controlling them, training them to suit herself. Except for the roses and trees, most of us got a little too unruly to suit her."

Nina hadn't grown unruly. Terrified Hattie would abandon her as her parents had, Nina had obeyed all Hattie's rules. She would have crawled on the ground and licked dirt if Hattie had asked it of her. Not liking that revelation about herself, Nina nervously adjusted the lamp wick.

Nina jumped as the jarring ring of the phone shattered a momentary silence between thunderclaps. Maybe it was JD.

Taking the lamp, she left her mother pouring another glass of whiskey in the dark and hurried down the hall. She grabbed the receiver on the third ring.

"Miss Toon?" an unfamiliar voice asked.

"Speaking." She set the lamp down and clenched her fingers in fear.

"This is Shady Grove Nursing Home. Your aunt passed away a few minutes ago."

TWENTY-THREE

JD winced as another jagged streak of lightning lit the horizon, but he judged the roll of thunder that followed to be at a sufficient distance for safety as he took the Harley into the turn at Hattie's Lane. He'd left Jackie with friends in town, but he couldn't leave Nina worrying about them. Briefly, he cursed rural telephones and their tendency to break down at the most inconvenient times, but he cursed out of habit. His mind was on the woman waiting in the house ahead.

He never thought about women. That he did now worried him as much as the weather. He didn't have time for worrying about anything other than Marshall Enterprises and the banking program Jimmy should have tested and submitted for copyright by now. The women who had floated through his life varied from necessary evils to inconsequential nuisances, but he'd seldom thought about them. They'd pretty well thought of themselves without his help.

But Nina was different. She didn't think of herself. She was so spaced out with her plants and garden and aunt and neighbors that she needed a keeper just to make sure she ate properly. He couldn't be that keeper. Hell, he'd be gone in a few weeks, and he had enough experience in long-distance love affairs to know they didn't work. But contemplating a casual affair with a woman as vulnerable as Nina nagged at his conscience.

So he'd better quit worrying about her and concentrate on Jackie instead. His son should have the attention and guidance he'd never had. That meant forging a relationship in a few short weeks that should have taken years to develop. He hadn't a clue how to go about it. Not any more than he had a clue what to do about Nina. Maybe he should steer clear of this relationship/commitment business altogether. What did he know about them, anyway? He'd never had a relationship in his life. What made him think he could raise a kid? And Nina . . .

Hell, he didn't know what he was doing with Nina. Building a botanical garden was a hell of a way of seducing a woman. He had his head screwed on crooked. He should be climbing in her bed and whispering sweet nothings in her ear, not setting up corporations and hiring lawyers. He'd be giving her ideas if he didn't watch out.

Hell, he was giving himself ideas.

Morosely, JD swung the motorcycle up the gravel drive, belatedly noting the absence of light from the old farmhouse. Damn, the electricity must have gone out. He hoped to hell it hadn't been a direct strike. His surge protector wasn't designed for that.

He roared to a halt in a flurry of gravel and mud. Forgetting his injured foot, he kicked the stand in place and yipped at the pain shooting up his leg. He hated being crippled. He'd never been sick in his life. Only Nina's concerned and admiring looks had kept him using the damned cane. He didn't have it with him now.

Grimacing as he hobbled up the porch steps worrying about his equipment, JD almost missed the huddled figure on the porch swing. As he caught sight of her out of the corner of his eye, his heart plummeted to his feet faster than his mind could kick in. He knew instinctively who it was, and knowing that, he could feel the pain and anguish emanating from her curled-up posture.

He had no experience comforting women. Had she been a man, he might have offered her a beer and a chance to talk. He wouldn't have to say anything, wouldn't have to find the proper words. Still, whether he knew what to do or not, he couldn't just walk away.

"Nina?" JD stopped hesitantly by the porch swing. When she didn't respond, he took the seat beside her. She was curled into such a tiny ball, it was like sitting beside a sleeping kitten. "What happened?"

He thought she shivered, but she didn't reply. Despite the storm, the air still held a humid heat, so she couldn't be cold. Hesitating to touch her in his drenched clothes, JD slid his arm along the back of the swing. "Your mother?" he asked tentatively, searching for clues.

She shook her head, then uncurled somewhat to rest against the seat back where he could caress her shoulder with his fingers. "Hattie," she murmured hollowly.

The emptiness of her voice shivered down JD's spine. Until this moment, he hadn't realized how much life and emotion Nina packed into her few chosen words. She seldom ranted or raved or talked to hear herself talk, but often her few words concealed a sly humor, a joy of living, an appreciation for her surroundings. He heard only emptiness now, and he knew what had happened.

He didn't know what to say. He'd buried his head in machines for so long that he couldn't communicate on any meaningful human level. He didn't think a stupid joke or a flattering phrase would work now. Those had been the extent of his social conversation for years. He couldn't order Nina to cheer up. He supposed he could mobilize a funeral without too much trouble. Maybe he should offer. But something unfamiliar gnawed at his insides, telling him that wasn't enough, not for Nina. Where was her damned mother?

"Oh, hell." Giving up on finding the right words, JD grabbed Nina in his arms, pulled her on his lap, and held her tightly. He rocked the swing with his foot and watched the lightning fade into the distance. "You knew it would come sometime, Nina," he said gruffly, then cursed himself for gross stupidity after the words blurted out.

She nodded against his chest. Her fingers curled in his wet shirt, and the warmth of them seared his skin. That wasn't all her touch heated. Sighing at the perversity of his wretched hormones, JD concentrated on her plight rather than his own. "Do you believe in an afterlife?" he asked idly, searching for a topic to divert his thoughts from the pressure of her rounded bottom against his thighs.

He thought she relaxed a fraction as she considered his question. Resting his head against the seat back, JD stared at the shadows on the porch ceiling. She couldn't weigh a hundred pounds soaking wet. He didn't think anyone or anything had ever felt so good in his arms. Maybe he should buy a dog if he was this damned deprived of companionship.

"I believe everyone has a soul," Nina whispered from somewhere below his chin, jarring him back to the moment.

"Yeah, I guess I believe that, too. I'm just not too certain I believe we all go to this place in the clouds and wear halos and wings." JD adjusted her more comfortably in his lap and was rewarded with her head on his shoulder.

"I don't think Aunt Hattie would much care for halos or wings," she murmured thoughtfully. "Sometimes, I think earth is hell, or at least some kind of purgatory we have to earn our way out of. But I don't know where we go from here."

"Maybe there's something to this reincarnation stuff. Maybe we keep coming back until we get it right." He'd really never thought about death much. He'd been estranged from his father too long even to notice his passing. But he'd read a bit over the years, and he liked this theory better than others.

"You don't think Hattie's right here, watching over us now? Her heart was in this house, you know."

"Maybe. But you wouldn't want her lingering here forever, would you? There's got to be a better place. And she had a lot of time to get ready for it. She might have passed right on over to the other side." JD relaxed and ran his hand up and down Nina's arms. Her voice had regained some of its liveliness. Maybe he'd helped a little. A small flicker of pride ignited inside him at the thought. Maybe he wasn't entirely hopeless. Maybe there was something to this reaching-out-and-touching-someone business.

"You may be right," Nina agreed slowly. "But I still think she would find some way of checking in. Hattie didn't like letting things go."

As if suddenly realizing where she was, Nina sat up, but JD tugged her back into his arms again. "It's nice out here. Don't go yet."

Obediently, she snuggled against his chest. JD rocked her until she slept. Then, reluctantly, he carried her into the house and up the stairs. There might be more to this reaching-out business than he realized, but he had a suspicion it was damned painful. Machines couldn't twist a man's guts into knots.

The odd peace Nina had found in JD's arms dissipated with the blistering dawn of the next day.

The phone rang so incessantly, she wished for another line just so she could call out. Word traveled fast in a small community. Those who hadn't heard about Hattie called about the garden. Both Matt Horne and JD's lawyer called, along with the newly appointed board of directors. Once Nina notified the funeral home, the sympathy calls began.

Helen got in her battered Cadillac and drove off, leaving Nina fending for herself, as usual. Perhaps it was for the best. She couldn't have borne speaking politely to her mother at a time like this.

As she sat at the telephone table in the hall, staring blankly at a framed daguerreotype of her great-great-grandmother before making the next call on her list, Nina looked up in surprise as JD slapped a coffee mug down beside her.

"You haven't eaten. I've fixed a fruit salad. Come and have some. I'll answer the phone while you eat."

She liked the idea of someone taking care of her entirely too well. She couldn't give in to the luxury of it. Shaking her head, she didn't even look up at him. She remembered how good JD's strong arms felt around her. She didn't have the strength right now for resisting temptation.

"Matt's pulled the power of attorney from the docket, but he wants Hattie's copy of the will. I have to search her desk for it."

JD caught Nina's shoulder as she stood, steering her toward the kitchen instead of the stairs. "I know what a will looks like. I'll look for it. Why in hell didn't he keep a copy?"

"Do lawyers keep copies?" she asked vaguely, too weary to fight. "Helen's down there with him now." She simply couldn't concentrate on legal niceties at a time like this. Hattie's death opened a gaping hole in her future, and she couldn't confront it yet.

JD's curse had a rather picturesque quality that almost made Nina smile. But the image of her mother in the position JD suggested seemed a little improbable, and she let it fade.

He shoved her into the kitchen chair in front of a bowl of cut-up peaches and strawberries. He'd used one of Hattie's cut-glass bowls from the china cabinet, the ones she saved for the entertaining they never did. Nina admired the prism of color created by the glass and the sunbeam from the window. If those bowls were hers, she'd use them every day.

But they weren't. They would go to Helen along with the house and the land and everything she'd worked for her entire life. She wouldn't even have a home anymore. If she thought about the town and their hope for a garden, she'd go looking for a gun for her head.

Too depressed to eat, she pushed a strawberry around with her spoon.

"Eat, or I'll feed you," JD commanded.

The phone rang again, and Nina started to rise. JD shoved her back in the chair. "Sit. I'll get it. And if that fruit isn't gone by the time I get back, I won't tell you if I find Hattie's will."

He strode off down the hall. Nina watched him go, admiring the straight set of JD's shoulders and the grace of his stride. He wasn't using his walking stick, she noticed.

She wondered how much they paid teachers in California. Would they accept a Kentucky teaching certificate? The idea of following JD to California was an insane one, born of desperation. The realization that it actually lifted her spirits for the first time today terrified her. JD had never given any indication that he wanted a permanent relationship. She shouldn't be thinking in such terms just because he'd held her for a little while.

That thought led down too many depressing paths, and Nina turned back to the fruit. It was too pretty to throw away. She nibbled at it until Ethel knocked on the back door, carrying a cake.

The day went from hectic to chaotic even with JD manning the phone. The regional newspaper heard about the garden and wanted to do a feature story. Distant relatives Nina hadn't seen in years called to ask about funeral arrangements. Tom returned with three more farmers, bulldozers, bushhogs, and trucks, and began clearing the bottomland. Jackie came home and took over the duty of answering the doors and collecting food, but Helen returned and sent him outside so she could entertain in the front room. JD reported he couldn't find anything resembling a will in Hattie's belongings, and Nina didn't have time to look.

She didn't even have time to mourn Hattie, she realized later that night as she stood in the drive, watching the last car drive away. She hadn't time even to begin figuring out what to do with her future. Maybe she'd better start packing her clothes and books before Helen claimed them, too.

JD caught her before she returned to the house and steered her toward the rose garden. "We need a minute to talk."

Nina shrugged him off. Everybody kept pushing her around, and she was damned tired of it. Angry over nothing, she stalked toward the rear of the house.

"The lawyer is filing a lien in your name against the property." Despite his injured foot, JD had no trouble keeping up with her, she noticed grumpily.

"How can he file a lien? On what basis?" At least legal talk could occupy her mind so she didn't have to think of anything else.

"On the basis of all the money you've spent on this place over the years. Even if a will is found, you'll have a claim against the estate. You need a list with approximate amounts. Accuracy isn't important. Just make it huge enough to prevent anyone from selling the place out from under you immediately."

"I haven't any idea how much I've spent. I've taught for eight years. Say I've had an average salary of twenty thousand dollars a year. We grew most of our food. The house is paid for. I paid the utilities, but they're not much. Almost my entire salary went toward taxes, insurance, maintaining the house, and expanding the gardens. Hattie's insurance covered most of her medical bills, and her pension paid her personal expenses. We lived simply. Do you have any idea how much that greenhouse alone cost?" Nina turned and stared at JD through the dusk.

He stopped and stared down at her. "Would a hundred-fifty-thousand-dollar lien pretty much cover the worth of this place?"

Something shaky churned inside her, but she nodded. "Pretty much. Farmland is cheap out here, and the house needs too much work to be worth much."

JD stroked her cheek, and Nina longed to lean into his

embrace, but she couldn't afford weakness right now. He dropped his hand as she stiffened and moved away.

"Then let Helen post all the for-sale signs she likes. Until a court settles the matter, she can't complete a sale without paying you first."

Nina felt an enormous burden fall from her shoulders. "It's that simple?" she asked in awe.

"For now. It's not a permanent solution. Unless we find Hattie's will, most of the property goes to your mother under Kentucky law, since her mother died intestate, too. A court will decide on the legitimacy of your lien. But the lawyer says that takes months, when and if your mother files suit for a judgment on the matter."

Nina nodded and wandered down the path between the rose beds. The tea roses filled the air with their heavy scent, and she drank it in as if smelling them for the first time.

"Matt has influence. He'll try to get the lien thrown out. Will it stop the phone company?"

"They're still working on that. Don't think about it now. Go to bed. Get some rest. You've had a rough day."

"Tomorrow's visitation. I'll have to sit down at the funeral home and listen to old women cry. Am I being selfish wishing I were a thousand miles away?"

In the dark, Nina could only sense JD walking in the shadows beside her, his hands in his pockets. She shouldn't cast these burdens on him. He was—for all intents and purposes—a stranger. But he was the only person she could talk to now that Hattie was gone. That was a terrible comment on her own life.

"No, you don't have a selfish bone in your body, Nina. You know your aunt's here, in these gardens, if she's anywhere at all. You'd be happier staying here, puttering in her roses. But instead, you'll go to the funeral home and help others with their grief. That's your nature. That's life."

Tears leaked from Nina's eyes, and she hastily brushed them

away. "Thank you. I haven't thanked you enough for everything you've done. I don't know what I would have done without you and Jackie. Why don't you take him down to Opryland or someplace for a few days, enjoy yourselves, instead of getting embroiled in all this? I can handle it now."

He halted on the path somewhere behind her. His voice came from a distance.

"We'll do that later. We'll keep out of your way these next few days. I'll see you in the morning."

Nina heard him limp away. She didn't think he'd been limping earlier. She wondered if she'd said something to hurt him. She couldn't imagine what. After all, he was only a tenant. He wouldn't be here long enough ever to qualify as a friend. She couldn't let herself think of him as anything more. That way led to disaster.

TWENTY-FOUR

The sun pouring through the high umbrella of the pin oaks scorched JD's back as he wielded the ax one more time and splintered the log into pieces. He knew he courted heat stroke out here, but the tension inside him needed violent physical release. Chopping wood seemed the safest activity.

He glanced over the yard to where Jackie hacked desultorily at the underbrush between the trees. Everyone had gone to the funeral service hours ago. He hadn't seen any reason for Jackie to attend. He'd planned on accompanying Nina, had even dressed for the occasion, but at the last minute, she'd told him it wasn't necessary. He hadn't known Hattie. Why should he go?

JD still didn't know why that brush-off had hurt. He didn't like attending funerals. She was right. He hadn't known Hattie. But for some idiot reason he'd thought Nina would appreciate his company. Stupid of him. She'd gotten what she needed from him. She didn't want any more than that. When would he learn people were like that?

He slammed the ax into another log. The month was almost shot. Maybe he should think about taking Jackie to Myrtle Beach after all. He didn't need the distraction of Nina and her gardens and her big, anguished eyes. Maybe he should go in and call Jimmy, see how business was coming along. He hadn't heard anything but the brief e-mail saying he'd arrived safely in L.A.

That thought led to the question about the still-unidentified body. The sheriff had said autopsies were performed in Louisville and took a long time, but there had been no reports of any missing persons. He didn't like leaving Nina with that question hanging.

He hadn't seen the Mercedes around lately either. Maybe it was all in his head. Paranoia erupted easily at times of stress. Nina probably thought him a crazy man. What did it matter what Nina thought?

"Hey, Dad, look!" Jackie stopped his idle weed-whacking and pointed in the direction of Hattie's Hill. "There's a truck full of pipes pulling in over there."

JD shaded his eyes with his hand and watched the flatbed pull off the road and onto the field. No one had apparently used that field in decades. The barbed-wire fence was almost completely buried under honeysuckle and wild roses. Whatever gate had once blocked the entrance had fallen off long ago. Only the mound over the roadside drainage ditch gave any indication that a drive once existed. Someone had recently bushhogged the tall grass out there, but no other work had been done to grade the entrance. The flatbed tilted slightly and halted just inside the fence.

Putting down the ax, JD glared at the truck's contents. He'd never watched the construction of one of those enormous steel-and-cable contraptions with which the cell phone people littered the countryside, but he'd wager that was just the sort of material they'd use. A uniformed man stepped down from the truck cab, confirming his suspicions.

"Those dirty, lousy, good-for-nothing . . ." Jaw tightening, JD glanced around, searching for the swiftest means of halting this invasion. He smiled grimly as his gaze alighted on the bulldozer Tom had left behind. He'd been spoiling for a fight. The phone company had just offered the opportunity.

"Jackie, go in and call the sheriff. Tell him the cell phone people are trespassing. Then start calling everyone you know and have them call everyone they know. Tell them to send people out here as soon as they get home from the funeral. Those damned thieves think they'll start while Nina's at the cemetery. I'll be damned if I'll let them."

Jackie watched as another flatbed halted on the road, this one laden with heavy equipment. "I don't know, Dad. It's gonna take time before anyone gets here. How will we stop them?"

"Don't worry about that. You just get on that telephone."

JD had never driven a bulldozer before, but he'd driven about everything else at one time or another. He had an affinity for machines. He figured he could at least move it forward. The devil inside him anticipated the battle with glee.

After the graveside services, Nina returned to the funeral home to pick up some of the potted plants people had sent. Knowing Hattie's love for flowers, many people had sent everything from giant scheffleras to blooming gardenias instead of the more traditional cut flowers. The bouquets had gone to the gravesite, but the potted plants would go home with her. They'd make a memorial more fitting than the cold stone monument she'd ordered.

With the seat down, she could crowd most of the plants into the hatchback. A truck would pick up the bigger ones. If she worried over the plants enough, she wouldn't think about Hattie's frail body in that miserable wooden coffin buried under six feet of soil. They should have been like Native Americans, the kind who buried their dead in trees, closer to God. That made a lot more sense than planting people in the ground.

Tears streaking down her cheeks, Nina drove carefully down the back roads toward home. Her mother had been at the service, piously applying a lace hanky to her lovely nose. She didn't know where Helen had gone afterward. She didn't care. The idea of living with that hypocrite until the estate was settled curdled her stomach, but she wouldn't give up Hattie's dream. She couldn't. It was all she had.

Her fingers clenched the steering wheel so hard she almost had to pry them loose as she rounded the bend and saw the traffic lining the road ahead. She braked the Camry and stared.

Pickups, battered Chevys and Fords, and tractors lined Hattie's Lane and the driveway to the house. Had they all come expecting some kind of reception after the service? That was crazy. Surely not. She'd never said any such thing. It wasn't the practice around here.

Her gaze drifted over the fields to the collection of heavy equipment the men had left behind the other day. She appreciated all their eagerness for the garden, but surely they hadn't come directly from the funeral to scrape off her fields. Still, there seemed to be an inordinate amount of activity around Hattie's Hill.

Parking the Camry behind a rusty station wagon, Nina rolled down the windows so the plants would have some air, then climbed out.

A bulldozer sat defiantly in front of Hattie's precious rose garden, the one that had begun their dreams of boxwood hedges, graceful arbors, and gravel paths. Their dreams had grown, but the rose garden on top of the only hill in the county was all the concrete evidence they had that they could carry them out. It was Hattie's pride and joy. And a bulldozer sat in front of it—parked facing away from the garden and toward the road, flanked by a bushhog and a combine. Had someone taken up equipment sales in her yard?

The crowd of people milling about almost verified that theory, except many of them still wore their suits and skirts from the funeral. As she squeezed between a Jeep and a semi cab parked on the far side of the road, Nina saw the scene more clearly.

A flatbed full of long pipes sat right inside her fence. Another flatbed with digging equipment blocked the gate entirely. The small logo emblazoned on both vehicles had a familiarity that twisted in Nina's gut. The cell phone people.

She wanted to turn and run.

She had no strength for a battle today. She'd just laid her aunt Hattie to rest, for pity's sake! Couldn't they leave a soul alone on a day like this?

Of course not. They assumed the property belonged to Helen, and she'd obviously made some deal for the right-of-way. They probably figured they could move now, in the confusion of Hattie's death, and eliminate the legal complications.

Furious tears stinging her eyes as they always did when forced into a confrontation, Nina strode up the hill and toward the crowd of people gathered between the two lines of vehicles. She wished for her shotgun. She couldn't argue right now. Her throat was clogged, and she couldn't think straight. She just wanted them all to go away and leave her alone. A shotgun would accomplish that faster than words.

Then she saw JD. Like a knight in shining armor, he rode the bulldozer as if it were his mighty steed, standing straight and tall in the stirrups, swinging his battle-ax and leading his troops. The sun glinted off the thick ebony of his ponytail and the bronzed breadth of his bare back as he waved a rolled-up paper like a sword. She couldn't hear his words from this distance, but they held his enemy in thrall. The cable men in their white shirts with their little blue embroidered nametags stared at him in consternation and no small amount of fear.

Friends and neighbors, their weathered faces grim and unsmiling, sat atop every piece of equipment they could gather in a short amount of time. Those without machinery held pitchforks and rifles, forming a solid line between the cable trucks and Hattie's roses. They didn't have to say a word. Their postures said it all. The tower would be built over their dead bodies.

Tears streaming so fast and thick that she could barely see, Nina stumbled over the rough ground in the direction of the battlefield. Though the sun shone hotly, she shivered inside, and her heart sobbed in tempo with the ragged gasps coming from her throat. The entire town had seen Hattie's dream, rallied behind it, and raced to the rescue. It might never do them any good, but on this day, it was like watching the sun rise after six months of darkness. She wanted to cry "glory, hallelujah," and laugh and hug them all.

The crowd parted to let her by. JD put down his ax when Nina climbed up on the dozer beside him. As she threw her arms around him, the crowd cheered and yelled. If he was the Music Man, this was the parade, and seventy-six trombones would start playing any moment now. She'd never felt so joyful in her entire life. JD's strong arm held her so tight, she knew she would never falter or fall again.

Shocked at this revelation, Nina hastily shoved it aside and turned to her friends and neighbors. Teachers who taught beside her at school, kids who had been in her classes, all had gathered around, and she grinned as her heart swelled. Caught on the flood tide of courage this turnout displayed, she could do anything. Catching the eye of the music teacher, Nina threw aside caution and gave in to impulse.

"Mine eyes have seen the glory of the coming of the Lord. . . ." Her voice trembled, but it carried. These people had just spent the morning singing hymns. They understood.

The music teacher caught the refrain first, her lovely contralto picking up on the first breeze they'd felt in days and carrying throughout the crowd.

"He is trampling out the vintage where the grapes of wrath are stored. . . ."

More voices joined in: deep bass ones, high childish ones. The song spread across the field with the breeze, growing larger, louder, more defiant. Women hugged, then joined hands.

Men laid down their weapons and wrapped their arms around the shoulders of their wives.

"Glory! Glory! Hallelujah!" rang across the field in such resounding chorus that surely even the clouds heard. A flock of quail squawked and soared to the heavens. Laughter broke out in the ranks as several of the cable men jumped nervously and eased toward their trucks.

The hallelujahs still rang loud and clear even as the phone trucks backed toward the road. Kids cheered and chased after them. The adults, tears of joy still streaking their cheeks, continued singing and hugging. They had won.

For now.

Sitting on the front porch steps, hugging herself, listening to the katydids and crickets sing, Nina held all that earlier joy inside, letting it fill the hollow places in her soul. Hattie had been there, she knew. Hattie had watched over them, egged them on, cherished the moment as much as Nina had. She hadn't lost Hattie. She would always be with her, singing songs and eating chocolate ice cream, smelling the roses in her garden. God bless Hattie, she murmured.

And God bless JD.

She'd changed from her Sunday clothes into jeans, but she could still smell the heat of him as he'd hugged her. The male musk and sweat had permanently imprinted themselves on her brain, as had the memory of his possessive grip when he'd grinned so proudly at her. She'd felt his pride with every cell in her body. No one had ever made her feel that way before. Hattie had occasionally patted her on the back and said "good work," but no one had made her feel that she was someone special, someone who counted, someone who was worth fighting for. All these new sensations swirled around in her head, and she couldn't untangle one from the other.

Nina just knew she wanted JD out here, sitting beside her, so she could explore her emotions more thoroughly. She knew they were dangerous, but she was feeling particularly brave tonight. For once in her life, maybe she could break out of this shell of fear and let her true desires emerge. Instead of keeping him at a distance as she'd done these last few days, maybe she could show JD how much she appreciated what he had done, how much she appreciated his friendship, how much she wanted that friendship to be something more.

The notion terrified her, but she was still riding high on a cloud of joy, believing that she could do anything.

She smiled as JD finally opened the screen door and stepped outside. They'd scarcely had a chance to talk all day. After the phone people left, everyone had lingered for cake and soft drinks. People had come and gone, changing clothes and coming back, working in the fields, hanging wire across the entrance to Hattie's Hill. JD had spent his time with the men, while Nina had spent most of hers in the kitchen with the women. That's the way things were done here. She hadn't minded. She'd rather enjoyed listening to the women sing JD's praises.

At supper he had seemed oddly quiet, and afterward, he had disappeared into his room, and she'd heard the clickety-clack of his computer keyboard. She'd thought once he finished his program, he had given up the computer, but she supposed he kept in touch with Jimmy and whoever worked with him back in California. She really should ask him more about the company he worked for, but the time had never seemed appropriate. Maybe she should ask now.

He didn't sit down.

Puzzled, Nina crooked her neck and looked up at him. "Is something wrong?"

A chill ran through her at the realization that her words echoed the ones he'd uttered the night Hattie died.

"I've got to go. I've booked flights for me and Jackie from Nashville tonight." He hesitated, then lowered himself to the step beside her. He didn't look at her. "I'm sorry, Nina. It's important, or I wouldn't leave like this."

The chill became something else, something colder that chased the joy away. She stared at his hawk-nosed profile. He couldn't go now, not when she'd just discovered how he made her feel, before he could teach her more. That was selfish of her. Concerned, she concentrated on JD. "Can you tell me? Can I help? You've done so much for me. . . ."

JD shook his head, and Nina noticed the band around his ponytail had come undone. She had the urge to run her fingers through his hair and smooth it back. She supposed California employers didn't care if their employees looked like hoodlums.

"It's nothing you can do. Jimmy's having a problem with the copyright. There's something wrong, and I can't handle it without going back. I'm sending Jackie home to his mother. Maybe everything will work out, and we can come back for a few weeks before the summer ends."

No, he wouldn't. Nina could feel it in her bones. No one ever came back here once they left. This was Nowheresville; she knew that.

All Nina's newly discovered bravery fled, but she forced herself to touch his arm, hoping JD would look at her. He didn't. "Will you stay in touch? I can't begin to thank you for what you did today. There're so many things I want to say. . . ." And so many things she couldn't say if he left her like this. Her heart ached with the burden of words longing to escape. If she said them, would he stay? Or run as fast as he could the other way? Experience had taught her the latter, and, biting her lip, she let caution prevail.

He turned then, and the bleakness behind his eyes shattered her soul. "You don't have to say anything, Nina. I enjoyed it. I wish I could stay. I'd say you made me feel at home, but I've never really had a home, so I probably don't know what I'm talking about. I'll leave my card on the desk in case you need me for anything. The papers on the garden are all filed, and the lawyers know more than I do. I'll probably be busy for a while, but I'd like to hear how things work out. If you get in a bind, give me a call."

Such cool, polite words. Nina removed her hand and blinked back the tears. He was right, of course. They led completely different lives. She'd known this would happen sooner or later. She'd just counted on it being much, *much* later. But he was telling her the project was all hers now. He was out of here. They would never explore whatever had been between them. Perhaps it was better that way, before she hurt herself too badly with fantasies of what would never be. In the real world as she knew it, they would write occasionally, exchange Christmas cards, and it would never be like this again.

For the first time in her life she'd met a man she could talk to, but he had better things to do than talk to her. That made sense, she supposed.

She didn't want to let him get away, though. She'd thought, there for a while, that he'd felt something for her. Maybe it was just a passing fancy, a moment's boredom, but she'd thought there'd been *something*.

Summoning what little courage remained, she tugged his sleeve. "Kiss me before you go?"

She tasted the regret as soon as his lips touched hers.

TWENTY-FIVE

"Look, Jackie, I'll make this up to you first chance I get." They stood outside the Phoenix rental car agency waiting for their car. "I promise. But if I don't do this now, I'll let a whole lot of people down besides you. Do you understand?"

Jackie gave him one of those sullen, resentful looks only a teenager could make, but he nodded grudgingly. JD had an urge to brush the mop of long hair back from his son's face, but he couldn't treat Jackie like a little kid. It would have been nice if he could have babied him once in a while, but he'd forfeited that right sixteen years ago. That knowledge would remain an ache inside him for the rest of his life, but looking backward was pointless. The issues they faced now were adult ones.

"What about Miss Toon? Are we gonna see her again? I promised Laddie I'd show him the fishing hole we found."

JD couldn't even think about Nina. Wouldn't. It confused the issue too much. He hurt in so many different places, he couldn't distinguish one pain from another, and he'd never been good with pain. For one brief moment, he'd thought he'd seen anguish in her eyes when he'd said his good-byes. Surely he hadn't put it there. She'd made it perfectly clear he was no more than a distraction from her problems. She certainly didn't need his problems added to hers. He was saving her grief, not causing it.

JD took a gulp of desert air and pushed Jackie into the rental car when it arrived. "We'll cross that bridge when we get to it," he promised. If he lived to get to it, he added mentally.

The day of Hattie's funeral, Sheriff Hoyt had arrived with pictures of the corpse Jackie had found. The sheriff hadn't needed to disturb Nina with the gory details. JD had recognized Harry's distinctive features instantly.

The grief sweeping over JD was as nothing to his fury. He meant to find the bastard who'd done this to a simple man like Harry, and then he'd send him to fry in hell.

Nina fingered the business card JD had left on the vanity he'd used as a computer desk: "JD Marshall, Chief Executive Officer, Marshall Enterprises." JD Marshall. Well, at least she knew who he was now, even if she didn't know what Marshall Enterprises was. It scarcely mattered. He hadn't called, and he'd left over a week ago.

She didn't know why she worried. She'd never thought of JD as a busy executive, but she supposed she should have. He'd dropped enough clues. No mere employee worked as hard as he did or took weeks away from his job and worked anyway. Why hadn't that occurred to her before? JD obviously knew his way around the business world. He could take care of himself. And a man like that wouldn't even think of a nobody like her once he'd returned to his own realm.

Still, she couldn't believe the long-haired motorcycle rebel she'd seen in him, the concerned father, or the man who had rocked her to sleep the night Hattie died—the one who had stood on a bulldozer and defied the establishment—could so callously forget that she existed. If she had a little courage, she would call this phone number on the card and make certain he'd arrived safely. But she had no courage. It had departed with JD.

Irritated with herself at that thought, Nina stuffed the card in her pocket and wandered toward the front room. The temperature had already zoomed to unbearable, but she'd watered everything early this morning when she couldn't sleep. Normally, she would work on the plans for the garden at this time of day, staying inside until the heat dipped later in the afternoon, but if she stayed inside much longer, she'd have to talk to her mother.

She couldn't talk to her mother. They'd reached an armed truce after the debacle of the phone company war. Nothing like suing your own mother to generate goodwill, but JD's lawyer had said that's what it might come to. She'd given the man the thousand dollars JD had paid her for rent as down payment on the legal battle to come. She didn't know where she'd find funds for the rest of his expenses. The lien she'd filed against the land was all that stood between her mother and the garden unless they located a will.

Nina glanced out the front window at the scattering of pickup trucks in the drive. Tom and the others still came over and worked whenever they had a break in their chores, but JD's departure had taken a little of the hope out of the enterprise. They knew an effort like this took money, and none of them had it. They didn't even know where to get it. Ethel had a nephew at TVA who was going to ask for industry donations, but it seemed pretty far-fetched to believe anyone would contribute to a private venture.

The phone rang, and Nina ambled over to answer it. She didn't have much heart for answering questions these days. She almost wished school would start so she could shake this monumental black cloud hanging over her head.

"Miss Toon?"

The voice sounded vaguely familiar, but Nina couldn't immediately place it. "Yes?"

"This is Jimmy MacTavish. Is JD still there?"

Alarm shot through her so fast, Nina almost dropped the

receiver. Clutching it with both hands, she waited for her heart to stop racing before answering. "He left days ago, Jimmy. He said there was some emergency back there. He and Jackie flew out of Nashville on Tuesday."

The silence that followed jangled more alarms in her head.

"I've talked with Nancy. JD brought Jackie home Tuesday evening. I thought maybe he'd just gone back there instead of coming here. I'm sorry to have bothered you."

"No, wait! Did Nancy say whether JD was flying out of Arizona? He left the motorcycle and your truck here, so he doesn't have any other transportation."

"She said he rented a car at the airport. Maybe he's at home and not answering the phone."

"Jimmy, let me know what you find out. He seemed awfully quiet when he left here, but I thought he was just worrying about that program." Nina clung to the receiver, unwilling to break this tentative connection with JD's world. Her overdeveloped sense of disaster was spinning out of control.

"He's right to worry about the program. Someone's already marketing it. I'm afraid he's done something crazy like going after his uncle Harry's friends."

That made little sense in the normal run of things, but Nina understood it in some vague manner. Shaking now, she stared at the daguerreotype of her pioneer ancestor. "Call me as soon as you check JD's house. I'm calling the sheriff. If you can't find him, maybe you should call the police out there."

She could tell by the way Jimmy said his farewells that he thought she'd gone off the deep end, but she couldn't explain her eerie prescience, not even to herself. She'd never tried explaining how she knew a plant was sick or a machine was about to die. She certainly couldn't explain how she knew JD was in big trouble. It could just be her worrywart gene kicking into action. But she couldn't ignore it, not any longer.

As soon as she hung up with Jimmy, she called the sheriff's office. Hoyt was actually in for a change. "Hoyt, something's happened to JD," she said firmly, in her best teacher's no-nonsense voice. Sometimes, even when she said the most insane things, people listened to her if she spoke with authority.

"Something better not have happened to him," Hoyt replied grimly. "The state police still want to talk with him. He was supposed to call them days ago."

"The state police?" Alarm shot through her with treble force.

"Didn't he tell you? Remember that body they found down by your place?"

As if she could forget it. Capping her impatience, Nina forced herself to be calm. "Of course, Hoyt. What about it?"

"They couldn't ID it, so I brought a photo over Tuesday for you and JD to look at. I showed it to JD first, and he said not to bother showing it to you, that he could identify the body. Said it was his uncle Harry from Las Vegas. The police out there have confirmed that Harry Marshall hasn't been seen in weeks. I thought JD was a mite upset, and I didn't want to pursue the matter what with everything else going on at the time. But he promised to contact the police as soon as he checked things out for himself."

With her back to the wall, Nina slid down and sat on the floor, resting her forehead against her knees. "He's disappeared, Hoyt. Something bad's happened to JD. Did he tell you about the Mercedes?"

"What Mercedes?"

She told him about the car that had followed them around, and then told him that JD was certain the van that had wrecked his truck had done so deliberately. Hoyt didn't take her seriously.

"I'll look into it, Nina, but we never found that van, and it's kind of hard looking for a Mercedes without a license number. If you see it again, you let me know. And if you hear from JD, tell him to get his ass back here or give me good reason why."

Nina continued sitting on the floor after she hung up. If she had any real psychic abilities, she should be able to tune in to

JD and know where he was right now. But all she had was this sense of impending disaster. She swallowed and tried to force herself up, but not until her mother sauntered down the hall could she even raise her head.

"What the hell are you doing down there?"

So much for motherly concern. Sighing, Nina tilted her head until she could see her mother's lined and heavily made-up face. "Praying. Have you ever heard of the word?"

"Nonsense. You're not praying. Hattie never much believed in that stuff." Helen stood there awkwardly for a moment, then turned toward the front room. "I'm listing this place for sale. I'm signing the contract this afternoon."

"Fine." Nina pried herself from the floor. "What do you expect to get out of it? Fifty thousand, maybe? How long can you live on fifty thousand?" She couldn't even summon the energy for anger. She'd known this was coming. They'd never found a will. Hattie probably thought she'd live forever. The whole mess was in the hands of the lawyers. They'd be the only ones to profit. She had no idea how it would work out, but she couldn't care anymore. Finding JD was her priority now.

That errant thought startled her so much that Nina almost didn't hear her mother's reply.

"It's fifty more than I've got now." Helen took a seat and picked up her cigarettes from the end table. She'd defied Nina's edict about smoking ever since the funeral.

"Brilliant thinking, the same kind of thinking that got you where you are now, I suppose." Wearily, Nina leaned against the doorjamb. "You've got a house that's completely paid for, land that provides sufficient food for a family, and you're going to sell it and do what? Buy a house in the suburbs and starve? Rent an apartment and eat off the proceeds until they're gone?"

Helen shrugged. "The Realtor says we can divide it up into lots and make plenty."

Nina gave a sarcastic laugh. "You've been talking to George. He's been trying to sell lake lots for years. Unsuccessfully, I might add. People around here don't want them. The lake floods every spring, the roads are inaccessible in winter, and the mosquitoes eat you alive in summer. The only people fool enough to want property out this far are tourists who don't know any better. And even they have sense enough to look at the places that already have electricity and roads. If you haven't noticed, the for-sale signs have been on those lots so long that they've about faded away. You're kidding yourself if you think that land will bring you anything. The house is all you've got."

Helen smashed her cigarette into the ashtray. "This house is a museum, for God's sake! You've got no cable, the TV dates back thirty years, and your electricity won't fry a turkey. And I won't even consider the plumbing. This is a technological backwater, and I'm getting the hell out of here before I turn into a dinosaur like Hattie."

"Fine, then get the hell out of here. JD gave the town its first opportunity to be more than a speck on the map, and you'll swat it out before they even have a chance. I'd buy the place from you, but I doubt I could make mortgage payments and still pay the insurance, taxes, and utilities. Good luck finding anyone else."

Nina shifted her shoulder from the wall and headed for the stairs. She couldn't think about the house right now. JD had helped her when no one else would. JD had kissed her when no one else dared. He'd stood behind her like a tower of strength even as his own world crumbled. She'd seen the bleakness in his eyes that night, but she hadn't reached out to help him. She'd been too busy protecting herself. She should have known. She should have seen it. Like the teenagers in her classes, he hid behind that tough exterior. But she, of all people, should have seen beyond that thin facade to the injured man inside. Damn, but she was a fool.

She didn't have time to consider all the implications now. She'd have to stop in town and pick up a few supplies and some cash. She'd never flown anywhere before. She wasn't certain how to make travel arrangements. She'd ask Julia. Julia had run a travel agency for a few years, until it collapsed out of sheer inertia.

She didn't even stop and think about what she was doing. Maybe that was the secret to courage. One just did it. With her entire world splintering around her, she no longer had reason for caution. Without JD, the gardens didn't stand a chance. She could sue Helen, but what was the purpose? She'd just thrown her thousand dollars away in a wild hope that something would come of it. If that wasn't reckless, nothing else was. So why shouldn't she continue careening down this insane course JD had started? He'd been there for her. She would do the same for him. A no-brainer.

So Nina didn't think about it. She just took it one step at a time. She took her savings-account book out of her desk, stuffed it into her purse, and walked out to the car. There wasn't much purpose in saving for taxes and insurance anymore, anyway. Or for another greenhouse.

Don't think about it, she ordered herself as she swung the Camry out of the drive. Think about JD. Think about what the sheriff had said. Someone had killed JD's uncle. Think about what Jimmy had said. Someone was marketing JD's computer program. Someone had stolen his dream as Helen had stolen hers. But JD wouldn't take any of this lying down. JD would fight.

With any luck, JD had the money for fighting. She didn't. But somehow, she knew JD's fight had gone past the lawyers and money stage, into something far more dangerous. That's why he had been hiding out here in the backwater of nowhere. That's why the van had rammed him, and the Mercedes had followed him.

Industrial espionage!

The words flew into her head just as Nina hit the main street of town. She read the newspapers, watched the evening news.

The competition in the computer world was fierce. Innovation made or broke a company. JD had something a lot of people wanted. And it sounded as if someone had found him and got it out of him.

She didn't like that thought.

So, don't think about it, Nina reminded herself. One step at a time.

She stopped at the pharmacy and picked up travel-size shampoo and toothpaste. On second thought, she grabbed a cosmetic bag, too. She didn't have anything decent for traveling. Thank goodness she'd bought that rolling overnight bag when she'd gone with the kids on a weekend to Nashville. She'd had to go to Paducah to find that.

Ed was busy at the counter, so she just waved at him, paid the clerk, and started for the side door. Julia's house was just up the back street and down the road. She could walk.

The instant she reached for the handle of the glass door, Nina saw it—the Mercedes parked in the alley beside the store. Tinted glass prevented her from seeing inside, but just the sight of the car spun her thoughts into panic.

Easing away from the door, Nina glanced back at the pharmacy counter. The Mercedes was parked so its occupants could see the main street and her Camry, and not this side door. But she'd have to walk out not three feet from the car's trunk. If the driver turned and looked over his shoulder . . .

She couldn't take that chance. If JD feared the Mercedes, she would be wise to do so, also. She wouldn't entirely desert Hattie's teachings. Some caution should prevail, though she needed to discover a new dividing line between caution and recklessness.

Ed looked startled as Nina circled around the counter, held her fingers to her lips, and slipped into his supply room. She knew the building had a back door.

Ed followed her, protesting vehemently, probably protecting

his shelves of expensive drugs. Why couldn't she be dealing with simple criminals, ones who just wanted drugs?

"Ed, I'm avoiding someone, all right? I'm not stealing anything. Go back to your customer. And unless that Mercedes parked outside is yours, I wouldn't mention this to anyone or you may have some very unpleasant customers to deal with. Okay?"

"Nina, are you out of your mind? Wait . . ."

But she let herself out the door before she heard the rest of his protests.

The heat of the parking lot smacked Nina as she hurried through the blinding sunshine. She needed her hat. She'd have to remember to pack it.

Amazingly, energy sang through her veins at the thought. Doing something was a hell of a lot better than moping and worrying. She felt alive again—alive, as JD had made her feel alive.

Another something she wouldn't think about just now. She'd done entirely too much thinking in her lifetime. If she ever meant to have a life, she'd better start doing instead of thinking for a change.

Once safely through the parking lot, Nina cut across old man Rafferty's backyard and into the street of residences behind the shopping area. Julia lived just a few blocks over, and the huge old shade trees would prevent sunstroke.

Julia looked surprised to see her but let Nina in without question. Along with the travel agency, Julia had once taught at the high school, too. After her husband's death, the life insurance policy had given her the freedom to try anything she wanted.

"First, I need to use your phone." Familiar with Julia's house, Nina hurried toward the kitchen.

"Nina, have you been out in the sun too long? Here, let me get you a Coke."

Nina accepted the glass as the phone rang in the sheriff's office.

"Hoyt, the Mercedes is parked in the alley between the pharmacy and Joe's. I didn't get the license plate, I'm sorry. It kind of startled me, and I ran."

"Nina, I swear, if this is some sort of gag like the one the boys pulled last—"

"It's not a gag, Hoyt. I don't know what it is, but JD was afraid of that Mercedes. He went well out of his way to avoid it. It may be nothing. JD may have been a paranoid schizophrenic for all I know. I just know the blamed car followed me twice, and it's out there again. Do what you like, Hoyt."

Nina slammed down the receiver and caught Julia's stare. Taking another swig of the soft drink, she thought quickly and found no easy answers.

"Just don't ask, Julia, 'cause I don't know. I need to get to Las Vegas as quickly as possible. How do I do it?"

"Why Las Vegas?"

Nina stopped with her glass in midsip and considered the question. Why Las Vegas? JD was from Los Angeles. He'd last been seen in Arizona. But Hoyt had said JD's uncle Harry lived in Las Vegas. JD had gone there, she had no doubt. She was insane. Whatever JD had was contagious. She was spending her life savings on a wild-goose chase.

"I've just got to do it, Julia. Will you help me or not?"

"Well, if you want a cheap vacation, you chose the right spot. There're all kinds of inexpensive tour packages to Las Vegas. Of course, if you mean to gamble your savings for funds for that garden of yours, you'd better have your lucky rabbit's foot with you."

Julia strode into the dining parlor as she talked. Nina followed and gaped in amazement at the array of computer equipment distributed around the room. Had JD known about this place, he'd have moved in here.

"When did you get all this stuff?" Nina asked, but she half

knew the answer. Julia had no family, no children. She never used the formal dining room for meals. She'd just accumulated years of expensive toys in here.

"I got the big computer when I started the agency. I've still got the 800 hookup. I'll check on air packages for you."

"You can do that? On the computer?"

Julia sat down and switched on the set. "Sure. I can check times, availability, and book your tickets. I don't have the agency system anymore, but there's a new place on the Web that isn't much different."

Nina watched in awe as Julia drew up airline schedules, hotel packages, and car rentals. "Will you want a car?" Julia asked idly as she clicked her way through the selections.

"I don't know. Can I get a taxi from the airport?"

"Sure. I'll give you a list of the cheapest car rentals in case you change your mind."

A printer spit out a professional itinerary, listing flights, hotel confirmation numbers, prices. Nina's rising excitement took a nosedive when she read the figures, but it was only money. And Julia had said these were the cheapest rates.

"This hotel won't be some kind of dive, will it?" Nina had some experience in hotel rates, at least. This one seemed amazingly low.

"It's one of the best on the strip, with a four-star rating. You might get a back room with a view of the roof, but it's in the center of everything."

The center of everything. Las Vegas wasn't Madrid. She couldn't stand in the center of the street and yell for JD to come out and play as the kids did here. How the hell would she find him in a place like Vegas? She didn't even know if he was there. She had definitely lost her marbles.

But she couldn't stay here any longer. She couldn't listen to Helen's plans for selling her dream. She couldn't play hide-and-seek with a mysterious Mercedes forever. And she couldn't bear doing nothing when, for all she knew, JD had disappeared into cyberspace.

She could be sensible, though. She would call Jimmy MacTavish and tell him where she would be. Maybe by the time she got there, he'd have some word of JD, and she could just have the best and only vacation of her life instead.

Maybe she would play the slot machines and make her fortune.

Maybe she should just buy a lottery ticket and stay home.

TWENTY-SIX

The dry, hot air of Vegas didn't faze Nina as she rolled her one suitcase through the sliding glass doors and out to the taxi stand. Even the airport hadn't been the hectic, crowded experience she'd feared. The rather laid-back atmosphere had given her time to look around and adapt to her surroundings.

The taxis, however, terrified her. She'd heard all the horror stories about taxis. Admittedly, most of them had been about New York taxis, but the same rules could apply. She had little experience in dealing with rude people.

Taking a deep breath, she threw her suitcase into the first cab in line and named her hotel.

"Hey, I heard they got a great show in there," the driver informed her as the car squealed away from the curb. "You ain't one of the new performers, are ya? Ya look like one. A dancer, I bet. How do ya balance the fancy headdresses with all the feathers?"

Nina let out her breath and laughed at her silly fears. A dancer! A taxi driver thought she was a dancer and not some poky schoolteacher from the outback of nowhere. Marvelous! Maybe she'd take on a new persona. The foolishness hid some of her anxiety.

With the same kind of questions she used to draw out her

students, Nina had the talkative driver telling her everything he knew about Las Vegas. He told her who owned which hotels, which ones were reportedly Mafia, the best places to eat, the best shows to see, and how to increase her odds on the slots.

The wealth of information she acquired was cheaper than a guidebook, Nina decided as she handed the driver one of her few precious twenties when they reached the hotel. Julia had advised her not to bother with travelers' checks and to carry plenty of ones. If she thought of spending them as buying information instead of the exorbitant cost of traveling a few miles, she might not expire at the extravagance.

Palm trees and vivid gardens held Nina's attention as the taxi drove off, but before she'd looked her fill, a bellhop ran to claim her suitcase. Unwilling to lose sight of her bag, she chased after it—straight into the first circles of hell.

Bells clamored. Sirens screamed. Red, blue, and green lights flashed blindingly through a smoky dusk. Disoriented by the sensory bombardment, Nina staggered onward. Cascades of coins jangled into metal trays. Zombies in shorts and sequins manipulated flashing machines that whizzed and whirled so fast, her head spun just watching. Surely this was hell. These people couldn't really *want* to live like this.

She couldn't stand it. Panicking, Nina searched wildly for the bellhop, the lobby, any island of sanity in this swirl of sensation. Surely she'd landed in the devil's hands.

The bellhop led her to a room fastidiously decorated in southwestern colors. With the draperies closed against the afternoon sun and the air-conditioning blasting out cold air, it had the effect of an icy desert. Nina dug in her purse and handed the bellhop a dollar and breathed a sigh of relief as the door closed behind him. She needed time to reorient herself again.

She flipped a switch that lit the shiny chrome and tile bathroom. The huge mirror encompassing the wall over the sink reflected her haggard image, and she grimaced at it before surveying the counter. Hair dryer, coffeepot, a basket of little coffee, sugar, and creamer packets. What would they think of next? Everything glass-enclosed and hermetically sealed and electronically wired. Scary.

She picked through the basket of amenities, latching onto one called "aloe skin refresher." She was paying for all this luxury. She might as well take advantage of it. Patting the moisturizer on her face, she searched for the thermostat. A person could become a Popsicle in here.

She couldn't find the thermostat, but she found the room service menu. It fell open to a page listing the various wines and champagnes available. Just what she needed right now: a bucket of ice and champagne. Maybe she could add to her list of new experiences and get bombed. The idea almost appealed.

The telephone had enough buttons to fly an airplane. Discouraged, Nina flopped backward on the king-size bed, testing it for bounce. It had none. A flickering memory of JD leaning over her on a bed half this size drove her back to her feet again. JD would know how to use that phone to full effect. JD would know how to use the damned bed even better.

Damn, but she didn't want to think about that.

She escaped to the bathroom to make some sense of her image, but she wasn't certain it was worth the effort once she got there. She rested her forehead against the cool glass of the bathroom mirror and tried assembling the scattered remains of her brain. The exhausting cross-country flight, the sensory assault of the casino, and the strain of coping with so many new experiences had drained and exhausted her.

For the life of her, she couldn't remember why she'd come. She must have suffered a temporary bout of insanity. Was there any way she could scream "Stop the train, I want to get off"?

Maybe if she went back outside among the palm trees and the flowers, she could get her head back together again.

That thought brought a new spurt of energy. A vacation. She

just had to look at this as a vacation. She needed to throw off the shell of the woman she had been and return as the woman she wanted to be, as soon as she figured out who she wanted to be. A vacation was a good start. One step at a time.

Not acknowledging the myriad worries chasing through her overworked mind, Nina hurriedly discarded the wraparound skirt and blouse she'd traveled in. Julia had advised shorts and casual clothes. Nina didn't own many, and she figured her favorite bib jean shorts wouldn't look right in a city. So she'd packed a pretty pair of pastel blue cuffed shorts and a matching T-shirt she'd bought for the Opryland trip and hadn't worn since. Aunt Hattie had thought they looked nice.

The little frill at the neckline looked childish, and she didn't like exposing her legs so much in front of strangers, but Nina was beyond caring at the moment. She needed to be outside in the sun and out of the hellish gloom of the hotel. She decided right then and there that she didn't like air-conditioning. Hell wouldn't be fire. It would be the dark cold gloom of air-conditioned rooms without windows.

Outside by the pool, Nina took a deep breath of hot desert air and let the sun fry her head for a while. She'd forgotten her hat. She supposed she could charge one. It would make a nice souvenir. She'd be happier if she could take JD home as a souvenir. She shoved that thought aside.

There weren't sufficient trees and flowers around the pool to satisfy her craving for nature. She needed to brave the casino again so she could reach the oasis out front. She'd seen waterfalls and a lagoon when she arrived. They struck her as fairly incongruous on a city street, but she'd take what she could get.

She almost got lost in the casino again. The place was a giant maze built to suck in the unwary, and she feared being gobbled by giants if she didn't find the right path. She couldn't go anywhere without traversing the casino, and she couldn't get out of the casino without fighting glittering one-armed bandits and their zombie attendants. Maybe she could suggest a new computer game for JD.

She might live in a technological backwater. She might concede that some technology—like computers—had some useful purpose. She would never admit that the artificial environment of this hell served any purpose whatsoever. Why the devil would anyone live here? She had second and third thoughts about JD's uncle Harry.

Nina finally escaped the maze and walked out the glass doors into the sunshine of the parking lot. She didn't see any benches or walkways through the palm trees on the other side, but she would sit on the grass, if necessary.

In late afternoon, the area was relatively deserted. Nina perched on a wall beneath the shade of a palm and concentrated on ignoring the street traffic beyond the lagoon. Begonias and impatiens spilled over walls and out of containers everywhere she looked. Evidently the heat and lack of water made it difficult to grow much else.

In these more relaxed surroundings, she could think again. She'd called Jimmy before she'd left. He still hadn't heard from JD, but he'd been out to his house. Someone had broken in and ransacked the place. JD's partner hadn't been able to keep the worry out of his voice. So she wasn't the only one who saw disaster ahead.

JD was in trouble, and she had to find him. How she thought she could do that was beyond imagining right now. She could check with Jimmy and find out where JD's uncle Harry lived, but if JD was in trouble, he wouldn't hide anywhere so obvious.

Jimmy had mentioned some financier from Vegas who JD didn't trust. If Vegas had a library, she could search the news files on him. But more than anything, Nina wanted to find JD.

The emptiness yawning inside her at that realization caused gooseflesh despite the heat. She could hear JD's laughter as he called her a Ninatoon, see the set look on his face as he dumped cartons of beer cans in the lake, and feel the comfort of his arms around her as he swung her on the porch swing.

She missed him.

She had no business missing him. He could never be part of her life. With Hattie gone, she just needed someone, and JD had wandered in. It didn't mean anything. Couldn't mean anything, she acknowledged. No matter what she felt for JD, he'd made it apparent he didn't return the feelings, not to the extent she wished.

But he had helped her with the botanical garden, and she should return the favor. Maybe he didn't need her. Maybe she was imagining the look she'd seen in his eyes. The possibility terrified her, but she couldn't back down now. She'd take the risk of making a fool of herself. JD was more important than a blow to her barely existent self-esteem.

As she watched the tourists stroll by, Nina realized she looked like a cabbage in a tulip bed. She must have *hick* written all over her. She might as well have worn her bib overalls. They would have fit in better.

Perhaps for safety's sake, she should blend in with the crowd more.

The idea hit her then, sprang up full-blown from the deep dark recesses of her wayward mind.

Ninatoons.

It would work. If JD were still alive and in Vegas, it would work. She wouldn't consider any other alternative.

Sitting on a cot in the garage garret he currently inhabited, JD shoved a stray hank of hair from his face and cursed an innocuous advertisement tucked between the personals and the want ads in the classified section of the newspaper. *Ninatoons are here! Call for an appointment.*

He didn't recognize the phone number that followed, other than to know it was local.

Nina was in Vegas.

He would kill her.

He stared at the small black-and-white ad a little longer. She'd had it framed and given enough white space to stand out, but buried in the back pages. How many people besides him would notice it?

Too damned many. Dropping the paper, JD stood and paced the limited floor space of his hideaway, thinking furiously.

Maybe it wasn't her. Maybe everything just reminded him of her. He saw Nina's face in his sleep, saw those huge eyes filled with concern as she leaned over him in his overturned truck, saw her grief at her aunt's death, saw the lovely flush of her cheeks after he'd kissed her. He should never have kissed her. He knew better. Those wide innocent eyes of hers had drawn feelings out of him he hadn't known existed. Somehow, he just hadn't been able to resist.

And because he hadn't resisted, she was here now. Dammit all to hell! Wasn't it bad enough he'd left one woman raising a child alone, now he had to drag another into this dangerous fray he'd embarked on?

He didn't have to call that number.

He couldn't *not* call that number.

Tearing at his hair, JD cursed. He didn't have all the evidence he needed. He'd tapped DiFrancesco's phone lines and burglarized his office. He'd found a trail leading back to Marshall Enterprises, but he hadn't traced the trail to the name of the traitor in his own organization yet. And all the while he searched, Astrocomputer salesmen were combing the country, selling the promise of his banking program to banks nationwide.

Unless they had the version he'd given Jimmy, they couldn't have it in production yet. But if somehow—God forbid—they had the finished version, it was only a matter of time before the first test programs were out there. Sales up front counted the most because once the actual program was on the market, every computer company in the world would attempt to duplicate it. Astrocomputer was stealing those all-important first sales he needed to pay off the loan. He would be ruined.

Unless he caught the culprit, hauled him before a judge, and got those sales returned to Marshall Enterprises—before Harry's killers found him.

He didn't have time for Miss Nina Toon.

The thought of those big eyes taking in the decadent splendor of Las Vegas hit JD with the impact of a freight train. All the air went out of him.

What if DiFrancesco saw her ad? Surely his goons would have found out her name by now.

He couldn't chance it. He had to get Nina out of here—immediately, if not sooner.

Providing it was Nina and not his overactive paranoid imagination.

Jerking his hair into a rubber band, JD grabbed his motorcycle keys and took the outside steps two at a time. He'd opened a bank account here using one of his Kentucky checks, then taken almost all of it out in cash to buy the motorcycle and for living expenses. With Harry's death, the police would be all over the place by now. He didn't want them tracing checks and finding him until he was ready.

Damn Harry.

The ache in the part of JD's heart where his ne'er-do-well uncle had once resided hadn't stopped hurting since the sheriff had shown him the grisly photo. Harry hadn't deserved to die that way. Harry only wanted to be friends with everyone. Harry had chosen the wrong damned friends and discovered it a little too late.

He'd get revenge for Harry's death when this was done. He'd see DiFrancesco and his goons hung from the highest rafters. If JD believed in God, he'd believe He reserved a special place in hell for monsters who took advantage of another person's goodness. But he didn't believe, so he'd take care of the matter himself.

Right now, he had to take care of a certain Miss Nina Toon.

JD stopped at the nearest library branch, checked the city directory, and cursed at the address given for the phone number in the ad. Why hadn't she just built a billboard that spelled out "Here I am"?

He wished his veins didn't thrum with anticipation as he wheeled his bike back on the highway. It would make life much easier if he could just dismiss Nina as a fool woman who couldn't leave well enough alone.

Unfortunately, JD knew better. Miss Nina Toon, in her unworldly manner, thought she could rescue the world, or at least any small part of it she inhabited. He had stepped into her world and thus had become fair game.

The knowledge that Nina had come to his rescue made JD uncomfortable. He'd always taken care of himself. He didn't need anyone else. Somehow, he would make that clear to Miss Nina. Then he'd send her back where she belonged, back to that safe little glass ball of a world that he could admire from afar, the kind of secure place he'd never known.

JD parked his bike in the hotel's side lot and made a quick reconnaissance of likely hiding places. He knew the desk wouldn't give him Nina's room number without calling her first. Now that she'd announced her presence to all Vegas, DiFrancesco's men would probably be watching. He'd rather not give out his name. Besides, he thought it a little too risky seeing Nina again in a room where the main piece of furniture was a bed. He remembered all too clearly the last time he'd entered her bedroom. His pounding need for her had escalated to dangerous levels since then.

He chose the island of palm trees and flowers in the parking lot. He knew Nina well enough to know she couldn't resist walking through here every time she went in and out. JD could just see her frowning up at that palm with a brown frond, wrinkling her nose, and taking the tree's temperature to see if it was ill. She probably watered the impatiens when they wilted in the afternoon heat.

He had plenty of time to sit here, watching the passersby for a shock of white-blond hair, and contemplate life with a woman like Nina. She'd want a house in a field of flowers. Dust might coat every stick of furniture, but the garden would be spotless. Or bugless. Or whatever it was one did in gardens. A woman like Nina wouldn't even notice if he didn't come home on time. She would be so wrapped up in some project or another that she'd forget supper as often as he did.

Why had his mind taken this circuitous path? He should be plotting ways of getting Nina the hell out of here instead of daydreaming fantasies of what he could never have. He was a practical man. He knew his limitations. He knew from experience that no female in her right mind could tolerate his habits for long.

Nina had.

He'd lived with her an entire month, and she'd not once commented on his habit of working all night or complained about his trail of peanut butter crackers across the floor. He'd ignored her, yelled at her, laughed at her, and generally been his usual rotten self, and she'd taken it all in stride—with unnerving complacence, actually. Only his kisses had left her flustered and uncertain.

JD's nerves twitched at such wayward notions. He caught the glimpse of white-blond hair through the trees with a rush of relief. He'd get this over with quickly and be on his way. His life had too many other complications right now to add a commitment-minded female to it.

JD nearly panicked at his first view of Nina strolling around the far end of the lagoon, swinging a shopping bag. He stared. His heart played a timpani against his chest wall. He caught the nearest tree to keep his knees from buckling.

What the hell had she done to herself?

She'd left her hair spiked and unruly as ever, but that's all he recognized. JD rubbed his eyes to push them back into their sockets. Maybe he was just seeing Nina in some stranger with similar hair. Stupid thought. No one looked like Tinkerbell but Nina.

Some Tinkerbell.

Her gold lamé knit top clung to every lovely curve, and the V neck gave hints of a whale of a lot more. Shapely legs encased in skintight leggings were enhanced by the addition of three-inch spike-heeled sandals. As she drew closer, he could see she'd darkened her cinnamon lashes and done something to her eyes that made them look even bigger and more lustrous than ever. JD had never realized how sexy her walk was until he observed the full sway of her hips in those damned white pants. He had the urge to fling every man whose head swiveled at the sight into the lagoon.

Prying himself from the tree trunk, JD stepped into her path, grabbed her elbow before the flash of joy in her eyes unnerved him, and practically dragged her toward the hotel.

He'd have that talk with Miss Nina Toon in private.

TWENTY-SEVEN

Oh, God, he looked terrible. He looked glorious. He looked gloriously terrible.

Watching JD's unshaven face as he hauled her through the casino, Nina's heart thumped faster. Dark circles shadowed his eyes. His hair could use a good scrubbing. The set of his mouth made his nose look even longer. He appeared savage enough to melt a path through the rows of slot machines.

And her crazy heart sang a song of joy. JD was alive! She'd done it! She'd found him all by herself.

She must have been out of her mind even to look. This wasn't the gentle man who'd rocked her on the swing. This was the motorcycle hoodlum who looked capable of murder.

That's what she got for doing and not thinking. Aunt Hattie had been right all along. Men were dangerous and couldn't be trusted. Use extreme caution in their company.

That didn't keep Nina from leading JD straight to her room. If he meant to murder her, she wanted it done quietly.

When JD slammed the door behind them and they were alone at last, Nina couldn't stand it any longer. Wordlessly, she flung herself into his arms and covered his stubbly jaw with kisses.

He stiffened at first, but then a *whoosh* of air left him and he held her tight, hugging her so close she could scarcely breathe. She hadn't been wrong then. He did feel something for her. She would just have to pray it was more than lust.

"Dammit, Nina, you're gonna get us both killed. What the *hell* are you doing here?" JD demanded, dragging his hand through her hair and holding her still.

Her heart pounded in syncopation with his as they stood, clasped in each other's arms. Nina dug her fingers into JD's T-shirt and rested her head against his broad shoulder, letting the dangerous vibrations between them escalate a little further. She'd never felt anything like this in her life. She wouldn't let it go readily. She'd discovered she had a really nasty stubborn streak.

"Do you have any idea how many people you've terrified by disappearing like that?" she whispered against his neck.

"You and Jimmy," he scoffed. "And you wouldn't have known if Jimmy had kept his mouth shut."

"I knew." Nina pushed gently away so she could see his face. She thought she saw sorrow and disbelief there, but she could never be sure with JD. "I just needed Jimmy's call to push me in the right direction. I talked to Nancy a little while ago, and she's worried frantic. Jackie's done nothing but talk about you since he came home. She doesn't want you disappearing from their lives again."

JD looked tired as he released her and brushed a strand of hair behind her ear. "Don't bring them into this, Nina. I've never been real good with people. Get out of here and let me handle this my way. I know what I'm doing."

"I'm sure you do." Nina stepped away and kicked off the heels. She hated shoes. "On the other hand, the police don't. Know what you're doing, I mean. You should have called Hoyt when you got here."

"I'll explain it all to the police later. Look, Nina, you've got to get out of here." He didn't move from the door as she stalked around the room, methodically putting her new purchases in their proper places, none of which was the suitcase. She could sense his irritation as he glared at the skimpy dress she pulled from the sack and hung in the closet. "What the hell is that, anyway? Some kind of costume?"

"The taxi driver thought I looked like a dancer. I thought I'd fit in better if I dressed like one." Nina smoothed the practically nonexistent fabric of the minidress. Maybe clothes did make the woman. She already felt like a new person.

"You don't need to fit in here. You're going home." JD moved menacingly toward the center of the room, fists clenched at his sides, muscles tensing for a fight.

"This is a free country. You can't make me. I paid a lot of money to come out here, and I mean to see the sights. I've never been this far west before."

Nina rather enjoyed getting under JD's skin. She'd get even for those times he'd treated her like a convenient piece of furniture. She'd remind him that she had a mind of her own.

Of course, right now, he seemed more focused on her cleavage than her mind. Deliberately, she bent from the waist to pick up a hanger on the floor. Her new leggings pulled taut across her backside, and her short-sleeved top gaped wider. JD had a side view of both. When she stood up again, she thought he'd strangle.

He made a quick recovery. His black glare could have curdled milk. "Anyone could have seen that ridiculous ad. Do you think DiFrancesco's goons haven't discovered your name yet?"

"Oh! That reminds me." Barefoot, Nina padded across the carpet and opened the desk drawer, pulling out a file folder. "I made these copies at the library this morning. Your DiFrancesco has a lot of interesting connections. Did you know he's on the board of directors of Astrocomputer?"

JD swore under his breath as he grabbed the file folder. "Dillon should have known this. What do I pay the guy for?"

"*You* should have known it," she pointed out in all practicality, "but you were too anxious for the money to look any further. Caution isn't precisely your byword."

JD flung the folder aside and glared. "Where did you get all this information?"

Nina gave him her best beatific smile. "I ask questions."

Obviously intending intimidation, JD caught his hand in her hair again. With the heels off, she stood considerably shorter than earlier. Nina knew the second his gaze drifted downward. Throwing her shoulders back, she gave him a good look. She'd hidden behind bulky clothes all her life because they made her feel safe, invisible. She didn't like teenage boys staring at her. But she wanted JD to stare. She wanted him to more than stare, she finally admitted. She gave him a good long look at what he was throwing away.

"Seen enough, or do you want more?" She couldn't believe she'd asked that. She'd occasionally whipped her classroom into line with sarcasm. She'd never used it on a man in her life. She'd never done a damned lot of things. Now was as good a time as any to start, even if she was shaking in her . . . well, her bare feet.

Nina's breath caught as JD suddenly slid his hand under her knit top and boldly fondled her breast.

"You're not wearing a damned thing under here," he murmured in surprise.

Nina couldn't have answered had she wanted. Her knees jellied, and the pulse in her temple pounded so loud she thought she heard bells. JD caught her with one arm, but his other hand didn't halt its sensual explorations.

"Nina, fight me," he warned. "Quit looking at me like that and slap my face."

Her lips quirked at this nonsensical command. She had never imagined any man looking at her the way JD did, as if he could swallow her whole. At the same time, he looked so miserable Nina wanted to stroke his face and tell him everything would be all right. Finally, things were beginning to make some kind of crazy sense. What she felt for JD was a hell of a lot more than friendship.

"Give me a minute," she agreed, although she was none too sure of that estimate. Her heart pounded so rapidly she thought she might be having an attack of some sort. "You just have to make up your mind what you want to do with me."

That startled him. Reluctantly, JD dragged his gaze upward, but his hand retained firm possession of her breast. Nina thought she might faint with the pleasure of it. She didn't want him to move his hand—ever. As his thumb flicked over her nipple, she closed her eyes and bit back an embarrassing need to moan.

"Do with you?" He seemed genuinely puzzled, as if awakened from a deep sleep and not certain where he was. "If you don't get on the next flight out of here, I think I might strangle you."

"Not precisely the answer I was aiming for." Keeping her eyes closed, Nina memorized the sensations of JD's muscular chest beneath her palms, the harsh brush of his jeans against her bare stomach, the strong fingers biting into her flesh. She might never feel this way again, so she needed the memory for her dreams.

"Let go, JD," she warned quietly. "If you're not going to finish what you've started, then have the decency to let me go."

He crushed her a little tighter, but she kept her eyes closed so she couldn't see his face. When he released her, she nearly fell at his feet.

"Leave, Nina," JD said, walking toward the door. "I don't need you."

That struck a ten-penny nail smack through her heart. Nina clenched her fists and retaliated in the only manner available—with honesty. "Maybe not, but I need you, and I'll not let anything happen to you if I can help it. I'm calling Jimmy as soon as you leave here."

JD halted with his hand on the knob and his head bowed.

"Don't, Nina. Don't do this to yourself. Go back to your June Cleaver life and forget about me. I'm not worth worrying over."

Nina bit back the harsh words burning her tongue. Maybe he really thought he wasn't worth worrying over. From what little she'd learned about his prior life, he hadn't exactly had a loving home. He'd practically raised himself. A man like that might have some mistaken illusion that he wasn't worth much. A man like that might need her more than he knew.

Hope and anxiety warred in Nina's breast at that revelation.

"I think that's my decision, JD," she said quietly. "I don't know what you're doing, but I can't leave here without doing what I can to help. We can do it together, or we can do it apart. Which will it be?"

"Damn, stubborn female . . ." JD swung his head and glared at her over his shoulder. "You have no idea—"

A knock on the door startled them both.

Nina raised her eyebrows questioningly. JD shook his head. Crossing her arms under her breasts, she held all her tightly strung nerves together until the intruder went away. Instead, the knock sounded louder.

"Miss Toon? Nina?"

Jimmy. JD jerked the door open, snatched Jimmy by the necktie, and hauled him into the room, slamming the door behind him.

"What the *hell* do you think you're doing here?" JD demanded harshly.

Jimmy straightened his necktie nervously, glancing at Nina over the obstacle of JD's shoulder. She shrugged and sat down on the edge of the bed, still holding herself together.

"Nina said she thought you were here, and I didn't want her getting into any trouble." Jimmy cleared his throat and gave JD's furious expression a nervous glance. "Nancy's out in the car. She wanted to help, too. Actually, she's been practicing the lecture she intends to give you all the way up here in the car."

JD shoved his hand through his hair and, defeated, turned toward Nina. "Now look what you've damned well done. Don't you have any idea how *dangerous* these guys are?"

"Then there's no reason for you to go against them alone. We're your *friends*, JD. You understood that concept well enough when you called in all my neighbors and fought the phone company. Why can't you accept it now?" Pushing down all the emotions and physical reactions JD stirred in her, Nina strove for reason. She couldn't help it if her voice still shook a little. Just looking at JD's taut, angry stance returned all the sensations he'd evoked earlier. Maybe he really didn't understand the concept of friends in relation to himself. The thought wounded her, and she clutched her fingers into fists so they wouldn't reach for him.

"I had a friend at BankOne call Astrocomputer." Jimmy jumped in before JD could present any further argument. "He talked to a salesman about the new program they're pushing. They claim it's in production and will be ready by September, but no one's seen a working version yet."

Steeling herself, Nina picked up the file JD had flung on the bed. "I don't have the computer access you do, but I've dug around and found financial reports on Astro. Remember, I teach accounting courses, JD. I can read financial statements. They have a serious cash-flow problem. They're way over-extended. My guess is that someone's calling due on their debts and Astro is trying to generate some cash to tide them over."

"So maybe they don't have the whole program, JD," Jimmy suggested cautiously, taking the file from Nina's hands and glancing through it. "Maybe they've got something and don't know what to do with it and they're just buying time while they figure it out."

"They're buying it over Harry's body," JD said through clenched teeth. "I want their heads. I want them locked up so long they'll rot before they ever get out."

An impatient rap at the door intruded. They exchanged glances, but Nina was the one who responded first. "Who is it?"

"Nancy. Is Jimmy still in there?"

JD grimaced, rolled his eyes, and stalked to the window, turning his back on the room and its occupants. Nina opened the door and let his ex-wife in.

"How's Jackie?" Nina asked, not knowing what else to say as Nancy passed her.

"He's fine. He's with my father," Nancy replied absently, her gaze traveling to the two men before returning politely to Nina.

"Jimmy shouldn't have left you out there in the heat. Should I send for some drinks?" Uncertain how else to behave in the emotionally charged atmosphere, Nina reverted to her Southern upbringing.

"Fine, give DiFrancesco's thugs an opportunity to come in here with an Uzi and mow us all down at once," JD commented from the window.

"He watches Sly Stallone movies, right?" Nina asked of no one in particular.

JD swung around. "Nina, this is serious! Harry's dead because of me. I don't want any other murders on my hands. The lot of you can get out now. It's me they want. I'm the only one who can crack the code on whatever part of the program they've got, and they know it. They won't shoot me, but they'll do whatever is necessary to get through you and at me."

"Fine, then we'll get at them through you." Not having any idea what she was talking about, Nina flopped down on the bed, crossed her legs, and let her mouth go where her mind dared not. "Jimmy, who had access to the program you brought back?"

Jimmy shrugged and shoved a chair toward Nancy. "JD hid it under a game program. I went in and transcribed it, but left it there. I made duplicate cartridges and put two in safety-deposit boxes at different banks. Then I took a copy and the transcription to our lawyer so he could start the legal processes. He keeps things like that in a safe. I've been playing with the copy on my drive so I could test it. My drive isn't hooked to a modem, and I've got it locked up with security devices. I don't think anyone could get in."

Nina glanced tentatively from Jimmy to JD. "Your lawyer?"

The two men exchanged glances, shrugged, and shook their heads. JD answered first. "Dillon's a dumquat. He can't even insert a disk into a drive. But he's handled the legal process on all our other software. He's experienced in that, if nothing else."

"I don't trust . . ." Nina and Nancy began in unison, then looked at each other and laughed.

"Lawyers." Nina grinned. "Can't you computer geniuses surf the net or something and find out more about your legal beagle? It seems to me there's a darned sight more information out there than either of you have bothered checking on."

"I can do that," Nancy answered softly. "I worked in a law office for a while. Do you want to see if there's some connection between this Dillon and anyone in particular?"

Nina thought JD looked properly bludgeoned into place. For a genius, he certainly had a lot to learn about people. With his hands in his jeans pockets, he paced up and down the length of the room, not looking at anyone. He wasn't about to accept with grace the fact that he was no longer alone.

Jimmy took on the task of explaining the Astro/DiFrancesco connection to Nancy, and neither of them paid attention to JD and Nina now. "The last I heard, the cell phone company was making some kind of deal with TVA to put the tower between the lakes," Nina murmured as JD lingered near the bed.

JD's head shot up, and for a moment, she saw a glimmer of pride. Then he glared toward the window again. "And your mother?" he asked.

Nina crossed her arms tighter. "She's listed the place for

sale. She has wild dreams of making fortunes on lakefront property."

"She can't sell it until you have your day in court," he reminded her, still not looking at her.

Nina didn't know if she could afford her day in court, but she didn't remind JD of that. He had troubles enough of his own. "Only time will tell. I think you should call Sheriff Hoyt, JD. The Mercedes was back in town when I left. He may have found out more by now. The police are on our side, you know."

That got his attention. Nina thought every muscle in JD's body stiffened as he finally met her gaze.

"Why the hell didn't you tell me that earlier?"

"When? While you were kissing me? Yelling at me? Walking out the door? Those aren't actions conducive to communication. Want to try talking now?"

"Dammit, Nina . . ."

Before he could elaborate, Jimmy interrupted. "Nancy and I are going to look for rooms. We'll let you know where we are as soon as we find some."

Before JD could protest, Jimmy pushed Nancy out the door and slammed it after them.

Defeated, he glared at Nina. "You won't leave either, will you?"

Silently, she shook her head. She could see the worry creasing JD's brow, but she couldn't leave, not even if her life depended on it. She'd never forgive herself if anything happened to him. She'd never forgive herself for putting this book away before she finished it. She wanted to see what would happen next, if there was any chance at all that something could come of whatever this was between them.

Giving a hefty sigh, JD stared blankly over her head. Then, with a shrug of resignation, he returned his gaze to her. This time, she saw the awakening heat in his eyes.

"All right. Go put on that skimpy little dress you had out earlier while I call Sheriff Hoyt."

Startled, Nina waited for explanation.

The corner of JD's mouth curled up in that reckless grin. "I'm taking you out to dinner and to see the lights of Vegas. You'll get your money's worth out of this vacation."

TWENTY-EIGHT

While Nina showered, JD ran down to the hotel shops and bought a clean shirt. He returned just in time to catch Nina as she stepped out of the bathroom in her new minidress. He thought his eyes probably spun in their sockets like the slot machines downstairs as he took in all that leggy magnificence.

"Maybe we shouldn't go out," he murmured thickly, while visions of what he'd much rather do played an erotic film before his mind's eye.

JD caught the flicker of disappointment in her expression before she could politely agree with his asinine statement. Nina was too damned innocent even to know what he'd just suggested. That thought scared him, but as usual, he ignored the warning.

"I'm teasing. You look gorgeous, Nina. I'm afraid someone will steal you if I let you out in public."

To his delight, her cheeks colored, and a pleased smile flirted around the edges of her mouth before she returned to practicality.

"You thought I looked like a clown when you first saw me," she reminded him.

"Yeah, and I'd just been bashed over the head, if you remember correctly. Actually, I thought you looked lik those big-eyed waifs they used to paint on velvet," he countered, "but I hadn't seen you in anything that looked like this." He gave the clingy scrap of fabric another lecherous look, for his benefit as well as hers. "You have no idea what that dress does to a man's mind."

Or other parts of his body, but JD figured he'd given her enough to go on while he took his turn in the shower. He didn't dare leave Nina alone long enough to go back for fresh clothing and his shaving gear. She'd just have to take him as he was tonight. He'd show her around town, give her her money's worth, and put her on the midnight plane out of here. Or maybe the dawn one. He showered faster at that thought. Maybe he'd think more clearly once he got some physical release.

Finished, JD dried off, wrapped a towel around his hips, and, realizing he had no comb, stepped out of the bathroom and asked Nina if he could borrow hers.

She sat at the desk table writing all her charge receipts into a little notebook. At his question, she glanced up, and her eyes widened into saucers.

He'd forgotten he wore only a towel and that Nina wasn't quite as sophisticated as his usual women, but JD didn't regret his mistake. His grin broadened as the decided look of admiration in her eyes momentarily soothed his bruised self-esteem.

"Still want to go out tonight?" he taunted her recklessly.

She gulped, nodded, and pointed at the brush and comb on the dresser. JD wasn't fooled. He'd scared her half to death, but he'd damned well opened her schoolteacher eyes. If she meant to run around rescuing men, she'd best learn everything that entailed.

Taking the comb back to the bathroom, JD toweled his hair and dressed. Pulling his new shirt out of the bag, he slipped a [illegible] of other purchases into his back pocket. Now that she'd [illegible] world, JD considered the tables turned. Miss Nina [illegible]me fair game.

[illegible]ything as he came out straightening his

cuffs, but she had on her high-heeled sandals and wore eye shadow and mascara. For him. She'd dressed up for him. JD thought he might burst his shirt buttons.

"You know you're going home first thing tomorrow, don't you?" he warned as he took her arm and guided her from the room.

"No, I'm not," she replied mechanically, avoiding looking at him.

JD couldn't remember ever having quite this effect on a woman before, and it tickled him no end. Usually, the women he went out with criticized his hair, his lack of tie, his choice of shirt, even the places he took them. He could learn to like Nina's kind of acceptance. She hadn't even complained about his beard.

"I'll get you drunk and pour you on the plane," he threatened, only half jokingly, as they rode the elevator down.

That brought a flash of irritation from her lovely eyes. "I don't drink," she informed him.

"You will," he answered knowingly. "This is Las Vegas."

Staring at the garishly adorned, half-naked dancers on the stage, Nina sipped unthinkingly at the champagne JD poured for her. Rock music pounded through her veins like jungle drums. Flashing lights and alcohol sang a siren call in her brain. But she knew perfectly well most of her spinning senses were caused by the man across the table.

Her feelings went way beyond infatuation, she'd admitted long ago. She didn't know much about lust, but she had a decided feeling the excitement, pain, and sheer terror roiling inside her right now went beyond lust, too. The man across from her tied her insides into knots with just one look. Though JD hadn't shaved or dressed up, she thought him the most handsome man in here. Even Pierce Brosnan couldn't compare. If she thought about his kisses, or the way he'd conjured up her garden and chased away her personal dragons, she would most likely swoon at his feet.

She sneaked a peek at JD again. Instead of watching the nubile young dancers, he was nibbling on shrimp and watching her. He winked when he caught her look, and Nina considered throwing the shrimp at him. But he'd gone out and bought that shirt just for her. It had probably cost him a fortune in the hotel shop.

He didn't look like a man on the edge anymore. He wasn't a stranger either. She could read the look in his eyes, and instead of alarm bells, it rang a clarion of anticipation. He was just waiting for her to say the word.

After the dinner show, JD took her dancing. Unless school dances counted, she'd never gone dancing in her life. She wasn't a great dancer. Neither was he. But together—together, they somehow became something explosive.

"It's the champagne," Nina murmured as JD led her from the floor after a slow dance that nearly had her in flames.

He circled his hand at the small of her back. "No, it's not."

Nina scowled. "Must you argue with everything?"

"Not if you tell me you're ready to go."

The smoldering look in his eyes could have ignited kindling. Nina was much more flammable.

She had known it was coming. He'd made it clear enough all evening. She'd exceeded the bounds of propriety by chasing him out here. Aunt Hattie would have been horrified. Aunt Hattie had died a lonely old woman.

Of course, if Nina looked at this carefully, she could summon up her mother's bad-girl image and know the danger she courted. Helen had sought men and pleasure and had shirked responsibility all her life, and look where it landed her.

Nina had worked dutifully all her life, and she hadn't fared any better than Hattie or Helen. So to hell with it. She'd learn from her own experience for a change.

Nodding once, she picked up her purse from the table. "I'm ready."

JD seemed almost as stunned by her acquiescence as she was, but he recovered quickly. Throwing a bill onto the table, he guided her through the dark maze of chairs and into the casino beyond.

Walking through the flashing maze of lights, Nina tried ignoring the humming in her head. She blamed it on the champagne, the man beside her, the sensory overload. As they came in sight of the door to the outside world, she couldn't bear the noise anymore.

Grabbing JD's arm, Nina halted and pointed at a lone machine near the door. "What happens when one of those things breaks down?"

JD glanced at the flashing slot machine and furrowed his brow. "I don't know. I've never seen one break down." He shot her a quizzical look. "Why?"

"That one's humming."

Any other man would have brushed her comment aside and hurried her out of here. Nina understood the tension in the arm beneath her fingers, knew JD had focused on one thing and one thing alone, and it certainly wasn't on that mechanical one-armed bandit. She liked knowing she had his complete attention, even if it was all sexual. She liked it even better when—without questioning—he pulled a quarter from his pocket.

Dark eyes gleamed as he handed the coin to her. "All right, let's see what happens when a slot breaks down."

Delight washed through Nina as she took the coin and heard his acceptance. He understood. He believed her. She just hoped she wasn't about to make a fool of herself. But then, neither of them knew what happened when a machine broke. Maybe it didn't do anything. It was enough to know he accepted the potential.

Biting her bottom lip, Nina inserted the quarter in the slot, hesitated, then pulled the handle.

Lights blinked. Little pictures twirled. Cards flashed. And then the machine screamed.

Nina covered her ears as dozens of coins poured into the tray and onto the floor, and the machine kept screaming.

Or maybe she kept screaming. People crowded around, laughing, pointing, handing JD hats and cups to scoop up the change, yelling their advice and questions. Blinking in disbelief at the cascade of silver, Nina stood frozen.

The laughter in JD's eyes as he handed her the money returned her senses. She loved it when he laughed. She loved it that she had the ability to drive away his fears, if only briefly. She loved it that he had believed her without question. She loved him.

Dizzy from that discovery, Nina had no idea how they escaped the noisy casino. The sultry desert air of the Las Vegas night slapped her back to reality.

Fluorescent lights blinked and gleamed along the strip as far as the eye could see. In the distance, the volcano at the Mirage erupted, spewing a firework display of glittering embers. Earlier, Nina had laughed at the battling pirate ships, gasped in awe at the volcano, gawked like a kid at the circus acts. She'd seen enough glitz, played enough games. She wanted something more substantial.

JD's hand holding hers as he hailed a taxi was the grip she needed. Just the grasp of his fingers had a reassuring effect. Maybe the champagne made it easier to admit what he did to her, but Nina didn't think alcohol explained this sensation. It came from somewhere deep inside her, somewhere that had stayed empty and alone for too long, somewhere that grew warm and expectant when JD looked at her as he was doing now.

The hotel he gave the driver wasn't hers, and startled, she looked at him questioningly.

He brushed a finger across her lips. "I know a better place."

Nina relaxed and let him hold her. He wasn't putting her on an airplane yet. Maybe by morning, he would have accepted that she couldn't leave without him. She could hope, anyway. She just had to keep from thinking about what would happen between now and morning. The newfound knowledge of love made it easier and more difficult at the same time. She had to throw away everything she'd ever learned about caution before she could dive headfirst into this spinning cauldron of the unknown.

In the darkness of the taxi, JD brushed kisses across her hair and played dangerous games through the fabric of her dress, escalating the drums pounding in her veins, providing the oblivion she needed. Thriving on sensation and not thinking could be habit-forming.

The taxi rolled down a drive carved from a jungle. Nina gaped at the lantern-lit trees, hanging baskets, and flowering vines. Surely they'd found Eden.

Instead of the glare and blare of a casino when they entered the hotel, they walked through a tropical garden of calling birds and trickling water. Utterly fascinated by the lush greenery, Nina scarcely heard JD as he arranged for a room and picked up the card key. Soft music played from a nearby lounge. People wandered jungle paths in every direction. It was too surreal to comprehend in her current condition.

They took another path out of the main stream of traffic, into a quieter world. The music and the jungle fell behind them. JD pushed open a glass door, and they entered a new scene, this one of moonlight and fresh air, emerald lawns and garden beds.

"Better?" JD murmured, swinging her hand while she took in the view.

"Much better," she sighed. "Thank you. It's perfect."

"A real oasis," he agreed. "Are you sorry all those coins didn't turn to riches?"

Nina didn't think it was her winnings he questioned. He'd

converted them into a neat stack of twenties for her. It didn't cover the price of her vacation, but it came close. But what was bothering JD went beyond money.

She smiled and wrapped both hands around his arm. "I'm not sorry about anything."

"Good." He pressed a kiss to her hair and stepped into the moonlight.

They said nothing more as they followed the path to patio doors overlooking the garden. Nina bit her trembling lip as JD unlocked the door with his card. This was it then. She couldn't turn back now.

She didn't want to turn back now.

He made it so incredibly easy. He closed and locked the door, slipped the key in his pocket, and pulled her into his arms. It was that simple.

Nina closed her eyes and drank in the bliss of JD's mouth pressed to hers. Her lips parted, and she tasted the champagne and chocolate they'd eaten last. Her arms found a natural perch around his shoulders. Her fingers pulled at his long hair. Her hips cradled in the heat of his without once flinching at the pressure there.

Her useless gown slid to the floor, and she merely stepped out of it along with her shoes. She hadn't worn stockings. Thanks to JD, she didn't wear her bra or panties for long either.

The bed had already been turned down. Chilly linen caressed Nina's back as JD lowered her across the mattress. He hadn't pulled the light-concealing draperies, and moonlight shimmering through the sheers illuminated his bronzed shoulders as his shirt joined her dress on the floor. Again, she thought him the most handsome man in the world. He wasn't pretty. He wasn't even good-looking. But she loved the character of his sharp nose and jutting chin, loved the way his dark eyes gleamed when he looked at her, loved the way his muscles rippled beneath the dusky whorls of hair as he discarded the rest of his clothing.

She thought she'd be frightened when he came to her naked, but she wasn't. Excited, definitely. Nervous, a little. But not frightened. JD kissed her lips and cuddled her breast, and it all seemed as natural as rain on a spring day.

They didn't say much. They would only have argued if they had tried, as they had argued off and on all evening. Nina knew JD still expected her to leave. She didn't know what kind of women he'd known in the past who would leave him without a fight, but she wasn't one of them. He wouldn't accept that. Couldn't, maybe.

She figured he thought of this as a one-night stand, a casual encounter they both needed to slake their lusts. She didn't believe in casual sex. She didn't much believe in lust, either. She felt something powerful, admittedly, something that intensified and grew to the point of explosion as JD's fingers explored and discovered the sensitive secrets of her body. But it wasn't just his fingers or the heat of his kisses causing the ache inside her. Those were purely physical sensations. What she felt was connected to the man in the swing, the man at the computer, the man on the tractor, all the men she'd seen in him these past weeks.

So as she melted in his hands, stretched to accommodate him, and accepted the thickness invading her body, she accepted the whole man, not just his physical parts. No other man but John David Marshall could have fit beneath her heart so neatly.

The flashing lights and pounding drums exploded inside of her then, and she forgot to think at all.

Through the grogginess of utter exhaustion, JD recognized the slender curves pressed against his side as he lay on his back. If he'd had any doubt, the throbbing in that part of him over which he had no control verified his suspicions. He'd awakened like this every night for weeks, and only one female of his acquaintance could cause it. And apparently, one release wasn't enough, even one as explosive and mind-blowing as they'd shared last night.

He still couldn't believe it. He'd rather count program line numbers than think of what Nina had given him last night. Their lovemaking had been terrifying—and spectacular. In the past, he'd used sex the same way he used his gym equipment, as a physical release of tension. What Nina had given him last night no way in hell resembled the sex he'd known. The knowledge scared him. And made him hot all over. He wanted it again, wanted to see if it had been the alcohol or the music or anything but this slender woman blowing the gaskets of his mind. And he was afraid to find out.

Cursing silently as a small hand moved cautiously against his skin, JD sought reasons why he shouldn't do this again. He'd known Nina's relative innocence since the beginning, but he'd ignored the warnings. She'd told him how she'd grown up with the men in town and saw them only as boys. She'd told him she'd rushed home to her ailing aunt after classes at the university. He'd known she hadn't had much opportunity and would never accept casual sex. And he'd done it anyway.

He couldn't believe the mind-boggling pleasure she'd given him last night. He understood the pleasures of the flesh well enough. But Nina had given him something incredibly more, something his logical mind couldn't name, something that felt insanely primitive. Nina had given herself to him and to no one else. Triumph and male pride and a primal possessiveness figured into the equation, all emotions with which he had little acquaintance. He had lost his mind. He should try it again while entirely sober.

JD groaned and captured Nina's hand as it curled in the hairs on his chest. "I'll hurt you, Nina." He didn't even know if his warning meant physically or otherwise. Probably both. He wanted so damned much.

Her stroking hesitated. Then she freed her hand and began a teasing trek downward. "Shouldn't I be the judge of that?"

Hell, yes, he agreed silently, as certain parts of him jerked to complete attention. She was a grown woman. Why should he think he had to protect her against herself?

As JD turned on his side and found Nina's mouth with his, he wished she were a machine he could set aside in the morning. Machines, he could handle.

Nina had always wondered how she would feel the morning after. As a young girl, of course, she'd thought it would be after her wedding night. As she grew older and occasionally indulged in a romantic movie or two, she'd wondered and daydreamed a bit. Now she knew. She felt wonderful. And she ached like hell.

The steady desert sun already poured through the thin window sheers. They never had pulled the draperies closed. Between the sun and the heat of the man beside her, she didn't even notice the air-conditioning. She felt warm inside and out. She felt more than warm, but she wouldn't think about that. JD had warned her, and she took his warning seriously. She'd wanted to know what it would be like, and now she knew. She wouldn't expect more from a man who obviously had his own priorities.

Nina smiled as JD pushed himself up on one elbow and glared down at her. His beard stubble had grown thicker overnight, and his hair looked as tangled as hers probably did. Worse. Hers was shorter.

"Are you ready to start our argument where we left off last night?" she asked cheerfully.

His scowl made her smile broader. Somehow, she'd quit being frightened of anything JD did or said. Perhaps love did that. Maybe familiarity bred complacence. Or maybe it just bred knowledge. JD would never hurt her. He would argue until the moon turned blue, but he would listen to what she said. In return, she didn't scare him either. She couldn't put him off with her snide remarks or baffle him with her weird ways. They fought on even ground.

"When does your flight leave?"

"My, we're surly this morning. Too much champagne?" Daringly, Nina rubbed a finger down his prickly jaw.

She could feel his response against her hip. She was sore, but not that sore. She wriggled a little closer and heard his intake of breath. So, he had a few interests outside of computers. She could deal with that.

"Nina, just answer the question. I've got things to do, and I want you safe while I do them."

She batted her eyelashes outrageously. "Ohhh, the big strong hero will protect little ol' me. Well, you just go on and do what you have to do, and I'll do the same. Fair enough?"

"Nina, I swear . . ."

Deciding this argument constituted a waste of time, Nina wrapped her arms around JD's neck and put a halt to it. If she only had these few minutes left, she could find better use for them than arguing.

TWENTY-NINE

When Nina lagged behind him at the pool, JD glanced over his shoulder and saw her wince. Just that tiny grimace ground him into jelly. With any other woman, he would never have noticed. But watching Nina as she lingered over a fallen bougainvillea bract twisted heartstrings he hadn't known he possessed. If he hung around her much more, he'd start believing in the impossible. He had to remind himself that he only understood machines, not airheaded Tinkerbells who could woo plants into jungles.

He slowed his pace as she caught up with him. Perhaps part of this jangling joy careening along his nerve endings had something to do with a perfectly legitimate male need to conquer. He took an inexplicable pride in knowing he was the first man to teach Nina the things they had done last night. He supposed it wasn't precisely akin to the first step on the moon, but it felt close enough for him. After Nancy, he'd stuck with experienced women. Not one of them had ever made him feel the way Nina did.

They took the elevator up to her room, and protectively, JD held his arm across the doorway as he unlocked it with the key she'd given him. He had wanted to shove her on the first airplane out, but she'd insisted on returning for her clothes and luggage. Knowing Nina's limited finances, he'd reluctantly agreed. But this was DiFrancesco's town. He wouldn't trust anyone.

One glimpse of Nina's new clothes strewn across the carpet, her dresser ransacked, and her bed linen flung across the room warned of the evil within. JD firmly closed the door on the wreckage inside. "I'll call security. Come on."

Nina's startled-doe look didn't help his temper any. He didn't want her seeing the world's evils. He'd just discovered he preferred her refreshing innocence.

"You're safe, that's all that matters. They couldn't have found anything of importance," he said curtly.

"That file," she reminded him, accepting his authority without pushing past to see for herself. "They'll know I've been looking into Astrocomputer." She caught his arm. "How did they *know*?"

"I don't think they followed me, or they would have been after us last night. Probably the ad. I told you they'd know your name by now." JD found a house phone by the elevator and called the operator. Fury flowed through his veins, but he knew how to control and direct fury. DiFrancesco had breathed his last free breath.

Security appeared immediately. As they scanned the room and took notes, Nina hastily gathered her scattered clothing. The file folder had disappeared. Security didn't seem much impressed with the information. JD hadn't figured they would be.

Once they were out in the sunshine again, Nina's small travel case tucked safely in JD's grip, Nina stopped and glanced around at the brilliant flowers. "So, that's what it's like in the real world. I've never had a burglar before."

She'd been robbed of her innocence twice last night. JD ignored a pang of guilt. She'd made the choice to follow him. He'd done what he could to prevent it. He would prevent any further harm now by putting his wide-eyed schoolteacher on the first plane out of here. She belonged in never-never land, not here.

JD caught Nina's elbow with his free hand and steered her toward the parking lot. At least she'd changed into shorts; she could sit the motorcycle on the way to the airport.

"We'd better check on Jimmy and Nancy," she warned, following him without protest this time.

"Why?" JD knew he sounded surly, but somehow, he couldn't stop himself.

"The message light was blinking on the phone in my room. I checked with the operator, and they had a message giving Jimmy's hotel. He didn't leave his name, but I bet your friend will have checked it out."

Damn! JD held her suitcase while Nina climbed on the bike behind him. He'd had a one-track mind this morning. He should have thought of that.

When Nina sat securely behind him, he handed her the travel case, waited for her to find a good grip, then started the bike. "Which hotel?" he asked with resignation as the bike roared to life.

The strip had little traffic this early in the day. JD hit the gas and steered for the address Nina gave him. Either Jimmy was cheaper than Nina at choosing hotels, or the town was full last night. Since he hadn't had any difficulty finding a decent room, JD assumed the former. He'd surrounded himself with pinchpennies. He just hoped these particular pinchpennies had survived the night safely. Jimmy was his better half right now.

JD hurried Nina through the lobby, even though he suspected she was still sore from last night. He'd make it up to her someday. He just couldn't do it right now.

"Rooms 302 and 304," Nina reminded him breathlessly as they reached the elevator.

JD caught her waist, kissed her forehead, and hauled her into the elevator. He had no experience in taking care of anyone. He hated this. He wanted to be back behind his computer where no human being could intrude upon him. But he held Nina closer all the same. A computer didn't smell sweet or feel soft like Nina.

Jimmy's voice answered the first door they beat upon. Breathing a sigh of relief, JD released Nina's waist. "It's me."

The door immediately swung open, and JD could see Nancy twisting her hands worriedly behind Jimmy. "You look like hell," JD said ungallantly, pushing past Jimmy into the room, dragging Nina with him. Jimmy slammed the door behind them. "What happened?"

Jimmy shoved his broken eyeglasses back up the bridge of his nose. "They ransacked my room last night while I was over here talking with Nancy. We heard them and called security, but they escaped before anyone saw them."

Talking with Nancy. JD looked suspiciously from his ex-wife to his partner, saw the flicker of guilt in their eyes, and blocked out all further thought in that direction. It wasn't any of his damned business what the two of them did. He just hoped Jimmy was prepared to face his bloodsucking girlfriend back home.

"All right, you're all getting out of here right now. This is my fight, and I'll fight it alone. There's no need for any of the rest of you to get hurt. Jimmy, get Nancy back home where she belongs. I'll put Nina on the plane. This has gone far enough."

Like the marine sergeant he once was, JD expected his troops to snap to attention. Instead, Nina wandered over to Nancy and whispered a few things he couldn't hear. Jimmy ambled in the direction of the bathroom and came back with a familiar file folder. He flung it down on the bed since the room lacked anything resembling a desk or table.

"Nancy and I thought we'd follow up on Nina's notes today."

Nina's eyes widened at the sight of the folder. "Where did you get that?"

Jimmy shrugged. "Picked it up yesterday while the two of

you were arguing. Figured we'd get some work done while you worked things out. We've gone through it once. There may be some other connections we've missed. We thought the library might have a computer we could use today." Jimmy plunked down in the room's only chair.

JD glared at him. "Are you out of your mind? These people killed Harry. They're trying to save a multimillion-dollar company. Do you think they'll let amateurs get in their way?"

Nina looked up from her conversation with Nancy. "What happened to those computers you shipped from Nashville? Where are they?"

"I picked them up in Arizona and stored them in a warehouse there. If they didn't follow me to Arizona, they can't find them. Now come on, we're getting out of here." JD waited impatiently for them to jump.

"Maybe Nancy and Jimmy can pick them up and work from there," Nina suggested tentatively.

Jimmy answered before JD could agree to anything. "Hell, no. JD will turn this town on its ear and get himself killed in the process unless someone keeps a rope on him. If we need a computer, I can pick up a laptop."

JD clenched his fists and glared at the roomful of people ignoring him. "Have you all lost your minds? You've got families, responsibilities. You can't risk your necks here. I can. This is my fight. Let me fight it my way."

Nina looked at Nancy and shrugged. "He hasn't figured out that even cavemen traveled in packs. Check out that lawyer first. I'll ride herd on the cowboy."

"Nina, dammit, you'll do no such thing. This cowboy rides alone." JD grabbed the doorknob. "Are you coming with me or not?"

"If you take me to the airport, I'll just catch a cab back. I've got lots of money now, remember." Leaving her suitcase, Nina obediently crossed the room and hooked her hand in the crook of his elbow. "Don't you think we'd better agree on a different hotel now that they've found this one?"

Fury and Nina muddled his mind. JD stared down at her as if he'd never seen her before. Maybe he hadn't. The fey creature who talked to plants hadn't struck him as the tenacious type, but he should have known better. She'd clung to her style of life for the sake of her aunt all these years, despite all the hardships it presented. Now her aunt was gone, and she'd been uprooted. She'd attached herself to him for some inane reason or another. And he'd let her. She wasn't any sappy clinging vine either. She was a rampant thistle who planted herself anywhere she damned well pleased. He must be out of his pea-pickin' mind.

"I'm taking you to the airport," he warned. "You'd better take your suitcase."

She shrugged and glanced back at Nancy. "I'll call you when I get there, and you can tell me what the two of you've decided. I'll join you later." She smiled up at him. "Okay, let's have a fun ride to the airport."

JD heard Jimmy snicker. He scowled, and Nina smiled wider. She'd do it, too; he could see it in her eyes. She should be terrified. She should be ready to go back to the peace and quiet of her little Mayberry town. Even as JD thought that, Nina reminded him of a minor fact he'd forgotten.

"They're back there, too, JD," she said quietly, no longer smiling. "Do you really think I'm any safer at home?"

"Dammit." He drove his hand through his hair, frantically looking for some escape, finding none. DiFrancesco would find her anywhere. She didn't have the knowledge to hide well enough. She couldn't stay with him. It wasn't safe. Still, the thought of Nina staying by his side brought a rush of warm air through some crack in JD's soul. He feared that crack like he would fear a crack in the foundation of his house, but the warm air stupidly lulled his fears. He wrapped his fingers around Nina's and squeezed.

"I'll tie you up and gag you and stuff you in a closet somewhere," he threatened.

That daunting smile of hers returned. "I hate bullies."

That did it. He wouldn't have her treating him like one of her damned teenage students. Keeping a tight hold on her hand, JD turned and confronted his friends. His friends. Some friend he made, dragging them into this. Maybe they'd give up and go home on their own. Until then, he couldn't let anything happen to them. "The hotels aren't safe. I've rented a security-protected house in the desert. I've been using the garage apartment." He dug into his pocket and threw the house keys at Jimmy, then scribbled on the notepad by the phone. "Here's the address and gate code. Open up the house and we'll use it for headquarters."

"Don't let anyone follow you," Nina chirruped beside him.

Jimmy grinned and saluted. JD knew damned well it wasn't for his benefit but for hers. Jimmy fell for any female with legs. He jerked Nina's hand and dragged her into the hall.

"I think Nancy likes your friend," she said calmly as JD hurried her through the maze of corridors. "Do you think Jimmy would make a good stepfather for Jackie?"

Hell, no. Well, maybe. He didn't want to think about it. Nancy and Jimmy? The whole damned world was coming apart at the seams.

"Don't you have some relatives somewhere you can visit?" he asked in despair.

"I wonder how much Astro stock sells for right now?" she murmured aloud, ignoring his plea.

Finding the motorcycle and practically flinging himself on it, JD glared at her. She was making him crazy on purpose. "Why?" he demanded, unable to withhold his curiosity.

"Well, I don't know a great deal about this business, but it seems to me if we could drive the stock price down, we could find some way of acquiring a large share of it. That's the way they do it in books, anyway." She shrugged diffidently as she swung her leg over the bike seat.

In shorts, that leg looked mighty good, and JD felt a surge of lust so powerful he thought he would drop the bike. What the hell was wrong with him? He never looked at women that way. Hell, he never looked at women. They just slinked in and out of his life all on their own.

It took a moment for her words to catch up with his errant brain. Stupid idea. He'd borrowed money to keep his own company afloat. He was worth quite a bit, but only on paper. He couldn't acquire another company just like that. Or could he?

The idea churned in JD's brain as he roared the motorcycle down back roads. Behind him, Nina remained silent, taking in the sights and sounds of the desert city. The hills and lush greenery she was used to must make this flat brown environment seem entirely foreign. He'd show her the real desert later. Right now, he had to get her somewhere safe.

He'd purchased a laptop the instant he'd hit town, so he didn't need to stop now. He didn't know if DiFrancesco had any means of tracing his calls, but he'd had to keep up with his business somehow. E-mail had seemed safest. Now, he had other ideas.

When he drove the bike through a security-protected gate with the use of a remote code, Nina gasped, whether at the technology or the garden beyond, JD couldn't say. He suspected a little of both. Nina would gasp at a garage door opener, he figured.

He'd never particularly noticed the towering palms or the flowering Joshua trees, but he saw the place through Nina's eyes now. It must look like some kind of tropical jungle. Maybe she wouldn't mind the desert so much in the midst of this oasis. He'd felt guilty keeping her away from the comfort of her familiar surroundings, her greenhouse and her roses, but maybe she wouldn't mind this for a little bit.

"You don't need to water them," he teased as he stopped

the bike and dropped the kickstand. "There's an automatic sprinkler."

"Really?" She climbed off the bike and gazed around as if she'd walked into wonderland. "How does that work?"

"It has a water gauge that judges when the ground needs more moisture. You'll get wet if you're not careful. Come on, let's get you inside." JD grabbed her elbow and led her toward the garage steps. He'd have to move her into the house when Jimmy arrived with the key.

"Is that a Rolls in there?" she whispered, glancing through the garage windows as she followed him up.

"The owner collects expensive cars. He's got a warehouse full of them." JD jerked open the door and practically pushed Nina inside. Even if DiFrancesco figured out where he was, he wouldn't dare trespass out here. Only fools messed with the owner of this place, and DiFrancesco didn't strike JD as a fool. An ass, maybe, but not a fool.

"Oh, my, isn't this lovely?" Nina twirled around in the middle of a worn Persian rug, admiring the bare white walls and the bleached wooden timbers of the chauffeur's apartment.

Everything in here was probably cast off from some earlier redecoration of the main house, JD had figured. He'd not thought anything of it. Judging from her delighted expression, Nina thought it enchanting. Of course, anything would look enchanting after that black forest of nightmare furniture she lived with.

"I'll print out the financial statements of Marshall Enterprises and Astrocomputer. You can study them while I check a few other resources." JD sat down at his computer while Nina roamed the room behind him. He wanted to watch her. He wanted to see what she did when she found the bed. He wondered if she'd considered the consequences of staying here with him. He wanted to test her availability right now. He focused on the computer instead.

"Did Marshall Enterprises belong to your father?" she asked

without curiosity as she examined a delicately woven dreamcatcher. "If it's not a public company, how will you obtain the financial statements?"

Damn. She'd spent two days investigating Astrocomputer and hadn't once picked up on his company. Any self-respecting gold digger would have found that out first thing. Although, admittedly, as she'd said, a nonpublic company wouldn't have a lot of information out there.

"I'm an officer of the company, remember? I've got access to the company files. I can access them with the right code word." Hurriedly, JD typed in those words, wondering if he should explain. It didn't seem particularly relevant at the moment. He'd lose the company and his shirt if he didn't stop DiFrancesco.

"That must be an interesting company," she observed from near the windows as the automatic sprinkler system shut off. "There aren't too many businesses in Kentucky that would let their CEOs look like you do. Or do you dress up when you go to the office?"

JD chuckled as he punched the button sending the financial statements to the printer. "My secretary expresses the same sentiments. Unfortunately, I'm in charge of dress code, and I don't give a damn how anyone dresses, as long as the work gets done."

Nina spun around, and JD could sense the admiration in her eyes, even though her expression was shadowed with the light behind her.

"You really are a CEO? That still amazes me. When I first saw you, I thought you were a motorcycle bum. I was afraid to cash your check."

JD stood up and crossed the room, capturing her in his arms while the printer clicked and whirred behind him. He nuzzled her neck. "I'm really a CEO, and I really can produce a list of corporate donors for your gardens, if we can just get your mother out of them. Is that what worries you?"

She smacked his chest, but the blow didn't hurt.

"You worry me. Your Mercedes friend worries me. Everything worries me. I've decided not to think about any of it. I'm on vacation."

"Some vacation." With that, JD gave in to temptation. He might prefer machines to people, but he was still a man. And she was a woman. A beautiful woman with a smile like the summer sun.

His ship might be sinking, but it could damned well go down under a shining sun.

THIRTY

Feeling more alive than she'd ever felt in her life, Nina stretched, raising her arms high above her head so her fingers brushed the petals of an exotic blossom she couldn't identify. She needed a gardening book. There were so many things she didn't know.

Aunt Hattie would have loved exploring this desert garden.

No, she wouldn't have.

Startled by that rebellious thought, Nina lowered her arms and stroked a thick-leaved plant beside her. Hattie didn't like change. Helen was right. Hattie liked controlling things. A garden like this one was uncontrollable. In this constant heat and sun, it either died or ran rampant beneath the automatic sprinklers. Hattie couldn't have controlled either. She would have disapproved of the exuberant bougainvillea spilling over the garden walls as much as she had disapproved of the honeysuckle on the wire fences. She would have despised the lizards darting about underfoot. And she would have considered the bountiful cactus blossoms as obscene as the wisteria vines she constantly hacked down at home. Neat tea roses she could control. Wandering vines had to die.

Astonished by that revelation, Nina sat down on a bench beneath the unidentifiable flowering shrub and stared blindly at the electronic gate. She loved Hattie. Her aunt had given her the security and mental nourishment every child needs to develop a strong character and mind. But she'd kept Nina neatly trimmed and in her pot by depriving her of the emotional encouragement necessary to brave the world. Had Hattie not died, Nina might never have followed JD, never seen this garden, never flown in an airplane. JD had given her that encouragement. JD had made her feel strong and proud within herself, capable of doing anything she applied her mind to.

Freedom. What a marvelous feeling!

With love warming her heart, Nina glanced up at the garage apartment windows. She'd left JD buried in armloads of printouts, staring intently at words spewing across a computer screen. He hadn't even noticed her departure. She supposed she should feel insulted, only she knew he applied that same intense concentration on her when the time was right. She still tingled inside and out from their last session in bed. She hadn't known what hollowness was until JD had filled her.

Maybe Hattie was right about some men, but Hattie had never explored beyond the boundaries of Madrid. There were good men in the world, men like JD. So, maybe he was a little dangerous. Maybe he shot off like a rocket in any direction that caught his interest. Maybe that wasn't so bad. And maybe—just maybe—her natural caution could balance his impulsiveness, and vice versa. Maybe. If she got the chance. Please, God.

Finding hope after so many years of hopelessness disturbed the rhythms of Nina's heart. The squeak of the automatic gate brought her back to reality.

Jimmy and Nancy still drove Nancy's little red Geo. Nina suspected Jimmy would have preferred a slightly larger car for his long legs, but he didn't appear in the least discomfited as he drove through the gateway. She thought she detected a rather smug expression of contentment on his face, much like the one on her own.

The gate creaked again as it closed, and Nina gave it a look of mistrust. She didn't think automatic gates should creak. But Nancy's excitement as she leapt out of the car distracted her from that thought.

"We've found it! We've found the connection! Where's JD?" Nancy waved the file folder as she hurried across the grass in Nina's direction.

"Watch the water sprinkler. It's just about time for it to go off again. It's rather like living in one of those fancy Kroger produce departments around here." Nina walked across to a pathway she'd discovered was safe from the misting sprinklers. She felt a twinge of jealousy observing Nancy's tanned, blond, Miss America looks. JD had once found this woman attractive enough to marry. Did he still harbor feelings for her? After all, she was Jackie's mother. It would only be natural.

Nina had no experience with jealousy. She didn't like the sensation. Hoping it would go away if she ignored it, she led the pair toward the garage. "He's working. We may have to hit him over the head to get his attention."

Behind her, she heard Jimmy chuckle, but she ignored that, too. She surmised some sexual innuendo behind that chuckle, and she wasn't used to that sort of thing aimed at her. The sad part was that he had every right to the thought, whatever it was.

"JD, we've got company." Leaning in the doorway, leaving their guests outside, Nina observed JD's broad, bare back hunched over the keyboard. He'd leapt out of bed with some frantic idea, and she hadn't heard an intelligent word from him since. She didn't get one now.

Shrugging, she closed the door and turned back to the new arrivals. "Better make yourselves at home over at the big house. Is your news important enough that I should bring him out of his trance?"

Jimmy grinned. "You haven't whopped him over the head with a keyboard yet? That's what most of his women do. He can be there all night otherwise."

Nancy smacked his arm. "You have the tact of an orangutan, MacTavish."

Nina laughed at Jimmy's surprised expression. "It's okay. I haven't tried the keyboard tactic yet, but thanks for the advice. If you understand financial statements, I'll bring some over to the house and show you what I've figured out. He'll come looking for us eventually."

Nancy smiled tentatively. "I never had that kind of confidence. I always hated it when he ignored me."

Holding the doorknob, Nina gave that brief consideration, then shook her head. "I'm used to being ignored. It's when he starts paying attention that I'm in trouble." She smiled when she said it, and Jimmy and Nancy laughed, though Nina had only half meant it as a joke. What JD did to her when he turned that formidable concentration in her direction scared her stiff. She didn't think she'd ever get used to melting into puddles.

She didn't bother tiptoeing into the apartment after Jimmy and Nancy clattered down the stairs. She figured JD wouldn't hear an atomic bomb if one exploded in his ear.

To Nina's surprise, he looked up the instant she closed the door behind her. He still hadn't shaved. He looked like a half-naked pirate. He grinned a wicked grin that had her tap-dancing heart twirling.

"I like it when you look at me like that. It makes me feel like Tom Cruise and Arnold Schwarzenegger rolled into one." He rose and crossed the room in her direction.

Nina halted him with a hand to his broad, bare chest. "It's not pretty faces and brawn we need right now. It's brains. So stuff it, Marshall."

"Brains?" He nuzzled her neck, making short work of her inhibiting hand. "You don't want me to just go out there and pump lead into the bad guys?"

Oh, damn. She was melting again. This couldn't go on. He'd turn her mind to mush, her knees to jelly, and leave her a muddy spot on the floor at this rate. Nina pounded ineffectually at JD's impervious chest. "Jimmy and Nancy are waiting. The wolf is at the door. And I don't think your security gate is working right."

She didn't know which statement brought his head up, but she breathed a sigh of relief when his thoughts finally found another focus.

"I'll take a look at the gate later. I'd better talk to Jimmy now. I've unleashed a dragon, and it may be better if you're all in China when it roars."

Before Nina could protest, JD hurried toward the bedroom. He hadn't even questioned her comment about the gate. He'd simply accepted it at face value, as he had the slot machine last night. How could she *not* love a man like that?

JD returned wriggling into a T-shirt. He caught up a wad of papers and, placing a proprietary hand at the small of her back, pushed her out the door.

"We've had this argument before, JD," she warned.

"I know. And you won. But you've done all you can do now." He caught her arm and hurried her across the drive toward the house.

"Where can we go that's any safer than this?" Nina demanded as he opened the side door and practically shoved her through.

"One thing at a time. Let's find Jimmy."

Silence shrouded the mansion, but JD seemed to know exactly in which direction to go. Nina shivered at the heavily draped, dusk-filled rooms. She definitely needed light and fresh air rather than air-conditioning.

Fluorescent bulbs lit the immense white kitchen as JD shoved through a swinging door. They caught Jimmy with the refrigerator door open and Nancy setting out rosebud china plates. JD didn't appear in the least surprised.

"What did you find?" he demanded as he entered, pulling Nina after him.

"Dillon," Jimmy responded from the interior of the huge refrigerator.

It took Nina a moment to remember the name. Dillon. The lawyer who filed copyrights. Of course.

"Damn. That's what I was afraid of." JD kicked a chair and dropped Nina's hand. "I just didn't think he had the brains."

"Probably doesn't." Jimmy emerged with a jar of jelly. "There's no food in here."

"There's no people in here." JD stalked up and down the sparkling black-and-white tile floor. "Dillon's got the whole damned program. If he's sold us out, Astro has the real thing. If we don't move fast, we'll be ruined."

"Nancy found us a new lawyer."

Nina noticed Nancy didn't say a thing. She continued laying out neat place settings, arranging the glasses in a symmetrical pattern, and letting Jimmy do the talking for her. Nina thought she might bust a gut if she'd had to keep quiet like that. Maybe Nancy knew something she didn't.

"I read those financial statements, JD," Nina reminded him, just so he'd remember she existed. She could see how JD and Jimmy worked together all these years. The dynamics might work well while developing computer programs. It left a lot to be desired in the corporate world. "It wouldn't take much to ruin Astro."

"Good, because that's just what I'm doing." JD grabbed a cracker from the box Jimmy ferreted out from somewhere. Smearing it with peanut butter he found on a shelf, he returned to pacing.

With an exasperated sigh, Nancy opened the freezer and began searching through it.

Jimmy stacked his crackers on one of the rosebud plates and, taking a chair, sprawled his long legs across the floor as he applied the jelly he'd found in the refrigerator. "Nancy's lawyer is an expert in copyright theft. He's filing a motion with the court in the morning and going after a search warrant for

Dillon's office. Dillon's a lawyer. He keeps copies of everything. He'll still have a copy of the transcript."

"Can we get the program into production immediately?"

Shaking her head, Nina pulled herself up on the countertop and watched the two men work. JD still looked like a motorcycle thug, especially with his week-old beard. But his constant barrage of succinct questions and commands explained his rise to CEO. She didn't remember his ever saying where he attended college. Maybe the marines sent him.

Nina chuckled as Nancy closed the freezer and stood waiting, arms crossed, to get the men's attention. "You could try tripping him," she suggested, indicating JD's agitated pacing.

Nancy shook her head. "He's too coordinated. He could walk an obstacle course talking like this and never hit anything."

"Pity there aren't any eggs in the refrigerator. We could use him for target practice. How about ice? If we slid it across the floor under his feet?" Nina asked hopefully.

Nancy looked startled, then amused. "Do you want to slow him down or just get his attention?"

Nina considered that. "Both. We have lots of useful information he needs to hear, but he's forgotten we exist. The man needs a lesson in delegating."

Nancy shrugged. "That's what happens with a lot of people who build their businesses from scratch. They're so used to controlling every detail, they can't delegate when the business gets too big for one man to run."

"Build their businesses from scratch?" It was Nina's turn to look startled. "JD built Marshall Enterprises?"

Nancy gave her a look of amusement. "His drunken old man sure didn't. I see he still hasn't learned to communicate the important stuff."

Either that, or he didn't want leeches draining him dry, leeches like impoverished schoolteachers from Kentucky.

She'd seen the financial statement of Marshall Enterprises. They weren't cash heavy. They were highly leveraged. But their profits had soared at a breathtaking pace these last few years. Her motorcycle thug was a multimillionaire.

So much for any errant thoughts she might have harbored about any kind of steady relationship. She'd just been an amusement for JD while he was stranded in the middle of nowhere. No wonder he kept trying to get rid of her. How dense could one person be?

Her small balloon of hope spiked, Nina collapsed inside. She knew how to take care of herself. She could go home, tend her garden, go back to school, live day-to-day as she always had. It wasn't a bad life. She still had to contend with her mother. Maybe she could work something out. She should have had someone check on her geranium seedlings.

"Nina!"

JD's sharp voice startled Nina out of her reverie. He never spoke sharply. She must have been daydreaming. Not looking at him, she slid down from the cabinet and searched for a glass. "What?" she asked with irritation, filling the glass with water.

"Explain to Jimmy about Astro's finances."

"Their last big game program bombed when your firm released the new edition of Monster House. Quicken's new banking program made their personal finance software obsolete. They've lost money for three consecutive quarters, a disaster for any highly leveraged firm. Which Marshall Enterprises is," Nina reminded them. "Not as badly as Astro, but you're in risky waters."

JD shrugged, took the glass of water she'd poured, and drained half of it before speaking. "Jimmy and I are the ones taking risks. We'd be the only ones hurt. We're not a public company."

"But Astro is. The stockholders are screaming. Banks are unloading their shares. From the printouts JD gave me, it looks as if they're overdue on several loans. They're teetering on the brink of disaster. One report says there's a demand for a new board of directors. I don't know where your Dillon stands amid all of this, but DiFrancesco is on the board, which undoubtedly means he holds a substantial block of potentially worthless shares."

Timidly, Nancy broke into the temporary lull following Nina's speech. "From what Jimmy and I can tell, the money Marshall Enterprises borrowed came from a consortium of Astro's stockholders. Jimmy's friend at the bank is searching the files, trying to follow the money trail. Dillon borrowed against his law firm to contribute part of the sum. I imagine that means he owns stock in Astro."

"Thank God we haven't gone public yet," Jimmy muttered.

"Dillon wanted us to," JD pointed out. "He and his friends probably would have bought us lock, stock, and barrel if we had."

"That's irrelevant now. Astro has your program, their sales are soaring on the basis of it, and their stock prices have just recently turned around. Without that program, you're stable, but jerk that program from Astro, and they crumble." Nina refilled the glass and sipped.

"I've already notified a contact at the *Wall Street Journal* that we're pressing a copyright-infringement suit against Astro. If this lawyer you've found is any good, he can have theft charges pressed. The news should break soon. I've already got it on the Internet. Astro's stock should start tumbling in the morning," JD announced with satisfaction.

Jimmy shouted in glee, and Nina lifted her glass in salute. JD would never stay down long. She'd be wise to follow his example. She just wished her heart were in it.

"If you announce your intention to go public with your stock, couldn't you borrow sufficient money to start production of your own program?" she asked.

"You're wasted teaching high school, Miss Toon," JD admonished. "You have a wickedly clever mind. However, I'm taking your earlier suggestion. Astro has production facilities that we don't. They've already sold the program across the country with a sales force we don't have. When Astro's stock plummets, I'm personally buying up every share that hits the market. I've notified my broker to buy when it hits the price I've designated. And I've given him a list of major stockholders to contact. My bet is that when the news of our suit hits tomorrow, the rats will scurry to flee the sinking ship."

"I want in on some of that action." Jimmy crossed to the telephone and began punching in numbers. "I've not squirreled away as much as you have, but I can manage enough. Hell, I'll sell the Corvettes if I have to."

"You have a Corvette?" Nancy asked in surprise. "We've been driving around in my little box, and you own a *Corvette*?"

JD handed her a peanut butter cracker. "A new Corvette, three antique Corvettes, a Cadillac STS, and the worst collection of Chevy trucks you'll ever find. He's certifiable."

"Never drove a Geo," Jimmy mumbled through a cracker as he waited for someone to answer the phone on the other end. "Foreign cars, hate 'em. But if Chevy—" He turned back to speak into the phone.

"Well, then," Nina said brightly, "sounds as if everything will end happily ever after. I guess I'd better get back to my geraniums."

"Good idea," JD said, capturing her against the counter. "Only one little problem."

Breathless at the close contact, Nina tried to make herself smaller. "Oh, and what is that?"

"I called the cops and had a long talk with them about DiFrancesco and my uncle. They should be searching his house for a weapon right about now. Guess who will be gunning for me when he finds out?"

THIRTY-ONE

"If they find the gun, they'll lock DiFrancesco up, JD. There's nothing to worry about." Nina eased away from him, pretending to examine a bush she'd already thoroughly examined earlier. It was easier than standing close to JD in the midnight garden.

It was impossible to escape JD. He came up behind her, catching her waist and pulling her back against him. Her head rested on his shoulder, and his encompassing arms offered the strength she'd never possessed. It would be so easy to pretend she could count on that welcome embrace forever. But she'd never had much success lying to herself.

"I just don't think going back to Madrid right now is the safest thing for you to do." JD's hand wandered, caressing lightly. "Staying with me is probably wrong, too. I could send you to San Diego. You could visit the zoo. Anything to keep you out of DiFrancesco's range until this is all over."

Nina shivered as the hand on her breast pulled erotic chords. She would never feel his caress again once she left here, she knew. He would immerse himself in his own world. He'd never have time to visit an out-of-the-way place like Madrid, Kentucky. The nearest airport was well over an hour away. But if she would never see him again, wouldn't it be easier to make the break now, before she fell any deeper?

"You said you talked to Hoyt and the Mercedes is gone. I'll be safe enough. Coming after me won't save DiFrancesco's stock from plummeting or keep the police from finding the gun if he truly did murder your uncle. He'll probably be in jail by the time I get home. I think it's best if I leave now, JD."

Instead of releasing her, he held her tighter. Above the tangle of palm leaves, a desert sky sprinkled myriad stars, and Nina wanted nothing more than to forget the rest of the world in JD's arms. He could do it so easily, chase away her problems, make the world go away. But she didn't think she could afford the price.

"Was it something I said?" he asked carefully. "I didn't mean to ignore you all day. It's just sometimes I—"

Nina vigorously shook her head. "Don't be silly. You didn't ignore me. You didn't say anything. I just came out here to see that you're safe, and now it looks as if you are. I've got my own life, JD."

He loosened his hold but continued idly rubbing his hand up and down her hip. "All right. You're worried about the garden. I can understand that. Just don't go yet. Wait a little while, until I'm sure it's safe."

His argument was scarcely persuasive, but his hand was. Nina tried stepping away, but cement encased her feet. The roar of a car engine caught her attention, and she jerked her head in the direction of the gate.

"JD, someone's out there."

It was well after midnight now. The owner of the house was in France. No one should be out there.

JD shoved Nina toward the house. "Warn Jimmy. Call the police. If anyone tries to breach the gate, it's supposed to notify security, but let's not take chances."

Nina caught his arm. "Wait! Where are you going?"

JD grabbed her by the waist, planted a hungry kiss on her

mouth, and pushed her away again. "Over the wall. If it's DiFrancesco, he wants me. I'll distract him."

"JD, you impossible idiot . . ." But he had already disappeared into the shadows of the shrubbery.

Slipping down secluded walks, JD hurried in the direction of the gate. He might know more about machinery than people, but instinct drove him to protect what was his. Nina was his. He'd not let anyone touch her.

He shoved through the shrubbery until he reached the base of the wall. He could hear someone fiddling with the gate. Why didn't the security alarm go off?

He hadn't thought DiFrancesco could find him so easily. If he'd thought at all, he would have figured the financier as the sort to run. But, as usual, he hadn't given it any thought. This time, his damned impulsiveness could hurt innocents. He'd never forgive himself if anything happened to Nina. She'd left her safe little world for his sake. He would protect her in the only way he knew how.

His foot found a grip between blocks of the wall. He could reach DiFrancesco before he broke through the gate. Quietly, he dropped into the darkness beyond the garden wall.

Staring uncertainly at the place where JD had disappeared, Nina started at the screech of metal. JD had never checked the gate mechanism. It might hold. She could just be indulging in her usual paranoia. But living in a house with erratic electricity had taught her caution.

Throwing a glance over her shoulder, deciding she was closer to the gate than the house, Nina dashed along hidden pathways to an observation point she had discovered earlier. She'd explored for hours this afternoon while JD worked. She put what she'd learned to good use now.

From the fountain wall she could see a low-slung black Porsche revving its engines in front of the gate. Behind it was the Mercedes. The damned Mercedes. Or one just like it. A man stood at the security gate, playing with the buttons that signaled the house. If Jimmy and Nancy hadn't already gone to bed, they'd know they had company now.

The gate creaked again. No security alarms clamored. For a terrifying moment, Nina wondered if the owner had returned from France. Did JD really have permission to use this place?

And then she saw the machine gun.

She didn't know a thing about guns. It could be an Uzi or whatever criminals used these days. She just knew it had a short barrel and a thick stock and didn't resemble any kind of rifle she knew. And JD was out there somewhere.

She thought she saw his shadow darting along the high block wall as the gate creaked open. She heard a shout as the man at the box shoved past the gate with his gun. She didn't hear any gunfire yet, but she wasn't waiting to take chances.

Hitting the control mechanism she'd found earlier by the fountain, Nina shot arrows of water into the air. The sprinkler system roared to life, soaking the guy with the gun. His curses turned the air blue as she dashed for the garage.

"He's over here, boss! I've got him!"

The shout coursed down her spine, but Nina kept running, praying.

"There's more in here. Grab him before they call security!"

More than one man darted through the gate and over the wall. Nina heard an ominous thud that very much sounded like a body landing on metal, hollow metal, like a car. The Porsche was easing through the half-open gate now. Where the devil was JD?

Panting, Nina located the side door into the garage. The Rolls had fascinated her earlier. After a dozen years of driving that tiny, rusty Camry, a luxurious car like this one couldn't have done anything else but fascinate her. It smelled new. The glossy paint glimmered even in the dim light of the garage. She hadn't dared turn on the engine, but she knew where the keys were. They hung on a board right by the door, neatly labeled.

The shouts sounded louder now. Whoever was out there had

scattered all through the yard, and the sprinkler system worked overtime to drown them. She'd never heard such cursing since the principal had invaded the boys' bathroom and caught them smoking. Surely, if these men had caught JD, they wouldn't still be out there running around in the water.

That thought exploded when she heard a triumphant cry from the direction of the gate. "He's here, boss! I got him. F—" The curse was cut off in an alarming screech of pain.

Praying harder now, Nina grabbed the keys and, with trembling fingers, swung open the car door. She didn't know a thing about driving a car like this one. She prayed it had an automatic transmission. She should have learned a standard, but Hattie couldn't drive. She'd had to teach herself.

She found the ignition, and the car rumbled to life. To her utter surprise and dismay, the garage door slowly opened of its own accord. She pulled a gear stick she prayed set the car into forward, and the huge automobile rolled in stately grace through the opening doorway.

Someone inside the house had turned on the floodlights. Thank God, Jimmy and Nancy must still be up. Maybe they'd called the police.

A sudden thought curled Nina's toes. What if those goons had cut the telephone wires? That's why the security alarm hadn't gone off when the gate opened. They were out here in the middle of the desert, entirely on their own.

So much for damned technology.

The sound she'd feared most rattled the night silence. Gunfire.

Oh, God. Oh, God, don't let it be JD. Not JD. It wouldn't be fair.

Nina floored the accelerator.

The Rolls didn't precisely roar. It glided. It glided faster. It rolled at warp speed directly toward the low-slung Porsche driving toward the house.

Hair-raising sirens screamed, cutting through the night air

like silver swords. Alarm bells clamored. Floodlights swept the gardens like a prison security system. And dogs howled.

Dogs? Nina didn't remember any dogs.

She couldn't worry about them now. The Rolls had taken on a mind of its own. Taking her foot off the accelerator hadn't helped. The huge machine rolled determinedly forward. The Porsche screeched to a halt, hesitated, and inched into reverse.

Silhouetted against the night sky, two men struggled on the wall. One had the very distinct physique she recognized as JD's. The other had a gun.

Helpless, Nina pounded the steering wheel until she located the horn and leaned against it as the car moved forward.

The Porsche hurtled backward faster. The security gates slowly swung closed.

From his vantage point on top of the wall, JD saw the behemoth car illuminated in the floodlights. Like the Silver Shadow it was, the car drifted majestically forward all on its own. He couldn't see Nina anywhere. JD prayed she had made it to the house, but even in his prayers he couldn't believe she'd found the alarm system and set it off. Nina wouldn't even know what an alarm system was.

He had both fists wrapped soundly around the barrel of the weapon that had threatened him earlier. The man holding it equally tightly had the advantage of height and weight, but he didn't possess JD's fury and fear. The idea of any of these goons laying hands on Nina gave him an impetus nothing else could have generated. With a cold-minded kick, JD's foot shot up under his opponent's guard, hurling him backward with a howl of agony.

He hadn't been a marine for nothing. Breaking open the weapon, he emptied the cartridges in the mud and sand of the garden below, then flung it toward the cascading fountain. Terrible thing to use combat training defending a damned computer program. JD regretted not using the weapon as a club against the other man's jaw, but he didn't have time for additional violence.

Leaping down from the wall, he landed just in time to see the gate swing closed as the Porsche geared into reverse. The gate screeched like a cyclops in pain. The Porsche hit it with a clash of metal on metal. The Rolls continued moving forward, slowly crumpling inch after inch of the small car's low-slung hood.

"Nina!" JD screamed, understanding now the source of the ghostly driver. "Hit reverse!"

Running, not bothering to dodge the streams of water shooting through the ground beneath him, JD lunged at the shadowy figure lurching from the driver's seat of the Porsche.

They toppled into the mud not inches from the wheels of the Rolls. JD grabbed the driver's wrist, knowing instinctively what he'd find there. The cold metal of the revolver brushed his fingers, but he couldn't quite grip it as he struggled with the man beneath him.

In the distance, sirens screamed. Outside the gates, the Mercedes frantically blew its horn, then roared to life. The man beneath JD fought for freedom.

In horror, JD watched as slender ankles raced toward him instead of away. He couldn't look up. Despite the man's smaller size, he fought like a demon. Terrified the gun would go off, he concentrated all his attention on keeping that one hand pinned to the ground. He couldn't get his knee into a position to do any good.

Damn Nina, she was running right for them. Was the woman insane?

Of course she was. Stupid question. Only an insane woman would have followed him into this mess.

A hard object whistled past JD's nose, hitting with a hideous thud and exploding mud in his face. Cursing, he tightened his grip, but the man beneath him collapsed and stilled.

Grabbing the gun from lax fingers, JD shook his head and finally dared to look up.

The remains of a potted cactus sat on his assailant's head, tilting dangerously to one side as the dirt from the broken pot washed away in the water from the sprinkler. JD's gaze followed the slender legs upward until his battered concentration reached the edge of trim blue shorts. With a sigh of exasperation, he wrapped a muddy hand around her ankle and pulled himself up.

Nina practically collapsed in his arms.

Exhausted, exhilarated, JD held her tightly and let someone else fight with the wayward security gate as the blue lights of the police cars spilled into the drive.

"Trespassing and assault charges should hold him for a little while." Newly showered and dressed in clean jeans, JD shoved his wet hair from his face and kept a close eye on Nina as she wandered the far side of the kitchen. She'd stayed a safe distance from him ever since the police had arrived. He couldn't blame her. She'd lived a sheltered life, and the instant he'd dropped into it, she'd been bombarded with reckless vans, dead bodies, and terrorist attacks. Her aunt Hattie would have shipped her off to an island somewhere if she'd been around.

JD felt like a dog begging for a bone as he followed her progress around the kitchen, but he couldn't tear his gaze away. She'd already told the police she was leaving in the morning and given them her home address. He didn't want her to go.

That was nonsense. He knew that. She'd hung in there through more than most women would have. But now she was leaving like all the others. The Marshall luck hadn't changed any, then. He'd hoped, but that had only been his own wishful thinking.

She looked so damned good, like the ice cream cone with sprinkles he could never have when he was a kid. All that vanilla hair stood on end from being washed without drying.

Flushed slightly by these last days under a desert sun, Nina's pale cheeks glowed, accenting the glitter of green eyes. She had on those blasted white leggings again, and JD could see every well-shaped curve as she polished china and neatly put it away. She'd made an accordion of a Porsche and turned a desert into a swamp, but she stood here neatly returning the kitchen to rights. Fool woman. Why did thinking he'd lost her hurt so?

"Did the police find the murder weapon?" Jimmy munched on cold pizza while Nancy poured him a drink from the remains of the bottle of Coke from the carry-out they'd ordered after the police left.

"DiFrancesco collected guns. It will take them a while." JD shrugged and looked at his own soft drink with distaste. He needed something stronger.

"Is he Mafia?" Nancy inquired uncertainly.

JD noticed Nina didn't say a thing. She just polished china until she should have rubbed the design right off. He shrugged again. "The police haven't found any connection. The other members of his consortium are squealing like pigs. They all swear they know nothing about theft or guns or murder. Maybe they don't."

"And maybe pigs fly." Jimmy washed the rest of the pizza down with a swig from his glass. "The mob mentality lingers in this town. Your uncle Harry had weird friends."

"Yeah, I know. He liked the casinos too well. And not the ritzy ones either. But DiFrancesco probably appeared legit to him. He did own a large hunk of Astro and probably half a dozen other businesses. Harry just thought he was a businessman."

Uncomfortably, JD thought of what else the police had told him. He'd never given his uncle enough credit. He didn't entirely know how to deal with that realization yet.

Nina darted him a look and finally spoke. "Why was your uncle Harry in Kentucky?"

Leave it to Nina. JD sighed and swirled the drink in his glass. "DiFrancesco or our burglar tapped company phone lines. And one of his goons followed me across the country. They planned on stealing the program and doing heaven knows what with it at first, but when they ran the truck off the road, things started getting dirty. One of Harry's buddies in the consortium must have warned Harry of his suspicions. The cops traced Harry from the Vegas airport to Nashville, where he rented a car. Harry was trying to save me."

Silence descended on the kitchen. Nina looked as if she wanted to say something. She held her hand out, then dropped it and turned away. That's when JD knew it was over.

Jimmy snorted but didn't comment further. JD was grateful for that. So, the Marshall bad luck didn't stop at women. It extended in every direction. What else was new? He could thank God he had brains and could worm his way out of anything. Unfortunately, right now his brain was telling him the Marshall bad luck could just possibly be the result of the Marshall tendency to leap before looking. Harry's end certainly gave evidence of that.

This time his recklessness could have cost him everything he'd ever wanted out of life. JD just wished his brains would figure some way to get Nina back over here again.

"It's late. There's not a thing we can do right now but wait and see what happens when the stock market opens in the morning. Why don't we turn in?"

Nancy's request caught JD by surprise. She'd scarcely said a thing all evening. She sent him a pointed look he couldn't interpret now. Damn, but he'd never understand women. He wondered if this meant she wouldn't trust him with Jackie anymore. Jackie. A great grinding ache dug into his soul. How could he get Jackie back and still have time to salvage his business and take over another? He had to put his son even before Nina. Damn. People demanded a hell of a lot more from him than machines did. He was afraid he didn't have what it took.

Jimmy obediently unfolded his lanky body from the chair and followed Nancy from the room with a minimum of "good nights."

That left Nina clearing the table and finishing up the rest of the dishes.

"Nina?" Tentatively, JD stepped forward. She retreated to the sink.

"Will you take me to the airport?" she asked in a monotone.

She kept her back turned toward him. JD ground his teeth and clenched his fingers into fists, not knowing how else to keep a grip on his temper. "Now? There's nothing going out now."

"There's a flight out first thing in the morning. I don't want to miss it."

"Nina, I . . ."

She turned, and JD flinched at the tears in her eyes. He couldn't handle tears. Not from Nina. They broke his heart in two. He could feel himself internally hemorrhaging.

"Please, JD. I want to go home."

He understood. He understood only too well. Nodding his head, not letting her see his agony, JD headed for the door. "I can get the bike past the wreck in the driveway. Is your bag packed?"

He walked out into the now-quiet desert night while his soul crumbled into ashes. She didn't want him. He couldn't argue with that. No one else ever had either. He wasn't even certain he liked himself very much, not after he'd let Harry down like that. His recklessness had cost one life already, and nearly cost the lives of the only other people he cared about.

Nina would be much better off in the safety of her own world, without him.

THIRTY-TWO

The excruciating heat and humidity of August had all but decimated the roses. Nina pinched off several black-spotted leaves and a heat-shattered bloom. No amount of tender loving care could produce lovely roses in this weather. But if she took good care of them, they'd come back in September and bloom for a couple of months more. A pity she couldn't salvage people the same way.

The bittersweet memory of her last conversation with Hattie echoed through her thoughts as she clipped the roses. "Nina takes after me," Hattie had said with pride. "I want my granddaughter to have the roses. Hank would have loved her." Tears stung Nina's eyes as she broke off another spent bloom. Why, Hattie? she cried inside, but she was past regrets now. Now that she knew some of the truth, she knew Hattie had loved her in her own way. JD had taught her that.

Even though she wore a wide-brimmed hat, the hot sun made her dizzy. Pulling off her gloves, Nina flung them in the basket she used to carry her gardening tools. Looking out over the flat bean fields and calm lake from her vantage point on Hattie's Hill, Nina experienced a modicum of satisfaction. Maybe, with time, she could again accept this land as a substitute for the life she would never have, a life she had glimpsed briefly through JD.

Pushing that thought aside, Nina picked up her basket and started down the hill. In the distance, she could hear the muted roar of a bulldozer leveling some of the scrub brush in the back field. The donations JD had solicited had been generous. The corporation could now afford to reimburse Tom for his labor. Already, outside money flowed into Madrid's coffers. Come winter, the men would begin building the boardwalk through the wildlife habitat—income they wouldn't have had otherwise. Even the governor had heard of the project and had visited with his entourage of reporters. His blessings had generated more donations. Through the magic of JD's confidence, her dreams were well on their way to becoming reality.

Some of them, anyway. Setting her basket in the toolshed, Nina wiped her brow with the back of her arm. JD had taught her to dream big and take action, but she hadn't quite got the knack of it yet. All the details bogged her down, but without those details, she'd spend her days moping and her nights without sleep. She would find her pace eventually, she figured.

She washed her hands in the kitchen sink, then dug out the brownies Helen had baked. They still didn't speak much to each other, but they'd developed a few patterns that reduced confrontation. Helen did the cooking because Nina didn't. Nina bought the groceries because Helen couldn't. Resentment lingered, but neither of them was in any immediate position to change things.

Heaping two scoops of Breyers chocolate ice cream on top of the brownie, Nina wandered toward the front porch. Shade covered it this time of day, and the fan she'd hooked up provided the only breeze on a day like this. JD would have heart failure if he saw the way she'd run an extension cord out the window. But JD was in California merging his company with the newly acquired Astrocomputer.

She still didn't have a computer and couldn't get e-mail. JD didn't write. She understood that. He'd called a few times, but she hadn't been in the house when he did, and she didn't have an answering machine. She hadn't returned the calls Helen had told her about. She didn't see the point. He had his world, she had hers. She couldn't find any conceivable connection between the two.

Nina bit back a sigh when she discovered Helen had already appropriated the porch swing beneath the fan. She still couldn't bring herself to call this woman "mother." She'd never been a mother to her. She was just some stranger connected by blood and obligation. Nina felt closer to JD than to her own flesh and blood. Odd, but it couldn't be helped.

"I've talked to Matt Horne," Helen announced as Nina took a seat on the porch railing closest to the fan.

"That should have been a spiritually uplifting experience," Nina murmured, dipping into her ice cream. Matt Horne would never get her vote, the lying, conniving bastard. The lawyer JD had found had proved his mettle thirty times over. Nina just wished everything she thought about didn't include JD.

Helen gave her a puzzled look. "I don't know what you're talking about. I'm not clever like you. Matt Horne is a decent boy. He's done his best for me."

"Matt Horne did the best for himself. Be grateful he was too lazy to cause you any harm." Nina didn't want to talk about how Matt Horne had sought her mother out and brought her back here to pry Hattie's farm out of her hands. She hadn't even asked how he'd known where to find her mother. She figured it was in his father's records somewhere. His father had been Hattie's attorney before Matt. Nina thought she'd much rather turn on an Andy Williams record, eat her ice cream in peace, and listen to the katydids than think about Matt.

Helen had sense enough to grimace at Nina's gloomy analysis. "Well, I'll admit your fancy city lawyer did a far sight better. I don't know why I never looked for my birth certificate."

"Because you had a baptismal certificate and that's all you

needed to get married. It's not like you ever got a passport or anything." Nina shrugged. The lawyer's revelation of Helen's true parentage had been something of a shock, to put it mildly. Nina still struggled with the concept.

"I always thought of Hattie as a dried-up old spinster. I knew she had a broader mind than my mother"— Helen corrected herself—"than her sister. She understood when I got pregnant with you. I just never realized why. I still can't believe it."

"I suppose we should have known." Nina licked her spoon and recalled lazy days on this porch with Hattie warning her of the dangers of men. "Most women don't despise men without reason. We should have asked her how she knew so much about them."

Helen chuckled. "Right. I can see that now. She would have looked down her long nose and said, 'None of your beeswax.' She didn't go to all the trouble of pretending Marietta was my mother just to spill the beans if we asked. I wonder whatever happened to my real father?"

"It was wartime, remember. That's probably why Hattie sympathized with your situation so easily. I bet if I ask Ethel, she can tell me who Hank Wheeler was. He was probably here on leave just long enough to get Hattie pregnant, then got himself killed when he went back to war. My word, she must have been almost forty years old! Can you just imagine?" Nina shook her head in disbelief at the thought. "I didn't think the military took men that old."

Helen shoved the porch swing restlessly. "It scarcely makes any difference, does it? I never knew my father either way. It just means the woman I thought of as mother died 'without issue,' as the lawyer put it. So the whole damned farm belonged to Hattie."

"It would have all come to you either way, whether you were Hattie's child or Marietta's." Nina tried not to gloat, although she'd been doing it privately for weeks, ever since her lawyer found the deed book. Hiding her secret elation, she scraped her spoon along the bottom of the bowl and didn't look up.

"Yeah, it would have been mine if the conniving old witch hadn't deeded the whole lot to you as a graduation present. I can't believe she didn't tell you."

"I can't believe she didn't tell Matt." Nina couldn't stifle her grin as she remembered Matt's face when her city lawyer had flung the deed and her mother's birth certificate on his desk. For a fleeting moment, she'd felt damned good. "Hattie's mental faculties were still sharp back then. She must have done it for a reason. If the stupid clerk had bothered changing the tax bills, there never would have been any confusion. It's about time they computerized down there."

Helen remained silent. Uneasily, Nina sneaked a peek at her. Helen had no money of her own, but she'd made some arrangement with one of the beauticians in town to have her hair done once a week in exchange for helping out around the shop. She didn't have a beautician's license, but she knew the business well enough. Just her polished, elegantly coiffed appearance gave proof of that. Not for the first time, Nina wondered how her mother had spent those missing years. They never talked about it.

"I know why she did it." Helen's harsh words cut the silence.

"You were her daughter." For some reason, Nina didn't want to hear what Helen might say. She'd had enough surprises for a lifetime. "She loved you. She always believed you would return. She took care of me for you. She had no reason to deed the farm to me unless someone told her you were dead."

"I was as good as dead, and Hattie knew it," Helen said bitterly. "I could have served time for the rest of my life. And she had to know that I had no way of supporting this place if I got out. She knew I'd sell it. So she deeded it to her granddaughter in hopes you would take care of me as I never took care of you."

Nina wished she could shut down her mind and not hear

what she'd just heard. It upset too many preconceived notions. She'd clung to an image of her mother as a glamorous party girl, swinging from man to man, drinking and making merry. She didn't want this other image shoved on her. Grappling with the idea of Great-aunt Hattie as her grandmother provided sufficient headache.

But once started, Helen proceeded relentlessly. "I killed your stepfather. Back then, people didn't know about stalking or care about spouse abuse. They thought a woman got what she deserved, that a man had a right to beat his wife if she didn't behave. I sure as hell didn't behave, I'll grant you that. I threw him out of the house when you were eight, but he wouldn't stay away. So I left you with Hattie and got out of here. He followed me. When he got the divorce papers, he beat me within an inch of my life. I moved again. I was going to get my beautician's license, but I was having a good time while I was at it, enjoying my freedom."

Having set aside her bowl, Nina clenched the railing so tightly she could feel splinters piercing her skin. She wanted to jump and run. She didn't want to believe any of this. But the anguish on her mother's face drew harsh lines in her perfectly made-up complexion.

"Richard found me again. I never knew how he did it. I didn't write to anyone so no one would know where I was. I was young and stupid and never considered consequences, but I did think that far. He found me in a bar and put me in the hospital again. When I got out, I bought a gun. The next time he came after me, I killed him."

"That's self-defense!" Nina protested, drawn into the story despite herself. "Any good lawyer could have gotten you off."

"Who could afford good lawyers?" Helen asked coldly. "I got a shiny new public defender who told me I was lucky not to get the chair for premeditation for buying the gun. Richard didn't have the gun. I did. Case closed."

Nina shut her eyes and dug her fingers deeper into the

railing. She didn't want to feel sympathy or rage. Maybe it would all go away if she just sat here and wished herself back to a few months ago, when everything was so much simpler. It wasn't going to happen.

"So you went to prison and never wrote again," Nina said between clenched teeth, remembering all those Christmases when she'd prayed for a card, for a miracle, for a Santa Claus she'd never believed in.

"Hattie knew where I was. It was a life sentence at the time. We both thought it best for you if you just forgot about me. We didn't know the laws would change so the governor could commute the sentences for abused women."

Rage exploded into Nina's bloodstream, burning like molten lava. Tears of helplessness streamed down her cheeks.

"All these years, and I could have had birthday cards, a mother's advice, words that might have made me feel loved, and you and Hattie threw them away?" Shattered, Nina wrapped her arms around herself and rocked back and forth, unable to comprehend the enormity of this revelation. "I wouldn't have cared if you were in prison!" she shouted. "I wouldn't have cared if you were in Siberia! I could have visited, sent presents, maybe known I had a real mother who loved me. And you're telling me Hattie prevented it? She didn't even tell us she was my grandmother, and you listened to her?"

Incoherent, unable to decipher her warring emotions, Nina slid off the railing and stalked away, ignoring her mother's stuttered excuses. She thought she might scream. She thought she might throw herself into the lake and see where it took her. Anything was better than this incomprehensible fog of rage.

She couldn't deal with these betrayals. She'd lost JD, lost the aunt she'd never really known, and gained a mother with the backbone of a toadstool. None of it made sense.

Maybe she should take a real vacation. School would start in another few weeks. She needed to get away and make sense of it all.

JD halted the Harley with his foot and turned off the ignition. Sometimes in wet weather the now-healed bone ached, but he didn't notice a twinge now. Not just his gaze but his entire being had focused on the crumbling old two-story farmhouse before him.

"Hey, Dad, I think I see Laddie back there. Can I go see what he's doing?"

Behind him, Jackie climbed off the bike and waited impatiently for some response. Dragging his thoughts back to his son, JD grinned ruefully. "You've still got that much energy after riding cross-country on this thing?"

Jackie's grin was almost identical to his own as he gave an ungraceful teenage shrug. "Well, next time, let's try an airplane, okay?"

JD laughed and waved his son away before he did something foolish like hugging the boy. Jackie hated being hugged, but JD had developed a fondness for displays of affection. He'd never known a mother's kisses or a father's love, but that didn't mean he couldn't love his own son. He just needed some practice. He could damned well learn anything he put his mind to.

A certain wide-eyed sprite had taught him that.

Glancing up at the house again, JD suffered a moment's trepidation. Nina hadn't returned his calls. He supposed he could assume her mother had never mentioned them, but he knew Tinkerbell too well to believe that for long. If he hadn't called, she would have checked with Nancy and Jimmy to make certain he was still alive. He'd defeated his own purpose by calling. Now she didn't need to check in.

It was possible that he was about to make a huge fool of himself. Once upon a long time ago, he'd been the butt of his father's drunken jokes and the laughingstock of the third grade because he was skinny and short and ill-dressed. He heartily disliked being laughed at. He'd turned himself into the class bully overcoming that particular distaste, and no one had laughed at him ever again. Did he really want to subject himself to the possibility of even more severe humiliation at Nina's hands?

He hadn't driven two thousand miles on a Harley to back out now.

He'd promised Jackie a few weeks at the lake before school started, and his son would have them. That's what JD told himself as he climbed the stairs to the front porch. Of course, if that's all he had wanted, he would have called first and made certain it was okay. But that wasn't all he wanted.

He scanned the porch, checking for diminutive sprites in the shadows, searching out details of changes since he'd been here last. They still hadn't installed a doorbell. He knocked, and while he waited, he frowned at the portable fan attached to the extension cord coming out of the window. The idiot would damned well electrocute herself one of these days. Somebody should look after her.

No one answered the knock. He hadn't driven all this way to be denied entrance that easily. Irritated, JD tried the knob. As usual, it swung open without protest. Not locking doors was another habit Nina should break.

"Nina!" he shouted into the echoing interior. Shadows filled the high walls and ceilings. Someone had actually closed the blinds. "Nina!"

No reply. Fighting a sudden panic, JD entered the corridor and headed for the kitchen. If he didn't find anyone there, he'd try the greenhouse next. He'd thought she'd be inside during the heat of the day. She courted sunstroke if she was outside.

Stupid of him to assume he would find her sitting here waiting for him. Maybe she was out fishing with Hoyt or arguing about Chinese chestnuts with Howard. Worse yet, she might be out somewhere with that overgrown puppy of a landscaper.

That thought made him twitch. He should have said something to her in Vegas when he'd had the chance, given her the reassurances a woman liked to hear, but he was lousy at doing the things women liked. And he hadn't been at all certain Nina wanted to hear them. Besides, if the risks he had taken hadn't panned out, he could have been bankrupt by now. How could he face Nina as a pauper?

Another stupid thought, he supposed as he stared at the empty kitchen. Nina had lived like this her entire life, and it didn't seem to bother her. He could have made another fortune. She wouldn't have cared about the money. But she did need to hear the words. He understood that now. Nina didn't have a lot of self-confidence.

Sure, she could defy phone companies and bungle-headed computer idiots like himself, but only because she fought for someone else. Nina didn't have what it took to stand up for herself. So she had left him. JD thought he sort of understood that, too. For a change, he'd actually spent a long time thinking about their parting. And one of the conclusions he'd reached was that he hadn't tried hard enough. He'd blamed his bad luck and quit rather than damage his damned ego.

Another conclusion he'd reached was that Nina would never have gone to bed with him if she hadn't felt something pretty strong. He didn't dare put a name to those feelings. He'd driven all this way praying he hadn't destroyed them. The time had arrived for action.

She wasn't in the kitchen. Cursing, JD strode out the back and toward the greenhouse.

To his amazement, instead of a pint-sized pixie reaching for the uppermost plants in this jungle, he found Helen McIntyre watering the granddaddy fern.

At his appearance, she put the watering can down and gave

his dust-coated, T-shirted attire a disapproving look. "Do you always make yourself at home like this?"

JD refused to be discomfited by a woman who would desert her daughter for twenty years. "I'm looking for Nina."

She returned to her watering. "She's not here."

For the first time since he'd embarked on this insane journey, JD felt fear. He should have kept calling until he'd reached her. He should have written. He should never have let her get on that airplane in Vegas. Damn, but he should have known better. Why in hell had he thought his luck had changed just because he'd found a woman who'd taught him to feel human again?

Gritting his teeth, JD tried again. "Where is she?"

Helen sent him a piercing look. "Why do you ask?"

"Damn it, Mrs. McIntyre, it's scarcely any of your business after all these years, is it? Just tell me where the hell she is." Clenching his hands into fists, JD generously refrained from jerking the watering can from the woman's hands and shaking her.

Helen slammed the can down on the table and glared at him. "Why the hell should I?" she demanded. "She's been moping around here for weeks, looking like someone had just run over her best friend. You made a few halfhearted calls and nothing else. She's been making herself sick with work, and she finally got smart and decided to take a vacation. You're too late to do anything about it now. School will start by the time she returns, and she'll forget all about a jerk like you."

Oh, God, no. JD took a deep breath and fought the tremors quaking through him. Moping. Working herself sick. He hadn't meant to hurt her. He was such a stupid ass. Why had he even thought he could reach out and touch someone like Nina without destroying her?

A worse thought struck him. Making herself sick. He'd taken precautions. Surely she wasn't? . . .

Oh, God, he had to find her.

Tamping down his raging fears, JD faced Helen with as much calm as he could summon. "It's extremely important that I find Nina. I won't hurt her. I want to take care of her. I'll do whatever she wants me to do. But I've got to find her first. Tell me where she is."

Helen scrutinized him carefully, as if she could somehow perceive his intentions from the cut of his clothes or the sweat pouring down his face. He should have dressed for the occasion. He should have worn some expensive polo shirt or designer pants or something. Maybe he wouldn't look quite so much like a motorcycle bum. Oh, damn! What if Nina hadn't told her mother that he had money? Maybe she really did think him a no-account hood who would never be here when Nina needed him. Oh, shit.

JD started to explain. He held his hand out, but the words didn't come easily. He dropped his hand again, then shoved it through his hair. At least he'd had the sense to get it trimmed properly for a change. It no longer required a rubber band.

As if that were the signal she wanted, Helen finally broke her silence. "I haven't been here to protect my daughter for twenty years, Mr. Marshall. It's probably too late to start now. But I'll tell you this—if you hurt her in any way, I'm coming after you. I won't have a damned thing to lose if I cut your testicles off."

JD winced at the image, but surprise that this well-groomed epitome of Southern womanhood could use such language prevented immediate reply. "I won't hurt her," he finally agreed.

She nodded and returned to watering. "She went to Los Angeles, said she had friends there."

THIRTY-THREE

Exhaustion overwhelmed JD as he climbed out of the taxi and paid the fare, but a strange sense of elation buoyed him as he turned toward the empty shell of a house he'd called home these last few years. He prayed hard and heavy as he shifted the bag of ice cream and reached for the gate latch. Joy washed over him when he found it unlocked.

Stupid, he reminded himself. She should never leave locks unfastened in a high-crime area like Los Angeles. Cautiously, he locked it behind him. Now that he'd found someone worth protecting, he'd have to quit taking risks.

JD couldn't wipe the foolish grin off his face as he hurried down the walk. He was probably operating solely on nervous energy at this point and couldn't be responsible for his stupidities. He'd left Jackie with Nina's mother, caught the first flight out of Nashville heading this direction, called Jimmy from the plane, and hadn't slept a wink in thirty-six hours. His brain was blatantly fried. But Jimmy had pulled it off. He'd persuaded Nina to stay here.

Thanking all the Powers That Be for their intervention, JD strode past the rocks and potted plants that comprised his yard. The plants were supposed to survive neglect. They hadn't survived his kind of neglect. The last time he'd noticed them, even the cactus had died.

He stopped abruptly to admire a single blossom on a yucca plant he'd thought he'd killed last winter. It hadn't looked this happy in years. Of course, it hadn't had a new pot and dirt since the landscaper had installed it either. The open bag of potting soil occupying the path indicated someone had corrected his errors.

Glancing around, JD grinned hugely. Every pot had fresh, moist soil. The bushes that had long since cracked their pots and tilted dangerously on root balls alone now proudly sported decorative clay containers and stood straight and tall again. They even looked alive for a change. Amazing what a little water could do. And someone to care.

JD hurried up the path. All Nina needed was someone who cared. He'd repeated that to himself like a mantra ever since he'd left Madrid. Maybe he was incompetent when it came to what women liked. Maybe he got along with machines better than with people. But he cared. He more than cared. Maybe that would be enough for Nina. He just had to let her know, and pray very hard. And feed her chocolate ice cream, he grinned to himself. The box he'd picked up on the way in from the airport was still nicely frozen.

He wouldn't find Nina in the kitchen, he knew that. And at this time of day, he wouldn't find her in bed, more's the pity.

He stepped onto the sun porch, uncertain what he would do but certain he would find Nina there. She wasn't. The blow struck him so forcefully, he almost staggered. She had to be here. He'd walked through the main living area and hadn't seen her anywhere.

The sun porch wasn't that big. She couldn't hide under the silly ironwork table the decorator had installed. He never sat out here. The blamed chairs were too uncomfortable. Besides, he was never home. But he'd expected Nina to appreciate the view of the city from the floor-to-ceiling windows. He'd had visions of handing her the ice cream instead of flowers, showing her he hadn't forgotten those times she'd sacrificed her treat for him. He couldn't believe he'd got it all wrong.

She *had* to be here. Surely she wouldn't have left the door and gate unlocked if she'd gone out. Another stupid notion. Nina thought locks were for nighttime.

Dread constricting his heart, JD returned uncertainly to the main room. The wilting plant in the front window no longer wilted. He had a cleaning service, so dust hadn't gathered in his absence, not that Nina would have taken care of it if he hadn't. A stack of papers in front of the television gave him some hope. Nina had worked in here at some time.

Not bothering with the papers, JD hurried down the hall to his personal quarters. The humming of his printer increased his step. That didn't make sense. Nina knew nothing about printers. Maybe Jimmy had locked her in one of the rooms, and he was back here messing around while waiting for his arrival. JD thought he'd hear Nina screaming curses if that were the case.

He burst into his office like a madman and stared in disbelief.

Nina glanced up from the computer and broke into a beaming smile. "You're back! Jimmy said he didn't know when you'd come in, so I've been amusing myself. I hope you don't mind."

Mind? He'd go down on his knees and beg her to play with the damned machine if it meant she would stay. Completely undone, JD couldn't find his tongue.

She was even more gorgeous than he remembered. She'd done something soft with her hair, so it kind of curled around her face instead of sticking straight up. She didn't wear any cosmetics except a smear of lipstick she'd almost chewed off, but Nina didn't need cosmetics. Her skin glowed from within, her eyes shone with their own light, and her smile—her smile could nail a man to the wall from half a room away.

"You're here," he said stupidly. Damn, but he should have slept on the plane.

She curled her fingers anxiously into her palm but nodded agreement. "Jimmy gave me the keys and said it was all right." She darted him an uncertain look. When he didn't seem furious, she gathered her courage and stumbled hurriedly through her practiced speech. "I thought it kind of presumptuous myself, but I'll admit I like seeing how the other half lives. You've got a lovely view."

The view from this vantage point was even better, Nina decided as JD flexed his shoulders nervously and stared at her as if he'd just conjured a demon. She was nervous, too, but that didn't keep her from admiring the muscular forearms driving his hands into his hair. He'd had that thick mass of black trimmed into a proper style that would probably look professional if he wore a suit. She couldn't see JD wearing a suit. She liked seeing him in well-worn jeans. She liked seeing him out of those jeans. She flushed and returned her gaze to the computer.

"Jimmy told me how to find operating instructions for this spreadsheet program. I've been playing around with it. It's fascinating. I push this little button, and it adds all these columns, but if I push this one, everything disappears. I thought I could use it for the bookkeeping system I'm setting up for the garden, if I can learn it."

"Nina."

His voice sounded strained, and she hastily looked at him again. Did he really mind if she played with his computer? Jimmy hadn't thought so, but maybe Jimmy didn't know what he kept on here.

"I'm sorry. Shouldn't I have played with it? I've tried not to mess anything up. Jimmy assured me you backed everything up and I couldn't hurt anything."

"Nina, would you do me a favor?"

He didn't sound any less tense, but he didn't sound angry

either. Nina nodded uncertainly. "Whatever you ask, JD." Foolish answer, but she meant it. Gad, how she meant it. She'd probably rob a bank if he asked it of her, because she knew it would be for a good cause. JD didn't know the meaning of selfish. He might not be a communicative man, but he was good through and through.

"Get up and come over here."

That, she could do, had been dying to do since he walked through that door. But she'd used up all her reserves of courage by flying out here without warning. Silently, she stood up and crossed the room. He smelled of soap and shaving lather, and she glanced at the travel kit and sack he carried in one hand. He'd washed and shaved. Had he known she was here?

As if just realizing he still held them, he glanced down at the items in his hand and flung them on the credenza. In the same swift move, he swung his arm back to catch hers, pulling her against him until they stood toe-to-toe.

Nina's heart thudded as her breasts crushed into the unforgiving hardness of his chest. She couldn't help herself. She curled her fingers into his shirt and tilted her head back to meet his eyes.

"Yeah, just like that." With an exhalation Nina almost translated as relief, JD crushed her against him and bent his head so their lips met.

Ecstasy. Sheer ecstasy blossomed outward from somewhere deep inside her as JD's lips caught hers and demanded surrender. Nina slid her arms over his shoulders for support and gave him everything he asked and more. Pressing closer, she offered what she thought he wanted. He could have her any way he liked. She just couldn't bear living without him any longer.

She'd thought she was running away when she'd boarded the plane in Nashville, but upon arriving at this desolate house with its dying plants and deserted air, she'd known she'd been running toward something far more important than botanical gardens and math classes. JD had once told her he'd never had a home. She could give him a home. She could give him the love he needed, teach him to trust people again. JD needed her as much as she needed him. She saw that now. She just had to make him see it. If this was how it was done, then this was how she would do it.

"Oh, God, Nina, now I know how my plants felt when you watered them." JD hauled her more tightly against him, rubbing her backside in a motion that reminded her of what that bulge in his jeans meant. Nina squirmed closer, kissing his neck and hanging on for dear life.

"I don't need a watering can for you?" she teased, licking his neck and discovering the delight of tasting him. He shuddered, and she did it again.

"Damn, Nina, we need to talk. We're two adults here, not hormonal teenagers."

He returned her to the floor, but she didn't release him. She faced him boldly. "We can touch and talk at the same time."

He managed a wry grin. "Maybe you can, but I can't. If you don't let go of me right now, I'll have that pretty little top off of you in the next five seconds. You don't have any idea what you've put me through these last few days."

"Oh?" Reluctantly, Nina released his shoulders, but she slid her fingers into JD's hand. She needed that physical reassurance right now. It gave her the confidence she lacked to do what she had to do. "I didn't know I'd done anything to you these last few days."

He flopped down on a sagging couch that had seen better days and pulled her into his lap. Nina thought this might not be the best position for conversation, but she didn't object. She wrapped her arms around his neck again and wriggled into a more comfortable position against his thigh.

"On second thought, maybe we ought to get this physical stuff out of the way and talk later."

Before Nina could respond to that provocative statement, JD

had her flat on her back on the wide cushions of the couch, his knees securely trapping her thighs as he again caught her mouth with his.

His tongue tasted as sweet as she remembered. Giving herself up to sensation, Nina explored the muscled arms preventing his heavy weight from crushing her. Even in this, JD was gentle. She knew she only had to back off, and he'd stop at once. She didn't want him to stop. She'd dreamed of this moment for weeks. For a lifetime.

The buttons of her ribbed shirt came undone, and Nina squealed as JD's mouth tugged at an aching breast. She hadn't known this was what breasts were for until JD had shown her. She dug her hands into his hair and let him plunder as he would.

She hadn't realized she'd worn this short skirt for just this purpose until JD shoved it up to her waist and cradled her hips in his hands. She felt wickedly depraved when he ripped off her panties and they were still almost wholly dressed. Maybe she had read one too many naughty books, but she responded eagerly to JD's hurried demands. Her need was as strong as his.

He spread his hands between her thighs and hesitated, searching her face for an answer to a question he couldn't seem to ask. She would need to be a mind reader to understand this man, but the task wasn't so difficult this time. Sliding her fingers over his smooth-shaven jaw, Nina urged JD's lips back to hers. She couldn't explain it any better than that.

He didn't hesitate any longer.

Nina cried out as he surged into her. Tears rolled down her cheeks as her body responded enthusiastically to its duty, arching to take JD deep inside, rising and falling rhythmically without need for thought, quaking with the joy he gave her. He teased her breasts, kissed her throat, and drove her straight into oblivion with his frantic release.

They collapsed in sweaty exhaustion in each other's arms. With the gradual return of her mind, Nina thought she should feel awkward lying like this with a half-naked man, their lower parts still joined and moist, the upper parts fully dressed. Instead, she knew only immense satisfaction. JD wanted her. She'd never felt like this with another man. Surely, that was a step in the right direction. Now, if she could only make him see . . .

He propped himself on one arm and gazed sleepily down on her. "I love you," he murmured.

Shock rippled through her, and Nina stared at his neatly shaved jaw with incomprehension. Maybe that was something he said to all his women. He hadn't said it before. She met his eyes, but his gaze didn't waver. It held her pinned as he challenged her to respond.

Gulping, Nina cautiously stroked his cheek. "You don't have to say that for my benefit."

"Yeah, I do." JD pulled her shirt closed and smoothed it tenderly over her breasts before looking at her again. "I don't think I've ever said it to anyone before, so it's kind of hard to get out, you know?"

The cold sensation of parting as JD sat up was nothing compared to the revelation of his words. Hastily brushing her skirt down, Nina struggled to sit up beside him. JD reached over and planted her firmly in his lap again. He hugged her close, and she rested her head against his shoulder. She liked resting her head against his shoulder. It seemed so right somehow, secure, as she had never known security.

"Yeah, I know," she replied in the same vernacular. Switching to her softer Southern dialect, she attempted to clarify. "You have to hear the words often to say them with ease. Maybe we should practice on each other. I love you, too. I don't have any idea why, but I do."

She felt JD's chuckle as much as heard it.

"I don't know why you do either. I'm pigheaded, blind, and stupid. I have no concept of what it takes to make a marriage. I barely have any idea what love is, but if it's this need to have you with me all the time, then I've got it bad. I've spent these last weeks worrying about you instead of worrying about the damned company. Every time I called up a financial statement, I thought of you curled up in that apartment, lecturing me on risk. When I learned I had control of Astro, instead of reaching for the champagne, I reached for the phone to call you. You weren't there," he said accusingly.

"I've been busy," she answered defensively. "All that money you solicited had to be spent somewhere. I've got bulldozers and tractors and construction workers all over the place."

"Yeah, I know." JD reached inside her unbuttoned shirt and cupped her breast in his palm. "I've just been out there. It looks pretty good."

Nina sat up so fast she almost clipped his chin. She jerked her shirt closed over his protesting fingers. "What do you mean, you were just out there? You were out there and didn't see me?"

He shrugged almost sheepishly. "I went there to see you, but you were here. Must have been some kind of mental vibrations crossing."

Nina stared at him in astonishment. "You went all the way out there when you're busy taking over another company and producing a new program and looking after Jackie? Couldn't you have just sent a letter?"

He wrinkled his brow in thought, staring at the ceiling. "Can't remember the last time I sent a letter. Could have been back in the service, when I wrote Nancy. Didn't have much luck then." He brought his dark gaze back down to her, and Nina shivered with the intensity of it. "Couldn't take that risk again. I'm eliminating risks in my life, Miss Toon. You see here before you a reformed impulse addict. I will proceed cautiously from now on. Will you marry me?"

In shock, Nina hesitated.

JD gave her a mischievous grin. "We didn't use any protection just then. You may have to marry me, Miss Toon."

Blood rushed to Nina's cheeks at the thought of carrying his child. She knew better than to think it possible after just one try, but she wouldn't put anything past JD. "I thought you were forgoing all risk, Mr. Marshall," she replied, too shaken to remember she had come here intending to make him marry her. "That seems like a rather immense risk to me."

"Nah." He shook his head and hugged her tenderly. "I know you too well. If I got you pregnant, you'd be here with a gun at my head and a knife to my throat demanding I do the right thing by our child. And then I'd have you right where I wanted you. So I didn't take any risks. You did."

So she had. She'd taken a huge risk. Stupid of her. But she'd had everything to gain and nothing to lose. Hattie had been wrong. Sometimes, one had to risk everything to gain anything.

Nina relaxed against JD's shoulder again. "This is ridiculous, you realize. We live two thousand miles apart. We might as well live on different planets. It will never work."

JD nuzzled her neck. "Of course it will work. I don't hum. Can't carry a tune."

Nina wondered if she'd heard properly. Or if they'd both gone mad. She glared at him. "You don't hum?"

He nipped her nape and slid a finger beneath her shirt, teasing a nipple. "If you don't hear me humming, then the relationship must be working. Isn't that how you tell when things are going to break down?"

Nina stared up at his grin in disbelief. "You're insane, you know that, don't you? People don't . . ." But of course, people hummed all the time. The smirk on JD's face told her that.

"See? I told you. Besides, anything that breaks, I can fix. Did you know your mother threatened to cut off my balls if I didn't take care of you?"

She'd believe almost anything at this point. Shaking her head and burying her face against his shoulder as his teasing finger made mush of her mind, she sought some sense in his words. "Why would she do that?" she asked warily. "She's never shown any concern for me before."

JD's voice lost some of its teasing quality. "Are you sure about that? We had a bit of a talk while I was booking my flight. She threw the prison thing in my face to see if she could run me off." He tilted Nina's chin up with his finger. "I think she protected you in the only way she knew how, by letting you think her dead and with the angels. She never knew a whole lot about love, Nina. Just think how old Hattie must have been when your mother was born. Helen didn't know you'd miss what she'd never had. She just did what she had to do and suffered for it, alone."

His words pierced her heart. Nina blinked back tears as she absorbed this new aspect of her mother. She hadn't really allowed herself to think about it, it hurt so much, but JD's version eased the pain.

"Nina, will you marry me?" he asked softly.

The question jerked her back to the moment. It was too much, too fast. She wanted to scream, "Yes, yes, of course!" but the habits of a lifetime were hard to break. "I don't know anything about being a corporate executive's wife," she warned. "You don't know anything about living in the middle of nowhere. I signed a teaching contract for this next year. I can't renege on it at this late date. Your company needs you at a time like this, or you risk losing everything. And there's Jackie. He needs your attention, too." Looking at the immensity of their problems, Nina groaned. She'd been an idiot to think just making him admit they belonged together would solve everything.

JD stroked her hair and ran his finger down her chin. "I told you, I've quit taking risks. I'm a family man now, and I've got to think of my family first. I know you won't like it here, and you can't give up all your responsibilities back home. But I can live anywhere. I *have* lived everywhere. Now, I just want a home and a family. Madrid is perfectly fine with me, but I'm hoping maybe you'll like my other idea a little better."

As the realization sank in that JD really meant it, really thought of her as family, warmth flooded through Nina. She tried not to look at him too adoringly, but she didn't think she could disguise her love very well. It would go straight to his fat head. She'd best keep things in perspective.

"What idea?" she asked with suspicion, but the way he grinned back told her he wasn't fooled. How the devil would she live with someone who knew her too well?

"I've been busy. I talked to your lawyer as well as to Helen. I know you officially own the garden now. So I called a few Realtors out your way. I had time before the plane left Nashville to stop and look at a few places they suggested. There's a place way out in the country near the state line that I thought you might like. It's modern, I'll admit, but they've buried all the cables underground so all you'll see is trees from the windows. It's about halfway between Madrid and Nashville. I know you're not used to commuting, so maybe when the weather is bad we can stay at your place so you don't have to drive far. I thought you might like a place of your own, so your mother could stay at the farm."

Now she knew why she loved this man so much. JD was so incredibly intelligent, he took her breath away. Staring at him now, Nina couldn't believe he was saying these things. There had to be flaws in the design, but she was too flabbergasted to see them. "What about your company?" she finally asked, too stunned to know what she was asking but understanding it was of importance.

JD pressed a kiss against the corner of her lips. "You're supposed to ask all about the house and ask when we're getting married and seduce me some more. Why am I not surprised that you ask about me first?"

Nina shook her head and smiled at his reaction. He really wasn't used to having anyone think of him first. She could change that. She might make a lousy housekeeper and cook, but she could make him happy. "Just answer the question, JD," she said boldly, knowing he wouldn't complain of her sharpness.

He didn't. He kissed her again, making her head spin. Then he answered.

"Astro's distribution headquarters are in Nashville. It's a central location, making it easier for the sales force to keep in contact. I'm leaving Jimmy in charge of Marshall Enterprises while I move in and look over Astro's operations. Ultimately, I'll have to hire someone more experienced in operations management so I can get back to R&D, but one of us has to stay on top of things. I volunteered. Jimmy thought he'd fallen off the planet when he was out there."

Nina giggled and relaxed again. Jimmy would definitely have been out of place in Kentucky or Tennessee. JD wouldn't. He'd adapted with commendable equilibrium from the moment he'd set foot in her house. Another reason she dearly loved this man.

"What about children?" She pushed him deliberately, probing for the flaw in this bubble of happiness.

"I've got a son. We'll have to do some juggling with Jackie's summer and holiday schedules, but I don't need more kids if you don't want any. But if you should feel so inclined, I'd kind of like watching a kid grow up. Maybe by now I've learned a thing or two I could pass on."

JD hugged her gently, and his finger traced a tempting path over her bare breast. Nina couldn't believe she had it all, everything she'd ever dreamed of and never thought to have. She knew better than to believe it would be perfect. JD was an impossible man who would forget she existed when he was busy with one of his projects. He wouldn't come home and he would forget to call and tell her why. He would yell at the kids and lose his patience. But he would never lift a hand to them. He would cry when they cried.

And he understood what she hadn't understood until now. She needed a home of her own, one that wasn't Hattie's or her mother's or anyone else's, one she could call her own. Maybe then she could get to know Helen a little better. Maybe, someday in the distant future, they'd have a real family, with a grandmother and children and a father for Jackie. Two fathers, if Jimmy toed the line with Nancy. And despite all their differences, they would be whole again.

Leaning back in JD's arms, Nina slid her hand beneath his shirt and reveled in his intake of breath as she plucked a sensitive spot. "My teaching contract is up in nine months," she reminded him sweetly.

It took him a second. He looked a little dazed at first. But JD always made nice recoveries.

This time, he carried her to the bedroom and did it properly.

The chocolate ice cream dripped and puddled on the floor before anyone remembered its existence.